Control Alter Delete

A Novel

Stella Whiteman

CONTROL ALTER DELETE. Copyright © 2015 by Stella Whiteman
All rights reserved.
ISBN-13: 978-0692439654
ISBN-10: 069243965X
Library of Congress Control Number: 2015906960
Soonscape Books
Philadelphia, PA

For Phil

ACKNOWLEDGMENTS

Many thanks to all the authors at the Rittenhouse Writers' Group and the Green Line meet-ups who provided me with invaluable feedback and helped me knock this novel into shape. Thanks are also owed to James Rahn and Karen Rile for facilitating such supportive yet challenging fiction workshops, to Ellen Sawyer for proofreading the manuscript and Paul Graff for his work on the cover. I am especially grateful to Katharine Beals and Louise Jones for their advice, interest and enthusiasm over many years.

My biggest debt is to my husband, Phil, whose encouragement has been ceaseless, and to my wonderful kids, Conrad and Yemisi. I would also like to give a special mention to my dad who set me up with a typewriter and a copy of Writers' & Artists' Yearbook when I was twelve.

Part One

1

Tuesday 12ᵗʰ August 2059

EZRA HADN'T MEANT to stare. He'd been hunching over a beer when they just appeared, those ankles, at the top of a staircase that led to the basement bar. A rich dark brown, they were slender and bare, save for the sandal straps curling up to the calves. White-skirted hips swayed with her descent. Breasts – round and high under a teasing little blouse. Necklace – askew, trapped on the point of a collar; blown by the wind maybe. Mahogany ringlets – all strewn around the shoulders. Eyes, large and almond-shaped, and staring right back.

Ezra was the first to blink and look away.

He lifted his pint glass off the beer mat and a new 2-D commercial for cannabis smokes began playing on its surface. The mini-movie showed wispy white smoke rings blowing from a blonde woman's mouth, then swirling into the cumulus clouds of a mountain scene. Maybe later he'd try one. He swigged his beer, recovered the mat and its ad with his glass.

The woman was still in the same spot at the bottom of the stairs, checking the place out, scanning the small stage in the far corner, then the gaming room to the side.

There was a tap-tap-tap of heels crossing wooden boards and while his gaze was cast down, deliberately to look composed, the woman's sandals appeared at the base of the stool nearest to his at the end of the bar. Thinking she must have something to say (else why would she come so close?) he glanced up at her face.

She was looking at her reflection in the mirrored wall behind the array of liqueurs, adjusting her necklace, her collar, her ringlets. Switching to her reflection now, he caught a flash of epicanthic eyes – green, large, weirdly bright, reflecting the glint of a bar lamp. Ezra gave a nod to the mirror-woman, a silent hi. She gave a snap smile. He'd wanted to say more, but he thought better of it. He had nothing lined up anyhow, and he'd rather say nothing than say something contrived. He took a swig of his beer. She looked intelligent, sophisticated. Probably the last thing she wanted was some stranger working her with a piss-poor wisecrack.

He continued sneaking glances anyway. He couldn't help it. She was extraordinary.

Her skin was darker than his. Just. And so surreally smooth it made his seem rough. And he'd never thought that before. Baby skin. That's what his ex used to say each time she'd smoothed her palm around his face. There was nothing craggy about his skin. It was this woman at the bar. She was particularly pristine. All over. Skin, eyes, clothes, those sandals with their unworn heels and scuff-free leather. He peered at the leather straps from the corner of his eye. Not orange. Not red. There was a name for that color. Something girly. Peach, maybe. His ex had her bathroom painted that shade. What was it called? Something to do with the sea.

Now the woman was looking at her shoes too, then looking at him suspiciously. He thought any minute she might come straight out and ask him what he was staring for.

Instead a deep voice cut in, "What can I get you?"

Mo, bearded, pot-bellied, was wiping his hands on a tea towel in an *Employees Only* doorway. A pathogen detection device blinked its *all clear* light on the wall to his side, making one side of his beard flash green. Moving out of the light, he approached the woman.

"Ready to order?" he said.

"Gin and tonic," she replied, after some hesitation.

The barman poured the drink, then moved to the cash register where the price flashed on the screen in a luminous blue. She placed her index finger on the pay pad. There was no immediate response, no little beep or red light to say that the transaction was processing. Just silence and a woman frozen, fingertip outstretched, pressing on the pay pad.

"Old equipment," Mo said.

"Good to know," she replied. "Glad it's your machine that's malfunctioning rather than me."

More silence, then finally the high-pitched ping of a transaction cleared. Mo jabbed at one more icon before ambling back though his *Employees Only* door.

The woman hoisted herself onto the bar stool, crossed her legs, smoothed down the skirt on her thigh.

Smoothing, smoothing – this action continued, despite there being no creases that Ezra could see. But then it seemed like more than a smoothing of the skirt, more of a slow massage along the length of her thigh, a deliberate pressing of her skin. The rubbing of an ache? He looked at her face. She didn't seem to be in pain. Just deep in thought. Her head, torso, and legs were motionless. The heels of her shoes were hooked over the rail at the bottom of her stool. But her hand kept moving, stroking her thigh.

"So," she said suddenly, "what's wrong with my shoes? You keep looking. Why?"

"It's their color. What color would you call that?" She looked down to her feet. The shiny heel of one sandal reflected a line of light. "Probably seems a dumb question."

"There's a story behind this color," she said, after taking a sip of her gin.

"Oh? A good one?"

"Maybe, but I don't think I should tell it. Not the whole thing anyway. A short version maybe."

"Why not the whole story?"

"It could be construed as risqué."

"Risqué? Now I definitely want the whole story."

"You're not getting it, though."

"No?"

"No."

"All right. How about the short version?"

Several seconds of silence, then finally she said, "It's funny how people can surprise themselves, isn't it?" Ezra waited for her to continue. "I chose these shoes to go with a dress the same color. I chose the dress because it reminded me of a hospital gown. I think," the woman said in a way that suggested she was about to deliver some grand conclusion, "this color has become a fetish."

Shoes, dress, hospital gown – he didn't know where this story was heading, but he found himself saying, "A fetish?" He hadn't really thought about colors being fetishes before.

"I was having a medical examination," the woman continued. Ezra had his glass to his lips as she said this. It remained there for a while, momentarily frozen. "I was given a gown. You know, one of those ones that have a single tie at the front." She pointed down to her sandal. "It was the same color as this. Exact same color." She shuffled back on her seat a little, crossed her legs, rubbed her thigh. "So, I put the gown on, and normally I'd feel, well, undignified I suppose – you know how those hospital gowns make you feel."

"Oh yeah," Ezra agreed, while wondering what medical problem she had, and how she could so openly describe getting undressed to a complete stranger. "Totally humiliating."

"But this time, well, d'you know what I was thinking while I was waiting for this doctor to examine me, waiting in this gown?" Ezra shook his head. "I was thinking this doctor is going to need me to remove this gown. What's he going to say? Is he going to say something formal like 'If madam could just remove the robe now,' or is he going to be nice and casual and say something like 'OK, let's have a little look then, shall we?'"

"What did you want him to say?" Ezra found himself asking, while trying hard not to look at her breasts.

"I didn't have a preference. I was just curious about how he was going to get the examination started, what kind of approach he'd have and how formal his speech was going to be."

"And how formal was his speech?"

"Not formal at all."

The long pause that followed made Ezra wonder whether that was the end of the story.

"Laid back? Colloquial?" he asked, trying to keep her talking, but somehow not really understanding what he was even asking.

She was silent for a while, seemingly working out the answer.

"No, not colloquial." The woman turned to face Ezra. Her eyes were bright and impossibly green. "He never said a word. Not a word. He just stepped up to the examination bench, stood right before me, pulled the tie undone – he was really calm about it – and nudged the flaps of the gown apart with his index fingers."

Though she was facing him square on, he couldn't help the fleeting glance to her blouse and the breasts beneath.

A career in medicine – now why hadn't he thought of that? If he could read the woman better, he might try that line on her, throw in some humor, but when he looked up once more, he found himself confronted by a piercing stare. What – was she upset now? Well, how was he supposed to behave with a story like that? And just as he was thinking that women were impossible, there was no working them out, she repeated, under her breath, seemingly to herself, "Never said a word. Well," she said with a tone of finality, "I wasn't expecting that."

She picked up her glass and took a long sip.

"So, that's the short version. How about the long one?"

"Off limits. Didn't I say that before?"

"Yes, you did."

"So, there you are – you'll just have to use your imagination."

He already was. She was there, in his mind's eye, in a loose hospital gown with a single tie at the front.

"And the color?" he said, aware how lame the question would sound. "Of the gown? Of the shoes?"

It wasn't even important. Just something he knew, but couldn't recall.

She looked down at her sandals again, but seemed to get distracted by his work bag positioned between their bar stools. A single pen poked from the end pocket, its clip pinching the leather and holding it in place. She was narrowing her eyes, cocking her head – he could tell she was scrutinizing the label, the words *Sense Surveillance*. She was peering at him intently now. Probably she was applying the corporate logo not just to his pen but also to him. When the hash commercial began playing on his drink mat, he decided against covering it up. It could serve as a distraction, could deflect any snide comment about the company he worked for. Not that he was ashamed of it. He had no problem defending his role in a global surveillance company. It was just he didn't want to get heavy, switch the mood – things had been panning out, weirdly, somehow sexually, in a way he really liked.

"Coral," she said.

That was it. He leaned back in his seat, glass cupped in his hand, resting on his lap.

From the corner of his eye, he saw her smoothing her skirt again, rubbing her thigh. Wishing she'd stop, he looked at the mat in front of him. The retina detector kicked in and the mat replayed the commercial. When Mo walked past, Ezra gestured to the Bliss packs on the top shelf above the brandies.

"Five pack?" Mo said.

Ezra nodded.

He was aware of the woman watching as he pressed his finger on the pay pad. Lights, bleeps, and transaction-complete-ping all over in a nanosecond.

He tore the cellophane off the pack. Offered the woman a smoke. She looked like she was tempted. He was surprised by her "No thanks."

He lit one for himself.

"I'm Ezra," he said.

"Lena," she replied.

***

Suzanne was determined not to let it get to her, but the low level whining was gnawing through her skull.

"I don't know what you want," she said to Adam. "I just don't know." But her two-year-old, squirming in his high chair at the head of the table, clearly couldn't give a shit about what she did or didn't know. He pointed frantically towards something (what, for Christ's sake?) on the table, and now between the whines came a series of irritated grunts. "What is it? Is it this? The tablemat? No? The spoon? The banana?" *What* was it? Shoe? Dishcloth? School of Journalism brochure? God what a mess – half the contents of the flat seemed to be heaped on this table, like they'd followed her around and hemmed her into the corner of the room.

Adam, still grunting, was pointing manically now. Suzanne followed an imaginary line from the tip of his index finger.

"Oh! I see," she said. Finally. The moment felt like a revelation. "You want the knife."

Another communication struggle over. At the back of her mind, though, was a niggling anxiety that Adam wasn't meeting milestones. One of the baby blogs had listed as normal a vocabulary of over a hundred words for a child Adam's age. Adam had five words, six if "naba" could count for banana. Should she worry or not? Would she know better if she were one of those serene and wise-looking forty-something mothers at the playground and not the twenty-year-old that she was?

Adam was grimacing and fidgeting beneath messy blonde hair, trying to heave himself from his high chair towards a knife with a wooden handle and a serrated blade.

"It's dangerous, Adam."

She whisked the knife away. He started whining again.

Don't lose it, she willed herself. But that was going to be difficult; she was still annoyed that Adam's tantrum earlier in the afternoon had interrupted her call to Sense Surveillance. It had been the third time she'd taken the police's advice and called to ask for access to surveillance data on her missing brother, and the third time Adam had wailed his way through her call.

Sense wasn't taking the case seriously, wasn't responding to her concerns – she'd wanted to say all this, but, with Adam tugging on her legs, she'd lost concentration and had failed to make herself clear.

She also had qualms. "You're an OMNI member," the Sense

rep had said, presumably looking over some data on her during that last call. Opposition to Mandatory Neural Implants – Suzanne could almost hear the cogs turning in the rep's mind: You campaign against us and our Resolve scheme, the most effective surveillance tool possible, yet when your brother goes missing you come running to us for help.

Suzanne was in a foul mood by the time she'd come off the line.

She'd marched Adam to Holland Park, inserted him in a swing, until something – the mesmerizing motion, the breeze, the view of roses arranged in rows across the lawn – had calmed them both down.

And everything had stayed calm until now. She glanced at the clock. Nearly six thirty. Where *was* Brin? He hadn't even called to say he was leaving the workshop.

Adam was still whining about the forbidden knife.

"Look," she said, casting around the mess of the room, the plastic bricks strewn over the floor, the xylophone with play dough squidged between its keys, "we could play with your puzzle." She put some pieces of the shape puzzle on the table. But all she received was a look of contempt. "Come on," – she nudged his side – "lighten up."

In one deft motion with his forearm, Adam swept the puzzle onto the floor.

She tried picking him up, holding him close enough to stop his flailing arms swiping her. But then he started pummeling his fist around her face, and finally tried to wrench himself free of her grip altogether. He arched backwards, seemingly as far away from her as he possibly could. His eyes were screwed shut and there were tears shimmering on his cheeks. His mouth was a great chasm from which his loudest yowl yet was now emanating. All this for want of a piece of cutlery.

"You're so dramatic," she said, suddenly finding the ridiculousness of this tantrum amusing. With his next wail she looked into his mouth, and marveled on his perfect little teeth, stain free, not a single cavity. But then she felt guilty for smiling because a blog she'd read recently said, "Don't laugh at your child's tantrums – take their frustrations seriously."

And then he started to swipe her harder and harder, and the more she dodged and scowled, the harder he swiped.

So, she put him down on the floor. Abruptly.

Unexpectedly, he was quiet. Suzanne watched him trot towards the armchair on the other side of the living room, watched him stop to glance back at her, watched him head towards the bookcase behind. Oh, for Christ's sake! What was Brinley thinking of leaving his carpentry stuff there? She raced past Adam and scooped two screwdrivers and a claw hammer from the shelf.

"Sorry Adam, you can't play with these. Dangerous, dangerous," she said, veering into a dark hallway with its broken solar ceiling light. She stepped over a safety gate and into the kitchen where she placed the tools on top of the fridge.

She stood in the kitchen, protected from her child by the safety gate, away from the ear-piercing scream.

She willed herself not to cry, and took a deep breath. "If you feel your anger rising," the blog had advised, "try looking at some pictures that have captured your child in cuter moments." Yeah right, she could see that working. But, since she had no other ideas, she marched back into the war zone and pulled the digi-frame from the upper shelf of the bookcase.

She plumped herself into the corner of the sofa and ignored Adam, whose tantrum, though he was still contorted in the middle of the floor, seemed to be on the wane. And, once she'd opened an array of images, Adam's outburst died down and was replaced by a look that said I'm still totally pissed off, but (and he was peering at her from the corner of his eye) I want to know what you're up to with that photo thing.

Suzanne swiped through the pictures. "This is *you*. At the beach. Do you remember?" His eyes switched from her face to the digi-frame and back again. "It's you," she said again. She truly liked that picture - bucket, spade, her beautiful boy. So what if it was a cliché? Maybe Adam had sensed her enthusiasm; he'd picked himself off the floor and begun climbing on the sofa. She had to be quick and make the most of this mood change. So, while he clambered onto the cushions, she lined up more images.

Somewhere among the numerous baby pictures were snapshots of the old house on Golborne Road that Suzanne had shared with Brin and all the rest of the OMNI crew, and somewhere among those was a picture of her brother. When she found it, she suddenly felt dismayed. Gavin, shown sitting at the bottom of a rickety staircase, looked skinnier and more disheveled than she remembered. From this photo, no one would ever know that he was blonde. His hair was dirty and straggly. Even now Suzanne remembered the smell of his clothes, their beeriness and smokiness. On one horrible occasion, too drunk to find a toilet, he'd returned to the shared house covered in piss. Perpetually embarrassed by his behavior, Suzanne was forever making excuses: he's been through a lot; he needs some support; if he could just stay here until he sorts himself out.

But he never did sort himself out.

Adam grunted at the picture.

"Yes," Suzanne said, "Uncle Gavin."

No one had seen Gavin for several weeks, not Suzanne, not her parents, no one from the old place on Golborne Road. And yet, in that house, Adam had always wanted to sit on Gavin's lap, and Gavin, who veered between drunkenness and withdrawal, had shown surprising patience with this little baby boy crawling around after him.

"Be careful with it," she told Adam when he suddenly lunged forward and grabbed the digi-frame from her hand. He was pointing at the image of a splintered baluster shown just to the side of Gavin's head. "Yes, it's broken, isn't it?"

Suzanne smiled at his apparent concern and stroked his hair. She looked at the picture too. Yes, that place needed some fixing, but OMNI had grown big there and she'd had a crucial role: researching Sense's proposed Resolve program, the safety of neural implants and the ethics of tracking people's thoughts. She'd put out press releases, edited newsletters, kept all OMNI's social network sites up to date.

She looked around her flat, at the magnolia walls with their recently acquired strokes of green crayon, at the window behind the sofa with its finger smudges on the pane. It was all right here;

not as happening as the old house, but a better place for kids – that was the main thing.

With her boy now absorbed with the images, she felt back in control. When the house comms system bleeped and Brin's voice, warm and earthy, came into the living room via the speakers, Adam didn't even look up. There was nothing to see anyway. The video was broken; the words *no signal* were the only things to appear on the screen.

"Hey you," Brin said, "everything OK?"

She was going to tell him she'd been worrying about Gavin again, but the sound of laughter in Brinley's workshop threw her. From the various voices, it sounded unusually crowded.

"Who's there?" she asked.

"Oh, Craig…"

"Who used to hang around the old house? What's he doing in the workshop?"

"Jamal texted him…" Suzanne could hear Jamal's deep voice in the background, interspersed with a heavy banging sound, presumably from whatever piece of furniture either he or Brinley was working on. "Think they're going for a drink,"

Suzanne noted the word *they're*. Had Brinley excluded himself from this drink? She hoped to high heaven he had.

"Who else is there?"

She could hear a chorus of laughter and now a woman's voice.

"Chalky, Sabirah. Quite a few of the old crew going."

He wanted to go. Suzanne could tell.

"Don't do this to me, Brin. I need a break."

"So, I can hear," he said. "It's in your voice."

"So, you're coming back soon?"

"Leave in ten minutes or so. Need to clear a few things."

Suzanne looked at the clock. Ten minutes plus the short walk – he'd be back just before seven. She clock-watched every day, but never said.

2

RINGS, GOWNS, DOCTORS – the conversation had come readily. That run of spontaneity was fizzling now.

"Shall I make things easy for you?"

"Easy?"

Exhaling slowly, Ezra stubbed out his reefer in a plain black porcelain ashtray on the bar.

"You're scrabbling around for something for us to do, trying to find out what I'm into. What kind of music, what kind of clubs…"

"That see-through, eh?"

Ezra grabbed his beer glass, took a long self-conscious swig.

"You know," she said, turning intensely green eyes on him, "we could just go in there and pick a game?" She'd nodded to the room with faint flickering lights seeping through the doorway. "What about Chamaeleon? They must have that loaded in there? Do you play?"

He could have said, "Used to. Not anymore." Because what was the point? He'd been through every level. No one had got anywhere near his score. But achieving that ranking had taken immersion. Even Mo, who made money out of these games, used to sidle up on occasion and say, "Why don't you give it a break?" One time Mo had even dragged him from the console back to the bar, to a fat battered cod and a heap of fries steaming on a plate and said, "For fuck's sake, Ez, you gotta fuckin' eat." Things had been messy back then; that split with Denise had been hard. But that was a couple of years back when Denise had finally had it with his gaming, whereas here was a woman actually egging him to play.

"I play now and then," he said.

"You any good?"

"He's been on a hiatus," Mo cut in. "Plus, he thinks there's no one as good as him. Maybe he needs showing otherwise."

"I'd be *very* happy to do that. You think you're the best, do you?"

Ezra shrugged.

"No, really," she said. "I'm interested. I want a good game. What's the point if it's not a challenge? Exactly how good are you?"

He pointed to the gaming room. Maybe some upstart had overtaken his score. He doubted it though.

"You can go and check if you like."

She slid off her stool and disappeared into the side room.

"Am I being see-through?" Ezra asked Mo.

"You're interested. It's obvious. So, yep."

Well, she was attractive. Strangely attractive. His biometrics training led him to look for certain patterns in a person's appearance: lips of a certain shape associated with a distinctive form of maxilla, a skull with certain proportions linked to a particular kind of stature. It was technically possible to predict someone's appearance from considering a single feature. Even something as detached as the bite marks left in an apple gave a lot away – with teeth leaving those kind of marks, the person would have this shape of jaw, if they had that shape of jaw, they would typically have this kind of frame. Theoretically, you could go on compiling a picture, so you'd get their height, their posture, even the way they walked.

Lena defied expectations; he'd not come across this mix of features before.

"So, you're not going to play with her?" Mo cut into his thoughts.

"I thought I was too see-through."

"Playing hard to get, then?"

"Not sure what's going on."

She'd been in the gaming room a while now. Maybe she was doing more than checking his score. Had she started a game with someone online? If he followed her to the console, he was bound to start playing. And where would that lead? A month-long binge on level 11 or whatever level people climbed up to these days?

There were more people coming in the bar now. Mo was taking orders for food. A djembe drummer and a couple of guitarists carried their instruments and amps to the small stage in the far corner of the floor. A saxophonist followed. Then a bloke in a baggy t-shirt headed towards the gaming room. Ezra felt compelled to see what Lena was up to. She'd wanted to play Chamaeleon, *invited* him to play. Was he really going to let that pass? He took hold of his pint glass and was about to cross the floor when she emerged in the doorway and headed towards him.

"Your score's pretty good," she said. She was cool, this woman. Even Mo, standing behind the bar pulling pints with his big brown hands, was casting her a sideways glance. And he was normally impassive. "But mine is better than yours."

He found that hard to believe, but asked with pointed calmness, "How did you manage that?"

"With this," she said, pulling a game controller from her bag.

It was a Helix gamepad. Translucent blue casing. Little black buttons.

"They've only been out a week," Mo said, cutting her a long look. "So, let me get this right…" his eyes were narrowing "…you switched that into my system, reloaded Cham 10, and *won?*"

She gave him a wink.

Mo shook his head.

"What about you, Ezra?" she said. "Don't you believe me either?"

"Sounds like a stretch."

"Well, you can go and check if you like."

Mo strode towards the side room before Ezra had formed an answer. Lena's half-smile remained fixed on her face all the while Mo was checking her score. Grew wide when he shuffled back behind the bar to say, "Still don't know how you did it."

"Already told you." She patted the Helix. "With this."

Ezra eyed the ribbed handles, the triggers and bumpers. He'd not seen a configuration like that before. He was regretting now not keeping up with the reviews. From the little he heard about Helixes, he knew that their motion sensors were vastly superior to any previous versions. No wonder she'd been underwhelmed by his scores.

"Game changer," he said, though he was too out of the loop to specify exactly how the game had changed. "What's so funny?"

"Are you in a bad mood?"

"No."

"You are."

Maybe he was.

"I'll have another drink, Mo. What about you?" he said, turning to Lena.

"A victory drink. Sounds good, why not?"

3

SUZANNE SAT WITH Brinley on a yellow sofa that backed onto a pair of sash windows. One window was open and a strong breeze wafted in, gradually dispersing the stink of Adam's last shitty diaper. The roar of a motorcycle burst into the first floor flat, then faded over cocksure voices – men, three, maybe four, laughing, joshing and going, Suzanne guessed, towards Ladbroke Grove station. She checked the clock hanging asymmetrically above the living room door. Twenty to eight. Probably they were headed for some bar or other. A lads' night out, she supposed. Their voices fading, she remembered her last night out.

It had been over five weeks ago when Gavin was still living with them, crashing here on the sofa. Some beers at the Lord Nelson, two minutes around the corner, that was all it was supposed to be. But Suzanne had worried that Gavin wasn't responsible enough to babysit Adam and that it was stupid to have gone out leaving her brother in charge. Brinley, who'd wanted to play snooker and had busied himself in the pub setting the balls into the triangle, had stayed surprisingly calm.

"Gavin's not so messed up that he can't text if there's a problem," he'd said, before adding, "I know I'm usually the negative one about your brother, but Adam's tucked up in bed, Gavin's watching some shit on the 3-D. What can go wrong?"

Plenty. Gavin could pull too many beers from the fridge. Get strung out on tranx tabs. Stagger over. Break something. Forget to turn the stove off. The possibilities were endless.

So, she and Brin had ended that night before it had got going and returned to the flat only to find Adam tucked up and Gavin sitting pretty much as Brin sat now, flicking through channels trying to find something to watch. That last night out had lasted three quarters of an hour, max.

A Sense commercial came on. Holographic images showing children, bed after bed, critically ill in hospital. An ominous minor chord came from the speakers accompanied by a deep and serious voice-over. *Who's plotting the next viral attack? With Resolve, we'd know.*

"Bollocks," Brinley said, turning the ad off. He swigged some beer. When they'd lived in the old house with Jamal, Anna, and Zoe, a commercial like that would have set them off for ages, on an all-night rail against neural implants. Not now, though – *bollocks* was just about their sum of things.

With Adam asleep in the bedroom and the doom-mongering voice of the commercial gone, the flat was quiet and still. Suzanne stretched out on the sofa and rested her calves on Brinley's thighs. He massaged her bare feet, his fingers occasionally reaching just under the hem of her jeans, fingering under her ankle chain, lightly fondling her lower leg. One of his knuckles bore a large dried gash, a carpentry wound from a week before.

She watched him put the bottle to his lips and scrutinized his stubble – it was getting thick. When he gulped down the beer, his Adam's apple and jaw muscles shifted and flexed. Watching this complex sequence of muscle movements, these contortions under stubble, she thought of her brother. Before he'd gone missing, Gavin had grown a beard. Not as defined as Brin's though, just scraggly, fair and patchy.

Brinley stopped glugging and turned towards her.

"What is it?"

She pulled her legs from his lap and faced him, cross-legged.

"I'm not getting anywhere with Gavin."

"You contacted Sense?"

"For the *third* time," Suzanne said.

"Well, you know they're not likely to take you seriously. I've said that before. I mean, they know we're attached to OMNI. They know Gavin was on the march. They've got that on camera. They'll probably say to themselves 'these people have got to be joking – they're out on the streets protesting about our services, now one of them goes missing, they come running to us for help.'"

Suzanne conceded that the Sense reps she'd spoken to probably had exactly that attitude. But what was she supposed to do? Her brother was missing. The police had shown her their records. If she doubted the intelligence, they'd told her, she'd have to take that matter up with the people who'd supplied it. Sense was her only chance of help.

She could see how this seemed like hypocrisy, though. How many nights had she spent sending feeds to all OMNI's social sites, fulminating about the evils of compulsory neural implants? Virtually all of her teens had centered on the issue, beginning with the project on civil liberties and surveillance she'd started as a fourteen-year-old.

That's why she'd veered towards Brin and all the other campaigners at their Golborne Road base. That's why she'd ignored her mum's continual griping that these "activists" and "hippies" she'd begun hanging around with were too old for her and a distraction from school.

"What are you doing with this man?" Suzanne remembered her mum whispering during a visit to the old house where she'd flashed puzzled glances at a table with Brancusi-style legs that Brinley had carved from recycled wood. "And what kind of carpentry is that?"

"Fine carpentry," she'd said, "He's just had an exhibition at the Hark Gallery…"

"*Fine*…" Suzanne still remembered how her mum had broken off the sentence to scoff. She'd regretted using the word *fine* – it must have made her seem all starry-eyed. "You're seventeen," her mum had said. "He's *eight* years older than you."

Looking back, she wondered whether there were more than just her parents who'd found her naïve. "Our little idealist," Jamal had called her in the old house one day when he, Zoe, and Anna had watched her pasting parts of her old school essay into an OMNI blog. The label had stuck and sometimes she'd found it difficult to tell whether the smiles that went with it were affectionate or patronizing.

Brinley shifted on the sofa and said, "The thing is, Suzanne, Gavin's not exactly the most sympathetic character, is he?"

Suzanne braced herself. So far he'd kept his feelings about Gavin out of the conversation.

"I know you're going to start moaning about the march." That was predictable – conversations about Gavin always took this turn. "Going on about how it was all Gavin's fault that the protest went wrong…"

"Well, he didn't help matters, did he?" Brinley had cut in before she could steer the conversation back to the matter of Sense's records. "He was never interested in anything we organized…"

"He was staying with us just to get himself together, sort himself out. You knew that. You can't act surprised that he didn't have his heart in OMNI. He was too messed up for that."

"I dunno…" head tilted backwards, Brinley shut his eyes. He stayed silent for a while, then said in a quiet, tired voice, "I don't understand how we ended up such a rump with people dossing around the house, doing little more than dropping tranx. Anna had the right idea…" Suzanne knew he'd bring Anna up "…separating the campaign from the old house. Setting up an office. Smartening up. At least it would have been the right idea if she hadn't split the group in two, leaving OMNI with a bunch of wasters."

"People like me and my brother, you mean? The rump?"

"Of course not you. The kids who used to lounge about the house whose only interest in the march was that it might get heated. I heard them. I heard them say that."

"You never heard Gavin say that."

"He might not have *said* it. But he got in on the violence. He's there on camera with a massive stick in his hand, pointing at a cop."

"I'm not denying that he acted stupidly. I'm saying it wasn't his fault he behaved like that. In any case, that wasn't any old copper he lost it with. It was one who'd been giving him a hard time."

"Oh stop it, Suzanne."

"Stop what?"

"Making excuses for him."

"I'm not," she said, but she knew that she was. She hated it when Brinley snapped; because it was so rare, it carried startling force. "I'm…I'm just looking at things from Gavin's point of view."

"Well, there are other points of view, aren't there? You give too much credence to his."

But someone had to give him the benefit of the doubt. Tired of his aggressiveness and drunkenness, their parents had given up on him, finally asking him to leave after he'd responded to a pep talk about getting himself together with a clenched fist that had only just missed their mum's head. Gavin was a mess. Suzanne had no problems accepting that. But he was also missing. That was the point.

"I just want Gavin traced, that's all. He's been missing for five weeks."

"He left London. That's what the police told you."

"And the police get their records from Sense and those records don't ring true." Brinley gave an impatient sigh. "Come on, you *know* they're questionable."

He stood and walked across the room and reached through the door into the unlit hallway. Then he dragged his toolbox into the lounge.

"When it comes to Gavin, Suzanne, I don't know much at all."

He rummaged through the toolbox, carefully scanning each compartment, lifting chisels, spanners, a rusty plane. He cleaned a wooden-handled screwdriver on already filthy jeans. Ignoring his question she said, "So, you think I'm wasting my time?"

"I didn't say that."

She waited for him to say more. He said nothing, just stood motionless but for his eyes sweeping the floor.

"So what *would* you say?"

Brinley didn't respond; hit by some memory, he'd snapped out of his trance. He walked over to the bookshelf.

"I thought I left it here," he said.

"The hammer? You did. I moved it to the top of the fridge where Adam can't stick it in his mouth like he nearly did this afternoon. Why's it more important to find your tools than talk about Gavin?"

Gesturing to the doorway, Brinley said, "The hall lights need fixing, the outside corridor too…"

"It's the solar storer. You told me that yesterday. It's not receiving enough energy from the panels on the roof. It's the landlord's job, not yours. You're just trying to avoid this discussion."

Brinley peered at her with a what-brought-this-tone-on look. Well, if it was difficult for him to get his head around, she'd explain it to him. "I'm trying to discuss my brother and you're more interested in your crummy tools. I get this from Adam."

"This what?"

"This not being listened to, this being ignored…oh, just forget it!"

She wished she hadn't lost her temper – it had made Brinley smile. She felt the sofa sag as he sat down next to her. "Look," he said, placing a palm on her thigh, "all I'm saying is that I think you've got a hard job getting anyone to look at Gavin's case." He was giving her a long look.

She avoided Brinley's eyes and sat rigid.

The breeze, still strong, wafted through the slit of the sash window. It felt cool on the back of her neck. She was silent a long while, but finally said, "I know Gavin annoyed you. He annoyed me as well. But you know he's got problems. And even forgetting about his problems, how faithful is Sense's intelligence? That's a reasonable question, isn't it?

"I s'pose so. But…"

Why did there always have to be a *but*? Why couldn't Brinley just agree?

"…it's possible he's fine, just taking time out of London as the records say."

"So, why haven't we heard from him?"

"Because that's how he is. He's not as responsible as you. You're worrying that something bad's happened. But maybe nothing's happened at all."

"Well, we don't know that, do we? I want to at least discuss it with someone at Sense." She paused. "I'm not getting anywhere, though. No one seems to be listening."

"OK," he said, slowly, as if he were really thinking things through, "OK, if you insist on pursuing this, then maybe you should forget the normal channels."

"What?"

"With Sense – you've been going through the proper channels, contacting Enquiries and the helpline…"

"But not getting anywhere."

"So forget that."

"And do what?"

"Go to the top. The directors and executives. They're so keen on getting the whole Resolve scheme through, selling it to the public, probably the last thing they want is some irate OMNI person raising questions about the veracity of their data. The directors might see this more than some rep on the phone."

"That might work," Suzanne said, seeing how it would be better to worry less about her seeming hypocrisy and instead use her position as a critic to her advantage. "I'll find a list of members…"

"Look at their profiles. Target the one you think will be most sympathetic."

"That's good…yes." The sounds of more young people talking, laughing, heading towards the tube station filtered through the window. Brinley craned his neck to catch a glimpse of them. "I'll contact Sense tomorrow," Suzanne said, quietly. "I'll do it first thing."

***

It was weird sitting at a bar, a little bit buzzed, scrolling through reviews of gaming controllers with a woman at his side who was indulging his interest.

"That's not the best review," she said, peering at his remote.

"Here… let me find you a good one. Good God! Isn't this screen a bit smudged?"

"Is it?" He was surprised she felt the need to reach in her bag for a tissue and give the screen a wipe. Hadn't he only just cleaned it a day or so ago? Or maybe she was fastidious. Fastidious and fidgety – she'd still been doing that occasional rubbing of her thigh.

The strap of a fold-up gas mask hung over the side pocket of her bag. At least they were on the same page about that; Ezra never went anywhere without his mask. The masks took up hardly any space. There was no excuse not to carry one. But maybe Ezra understood this more than most; with a brother-in-law killed by the encephalitis from the 2055 attack and a niece, four years down the line still suffering its effects, his memory wasn't short.

He turned away from the gas mask, towards the musicians on stage. He wanted to keep things light with this Lena, not get all serious about bio attacks and the like. He watched the drummers on stage for a while, then picked up a menu.

Lena said she wasn't hungry, so Ezra got ribs and fries for himself.

She slid his info-remote across the bar and showed him some reviews on Gameware Forum. He was tempted to study each post, but feeling a need to show some reserve, he said, "Thanks. I'll have a read later."

When his food arrived, she extended pincer fingers and plucked a fry from his plate. Wordlessly, he just pushed the plate between them. No verbal niceties. Just doing as they pleased. He liked that.

He normally swayed to the lowest drumbeats, but the guitarist was something else. His slides were impudent, sweeping suddenly from high to low, growing faster and faster until finally they merged into a metallic twanging dissonance. Ezra was blown away. The whoops and claps of the crowd became the most prominent sound, and the djembe drumbeat a calming layer. Ezra let its slow heavy rhythm pound through him. Steadied now, he turned to Lena. Nodding in time to the bass, she surveyed the musicians on the stage, the shifting crowd, the huge wall hangings with their geometric patterns on indigo cotton. She looked relaxed too.

Ezra felt good.

She flashed him a mischievous smile, and then extended her pincer fingers to his plate again.

But then she was distracted. Mo, the barman, had caught her attention.

"What's his problem?" Lena asked, nodding towards Mo's huge frame, which jutted against the pay pad on the bar. His expression, Ezra noted, was thunderous.

"What's up, Mo?" Ezra called out.

Mo walked over angrily muttering to himself, throwing filthy glances in the direction of the exit. Ezra swung around to look. Lena looked too. There was no one there.

"Who's bothering you?" Ezra asked.

"Well, I'll never know, will I? Skinny bloke, tall, that's about the sum of it."

"With jeans?" Lena said.

"Maybe." Mo shrugged his shoulders. "Dunno."

"Fallow colored?" Both Ezra and Mo looked at her blankly. "Skin color. Kind of... medium brown. *Fallow.*"

"Don't know about *fallow*," Mo cut in. "He never paid. That's all I care about." Mo waved a receipt in front of Ezra and pointed to the empty fingerprint box.

"Did a runner?" Ezra asked.

"Three scotches, a steak, plum tartlet with crème fraîche, for fuck's sake. Thinks I'm a fucking charity." Mo scooped an empty beer bottle off the bar and lobbed it into a recycling bin. "I still get good acts in..." Mo was nodding to the musicians who were on an interval and swigging back beers "...and I keep the place looking spick, but truth is I'm not making anything right now. Fuckers like that don't help."

"Shit," Lena said. "That's awful. Can't you help him out, Ezra? Tap into your surveillance records and everything with that little gadget you've got in your pocket."

"If that's what you want," Ezra said to Mo, knowing the chances of that were zero. It was doubtful the bar even had cameras inside. The place was mellow enough but plenty of times, usually later in the night, people would pass tabs around, snort X dust, and occasionally there'd be some friction. From a few quick glances around, Ezra saw no evidence of surveillance equipment.

"Nah," Mo said, confirming this. "No cameras. My prerogative. It's a private space here."

"What about outside?" Lena said.

"What about it?"

"She's right, Mo, there are cameras on the street. We could get his details from looking at the footage of him leaving." Ezra felt that he should make the offer. It was shit that this man had got Mo running around serving him drinks and food, then hotfooted it before the bill had hit the table. "You just need to file a complaint…"

"File a complaint? What, with the police? Yeah right," he huffed.

Ezra pretty much expected that reaction.

"Fallow," Ezra muttered to himself when Mo walked the length of the bar to serve a short blonde on stilettos.

"I suppose that sounds pretty imprecise to you, what with you being in Sense with all your face recognition systems and skin matchers and whatever else it is you've got."

"It *is* imprecise," Ezra said. On his remote he pulled up a skin color swatch and showed it to Lena. "What color was he? Make your selection." Lena hesitated over a group of close colors. "Somewhere in this range?" he asked. She nodded and Ezra pulled up the spectro numbers. "BF4400Y add or minus a variation factor of 4%."

"Not very romantic. I think *fallow* sounds better."

"And you…" Ezra took Lena's hand and turned it over so her palm faced upwards. He pointed the sensor of the remote towards her pulse, "…you are A13200X."

"I think I prefer *cinnamon* myself."

"Cinnamon. Very poetic. And how would you label me?"

"A darkish fawn."

It had a nice ring to it. But were these labels of hers loaded in some way? Why was she cinnamon? A spice – well, she was sort of spicy, he supposed. Why was he darkish fawn? The spectro-codes were better. They were precise and neutral.

"And your friend, Mo – he's reddy-brown like a conker. Just not as shiny," she added.

"S'pose he wouldn't be right now."

"Suppose not," she agreed.

There was a bleeping on Ezra's remote. A message from Systems at Sense. He logged in to the intranet for details. *Network maintenance necessary. Disruption level: negligible.* He was relieved to see the word *negligible.* Having to pack this night in and head off to deal with some work emergency would have been a crying shame.

Instead, he put his remote away and turned back to his plate of food. The bar was warm and crowded now. When he picked a ketchup-drenched fry, his arm got nudged by someone behind. The sauce splattered his shirt. Annoyed, he swung around and found a scarlet-lipped woman looking embarrassed, saying sorry over and over.

He couldn't bring himself to say, *it's OK.* He hated looking messy. Instead, he focused on wiping the stain off with a napkin.

"You need to get that out with water. Maybe soap," Lena said. "The sooner the better."

"Yeah?" This was a good shirt, from Duke Street. He didn't want it ruined. He slid off the barstool. "Back soon, then."

There was a strong stench of bleach in the toilets. Ezra grabbed a rough paper towel, dampened it and dabbed at the stain. By the time he finished, there was a large watery patch that was sticking to his chest and still a reddish mark in the middle. Have to do. He threw the soggy towel in the trash, then stood before a mirror with a little crack in its corner, willing himself not to delve with Lena, to just keep things spontaneous.

The muted bass line pulsated through the walls. He imagined Lena still nodding her head to the rhythm. She liked this bar. He was pleased about that.

Reflected in the mirror was a condom machine. He didn't want to ruin things, come on too strong, not if she didn't want. But, still staring at the machine, Ezra remembered how her gaze had swept over his face and lingered on his lips. She might want. He didn't know. But even so, he thought, as he found the change to put in the money slot, she might.

Ezra got the Durex and left the toilets. He passed around the back of the crowd gathered in front of the drummers, bustled past people dancing, picked his way to his place at the bar.

Lena wasn't there. Her glass was empty. There was a black rectangular plate on the bar with a receipt on top. Ezra picked the piece of paper up.

"She's paid," Mo said.

"Paid?" Mo was avoiding his eyes. "You mean she's gone. Are you serious?"

Mo nodded, looked slightly awkward. He *was* serious. Fuck.

Thinking that he'd got it wrong, Ezra scanned the room. There'd been something between them, a spark, a connection. How could she just up and leave? Had he said something to turn her off? What? He ran through their conversations. Couldn't find any place he'd got out of line. *She* was the one who'd led things – all that talk about the fetish, the gown, and getting undressed, then asking him to play a game. And she'd seemed all relaxed, nodding her head to the music, helping herself to his food. How could she walk out on him after all that?

He fixed on the door of the women's bathroom, wondering whether she was inside.

"She's not there," Mo said. Ezra turned around to face him. "She said to say thank you – she had a great time. Not your lucky night either."

"Fuck."

Ezra snatched up his glass. It was empty. Mo filled it up without being asked.

"Here you are, Ez. Have one on me."

4

Wednesday 13th August 2059

EARLY MORNING EZRA drove his Viper to Sense HQ, car window open, sound system playing an aggressive guitar. He switched to the fast lane, overtook a bus stopping alongside a hoard of severe-faced people, clocked their disapproving stares as he tore past. It was Lena, the way she'd messed him around; she'd made him go all juvenile and foul-tempered. If she'd just said something to his face like *look, I've had a nice time but...*but what? What would she have said? Was she married or something? All Ezra had to do was park his car in Sense HQ, take the stairs to his workstation in the Anomalies Department and enter a series of passwords to get all the answers he wanted. Not just from the snapshots and half-thoughts clogging social network sites, but from properly catalogued surveillance data: biometric records, files listing each place she'd lived and worked, time-stamped video showing every trajectory she'd taken through public space including exactly where she'd gone the night before.

Simply having her first name and a vivid memory of her looks would allow him to build up a profile in a matter of minutes. It would be a cinch to manipulate facial recognition software, find a good match in the database and determine some basic facts. Ezra had a good memory for faces; everyone in biometrics did.

Even if the visuals turned out to be insufficient to give Lena a positive database match (something he seriously doubted given the strange brightness of her eyes), he could always tie in voice records for added corroboration. Struck by her appearance, he hadn't paid much attention to how she'd sounded as they'd talked. But now that he was thinking about it, he recalled her voice was a little lower than average with maybe some scratchiness too. Could be a number of reasons for that. A common one was smoking. Fleetingly, he wondered what damage his occasional smoke did to his own vocal folds. The thought compelled him to clear his throat as he swerved around a bend in the road. Though Lena hadn't smoked the previous night, it looked liked she'd struggled to say no when he'd offered her a Bliss. Was she an ex-smoker? Or *user* as his sister would disparagingly say? Ezra gave a loud groan. Why was he even churning this over? It wasn't as if Lena had vanished without a word. She'd paid for the drinks and asked Mo to pass along her goodbye message. He should just write her off. Safest bet, though fucking unfair.

He floored the accelerator, veered past a black cab and a self-drive white van. Slumped against the headrest, he turned his head to the window to catch some fresh air.

But instead of a windblast, there was a problem with the gear change. He slowed down, changed back to first. There was a faint juddering and straining before the drive became smooth again. Approaching a traffic light at the Strand, he realized the taxi he'd passed earlier was drawing alongside. Its mustachioed driver was looking at him, triumphantly it seemed.

Ezra edged slowly around the island in the middle of the Strand with its solitary white church, then past the huge revolving doors of Sense Surveillance HQ. He bounced over two speed bumps, installed with tire identification scanners, then descended into the underground garage and brought the car to a standstill. Too bad John Durrant had left HQ; he had a knack with cars. A couple of times after work he'd flipped up the Viper's bonnet right here in the car park, once to set the alternator right, another to replace a valve. He would have had a play with the clutch as well, if he hadn't jacked in "all this corporate London shit" for a hermit's life near Colchester. Just as Ezra was about to instruct the comms system to call him he noticed the time: 08:45, glowing in red on the clock. He'd contact John later. Too early now; now that John didn't have anything to get up for, other than a day's fishing for carp in Ardleigh Reservoir.

A black Jaguar XZ3 slid into a parking space opposite, Cunningham from Contracts behind the wheel. Corporate climber – that much was obvious. A hotshot who'd headed London Transport Surveillance a couple of years back and was now eyeballing senior positions at Sense. Ezra kept tabs on him, especially since he was making a mark wheeling in Resolve technology with its powerful psycho-monitoring capabilities. "The ultimate technology," Cunningham had boasted in a presentation to senior staff. "A tool not only for reading people's real-time brain scans to see who was intending to commit a crime, but also a means to set them right." Ezra had no doubt that transmitting electrical "off-put" signals to individuals about to break a law sounded authoritarian and scary, but slowly Sense was making inroads in bringing the public on board. And Cunningham's PR efforts, to Ezra's annoyance, had been responsible for a lot of that success.

From his driver's seat, Ezra watched Cunningham finish his long-legged stride to the elevator. The stride seemed faster than usual. His face looked grave, thunderous even. Under some sort of pressure maybe.

Ezra pressed a control and the dark windows rose smoothly until they were shut. He got out of the car and took the stairs up to the nearly refurbished atrium.

Premises staff were busy installing colossal palms into vast blue pots. Ministers needed impressing, Ezra supposed; whenever they came to see if Sense should have its contracts renewed, their feel for the place would count. His gaze swept upwards, following the trunk of one of the palms, and settled high above enormous fronds on a slowly shifting large grey cloud that could be seen through the glass ceiling. Pricey plants probably wouldn't hurt Sense's image.

John had always been more cynical. Before he'd left, he'd been on a perpetual eye roll at all the "showy shit" the company pulled.

Ezra jogged the twelve floors to the Anomalies Unit, passing the Systems and Personnel departments on his way up. He slowed when he reached the training floor where he'd taken his biometric analysis tests. The smell of screen cleaner in the white-walled exam room would always be vivid in his memory, as would the training exercise where the examiner, Alex Fenton, had played an unlabelled video file of a young brown-haired woman waiting at a bus stop. Ezra had been surprised that the test had used live data, but had quickly matched her facial dimensions, iris characteristics, posture and gait to records in the database and determined that her name was Deborah Harrington that she was thirty-four, unmarried and lived in E17. He was good at this stuff, had been pleased with the test, but when the video had shown Deborah pulling out a cell phone from her Hynek handbag, Fenton had got weird and said, "Intercept that call." Ezra had known that there was something off about that, had even queried the behavior with Personnel. Their reaction was clinical; quickly they'd determined that Fenton was stalking and by the end of that day he'd been sacked.

Definitely, Ezra had to draw a line under any urge he had to look up Lena.

When he reached his office he saw an incoming transmission signal blinking on his desktop hologram unit. From the directors, no doubt. They'd been getting in early, issuing innumerable commands, convening countless meetings in the run up to the government's vote on Resolve. Immediately he flicked the *receive* control. The 3-D image of Monica Parks appeared. Neat blonde hair, black shirt, cream jacket. Icy, a lot of blokes said. Ezra sometimes thought that, but more often thought composed. Right now, with the Resolve vote imminent, Ezra was impressed with that coolness. She could be tough when the need arose. Intolerant of staff who took their people-watching too far, she'd been the one to sack Alex Fenton. She'd also taken the time to personally apologize to Ezra when he'd complained about the weirdness of the test. Maybe he was egotistical, but he could still recite the feedback she'd given on his exam: "You have integrity, initiative, composure, superlative technical skills. Your test, unconventional as it was, shows you possess these qualities. You could go very far within this organization. How would you like to be on the fast track to management?"

He'd liked the idea a lot. Had already climbed high, become Head of Anomalies with a team of a hundred tracers. He could see some of them now just outside his office. Dexter Sayle was closest, checking some data on his screen, spooning himself some cereal from a plastic carton as he worked. Ezra had weeded out the wasters and built an efficient team. He had no intention of throwing away his success by delving into private records. Not for Lena. Not for anyone.

"We need your help, Ezra…" the hologram unit showed Monica speaking from behind a large desk, with an antique Korean bottle to her side "…help with a complaint."

"Who's complaining?"

He sat down and faced the hologram.

"Suzanne Dixon."

"Dixon?" He'd heard the name, just needed to recall how. "One of the OMNI people?"

"That's right."

"What's her problem?"

"Her brother's missing. Has been missing for five weeks."

"Has she been to the police?"

"She has. But she doesn't accept what they told her."

"Which was?"

"That the final surveillance data on her brother show Gavin Dixon on a train that left St. Pancras for Prague on the 10th of July."

"That's what our records show?" Ezra asked.

"That's right."

"So, he's not an anomaly. He hasn't dropped off our records inexplicably…"

"No," Monica said.

"…and he hasn't suddenly appeared on our surveillance footage without explanation." Monica was shaking her head gently, looking, as always, serene. "So, this is a matter for Enquiries, not

Anomalies." Ezra looked through the glass partition of his workspace, over to the banks of tracers occupying the vast floor. They were poring over data-tables or scrutinizing visual recordings or listening to audio info with interference-eliminating head gear – all were dealing with real anomalies: sudden disconnects in intelligence, breaks in the record of people's movements, sudden appearances or disappearances. All his tracers were working flat out to square up these glitches. With Gavin Dixon, Ezra couldn't see anything that needed squaring. "Why can't someone in Enquiries talk her through the footage?"

"She's tried Enquiries, several times apparently. So now she's gone higher. Actually, she specifically targeted me." Ezra could understand that. If he had to complain to a director, Monica, with her charitable foundations and sponsorship of art galleries, had a more humane, less profit-centered profile than some of the others. "And my belief," she continued, "is that we should keep her happy." Because she was vocal, Ezra surmised – an OMNI member bearing a grudge and pumping out bad publicity was not what the directors would want right now. "I know that her brother's departure is all on record and explicable and strictly not an anomaly. But the thing is Suzanne Dixon *thinks* it's an anomaly somehow. And my belief is that she might benefit from someone senior talking her through how it's not."

Monica's blue-grey eyes were fixed on Ezra.

"Me?" Was she serious? He had an entire department to run. He didn't have time for pissy little complaints like this.

"I think you'd be good for this. Plus, I think it would be good for her to see that we're taking her seriously."

Ezra was silent for a while. Knowing she was going to insist, he said. "OK... OK, I'll deal with this real quick."

"Thank you, Ezra," Monica said, her eyes somehow seeming a little brighter. Forthright and polite and always so poised – was there ever a time she didn't get what she wanted? He watched her figure disappear from the hologram platform.

Beautiful, but out of reach. The kind of night he'd had with Lena – he couldn't see that with her.

Ezra switched on his text editor to write a pointedly sensitive message to Ms. Dixon.

***

Standing in the kitchen, holding the broom cupboard open, Suzanne hesitated at unhitching the mop from its hook. A revulsion was stopping her scrubbing the Bolognese sauce splatter congealed on a linoleum tile in front of the oven. Everything she needed was in the cupboard, right there in front of her – the mop with its raggedy head, the bucket strewn in a dark corner and the bottle of Econo bleach on a dusty top shelf. Half of her was saying *fill the bucket, dunk the mop, wipe the mess.* But the other half was intensely repulsed even by the idea of this chore. In a sudden decision to stop being ridiculous and deal with things, she grabbed the bleach bottle and unscrewed its top, but the chlorine fumes, unexpectedly strong, made her nauseous.

A message alert bleeped. She headed immediately for the computer in the living room, relieved to get away from the bleach.

With Adam asleep on the sofa, Suzanne was careful to avoid the floorboard that creaked in the middle of the room. She approached the computer, temporarily stationed on the end of the dining table, and checked her messages. She'd only written to Sense some two hours before, but there, already, was a reply. Probably just confirmation that they'd received her complaint, nothing substantive surely – it was too quick a response for that. She opened the message and read:

RE: Gavin Dixon Case KGXISN33
Dear Ms. Dixon,

    In response to your communication regarding your brother, Gavin Dixon, who our records show was initially reported to the police as missing on 14th July 2059, I would be pleased to assist you gather information on this case. I would like to offer you an appointment time for tomorrow…

Suzanne could hardly believe it. Tomorrow. God! To meet with someone in senior management? She checked the message for a name and read: *Ezra Hurst, Head of Anomalies Unit.* Not Monica Parks then, but still a departmental head.

Later, she texted Brin, but getting no instant response she decided to call. Several rings passed. Were they all so engrossed with their little creative projects – Brin and Jamal with their Brancusi-style furniture, Zoe with her ceramics and Sarah with her silver jewelry – that they couldn't get to a phone? When finally Brinley's voice came down the line, Suzanne could hear laughter in the background and Jamal (she knew it was Jamal) doing riffs on his guitar. Did they do any work there?

"Hi there," Suzanne said, to Brin's hello, a hello that still contained the laughter of some workshop joke she'd had no access to.

"Hey you. What's up?"

"Sense got back to me about Gavin."

"They did?"

"They want me to go in…for a meeting."

"So it worked, then, going in all high level?"

"Seems so," she said, still hearing some background laughing, Jamal scaling his guitar and, faintly, the banging of a hammer. So, at least one person there was working. Suzanne was struck by the noise in the workshop, the freedom to make it anyway. She looked over to the sofa when she heard a rustling of Adam's blanket. "Looks like I'll finally find out about Gavin," she said quietly, then seeing Adam fidget his way into a ball shape she stepped over the floorboards that creaked, and took her mobile to the kitchen, out of earshot from her boy. "Can you look after Adam then, tomorrow, when I have this meeting?"

"Course…" Brinley said, "You OK? You sound down."

"Bit tired maybe." With the phone to her ear, Suzanne stared at the bottle of Econo bleach, lidless on the kitchen counter. Keeping her face away from the fumes, she began twisting the lid back on with her free hand.

"You must have written a pretty sharp complaint for them to get back to you so soon. That's something, eh?"

Still, she felt she could tell what Brin was really thinking: *that's something, but that's it. You'll get the meeting, then be told the position is the same as before. No new information. No more help.* It was something she half thought herself. Were the people at Sense asking her in to gloat? *So you want our help, do you? After you've been so busy protesting against us.* This Ezra Hurst had been all polite in the message, but what were his real feelings?

"Shit," Suzanne said, when the bleach bottle lid slipped from her hand.

"What's the matter?"

The acrid smell of chlorine hit her again as she said, "Nothing...nothing." Then grimacing and pulling away from the fumes, she added, "What time you coming back?"

"Maybe a bit later, especially if I've got Adam tomorrow." Always a trade-off, Suzanne thought, while listening to more muted laughter through the earpiece. She wondered whether Jamal, Zoe and the rest would all be sticking around after hours too. "So, see you later then," Brinley said. How much later? she wanted to know, but didn't ask. "OK?" came Brinley's uncertain voice.

"OK."

***

When Ezra checked his messages at the end of the day he saw that the Dixon woman had accepted tomorrow's appointment. Pointless meeting, he thought. He'd checked the surveillance data. She'd already been given every relevant fact about her brother. Sense had nothing more to add. Still, he'd have to go through the motions, keep the directors happy. And ignore her campaigning and protesting. He wasn't so bothered about her hypocrisy. It was the naivety he couldn't stomach. The idea that the world was a place where everyone could be trusted, where everyone had good intentions and no one needed monitoring. Well, he thought, clearing some papers into a drawer, he'd keep things with Ms. Dixon as brief as possible. Meet, discuss, close. That's how it'd be. Half an hour max, then out of his hair.

He exited Anomalies and headed towards his car.

Taking the stairwell, he checked his watch. 17.52. That was about the time Lena's feet had appeared at the top of the Tavern's stairs. Maybe she was perched right now at the bar. Quick stroll round the corner, down towards the Thames. Would only take five minutes to check the place out. His pace to his car faltered. Even if she was in the Tavern would it seem too eager to turn up? Go chasing after her? She'd upped and left without a word to him, and that, now he was thinking about it, was pretty piss-poor. Chances were she wouldn't be there. Forget it. He'd go home. Ezra picked up pace and walked briskly to his car.

Down in the car park, when Ezra turned on his engine and put his foot on the clutch, he felt a glitch. He raised the clutch slowly and reversed. The indigo jag was opposite. No driver. Good. If Ezra was going to stall, he didn't want Cunningham smirking in the background.

"Durrant's number. Dial."

"Dialing," came the system's response.

John," Ezra said, when he heard a click on the line.

"Yeah?"

"It's me. Ez."

"Oh… Hello, Ez. What've you been up to?"

"This and that," Ezra said. Maybe he'd tell John about Lena some day. He just didn't want to go over it right now.

"What's up?"

"Car. The clutch, probably."

"It's your driving. Told you that before. You keep riding the clutch the way you do, you're going to wear it…"

"It's not my driving."

"So what is it, then?"

"Dunno. That's why I'm calling. I'll bring it to you. You can take a look."

"What? You wanna bring it out here with a broken clutch? It won't make it."

"It'll make it all right," Ezra said. He'd be in fifth most of the way. It was only the low gears causing the problem. Fifty minutes or so, then he'd be at John's. The car had been on the charger all the time it had been parked. Battery was nice and full. "I'm bringing it up."

"You serious? I'm telling you. You'll destroy the clutch."

"I'll get to you. It's a small problem. It'll be OK."

"What do you know?"

"Trust me."

"Yeah, right."

"Hour and a half. See you then."

"Back of a tow truck. Fifty quid."

Oh yeah, John liked betting. Ezra had forgotten about that. But John hadn't felt the glitch the way Ezra had. It was minor. He'd get out to Colchester OK. "All right," Ezra said. "Fifty quid."

Three hours later, when Ezra arrived at the back of a tow truck he paid the breakdown man first, then resentfully gave John his fifty quid.

It was dark by the time he'd arrived. The car needed pushing into John's garage, which had a powerful central ceiling light. A mix of precision tools and angling tackle was strewn around: scattered on benches, dangling from hooks on the walls, heaped in piles on the concrete floor. There was also a smell of fish.

"Gutted a bream in here earlier," John explained, flipping up the Viper's bonnet. "Was a giant one." Ezra looked over to a beaten up wooden bench where some bloodstains remained. "It's in a pot now. Stew. Want some?"

Ezra shook his head; the fish had no appeal.

He glanced about the garage, spotted some surveillance and security gadgets he'd picked up from expos – a variety of cameras, even a parabolic microphone. "Just wanna know how these things work," John had said, when he'd pocketed a tapper from an expo in Bristol back in 2057. And, true enough, the tapper lay in bits on a low shelf, all its circuits exposed.

Ezra brushed cobwebs off a small broken window. The frame had dry rot; left a black-brown gritty smear on his fingers. Through the window he saw a large yellow light beaming out of the open backdoor of a decrepit house.

"That's the kitchen," John said. "Have a poke about if you want. Get some drinks. There are cans in the fridge."

Scuffing his way across a gravelly yard, Ezra heard a clank that came from the garage, probably John tossing some wrench onto the concrete floor. Apart from that there was nothing. No sound.

There were no other buildings around. Just one narrow lane, deserted right now. He looked up at the house. Small, old and ramshackle with several cracked windows. He walked into an unmodernized kitchen with a dusty floor and a fishy smell. A big pot sat on top of a dirty gas cooker. Turn-of-the-century wiring dangled from the ceiling. New lights, solar storers and energy emitters lay on a cluttered wooden table, still in packets waiting to be installed. John had his work cut out renovating this old shack. Not something Ezra would ever take on. He eyed the old soapstone sink in the corner. It was half polished up. Probably would look good when it was finished. Then he poked his head into the hallway. Peeling wallpaper. Bare floorboards, many misaligned. At the end of the hallway was a living room. Basic but comfortable. Sofa, armchair, hologrammer in the corner with a static nude on the platform. Reclining with a copper sheen to her skin, it was a typical John creation. Ezra smiled. John used to do this 3-D art stuff in London. Nearly always the same subject: nudes, reclining, leaning on one arm, knees drawn upwards, legs slightly (always slightly) parted, or almost closed, depended how you thought about it. In any case so close together you could barely see anything between. This copper woman was no exception. John's nudes were always like this, the silver ones in London – Ezra had inspected them all. The color palette on the control pad of the hologrammer was set to metallic hues. Copper 23, to be exact. It was clever, what John did. Captivating. But Ezra never asked him what was going through his head. Everyone had some weird shit going on, shit beyond analysis.

Ezra left the room, got a couple of beers from the fridge and took them back to the garage. He'd begun thinking of Lena again, wondering where she'd gone, but stopped when he found half his Viper in bits on the garage floor. "Jesus Christ! Are you taking the whole engine out?"

"Got to." John replied, "Then you got to get it away from the transaxle."

Squatting on the floor, John was studying the flywheel. After a moment he rooted through a box of tools, found a big screwdriver, rejected it in favor of a bar. Gently he used this to pry a couple of plates apart. He pried a long time, until he suddenly leapt backwards when the plates fell and clanked on the concrete. "They're bastards for getting your toes," John said.

"So what you going to do?"

"Gonna put that clutch in," he said, nodding to a unit to his side. "I ordered it soon as you got off the line. Did a search for used ones. Had it delivered." He nodded to the bench. "There's the receipt." John stood, grabbed his beer from the bench, pulled off the ring and took a swig. "See, I knew you'd need another one. I know how you drive. You're too aggressive…"

"Aggressive!"

John kicked at Ezra's old clutch.

"Look, you can see all the springs and pads, how they're all worn down." Ezra looked. Were they worn? Maybe? He pretty much had to take John's word for it. "Had to give some time or other."

"All right," Ezra said, seeing John smirking. "You got your money. How long's it gonna take?"

"To fix? You're gonna be here a long time. You might as well kip on the floor and set off in the morning. Get up early. You'll get a nice clear road."

5

Thursday 14th August 2059

TAKE OUT THE 5.30 start and the boozy head, the drive back
to London was straightforward enough. The clutch seemed
smooth. Slight squeal maybe, but not the slipping of before. Fish
stink – that concerned Ezra more. The smell seemed to be seeping
out of his clothes and swirling around the car. He'd already been
on the Net and put in an instant delivery Ready to Rumble order.
Hopefully, the package of clean clothes (no need to specify size or
style, Ezra's details were on record from the last time he'd crashed
some place), toothpaste, toothbrush, washcloth, razor, deodorant,
should be waiting at reception for him when he arrived.

It was. The receptionist, a twenty-something redhead, dutifully
passed him the package. She had the good grace to keep a straight
face. She was new though. With the last front-of-house, he'd never
have heard the last of it.

Ezra cleaned up, got some coffee and took the stairs to the
Anomalies interview room.

With Suzanne Dixon due in half an hour, he downloaded a

large directory of files on her brother, Gavin. The footage of his last recorded movements at St. Pancras Station carried the date Thursday 10th July 2059. Coffee cup in hand, Ezra relaxed in a swivel chair and looked at the wall screen. Seemed straightforward enough. The footage showed Dixon (grungy? punky? – Ezra could never get his head round such ugly styles), pacing around the concourse, until the 11.55 Euro Express to Prague came in, then he loped along platform seven and boarded the train.

Ezra scanned a police memo that had been cross-referenced to the recording: Suzanne Dixon had reported Gavin missing on Monday 14th July; the police had shown her the St. Pancras camera data; she wasn't satisfied with that account; they'd referred her to Sense, basically, Ezra inferred, to get her out of their hair. Not that Ezra had anything more to add. He'd be going over exactly the same footage. All right, this Dixon hadn't contacted anyone yet, but some people were like that, young men especially.

Ezra was struck by the police reference number; it indicated that Gavin Dixon had been the subject of other enquiries and that the police on at least two other occasions had tapped into Sense intelligence. Ezra ran a search to find out more.

Dixon was listed on surveillance data of the big OMNI protest in Central London on Saturday 22nd March 2059, nearly five months ago. Ezra remembered seeing the protest on the news. OMNI had huge support then and this protest had been heavily publicized.

Ezra had resented that campaign. Still did. Why wasn't it obvious that there were times when security was of overriding importance, like back in 2055 when the Hedexa virus was released by some lunatic or militant, whoever the hell he was, killing 549 people? If Sense had already had Resolve in place, he would have been stopped the minute he'd started plotting. So what if it meant tapping into people's internal monologues? Ezra had no interest in sifting through the vast mass of shit most people were thinking. The Resolve software would pass over harmless stuff. But if someone was pulling together concepts like *Ebola virus, dispersal, covert* – then, why not dig further, root through their mind? Then what had happened to Ezra's niece might not happen to some other little girl.

Irritated now, Ezra remembered the details of OMNI's demonstration: thousands had turned out for the march, but some had broken off and gone their own way, gone to West London, around the Portobello, where things had quickly got out of hand and the march had turned into a riot. From looking at the reference log, Ezra could see that Gavin Dixon was one of the Portobello protestors.

Curious, Ezra uploaded the footage. It took a minute or so to get sensitized to the images. His eyes darted up and down and across the screen, to cars engulfed in orange fireballs – two upturned, one on its side, all windows smashed; to figures in balaclavas, scrambling, shrieking, charging and roaring; to a phalanx of policemen in riot gear, and a water cannon blasting at a woman's feet, sending her crashing to the ground.

Everyday street items all out of place: antique dustbins, aluminum and corrugated, clanking along the middle of the road, their lids, snatched up as rioters' shields; crude missiles formed from protest placards; bottles, planks, a road works sign somersaulting through the reddened, smoky air.

There were screams and sirens, shattering glass, a searing wail of agony, urgent voices and the clicking and crackling of a police radio.

He watched a figure on the screen grapple with a white balustrade of a rickety fence, then boot the bottom horizontal plank until finally he wrenched the piece clean away. Javelin now, point facing forward, high in the air. The man edged forwards towards a solitary policeman. Was this Gavin Dixon? Ezra placed a cursor on the image of the man's rage-filled face and called up details from the database: Gavin Dixon, d.o.b. 2035. Jesus Christ! Where did this seething aggression come from? Why was this twenty-four-year-old so wound up?

With a sudden explosion in the background, Dixon spurted around a blazing car. When the policeman toppled in the blast, Dixon raced forwards, one arm bent at the elbow ready to deliver the spear, the other arm straight out in front as a counterbalance, his expression one of total focus, total determination. The cop quickly straightened himself up, faced Dixon straight on.

Ezra jabbed *replay*, focused on this cop, noted the supercilious expression, the mouthing of – what? Some taunt? Ezra upped the volume to catch the word.

Cretin.

Destroy. That was the mode this Dixon had gone into – it was there in hate-filled eyes and a deranged but efficient, pummeling of the policeman's mouth. On the screen, the policeman rolled on the ground, choked, spat out blood and what? – splinters of wood? Pieces of grit? Oh Jesus! Teeth. He'd never say *cretin* again. No doubt about that.

Ezra pressed *stop* and breathing out, leaned back in his chair. The image of Gavin Dixon, blood-stained spear in hand, remained frozen on the screen. Futile, Ezra thought – the protestors had undermined their own argument. The news networks were more interested in this anarchy than they were in OMNI's message.

From the corner of his eye, Ezra caught a movement by the entrance of the interview room, a flash of blue.

"Oh right," came a sarcastic female voice from the doorway where a woman stood, staring disapprovingly at the screen. "I see we're going to get off to a good start."

Shit. Suzanne Dixon, fresh-faced and dressed in a man's denim shirt, was standing at the entrance. She was early and Muriel, the receptionist, now sheepishly retreating, had waved her over before Ezra had had time to straighten things up.

Ezra offered Suzanne a seat to the side of his desk. He grabbed two files from the space in front of her to give her some room.

"That's not the real Gavin," she said, looking at the image of her spear-wielding brother still frozen on the wall screen. "Don't let that be your only impression of him."

Ezra glanced back at the screen, the image of the wooden picket aimed in the direction of a policeman, Dixon's arm brought back for maximum thrust, the clenched teeth and lips twisted with rage, the hatred in his eyes – it was still the expression that fascinated Ezra. From the corner of his eye, he noticed Suzanne shift in her chair.

If the idiot receptionist hadn't let her in early, Ezra wouldn't have felt so defensive, and ended up asking, "What impression should I have?"

"The real Gavin," she said, "is clever and tame. Not one malicious bone in his body." She hesitated as if she were waiting for Ezra to challenge this description, but it was so far away from what he'd just seen, he had no response. "You have no idea," she said quietly. She gave a small sigh, then continued, "He was always very studious as a kid. Right from a young age he was fascinated with math. Shapes and patterns – he was always pulling objects around, squidging soft balls, tangling up strings, trying to see what contortions he could come up with. He did a project at school when he was about eleven on the mathematics of shoe lacing. D'you know what he said to me once?" Ezra shook his head. "He said, 'Did you know that if you have a shoe with eight pairs of eyelets, there are over 50 billion ways of doing the lacing?'" Ezra's eyebrows must have raised, because the next thing she said was "I didn't believe it either, but I looked it up on the web and I found it was true."

This creamy-skinned girl seemed too young to be in his office raising serious questions. Most times it was the parents who looked for missing kids, not siblings. And, glancing at her face, the fresh complexion, Ezra judged she was the younger sibling too. Very early twenties, probably. She didn't try with her appearance – no snappy hairstyle, no sharp clothes. Unsophisticated – maybe that's why she seemed young.

"God, that project!" Something had made her smile. "Gavin did a presentation on the properties of the different lacing arrangements. The whole family had to scrabble around finding shoes to give him for this bloody presentation. He took dozens of different shoes to school with different types of lacing: zigzag, criss-cross, serpentine, star…" She sighed again. "When he went on to university he got a first for math. He was post-grad in topology, you know. That's what he was engrossed in – the geometry of complex knots. Folds as well." Suzanne was now bending and straightening her arm, pointing at the crease in the elbow of her denim shirt. "He'd look at the patterns in a material and see what new arrangements you could make if you put in a crease or layered one kind of fabric over another."

"Well," Ezra said, "I'm sure there's more to your brother than the little I've seen."

"Yes, there is."

"But what I need to discuss with you are the dates and places Gavin was last seen." He had to take control now; he'd spent enough time on appeasement. "I want to show you the last security data we have for Gavin."

Ezra pressed a control on the workstation and a screen rose from a slit in the desk just in front of Suzanne. They watched the footage of Gavin at St. Pancras station, milling around the concourse.

"Same jacket," Suzanne said quietly. She was staring at the image of Gavin in a dirty green jacket. There was a large rip where one sleeve joined the shoulder and further down was a raggedy cuff. "He used to wear that jacket all the time."

Ezra glanced from the desk screen to the wall screen where the frozen image of Gavin with his bloodstained spear remained. It was true. He was wearing the same jacket in that footage too.

"Looks like it's seen better days," Ezra said.

"Yeah, he never used to walk around like that. He was always so tidy. He used to dress very boring." She was peering at the screen, watching the skinny figure of her brother walk along the platform, then step towards the train. She continued peering as the footage showed him shuffle through the carriage, then finally pick a seat. "Doesn't make sense," she said.

"For Gavin to get up and go?" Suzanne didn't say anything. "Well, that's the record we have."

"Well, I'd like to show you another record," she said, after a moment's silence. "Go on the Net," she said, gesturing towards the control panel. "Put in BBC news 3rd August 2056."

Curious, Ezra obliged. He found the archived news stream. The top story was the Maglev train crash at Manchester Piccadilly Station with images of fire-fighters, paramedics and police officers grappling with the mangled wreckage. Ezra looked at Suzanne uncertainly, waited for her to expand.

"Gavin was due to make a speech at a conference on topology.

There were people flying in from all over the world. He was traveling up from London. This is the train that he took."

"He was in this crash? Was he…badly hurt?"

"Coma for fifteen weeks, just tubes keeping him alive. Then when he did come around, all he did was try to pull them out. Must've been pain or discomfort or something. Took him months to relearn just the basics – feeding, grooming, recognizing people. He's come a long way, thank God. But he's not going back to academia. Can't concentrate now. Can't deal with complex information…and he knows what he's lost," Suzanne added, suddenly peering at Ezra, like she really wanted him to understand this. "So, now he gets frustrated, depressed, angry. Hit mum on more than one occasion. She had enough in the end. That's how he came to stay with us."

"He lived with you?"

"Twice," Suzanne said. "First in the old house with all the OMNI crowd. There was this Czech man who used to hang around there. Lukas Čapek. Gavin and him talked about traveling. Well, it was mainly Lukas who talked. He used to tell stories about Prague, and…poor Gavin…he was interested in hearing about Prague because that was the venue for an important math conference this year. But this is what you need to understand," Suzanne said, peering at Ezra, "Gavin's *never* been on a train since the Maglev crash." The hard look she was giving Ezra seemed interminable. "Never," she said again.

Ezra wasn't sure what exactly she was trying to say. He'd shown her the footage of Gavin at the station, pacing around the concourse, looking (and this made sense to Ezra now) pretty anxious.

"But you say Gavin talked about going to Prague?"

"He did," Suzanne conceded. "Lukas elaborated on places he knew, people he could visit. When Gavin started looking at travel sites we were all surprised. I worried about the idea, what he'd get up to, but he tried to book a flight…"

"A flight?"

"Yes, but he was prohibited from flying. He was considered dangerous after the attack on that policeman. The police were sore that the case never got to the court, but they made sure he was sectioned under Mental Health. He was banned from flying. Too unpredictable. Too much of a security risk to have on a plane. Gavin stopped saying anything about going. He never said much about anything, not about OMNI or the campaign. Most times he just sat there, saying nothing, just drinking. It was those times I used to talk about what he could do to get his act together. I suppose I never really accepted that the old Gavin was unrecoverable." She was silent for a while. "Can you close that file?" She nodded to the image of Gavin on the wall screen. Ezra closed the file. He felt bad that she'd even seen it. "So, you see, that's not the real Gavin." Then she added quietly, "Really, it's my fault he's gone missing."

"Why do you say that?"

"When me and Brin found our new flat, Gavin came to stay. But he got too much in the end," she said, looking down to the floor. "He'd get drunk and leave his tranx tabs lying around. The last day I saw him he was sprawled on the sofa, completely out of it. His pills had fallen on the carpet and my boy, Adam, had crawled over and put one in his mouth."

"Oh Christ!" Ezra said, the words slipping out quietly.

"I managed to get the pill out, though. Adam was all right. But I got Gavin by the collar and gave him a right old shake and yelled at him that he needed to get his act together. Go to the Czech Republic like he'd been discussing, drive down there or something with some of the Czechs that Lukas talked about. Do something, anything, just get out my sight. That's exactly how I put it: *just get out of my sight.* So, he walked out…and I haven't seen him since."

Ezra's office seemed eerily quiet when she finished. He stared at her now, as he had throughout that whole quick fire monologue.

She was looking down towards her shoes. Tatty trainers and an arrangement of laces he'd never seen before. A star pattern with the string forming a great clump in the middle.

"It's called devil lacing," Suzanne said quietly. "Apparently, it's *dense.* No vertical or horizontal segments. Just diagonals that cross at the center."

She had way too much on her plate. Early twenties with a kid.

Jesus, the last thing she needed was to beat herself up about this missing brother.

Ezra scrutinized a data log on Gavin Dixon, the initial complaint she'd made to the police, and their subsequent dismissal. "Strobo camera JF290 records your brother leaving St. Pancras station on a 11.55 train on 10th July 2059". That's what the police had told her. From checking over the footage, Ezra knew it was right. And hadn't Suzanne just said that she'd told her brother to go off to the Czech republic?

Some people just jacked it in. Took off suddenly in a screw everything gesture. Ezra had to think of some way of getting Suzanne to see this. She should leave satisfied that Sense had done everything in its power to help and, anyway, he now felt for this girl – even without Monica on his back, that's what he wanted for her. Well, he'd shown her how things were. Was she satisfied? From a glimpse of her expression, severe, withdrawn, mouth down turned – it didn't look that way.

Ezra leaned across the control desk, scanned through some of the previous images, looked for the clearest. He stopped the footage at the point where he was at the gate.

"We need to concentrate on these last images, especially if, as you say, he wears the same stuff all the time." The printer was purring at the edge of the workstation and multiple pictures of Gavin shown at Gate seven were emitted. "These contacts in Prague Gavin was told about. You need to track them and anyone who might know where he is over there, and distribute these pictures."

"Did you hear what I told you?" Suzanne replied. "Gavin never went on a train after the crash."

Momentarily, they stared at each other in silence, then Ezra said, "Let's start with the intelligence we have, shall we? Then, take things from there." Suzanne looked doubtful. But, finally, she accepted the pile of pictures Ezra was offering.

When she pushed her chair back and stood ready to leave, one of the pictures dropped to the floor. Ezra picked it up, then he rooted through the desk drawer, pulled out an elastic band and offered it to Suzanne. She rolled up the pictures, eased the band over the paper cylinder and left the Anomalies interview room without saying goodbye.

6

TEN TO TWO. Ezra strode passed the lifts and took eight flights of stairs to Directors' Level at a light jog. There were rugs in the reception area. Deep reds and blues with little angular patterns. Six-foot tiger holograms were spaced along the corridor, beamed straight from the New National Gallery in Seoul. Cunningham was just leaving, heading towards the lift, his face unnaturally reddish, expression severe, troubled even. Seemed to Ezra that Cunningham hadn't even noticed he was there.

Presumably the directors were seeing all the departmental heads. Contracts, PR, Anomalies, Events, Technology, Finance, Customer Relations – each department needed to be running smoothly if Sense was to get the Resolve contract. The way Cunningham was behaving, all stiff and self-absorbed, made Ezra wonder what his meeting with Monica would bring.

Director's Level – there was a side of Ezra that aspired to this god's eye view of the company. The thing was, and he knew this worked to his advantage, he didn't come across as ambitious. With each of his promotions, people around him had been surprised.

And that's how Monica Parks had operated too. She'd stood

out to Ezra partly because she was attractive, partly because they had the same modus operandi. And Ezra, since he'd joined, had watched her go far.

He pushed open the door to her office when her PA buzzed him in.

Her large white desk dominated the room. Monica along with two security guards was to the side of the room by a display case into which an antique ceramic bottle was being carefully positioned. She liked East Asian artifacts. Pottery like this and the tiger holograms had only appeared once she'd arrived on Directors' Level.

"Won't keep you long," Monica said amiably. "I'm re-installing the bottle," she said. "It's just been restored."

While Monica and the security guards concentrated on positioning the vase, Ezra paced over to the window. He glimpsed the small church down on street level, its white spire gleaming in the sun.

Ezra had connected with Monica there once, briefly, a couple of years after he'd started at Sense and a few weeks after the 2055 bio attack. As with now, there'd still been confusion about the identity of the perpetrator and the motive, and updates on the attack were still making headline news. But central London had started working again and people had begun carrying their masks rather than wearing them. Ezra had been sitting in the church, the organ playing in the background, and Monica, who he hadn't even realized was there, had crossed the marble floor and faced him.

She was holding a bunch of yellow leaflets in her hand, looking serious, her blonde hair styled impeccably in a bob around her shoulders. He'd felt a need to explain what he was doing there.

"It's calm in here," he said. At least it was once the organist had stopped.

Ezra crossed the Strand near enough every day, passing this church on its own little island in the middle of the street but never paying it any attention. He'd just dodge double-deckers and black cabs along with every other worker dashing out of the office for lunchtime refuel.

But that day the church had stood out – all bright white

between two lines of blood red buses streaming either side. The low organ hum seeping through the door had drawn him in. "Dunno," he said, "just had an appeal…I'm not religious." "Me neither," Monica said. She gave a half smile. "Perhaps I'm a hypocrite."

Ezra was surprised. He'd pegged her as a churchgoer. He'd seen her dodge traffic on the Strand and head into the church a number of times. "Thought you were a regular," he said.

"A regular? No. Sometimes I come. It depends on who's playing, you know," she said nodding towards the organ, "the recital." He glanced up at the mammoth complex of gold pipes. The organist had jet-black spiky hair and was folding his manuscript, wedging it into an old leather bag.

Monica waved to him. "You raced through that," she told him, as he approached.

"Too rushed?" He tightened the straps on his bag. "Lots on right now."

"I shouldn't criticize, should I?" Monica turned to Ezra. "Anthony plays the organ just as a little hobby. It's a surprise he finds any time to play. He's normally tied up in meetings all day. Do you like Bach, Ezra?"

"Sounded impressive enough," Ezra replied. "Don't know too much about it."

Anthony gave him a small smile. Supercilious, Ezra thought. They came from different worlds, these two. Monica with her interest in classical music and the art world, East or West, it didn't matter – she was a different kind of animal from Ezra, talking as she was, about the Members Only evening at the British Museum. She and the organist would both be there, checking out a celadon glaze exhibition, whatever that was. Before he left, the organist threw a pleased-to-meet-you nod at Ezra. Ezra threw one back.

"Anthony was playing Fugue in D," Monica said. "I like Fugue in D." She looked around at the empty chairs. "Evidently nobody else does."

"I wouldn't know," Ezra said. Church music wasn't normally his thing, just matched his mood that day.

He glanced at the pile of leaflets in her hand, and Monica,

presumably reading a curiosity, said, "Just some information about New Way – an organization I help with." Ezra knew about her interest in New Way. The Christmas card she'd sent him and all the other Departmental Heads had the New Way logo on the back along with the information that the organization was a registered charity providing safe houses for women. "I'll pin a leaflet to the notice board and leave the rest on the table at the front. The reverend said it was OK." She hesitated. "Are you OK, Ezra? I heard about your niece, how she got caught by the virus…how is she now?"

"Encephalitis… stable now…but will come out of hospital a different little girl… with fewer opportunities."

"I won't intrude on your quiet time," Monica said, "but I just want to say I'm very sorry."

Ezra mumbled a thanks. Everybody was sorry. It was good of her to say so, but it didn't change things.

"I need to get back," she said, "but you – maybe you should take your time."

And Ezra had sat in the quiet of that church several minutes more.

She'd been in Personnel then, but had moved up to quickly to Special Assignments and then to this office on Director's Level where Ezra stood now. Installing ceramic pieces like this bottle, she was making her presence felt.

"Is much known about it?" Ezra asked, seeing how satisfied she looked with its position.

"Actually, yes, there is a story behind it." She was watching the security guards as she spoke. "Supposedly there was an aristocratic woman who became bedridden with fever and terrible cramps. Her doctors told her that they had no cure for her, that she should bring her family near to see them for the last time. Well, she did no such thing."

Monica walked around the bottle and a helmeted security professional, who was bending over it setting its laser locks, then beckoned Ezra over. Smiling, she said, "Instead, she ordered this wine bottle to be made." Pointing to the stylized plant motif, the leaves splayed and stretched, horizontally around the bottle, she said, "The plant is ginseng, and ginseng was thought to engender longevity and vitality. The potter was told to pay particular care to the depiction of this plant. Either that or he would find himself expelled from her palace. The idea was that the imagery would infuse the wine with special powers so that she would become well and flourish. It's an early Koryo piece, from one of the Ganjingun kiln sites," she added. Ezra looked at her blankly. "Circa 950, something like that."

"It's all safe and sound now?" the helmeted security guard said, stepping back from the display.

"And let's hope it stays that way. Anyway," Monica's smile was big now – Ezra hardly ever saw her smile so widely, "I didn't finish my story."

"No?"

"No. The ending is that the aristocrat, contrary to what her doctors had said, did become better and a celebratory vase was made, identical to this one, except that on the new vase red berries were added to the ginseng imagery."

"And is there really such a vase?"

"Yes," Monica said, "and it's far more precious than this." After another look at the bottle, she checked her watch and said, "Anyway, to work." She took a seat behind her white desk, the towers around Covent Garden behind her. "So, you're on top of things?" she asked as Ezra took a seat facing her.

"I believe so. Clerical error, equipment failure, sabotage, fraud – in every major category the number of anomalies is down."

"And the fraud problem at the Passport Office?"

This was Ezra's biggest problem, but the results weren't in. "We should see that hole stitched up very soon."

"And you have reviewed the Dixon case?"

"Yes."

"Are we able to help the sister, Suzanne?"

"She was here a short while ago. I showed her the surveillance footage we have of Gavin's last movements..."

"The same intelligence the police gave her?" Ezra nodded. "I suppose the question is why she wasn't satisfied with that information in the first place."

Ezra told Monica about the Euston train crash and the fact that Gavin had never, to Suzanne's knowledge, got on a train since.

"So," he wrapped up, "she's having a hard time understanding why her brother would do a sudden turn around and be OK about rail travel."

"Yes," she said, after a moment of silence, "I can see why she'd find that difficult, but she must understand that we're in the business of supplying intelligence, not psychological explanations. Not yet, anyway. Of course, if we had the contract for neural implants.... There is an irony there that she's so opposed to their introduction. Anyway, I trust she left satisfied." Monica's eyes, grey-blue, were unblinking and piercing. "The last thing we need is an aggrieved OMNI supporter renewing a publicity drive against us."

To Ezra's mind it was unfair. He'd felt sorry for Suzanne earlier, but there were other cases of missing people, with relatives demanding access to surveillance data, seeking clues to their whereabouts. Most of these people weren't having Sense tread carefully around them, afraid of some damning publicity. From a twenty-year-old. Christ! She was only just out of school.

Monica was rising from her seat. She'd not said much in the meeting. But Ezra supposed she'd done what she intended to do: reiterate the importance of handling the Dixon case. He understood the reasoning but didn't like it.

When he returned to Anomalies he picked up the picture of Dixon that lay on his desk. He'd given the sister a way forward: copies of the last images of her brother, she should hand them around, jog people's memories. Monica had seemed satisfied too, and her standards, Ezra reflected, were about as high as you could get. So, as far as that case was concerned: done and dusted. He put the picture in the bin.

7

NO STROLLER BLOCKING the hallway. No noise from upstairs. Guessing that Brin had taken Adam to the park, Suzanne climbed dusty stairs to her second floor flat. A faint but putrid odor hit her when she opened the front door. She traced the stench to the bin in the kitchen, placing the roll of Gavin pictures on a countertop on her way. The bin was too full to close properly and the slime of blackened avocado was stuck to the inside of the lid. Suzanne hauled the black liner and all its stinking contents from the bin and dragged it back down the stairs to the street. She really shouldn't let the rubbish pile up like that, stink the whole flat out, but she'd been so tired lately. She felt exhausted now climbing back up the stairs.

She hadn't expected much from the meeting with Ezra Hurst and she hadn't got much. She'd registered her problem and had a point man now. He seemed all right. Better than some of the people Sense had sent to public discussions about making implants compulsory. Vincent Cunningham was the smarmiest. At least this Ezra Hurst wasn't like that. And she might as well distribute the pictures he'd given her; she had nothing to lose. Maybe tomorrow. Not now though. Right now she just wanted to sleep. Fatigue engulfing her, she couldn't be bothered tidying the toys strewn in every corner and the clothes crumpled on the carpet.

She rearranged the cushions on the sofa, stretched out and switched off.

***

Suzanne woke up on the sofa to the sound of Adam grunting and the smell of bacon frying.

"Hello," she said, smiling at her boy who was in the middle of the living room surrounded by copies of the Gavin picture she'd got from Sense. He was jabbing at one with his finger.

"That's Gavin, yes. Uncle Gavin." She looked up at the clock. 5.55. God! She'd been asleep three hours. "Why didn't you wake me up?" she asked Brinley who, fish slice in hand, suddenly poked his head into the room.

Suzanne could hear fierce sizzling in the background. Too high for bacon. But she kept her mouth shut.

"You looked like you could use the sleep."

"I just came in and…"

She'd been out like a light.

She'd had this kind of overwhelming tiredness when she was pregnant with Adam. Back in the old house she'd shared with all the others, she'd just suddenly announce that she *had* to lie down and rest.

She glanced to the School of Journalism prospectus on the stool to the side of the sofa and the form she'd already torn out and started completing. Was she really going to have another baby? She wanted to train, work, have enough for a sitter so she and Brin could have a decent night out, not be stuck in the flat listening to people outside, like those she could hear now, their voices and laughter coming through the slit of the open window.

"You OK?" Brinley asked.

Suzanne nodded. Not wanting him worried, she said, "So, you didn't get back to the workshop?"

"It doesn't matter."

Suzanne felt herself blushing. It did matter. He'd said he was busy. "I'm sorry," she said.

"Don't worry about it." He gave her a concerned look. "So, Sense – any help?"

Not really, Suzanne thought. But Brinley had taken all this time off, so she groped around for some constructive reply. "The man I was talking to seemed sympathetic. Went over same surveillance stuff the police showed me…."

"Did you tell them Gavin doesn't do trains?"

"Yeah." Suzanne nodded over to the pictures now strewn over the floor. "We're supposed to distribute the pictures, ask who's seen him."

Adam was jabbing at the picture again as he toddled over to her.

"Yes," Suzanne said. She pulled him up to her belly. "Uncle Gavin." You miss him? She wanted to ask this, but didn't. She didn't know where Gavin was, when he was coming back, why he'd suddenly left, and not knowing how to put all this to a two-year-old, she left it.

"Bacon and omelet?" Brinley asked from the doorway.

Suzanne visualized a nauseating greasiness.

"Not really hungry," she said, glumly. "I'll get Adam ready for bed."

His pajamas were still scrunched up on the sofa where they'd been taken off in the morning.

"What is it?" Suzanne said to Adam who was still pointing at the picture. Holding his pajamas she sat cross-legged and faced him straight on. He wasn't going to get dressed for bed until she'd commented on the Gavin picture he was holding. If only he had more words.

"He was your buddy, wasn't he?" she said, struggling for the right lines. "Sometimes people have to go off and do stuff." What stuff? What did Gavin have to do? "We'll hear from him soon…hopefully," she added quietly. Adam was still gripping the picture, studying it. Suzanne looked over the image of Gavin. Long, straggly hair, looked more brown than blonde, probably dirty, Suzanne guessed. Tatty green jacket – also dirty. Adam was pointing to the seam of the right shoulder. "Yes, you liked playing with that, didn't you?" Making a bad thing worse. It used to annoy

Suzanne the way Gavin would just sit on the sofa letting Adam tug at the frayed edges of the seam, intently watching him turn a couple of loose stitches into a three inch hole with fibers so ragged they formed a soft green fur around its edge. But then Gavin would probably have behaved the same way when he was at university.

Tangling and untangling – that's how he used to describe the math he was into to any layman who cared to ask. Ultra-complex knots and folds had been his prime source of fascination. The fraying and folding of fabric – there were corresponding equations. Gavin was seeing polynomials and making mathematical models where others just saw strings. At least those were his talents before the crash.

Adam was giggling, pointing to the hole on the shoulder of the jacket. Had she made too much of it before, pulling him off the sofa the way she used to, telling him not to rip at people's clothes. Maybe it had been Gavin's expression of bewilderment that had bothered her more than the hole itself, and the quiet but tortured sigh he gave, signifying that the wherewithal for explaining why holes like these were interesting was something that he'd lost.

Now that Suzanne was looking at it, the hole didn't even seem so bad. In her memory the hole was way worse than that. Was that part of the problem for Gavin – that she just blew things all out of proportion? Was that why he'd upped and left?

Adam stopped his giggling. His mouth formed a little O shape and, with obvious effort, facing Suzanne straight on, he slowly said, "'Ole."

"Hole! Yes, hole." Another word. Number seven. She should put it in a sentence. "The *hole* needs stitching, doesn't it?"

Adam smiled at her, then repeated, "'Ole."

"Yes," Suzanne said, smiling. "He said *hole*," she yelled to Brinley who was in the kitchen loading up the dishwasher. "Hole. Well done."

8

Friday 15th August 2059

THIS MORNING THE clutch *felt* fine – no problem changing gears, no slipping or crunching, but there was still a squeal, loud enough now to turn a girl jogger's head as he entered the tunnel leading to the Sense Surveillance car park. The acoustics of the underground concrete car park amplified the screech as Ezra drove into his usual space and, in his rear view mirror, he noticed Cunningham emerge from his jag and toss him a haughty look. Ezra needed to contact John, get the squeal sorted out, get that supercilious smirk wiped off Cunningham's face. He checked the clock. 08:25. Too early to ring John? Fuck it, the car needed sorting and, if John was still in bed, all he had to do was roll over and go right back to sleep.

"Yeah?" came John's voice after a few rings. He sounded groggy. Ezra wouldn't keep him long.

"Car's playing up, John."

"Jesus, Ezra! What time is…."

Ezra hit the window control, rolled the glass downwards, then shifted into reverse, shunted backwards from his parking space, then forwards letting the squeal reverberate through the open windows hopefully down the line to John's ear.

"You hear that?" Ezra said.

"All right. I'll deal with it. Sometime when I'm awake. Ring me later. Jesus!" John hung up.

Up in Anomalies, when he opened his office door, he saw that someone was leaving a video message on the wall screen in his office. Getting closer to his workstation he saw that it was Mo. Ezra hit *talk*.

"What's up, Mo?"

"I need your help." Mo's voice was tired. His skin (conker-colored, the thought suddenly came to Ezra) seemed thick and craggy. Too many all-nighters in the bar. "Take you up on tracing our fallow man," he said.

"Oh yeah, the one who did a runner? You filed a police report?" Ezra was surprised; he'd never known Mo to get the police in on any ructions.

"He pulled the same number on Angus last night."

"Angus?" Ezra wracked his brain. "At the Bass Clef?"

"Yeah, only when Angus took after him, he turned round and stuck a knife in his lung…"

"Shit."

"…so, I wanna know who we're dealing with."

"I hear you." He was about to tell Mo that to access surveillance data he'd need a signature or thumbprint on a police permission form, but then, in the scanner tray, he saw that it'd already arrived. "You remember what time Mr. Fallow ran off?"

"Not long before your bird did."

Ezra winced. "I'm doing you a favor, Mo. No need to rub it in."

"Sorry, mate."

But then it struck Ezra that tracking Lena would be easy: get the footage from the cameras outside the bar, find the point at which Lena made her exit (checking out what direction she headed off in while he was about it), rewind five minutes worth of data, find Mr. Fallow and run a query. Two birds. One stone.

"Leave it with me," Ezra said, taking off his jacket.

He didn't feel so hot now, but it was a new thing to feel hot at all after jogging just a few flights of stairs. Yesterday's Ready to Rumble pack was still there in his drawer, soap and wash cloth still inside. He'd clean himself up after he'd looked up the footage outside Mo's club.

He tapped in passwords and access codes and pulled up the security footage for Tuesday 12th August 2059, exterior Temple Tavern.

Ezra estimated the time Lena left to be just after eleven. Quarter past, something like that. He plugged in that time. No record of her leaving. He rolled the footage backwards. 23.06: Mo's man was shown slipping out of the bar, then sharply exiting onto a busy street. He strode towards Embankment, kicking a discarded cigarette carton as he went. Ezra ran a search on him. Got name, address, everything. That was easy.

Now Lena. She must have left a bit later than Ezra thought. Ezra rolled the footage forwards to 23.15 again, waited for the footage to show Lena going out of the doorway. But mostly people could be seen going in. 23.27 – still no Lena. But she had to have left before this time. After Mo's man had done his runner, Ezra had talked to Lena for…what? A couple of minutes? They'd both listened as Mo had ranted about being stitched up, then they'd talked about this and that. Complexions, as Ezra recalled. Then some woman had knocked into him and he'd ended up with food dropping onto his shirt. He'd gone to the toilets to clean up and when he'd come back, she'd gone. That couldn't have been more than ten minutes after Mr. Fallow's disappearance. The footage was now carrying a time of 23.37. And the only person the records showed as leaving at this time was Ezra himself. With a large ketchup stain on his shirt.

So what happened to Lena? Why wasn't she on the records?

He had her first name. And her description. He could run a query. It was worth a try. Ezra typed "Lena*" and made selections from likeness images to convey the shade of her skin, those almond green eyes and black-brown ringlets. Height, size, posture, weight – he was surprised at how much detail he could remember. He even had her exact complexion code. Checking his info-remote, he saw it was still stored: A13200X. He retyped the location of the bar and gave a longer range for time of leaving. Feeling confident he'd get a hit, he pressed the *submit* control.

No results came the database's reply.

This couldn't be right. He must have entered the data wrongly, hit the wrong controls or something. Slowly this time, he repeated the procedure. *No results* came the response again.

Ezra slumped back in his chair.

Stumped.

***

Pregnant. Suzanne finally admitted to herself that this could be true. She should do the test, get the sweat strips, stick them on her hand and see. They sold them in the pharmacy around the corner. She'd seen them there a few days before. And ignored them.

Adam had his shoes on and was waiting at the living room door, facing hallwards. She'd got his nappies, wipes, snack, drink, distracting toy, change of clothes together. All of this times two? How would she cope?

The computer's link lights were flashing. Stepping on the creaking floorboard, she crossed the living room to turn it off. The School of Journalism's Enrollment page was still showing. She'd submitted the application form. Probably she should have put more effort into the *reasons why you're interested in this course* section; no doubt that's where they'd check out her writing ability. Citing the press releases, newsletters and web content she'd produced for OMNI – would that be enough? She watched the green link light fade on the terminal. Half-hearted – that's how she felt about things right now.

The window needed closing. She squeezed between the arm of the sofa and the bookcase to pull it down. Yellow – stupid color for a sofa, she thought, noticing yet another amoeba stain on the fabric. Her foot nudged something on the floor. The digi-frame. She stooped to pick it up, saw an image of her brother again. He was shown sitting on the staircase in the old house with the broken banister post in the background, the post Adam had pointed at so incessantly just the other day, just like he'd been pointing at the ripped jacket in the photocopies yesterday. Gavin was wearing the same green jacket here too. Dirty and torn at the shoulder. Suzanne's eyes widened as she scrutinized the ripped seam. It was frayed, but – she pulled the photo up closer – way more frayed than in the photocopies Ezra Hurst had given her. She was sure.

"G…g…" Adam was tugging on her jeans pocket now.

"Yes, *go* – we're going out. Just one second."

She crossed to the table to check the photocopies. She was right. The jacket tear in the station picture was nowhere near as big as in the staircase photo. But the staircase photo was the older picture by some three months. So, the hole had got smaller? How? Mentally she ran through the dates again. She was sure she'd got them right. What would Ezra Hurst say about that? Determined to bring this up with Sense again, she found an envelope for the photos and put them in her satchel.

With Gavin still tugging her towards the door she pulled a mobile from her pocket and phoned Brinley's workshop.

"Did he stitch it?" Brinley asked her once she'd told him about the pictures.

"Stitch it? What? You mean get a needle and thread and…" she could hardly believe Brinley would think this, "…*sew?*"

"All right," Brinley conceded, "unlikely."

"Of course it's unlikely," Suzanne said, swinging the satchel over her shoulder, then guiding Adam to the stroller at the bottom of the hall staircase.

"So what do you think?"

She stayed silent for a while, then said, "I don't know…but maybe Sense… this Ezra Hurst – maybe he should explain it. I mean it looks like someone's… tampered…yes, tampered with the station images."

Suzanne had the phone pressed hard to her ear waiting for Brinley's response. It was a long time coming. She felt herself getting irritated. Irritated by the darkness of the hallway and the staircase, so narrow that the satchel on her shoulder scraped and scuffed the wall as she picked out steps in the dark. Then irritated with Adam for standing in the doorway while she tried, one-handed, to maneuver the stroller out of the passageway onto the street.

"Why?" Brinley's voice finally came into her earpiece.

"Why what?"

"Why would anyone *tamper* with the footage?

"I don't know. That's for Sense to explain."

"So, that's your next mission?"

Her next mission was to go to the chemist. Why hadn't she told Brin about this? It didn't seem right telling him now, not over the phone, while he was sanding some table or whatever he was doing that was making that scraping noise in the background. At least there was no twang of Jamal's guitar this time. It sounded like real work was going on. She'd tell him when he came home. The resolution made her anxious.

After the phone call she walked along Ladbroke Grove to the Express Pharmacy. She entered the shop, purchased the pregnancy strip, avoided eye contact with the glossy-haired, thirty-something pharmacist standing there all superior in her white coat. Suzanne stuffed the plastic bag containing the strips in the stroller basket and stepped back onto Ladbroke Grove. She heard a repetitive sound –bah, bah, bah – but didn't focus on it until Adam's hand, pointing at something in the distance, flashed across her field of vision. She looked down at Adam in his stroller. His face was craned up to meet hers, then once he had her attention he pointed again at a solar bus cruising noiselessly down the street. "Bah…bah."

"Bus! Yes." Suzanne smiled at him. "Where's the bus going?" she said in a deliberate singsong voice. She squinted at the number. 23. She'd taken the 23 to Sense's headquarters two days before. Would this Ezra Hurst agree to another meeting to discuss the discrepancies on the photos? He should do. There was, so far as Suzanne was concerned, an overriding need for an explanation. The bus was stuck on a red traffic light and while Adam was engrossed with watching it, she pulled her mobile from the stroller basket and dialed Ezra Hurst.

"It's Suzanne Dixon. There is something urgent I would like to discuss with you immediately."

After a pause, his reply came: "So urgent you must be seen at once?"

The traffic light changed to green. The bus cruised towards her.

"Please, I don't like problems." She suddenly felt tearful, then stupid for feeling that way. "I just want to get things sorted out."

Another pause.

"All right, Suzanne. Come in now."

Suzanne waved at the bus, swung the bag off her shoulder, checked she'd put the pictures in. Yes, the envelope was there.

"Thanks," she said to Ezra. "Bus ride!" she said to Adam.

9

EZRA HAD RUN the same footage several times now. No evidence of Lena leaving the bar. He'd set up queries, run searches. Nothing. Supposedly FETCH was the best software to set up a refined search containing multiple unknowns. But Ezra hadn't learnt FETCH properly. These days he didn't have time to keep up with the specifics of each new program. Not like he used to. Moving up the management ladder had taken him away from all that. Now he had to depend on other tech heads to provide the skills he used to have himself. He looked across the vast floor of the Anomalies Unit to the wispy-haired Sayle who was sitting hunched over his control pad. Course, Sayle was the best at FETCH. Ezra didn't like the fact, but he'd have to bite the bullet and ask for his help to trace Lena.

"Sayle," he yelled across the floor. Sayle spun around in his swivel chair. "You have a minute?" Sayle stood immediately, walked quickly over to Ezra's office.

"How is this possible?" Ezra asked after he'd explained the problem of the missing data.

"Interesting," Sayle replied, immediately engrossing himself. "Run FETCH. That should help."

"Don't have time," Ezra said, not wanting to admit that he hadn't got to grips with the software. "Suzanne Dixon called in. She'll be here any minute. Need to prepare."

"All right, Ez. Leave it with me."

Sayle scribbled down some reference codes from Ezra's screen, then strutted back to his desk. Leaving a personal matter with Sayle wasn't something Ezra was happy about. But what choice did he have? He was pissed off – with himself mainly, for getting so out of the loop on the technical side. He should spend his evenings in, sharpening his skills, not go shooting up to Colchester for a piss-up with John or hanging over the bar of the Tavern.

Moodily, he headed to the secure interview room where a takeaway food carton remained on the desk. A shiny badge slipped onto the floor as he tossed the package into the bin. It was a little square with a moving image of Magnifico Mouse. When he picked up the badge his body heat set a short flexi-film in motion. A cartoon of a female mouse with huge eyes and ludicrously long lashes scampering away from a snarling cartoon cat. Ezra tossed the badge onto his desk.

He switched his mind to Suzanne Dixon and just as he wondered what the *very urgent* matter was that she wanted to bring to his attention, there was a ping of an elevator and she began walking towards him. She was pushing a flimsy stroller. It contained a bug-eyed kid with a mop of blonde hair. She hadn't said anything about bringing a kid. Would have been nice if she'd asked.

Supposing she'd distributed pictures and had found something out about her brother's whereabouts already, Ezra had agreed to this impromptu meeting. But now that she was here in his office, in the same blue denim shirt that she'd worn the day before, with her son staring at him silently, he found himself being asked for his opinion on the state of Gavin's clothes.

"I'd like to know your thoughts?" Suzanne said.

"My thoughts?"

"On the hole on Gavin's jacket – why it's smaller here," she pointed at the picture showing Gavin on the forecourt of St. Pancras station, "than it is here." She was loading a picture into her mobile and now showing him an image of her brother sitting on a staircase. "That was taken in the old place we all lived in. Not exactly sure of the date but would've been something like six months ago. Definitely before March because we all moved out after the protest."

Suzanne slid the picture and her mobile across Ezra's desk and pointed at Gavin's green jacket in both images.

Suddenly Adam leaned forwards, straining in his stroller straps.

"'Ole," he said, excitedly. "'Ole."

"That's right," Suzanne said. "Hole."

Both mother and son were fixed on the ripped sleeve shown in the picture. Then, turning to face Ezra, Suzanne said, "Why would the holes have changed like this? Got smaller instead of bigger?"

He gave her a long look. She was difficult to read. There was definitely an implied accusation in her words. But her voice was flat, tired sounding. And there was something slow motion about the way she'd slid the objects across the desk towards him.

He had no idea what might account for the discrepancy in the photos. Maybe there was a resolution problem. Or she'd got the dates wrong. How could he possibly know?

"I don't know about these holes," Ezra said.

"Doesn't it strike you as unusual? Something needing an explanation?"

"If you're sure you've got your dates right, then, of course, it would be intriguing."

But the most probable explanation was that she'd got them wrong.

"How can a security video from an earlier time," she said, "find itself in a later recording?"

"So," Ezra took a deep breath, leaned back in his chair and concentrated his mind, "let me get this straight: you're saying that somehow Sense has mixed up the timestamps of this footage." He looked up and they both held each other's gaze. "How could that be?"

"I don't know," Suzanne said.

"Well, I don't know either. So, where do we go from here?"

"How could that St. Pancras recording, the one of Gavin getting on the train, how could that be checked?"

"Checked for?"

"Tampering."

Tampering. Ezra needed to cut this meeting short. He shouldn't be surprised that she might pull some paranoid theory out of the hat. She was an OMNI activist after all, had worked relentlessly on spreading the idea that Sense only wanted to implement the neural chip program for purposes of state sanctioned mind control. And she'd carried on promoting those ideas even in the face of a series of viral attacks that could have been prevented if Sense had had access to a national neural database that could have determined who was planning what kind of crime and when. This was what surveillance was all about. Ensuring safety. And that was what his job was all about. Not wasting time on the ruminations of some young conspiracy theorist. He struggled now to keep the sarcasm from his voice: "Check for tampering – you trust me enough to do this?"

"I don't have much choice really, do I? The footage is Sense property and you're my contact."

Ezra could feel himself scowling. He shouldn't be her contact as she'd so bluntly put it. He should be assigning teams to eliminate known anomalies, securing the surveillance net as efficiently as possible, especially on the passport fraud. The team working on that problem was running into all sorts of difficulties. Enquiries should be dealing with this Suzanne Dixon, like they dealt with most other people who had concerns about missing relatives. She should not be here in his office using up his time. Next time he met with Monica he'd tell her that.

"I could check for *tampering*, but I have to tell you I don't expect to find evidence of any such thing." He'd give the video a quick once over, get her off his back. "In the meantime, if you could continue distributing the pictures of Gavin...have you started that yet?"

"No...not yet."

"You haven't? Well, I think you should. Because it's my

opinion, if you're interested, that that is how you'll dig up information on your brother. What was the name of the Czech man your brother used to hang around with?"

"Lukas Čapek."

"Why don't you pay him a visit, find out what he knows?"

"I don't know where he lives now."

"But Gavin and this Čapek were friends?"

"Yeah. They used to sit around talking. Didn't always seem healthy to me." She paused for several moments. "Anyway, I don't know where Lukas lives now. I tried looking him up, but couldn't find him."

"You couldn't. No problem." Ezra tapped keys on his terminal. "How do you spell his name?"

"C with an accent. You know, like a little v that goes above the letter.

"With an accent," Ezra repeated quietly, sitting motionless. He had to think for a second how to get these special characters up. God – what was happening to his skills? Simple stuff like that, he never used to have to think about.

"Diacritics," Suzanne said. "I think that's what those things are called."

"D'you know his date of birth?"

Ezra asked Suzanne several more questions and entered her answers straight into the database.

"Here you are – this is his address."

"Really? You have it?"

"Of course, we would be a very incompetent surveillance outfit if we couldn't provide a simple address." Then passing her a piece of paper with an address in Lancaster Gate written on it, he said, "Here."

Adam lunged forward in his stroller, reaching out for the note.

"What? You want this?" Suzanne said, smiling at him. "It's just a piece of paper. And mummy needs it. It's important."

But Adam was intent on getting the paper. He began squirming in his stroller, trying to break free of the straps, his whining building to a crescendo.

Ezra remembered the shiny silicone badge he'd found in the

takeaway packaging.

"You like Magnifico Mouse?" he said, proffering the badge.

Instantaneously, Adam became engrossed with the moving image – the purple cartoon mouse. So, sometimes this shit did serve a purpose.

Ezra stood – a hint, hopefully, that he wished the meeting to end. Suzanne took it; she reached down for her bag, an old brown satchel.

"So," Ezra said, "you have your task and I have mine."

He accompanied her to the elevators.

"And when will you let me know what you find?" she asked.

"From checking the data?"

"Yes."

He wouldn't find anything – he knew that. But going through the motions, he plucked a timescale from the air and said, "In the next couple of days."

She nodded. She was going to hold him to that, Ezra could tell. There were things he didn't get about her: the idealism, slobbiness, but there was still something admirable. She was headstrong and earnest. If he weren't so pressed, he'd find that endearing.

A lift arrived with a ping. Suzanne wheeled her son inside. The doors swished shut and she was gone.

On the way back to his desk, Ezra stopped at Sayle's workstation. Looked at the query he'd set up. The logic was complex, involving terms Ezra didn't recognize.

"How's it going?"

"Nothing yet," Sayle said, without looking up. "I'll find out something, though. Just you wait."

Ezra said nothing, knowing he had no choice.

***

Suzanne awoke on the sofa to find Brinley kneeling next to her.

"Two sleepy heads," he said, stroking her hair. Adam was draped across her belly. She hardly remembered how they'd both came to end up so tired after a short bus ride to Sense and back.

She felt her eyes prickling, tried to stop the tears.

"What? What is it?" Suzanne heard the concern in Brinley's voice, she found it difficult to get the words out. She nodded to the palm strips poking out of her satchel at the foot of the sofa. Brinley pulled out the little pack, studied the label.

"You're pregnant?"

"Think so," she said.

He peered at her, his face full of surprise. While she wondered whether his lips were turning into a smile, he picked at the cellophane of the pack.

"Well, let's know so, eh?"

He pulled the strip from its little envelope and stuck its jelly side to her palm. They both peered at the results patch. Four, five seconds of silence with nothing changing, then a murky yellow line appeared that slowly became green. Even before it had changed to blue, Suzanne knew.

"Come here," Brinley said, nudging Adam off her belly and pulling her towards him. "Everything's going to be all right."

"We never go anywhere. We…"

"Can work on that so that we do…"

10

16.45. IT WAS later than Ezra thought. He'd spent most of the afternoon glancing over to Sayle's desk, hoping for progress on the Lena case while scrutinizing stats from his team leaders. But Sayle's back, hunched over a workstation in the distance, was all there was to see.

Seeing the pictures of Gavin Dixon on his own desk, Ezra supposed he should at least have a look at this problem.

Into the computer's search field, Ezra entered a date: Thursday 10th July 2059. Time: 11.50. Place: St. Pancras Station, concourse. The computer churned up a list of cameras with their grid positions around the station. Ezra ran his eye down the various camera models. Most were Eagles, not very versatile, but robust and reliable. Two were Cam-catch A's, good for capturing details in congested areas. But two were Cam-catch B's.

Ezra's eyes narrowed as he tried to remember the facts about the B's. John, before he'd left Sense, had ordered a number of them for various ports. In fact, Ezra had been with him at the expo in Bristol, when he'd been – Ezra remembered John's words – *blown away* by the superior resolution of the images, especially at huge magnification levels.

But Cam-catch B software had turned out to have a number of vulnerabilities which a hacker named Feist had been able to exploit, leaving John with a case of massive data corruption on his hands. Nonchalant despite having the directors breathing down his neck, John had said, "Give me a couple of days, I'll iron out the glitches."

He'd occupied the workstation just over from where Sayle sat now. There was a glass partition between Sayle's space and John's. Neither man had liked being on view to the other. Ezra found Sayle's prying annoying enough, but John used to get incensed, especially when he had the Cam-catch B problem to untangle.

"That's going to take more than a couple of days to sort out. The data's mangled – you're never going to get that straight." Sayle used to come out with some version of this line whenever he crossed John's path.

"Oh, ye of little faith," was John's usual reply.

But for all Sayle's downsides, Ezra knew he wouldn't say that a computer problem would be hard to solve unless it was true. And Ezra clearly remembered Sayle's incredulity when John had sent out a memo with the single word *Sorted.*

The data had been unscrambled. The record of events from all Cam-catch B cameras had been retrieved. The footage was there for posterity, for anyone who wanted to scan it.

And Ezra supposed he should scan it, the St. Pancras recording at least; he'd promised Suzanne Dixon he would. He hit *play.* There was Gavin Dixon picking his way, erratically, through the concourse crowds. Ezra peered at his image. Christ! This boy was a mess. Was he high or something? Why was he walking so erratically, circling the concourse, like he didn't know what he was doing there? On edge – that's how he seemed. Ezra supposed he would be, if, as Suzanne Dixon had said, this was his first visit to a station since he got all smashed up in the train crash.

What was it Suzanne had asked him to take note of? The hole on the jacket? The cuff? No. The shoulder. He saw it now: the frayed seam. Ezra estimated about two inches long. Then just as he made this estimation the hole changed or at least seemed to. Ezra replayed and watched. He'd seen it right. At 11.55 the hole seemed to become smaller and less raggedy and remained that way, Ezra could tell by zooming in close, as Gavin Dixon picked his way to the gate at Platform 7 where he finally boarded the 11:59 for Prague.

Was this quirk, this thing with the hole, some part of the Feist corruption? Some glitch that John had failed to unscramble? Feist was behind bars now, but Internal Security had an in-depth analysis of all of his tactics – handing those over was part of a deal that shaved years off his sentence. Ezra sat back in his chair, closed his eyes and worked out a plan of action. Quick call to Internal Security. They'd confirm that Feist caused the discrepancy in the footage (that seemed to Ezra the best explanation). Contact Suzanne Dixon with the news. She'd have her explanation. Case closed.

"So… that's how he did it," Sayle said cryptically.

Ezra hadn't heard Sayle sidle up to his desk. He felt uncomfortable finding the man leaning right over him, peering intently at the screen with its image of St. Pancras Station.

"Feist?" Ezra replied, wheeling his chair away from Sayle. What was Sayle getting at exactly? "That's how Feist did what?"

"Not Feist," Sayle said, "he hasn't got anything more to give us. Internal Security squeezed every ounce of information out of him. No. Not Feist. Durrant." There was an underlying triumph in Sayle's voice, and as if to emphasize this, he added (unnecessarily, Ezra thought), "*John* Durrant."

"What did John do?" Ezra asked cautiously.

"Used a continuity program." Sayle said, his eyes darting over the screen, as if he were finding elements in the imagery to confirm the diagnosis.

"To unscramble the data?"

"No. That's just the thing. He didn't unscramble anything. He couldn't. I knew he wouldn't be able to. The data from those B cameras, once it was corrupt, that was it. Irretrievable. Didn't I say that all along?"

Ezra wasn't about to give the pleasure of agreeing. All right Sayle was helping him out on the Lena thing, but John was his friend.

Sayle launched into an explanation: "When Feist attacked, certain sequences of data from Cam-catch B cameras were damaged."

"I know that." Ezra said, irritably. Sayle didn't need to speak to him as if he knew nothing about the sabotage. There were a few programs he needed to get up-to-date with (and continuity software, he supposed, was another type that should be added to the list), but he wasn't completely clueless.

Sayle's annoying school tone continued. "Typically, there'd be a sequence of OK data, let's call it sequence one, followed by a sequence of corrupt data (sequence two) and then another sequence of uncorrupted stuff. Three."

"Didn't John unscramble all those middle sequences? Set them all right with a neat fit between the unaffected data?"

"That's what he said he did. That's what he should have done. But he didn't."

"So what," Ezra paused, "in *your* view did he do?"

"See this," Sayle said, pulling up a spare wheely chair and manipulating keys on the control pad that changed the image on the screen into a page of program code. John used continuity software, which uses inferential tools. If a person's movements are missing from the surveillance record – say you've got a small business that can't afford to cover every square foot of its premises, has some points uncovered by security equipment, then you can have minimal cameras at a few select spots picking up a person's trajectory at disjointed points: say, point one and point three. Then the software infers and inserts the most probable trajectory for the missing point two…"

"Most probable trajectory," Ezra repeated, slowly. "There was some court issue with this recently?"

"Yes," Sayle said, "The most probable trajectory inserted by a computer trying to infer a person's movements is not the same as a security camera providing a record of something that actually happened. The courts are struggling with the use of this software, not knowing whether to present continuity filming to support a case or not."

"Well, strictly they generate hypotheses, don't they? Not recordings. Visual hypotheses – film stories – about what happened at a time and a place where there were no actual witnesses or cameras."

"True," Sayle said. "But in every experimental situation where the software's predictive capabilities have been measured, they have a more than ninety-nine per cent chance of making accurate predictions."

"But not a hundred."

"And that's the problem for the courts. It's so close to a real recording, it almost is a real recording. There've been test situations where viewers have been totally unable to distinguish footage derived from a series of cameras recording in sequence, from footage with only half of those cameras working and the rest of the footage inferred by a continuity program. The police love the software. You can get really sophisticated reconstructions."

"So," Ezra said, "If you can disguise all indication that a piece of footage is computer generated, rather than a real recording, how is anyone ever supposed to tell the difference?"

"Because Systems have come up with a way of identifying covertly spliced footage. That's why they've been so busy down there – they've been going through all the backups at every storage center, running them through this new package. Anything that comes up as a secretly spliced sequence gets a red SSS code." Sayle had minimized the imagery to the top right corner of the screen. The rest of the screen consisted of camera co-ordinates, software information, chunks of code. "And what do we have here?" Sayle said. He was smiling. Ezra wheeled his chair closer to the screen and peered at the letters, emboldened and red: SSS.

Was this really the John Ezra knew? Someone who would get the directors off his back by slotting some secretly spliced sequence, a story – OK highly probable story – but a story nonetheless into something that was supposed to be a faithful recording of events? He must have known that was an act of gross misconduct.

Ezra didn't want to believe the dirt Sayle was dishing up, but certain facts were hitting home, certain memories. One was now replaying vividly. The Security Expo down in Bristol. He'd gone there with John, who aside from skulking off to fish on some Avon tributary, had spent most of his time testing out trajectory inference packages. "A must-have," John had said, and back at HQ he'd convinced the directors that testing con software was essential.

Undeniably, John had the skills to manipulate the data. But why would he do that? He was under pressure. That was true. Would he go that far, though? What disconcerted Ezra was that he couldn't rule it out. John wasn't totally straight. Ezra had been on too many conferences and trips away to think John incapable of twisting things. Usually small time stuff – the skulking off to do his own thing: fishing, drinking when Sense was picking up his expense account tab, pocketing the odd gadget which strictly should have been listed on some Sense inventory and been housed by some officer in the Equipment Division.

There was something bigger too: a year or so back there'd been some difficult anomalies, old missing persons' cases. The police had been requesting updates on cases so old even the families had stopped asking questions. There'd been a lot of conflicts in the available security data. Fingerprint records not matching credit card biometrics. Iris scans not matching the portraits to which they were supposed to be linked. Looked like forgeries were involved, human trafficking in some cases. The crimes were several and complex. Too complex for the police, hence their constant requests for the latest surveillance data. Harangued, disinterested and ultimately unable to make sense of these cases, John had effectively masked the records, near enough deleted the files, until Ezra had picked up on it. "No one's looking for these people, Ez," John had insisted.

"Are you insane? The police are looking," Ezra had replied.

"Well, that's all about getting numbers down." John scoffed. "It's not like their families are looking for them. Not their mothers, fathers…"

"All the more reason for us to do things right."

"Why? What's the point? Why should I spend my time on cases no relative gives a shit about?"

Ezra's answer had been immediate, forceful: "Because that's our job. Everybody should have their rightful place on our system. Sort it out or get another fucking job."

So far as Ezra was concerned, there'd been that one off thing with John, one big off thing anyway. But had John pulled even more shit and kept it under wraps?

Ezra peered at the imagery of St. Pancras station on his monitor.

"You're sure about this," Ezra said to Sayle.

Sayle placed the tip of his finger under the red SSS letters on the screen. "How sure do you want?" he said.

Ezra nudged Sayle away from the control panel, switched back to the original footage. He zoomed in on Dixon and said to Sayle, "Watch this." Ezra was pointing at the seam on the shoulder of Dixon's jacket. "This is the image at 11.55." He let the footage play. It showed Gavin weaving around the concourse distractedly until 11.56.23. "Look," Ezra said, "now the hole on the jacket is suddenly much smaller."

"Interesting," said Sayle. They both watched the footage of Gavin, now part of a crowd heading through the gate at Platform 7.

"Would splicing something in with continuity software turn up that kind of discrepancy?"

"Only in a rare kind of instance." Sayle said. "See, the software only works on the basis that people's moves are, to a large degree, predictable, that intentions can be deduced from histories; that, in other words, people act as rational agents. Now if someone's not behaving rationally…" Sayle reset the footage to the point where Gavin Dixon first arrived on the concourse. "He's wandering about here, not looking very together…probably difficult for the software to make decent inferences based on behavior like this…"

"So what happens in that case?" Ezra asked.

"What happens then is that the software might plug into previously stored records from earlier times, days, weeks, maybe even longer, copy movements, mannerisms, gait patterns, then paste the whole trajectory into the relevant setting."

"So," Ezra said slowly, thinking the information through, "this image of him walking through St. Pancras has been copied from footage of him in an entirely different location."

"It's possible," said Sayle. "Could have been copied from a number of earlier recordings, then all patched together to make up a coherent picture of his movements in the station. Normally con software can just stitch up a story from recordings of close events, but if the subject's very irrational...well, d'you know this man's history? Does he have any problems?"

"Fifteen week coma. Massive brain damage. Drops tranx tabs on top."

"So, there you are. Software's going to struggle more in a case like this." Sayle nodded towards the image of Gavin, tapped the shoulder-hole. "Little hiccup like this, uncommon, but in this kind of case..."

"Makes sense," Ezra said. Or at least it sort of made sense. If everything Sayle said was true, what did that say about John? That's what Ezra needed to work out.

"D'you remember when Systems were scrutinizing old backups? They were onto something about data veracity, though they didn't go into details at that time. That's exactly when John left."

The same thought had already occurred to Ezra.

John's announcement that he was leaving had been inexplicably sudden. One late afternoon he'd begun rooting through his drawers, clearing his desktop. Ezra had finally sauntered over, "What you doing?" he'd asked.

"Had enough of this shit," John had said. "Give you a buzz, all right?"

Now Ezra was going to do the buzzing, if only to get his side of the story. He dialed John's number.

"Don't tell me," John said, on the first ring, "it's about the motor?"

"The car does have a problem, but there's something else too. Some anomalies I'm having problems with, thought you might be able to help."

"Anomalies? Jeez. I doubt I'll remember anything useful. I've left, remember. What's wrong with the car?"

"Clutch again. Squealing. Didn't you hear it when I phoned before?

A moment of silence.

"What? You're gambling on bringing it up again?"

Ezra hadn't planned on it, but the way this phone conversation was going (and it struck Ezra that John was being deliberately evasive), he figured he'd get further meeting face-to-face.

"I think it'll make it."

"Like last time, you mean?"

"It's not so bad as last time."

"No? Well, I'm curious what the problem is..."

"I'll bring it up then, all right."

There was a moment's hesitation, then, "All right."

When Ezra came off the line, he found Sayle staring at him.

"Are you driving up now?" Sayle asked.

"Got to hear it from John. Hear what *he* has to say."

Sayle was still sitting in Ezra's workspace. Ezra made a point of having to lean over him to print out another station picture of Gavin Dixon. Finally, Sayle rose and stood back.

"I'd be interested in hearing what John has to say for himself."

"Me too," Ezra said, rolling the picture and stuffing it in the pocket of the jacket hanging on his chair. "So what about Lena? Did you come over here to tell me something?"

"Oh yes..."

"What?"

"Well, to ask you something actually."

"Oh." Ezra felt disappointed. "What?"

"Lena's complexion code: A13200X. Are you sure that's right?"

Quickly Ezra checked his pocket info-remote. He nodded.

"There's something not right about that," Sayle said quietly. "I'll work it out though," he said, walking into the main passageway alongside Ezra. "Eventually."

On his way to John's, Ezra only stopped once on the M11 to top up his batteries at the fast charge station. The Viper made it all the way this time, but with a squeal so loud it brought John out of his shack before Ezra had turned into the drive. "It *is* the clutch. Shit. Must've had too many beers or something," John said once Ezra had parked and opened the car door.

"You know the cause?"

"Must've left grease on the clutch plate. Thought I'd cleaned it up good…" He huffed, displeased. With himself for screwing up the fix or with Ezra for coming over again? Ezra couldn't tell. John was acting all helpful, opening up the bonnet, poking around, but there was something grudging about it, and now there was a silence.

John heaved a big box of wrenches out of the garage and across the gravelly yard. No need for the garage lights this time – Ezra had arrived before sundown. The house seemed even more ramshackle than before, now that he could see its cracked windows, rotting frames and peeling exterior paint. And *so* remote. He'd known it was a house standing alone before, but in the dark that hadn't properly hit home. Now that he was viewing the narrow lane, he found there were no other buildings in sight.

Turning around, Ezra found John lying half underneath the car.

There was a long series of spanner clanks and thuds, followed by a moment's silence.

"So," John said finally, sliding out from under the car and standing to face Ezra, wrench in hand, "What is it? What's brought you here?"

John was on the defensive, Ezra could tell. His heartbeat quickened as he made a quick fire decision about how to bring up the data splicing.

"Need to pick your brains."

"About what?"

"One of the Cam-catch B recordings…" Ezra was careful about this. There were questions John needed to answer about all of the Cam-catch B data, but weighing in all heavy-handed was not how Ezra wanted to play it. He'd ease into the subject gently, take a specific problem. He pulled the still of Suzanne's brother from his pocket. "Gavin Dixon," Ezra said, "a case I'm working on…" Ezra held out the picture. Wiping his hands on an oily rag, John glanced at it from a distance. There was no sign of recognition on his face.

"What about it?" John asked, heading back to the bonnet again.

"The footage seems to have some irregularities. It was one of the streams you were…unscrambling after the Feist virus. D'you remember any problems?"

"With this person's data?" John asked nodding towards the picture in Ezra's hand. John was squinting at the image now, still with no flicker of recognition. "There were thousands of problems. How d'you expect me to remember that particular one?"

"Not sure what I'm expecting," Ezra said. "Just want to hear what you know about it."

"Nothing," John said. "That's the thing about leaving all that…" *corporate shit*, Ezra thought, predicting John's next words, "…corporate shit behind is I don't have to remember anything. I can pack my rod and bait, head off to Aylsham and fish for roach or bream or whatever the fuck I want and just forget everything."

Ezra knew he was going to have to toss in the issue of splicing, gauge John's reaction. But John could flare up, Ezra had seen him lose it in the Tavern a couple of times. He didn't want that happening, not with his car up on a jack and out of action.

"You taking the whole engine out like before?" Ezra asked.

"You know what?" John said. He suddenly seemed brighter. "After you came up last time, I thought this is stupid – poking about for hours the way I did. I mean, I like messing about with cars enough, it's just when there are gadgets that do the job much quicker, seems stupid not to use them. So, I got an Auto-Tron off the net…" John disappeared into the garage and came out with a machine that stood as high as the hip. "Self-assembly unit," John said. "Multi-functional. Just tap in the registration – make and model come up automatically, as you Sense people know…" John smirked when he said this. Ezra had been trying to give John, *wanting* to give John, the benefit of the doubt, but this smirk was irritating, especially hooked with the disingenuous phrase *you Sense people*, as if John had no connection to the company. Ezra felt his adrenalin spike – a faint turbulence in his gut that came with the knowledge that he was going to bring up the splicing allegation soon. "...once the car details come up – here, see," John said, pointing to the miniscreen on the unit, "here's your car." Ezra looked and saw the details. "Now," John continued, "I just put in the problem I want diagnosing and fixing...actually, I don't need a diagnosis. I know what the problem is. Grease on the faceplate. Sure of it. Mustn't have got the grease off my hands before I hooked it all up to the crankshaft. Jesus! Can't believe I did that. Too much beer, Ez. It's no good."

For all Ezra knew the allegation about John could be way off the mark, John might've been completely above board no matter what Sayle had said or what SSS flags were coming up on data he'd supposedly unscrambled. He was here to get John's side of the story, but something (and he couldn't say what) was telling him it wouldn't be good. "So, I can skip the diagnosis," John was saying, "just plug in that I want the faceplate leveled out and smoothed over – wire brusher will do." John was tapping in the instruction as he spoke. "Now we leave it to do its work."

"Which takes how long?" Ezra asked as he watched the Tron assemble itself a pair of sturdy metallic pincers.

"Get the clutch out, fix it up, put it all back together? Six, seven minutes. I tried it out on the old Volvo over there." John pointed to an antique car, all beaten up and scabby, just beyond the garage. "That's how long it took with her. Course, if you don't know what you're looking for, don't know what questions to ask, then the whole thing takes a lot longer. But I do, so we should be done very soon."

"Listen John, there's something I want to discuss with you..."

"To do with what?" John asked. "The anomaly you mentioned? What was the name?"

"Dixon."

"To do with him?"

"Kind of. It came up in connection with that. The Cam-catch B footage you went over – Systems have been through all the backups – a lot of it's showing up as sequences that have been spliced in...with continuity software."

John, who had looked away from Ezra, watched the Tron speedily dismantle plates and springs. It was remarkably noiseless in its maneuvers. Ezra found the quiet unsettling.

"I need your thoughts, John. This is data affecting my caseload."

"Con data streams are indistinguishable from original recordings. They shouldn't affect your caseload."

"Are you saying that the allegation is true?"

"*Allegation?* You make it sound like I did something completely heinous. There wouldn't be *any* records if I hadn't stitched them together the way I did. There would be nothing to look at, nothing to go on. That's the reality. With this Dixon – you now have the most likely story about what happened to him. If I hadn't put in the continuity piece, you'd have nothing – just a corrupt set of data."

"But we don't have a real recording of what happened at the station..."

"You wouldn't have that anyway. It was scrambled, remember, Feist threw a virus at the databanks. You're better off with the work I did. Everybody is."

"You're saying you weren't trying to cover your own arse?" Ezra said. "I mean, the B's had vulnerabilities. You installed them. It was your problem to sort..."

"OK...OK. Why you looking at me like that? I've left you with data to work with. How many times do I have to ram that point home?"

Ezra got John's take on it – OK, not strictly above board, but something almost as good. What was the big deal? He could see how, for John, it made sense.

"Trouble is," Ezra said. "Probable stories are not high enough standards."

"So, I gathered – I guessed that when Systems started crawling through the databases and all the backups."

"So you left."

"Well, you know I never had my heart in it anyway. Should've got out sooner. Look," John said, nodding towards the Tron, "here's the wire brusher." Ezra glanced at the machine with its self-assembled pincers, which quietly whirred as they leveled out the faceplate with a steel brush. "Three minutes," John said, "you'll be back on the road, if you've finished your interrogation, that is."

"Just wanted your side of the story, John, that's all."

"So now you have it. Mission accomplished, eh? What? Why are you looking at me like that?"

"This hasn't been much help to me." Ezra pointed to the image of Gavin Dixon. "This probable story you concocted for this Dixon lad has got glaring holes in it..."

"Shouldn't be any problems..."

"But there are. His sister's already picked up on them." Ezra tossed the picture onto a battered composting bin. "What do you propose I tell her?"

Instead of answering, John busied himself with disconnecting the Tron from the car, then getting it off the jack. Not John's problem, Ezra guessed – he'd packed in all that corporate shit. For what? A shack in the middle of nowhere with a dilapidated kitchen and his latest holographic nude in the living room all bronze-skinned and shimmering?

"Dunno what page you're on these days," Ezra said.

John had already headed off towards his shack. Ezra got in his car and reversed slowly over the gravel drive, listening for clutch squeals. There were none.

11

WHILE BRINLEY LAY on his back on the floor rough and tumbling with Adam, Suzanne knelt on the sofa, looked through the window and watched the street scene below. A solar bus glided smoothly along, and a cyclist rode, no hands, with a cap on his head and a French stick casually tucked under his arm.

"It's beautiful out there," she said. She hadn't realized it all day, not even earlier on the bus when she'd taken the pictures to Ezra Hurst.

"Why don't you get outside? Go for a walk?" Brinley replied.

She mulled the idea. Early evening stroll in the beautiful warm. Good for her. Not just her. She visualized, cartoon oxygen bubbles floating through a cartoon umbilical cord to a bean-sized humanoid. At least she supposed it was bean-sized. She had no real idea and had avoided the facts. Working out due dates, scheduling scans and genetic analysis, considering personalized GM therapies, nutritional supplements, pharmaceutical intervention – she needed to set these wheels in motion. For the last three weeks, at least, she'd had her head buried in the sand. Time now to take it out and think things through.

Looking out of the window, she reckoned she could head along Ladbroke Grove, take a shortcut to Notting Hill Gate, cross over Bayswater and go round Kensington Gardens. It'd been Brinley who'd first got her into the parks. Initially that had struck her as a way in which their age difference showed. Not that she minded strolling past Duck Island in St. James's Park or by the rose beds along Birdcage walk, but Brin had been really into it. He'd want to spend entire Sundays doing all the Royal Parks – Hyde, St. James's Green, Kensington Gardens – one after another, walking for miles, linking them all up. It had seemed old-fogeyish, but then she'd got into it herself, especially when Adam was tiny, even began suggesting trots around the Serpentine with the stroller.

"Yeah, I could do with a walk," she said.

"So, take one. Me and imp here can hold fort, can't we?" Brinley stuck a tickling finger into Adam's side. Adam doubled over in a fit of giggles.

"All right," Suzanne said. "I will."

It felt strange walking out of the door empty handed. No stroller, diapers, or toy. Nothing. It felt good. So did the warm evening air.

She took a short cut to Notting Hill Gate, crossed over Bayswater and decided on the North Flower Walk in Kensington Gardens.

If she carried on in a straight line, she'd hit Speakers' Corner where she'd first met Brin. It seemed silly now, the way, four years ago, she'd carried her interests to an extreme and fulminated on the dangers of psycho-surveillance in public in Hyde Park. To most people passing she'd been, like every other speaker, a curiosity with an axe to grind. Even Sally Brett, who used to sit next to her in school and who was a collaborator on the project was giving her strange looks that day at Hyde Park. Suzanne had realized then and remembered now that Sally Brett had only come in on the Speakers' Corner idea for a giggle. From the way that Sally had thrown her embarrassed glances from behind the long strands of hair dangling over her face it was clear that she hadn't taken her views *that* seriously.

But Brin had stopped and listened, told her about OMNI,

asked her if she wanted to meet the others in the group and help out with the campaign.

Brin had a real fervor then. They plotted endlessly. He was good at bringing new people on board and creating a buzz around OMNI. She'd started forums, newsletters, getting Sense worried enough to send representatives to meet them and find out their views.

Hyde Park was also where the protest was scheduled to meet. But instead of getting their message across, the riot had started and she'd ended up in the police station fretting about Gavin's violent outburst and his being put in custody.

Walking all the way to Speakers' Corner suddenly lost its appeal.

She'd maybe go to the Serpentine, perhaps rest at the fountains. Not too far from where Lukas was supposed to be living these days, though Suzanne wondered how he'd managed to get so upmarket in such a short space of time. Even to rent out a shoebox, he'd have to be flush. How could he afford it? She wasn't aware he had money when he used to hang about the old house in Golborne Road, sitting there unshaven with his great big jumpers, boots and jeans. Feeling inside the shirt pocket, she found the paper scrap that Ezra Hurst had written Lukas's address on that morning. Lancaster Gate. That was somewhere on the other side of Bayswater Road. Not too far away. She walked in that direction, checking the piece of paper. After ten minutes or so she found the right house number. This, according to Ezra Hurst, was where Lukas was supposed to be living now. Spotting a bench to her side, she veered towards it, just avoiding a collision with a speeding cyclist. She stared at the house. Georgian? Palladian? She had no idea; she didn't know much about architecture. Brinley would probably know. It was a big thing for him to get a good feel for a building before he designed any piece of furniture to put in it. He'd be able to classify the two thick pillars supporting the porch roof and spiel on particular features of the house, the heavy black doors, probably even the big brass letter box and knocker.

Suzanne glanced up at huge arched windows. One window on the top floor was open. Flat B, she reckoned would be housed on the second floor. She squinted up at the windows. They were fronted by a white stone balcony that supported two potted miniature firs. Impossible to see anything through the window at this distance. Either the room was dark or the curtains were drawn. She couldn't tell which.

She became aware of a man, turning towards her and slowing down as he passed her bench. She hated men eyeballing her, looking her up and down. He was a sharp-suit, clean-shaven, chiseled features, slicked back hair, sunglasses, shiny black leather shoes. Suzanne was wearing an oversize shirt, not even hers, Brinley's, with beaten-up trainers and ill-fitting jeans. When the man turned away from the main park path and took steps towards the street, she continued her scrutiny of the middle floor flat. She stood up, edged nearer, walking over the grass now, to the side of a bed of begonias. No – too dark in the house to see anything.

"Suzanne?" She glanced to her side. The sharp-suit was heading her way. "I thought it was you."

Suzanne had little to go on. The beardlessness, sunglasses and suit were all new. But the voice was the giveaway. Deep, earthy. Those two syllables *Suzanne*, articulated in a slow baritone as always, were enough.

"Lukas!"

"Hello," he said. There was surprise in his voice.

"God, I hardly recognized you."

"And I wouldn't have noticed you if you hadn't been eyeing the street so suspiciously."

"Do I look suspicious?" Lukas was smiling at her, but she found his tone hard to read. He was always like that in the Golborne Road house – his tone always accusatory. She gave him a puzzled look. He responded immediately.

"We've had a lot of break-ins recently. We tend to notice people who look like they're sizing things up – neighborhood watch and all that." He smiled. "No offense."

Just vaguely, though, she was offended. Not so much by Lukas's words, but the way he'd delivered them – with a patronizing smile and a glance over her clothes. She knew he'd pegged them as cheap. It reminded her of how he used to be in the old house. Silent usually, looking casual enough sprawled on a sofa, but nearly always observing the comings and goings of different people, the minutiae of their interactions. The only times he did pipe up were to criticize some publicity piece she'd put together, a web page, a press release or newsletter. "That's too hard-hitting," he'd say. "You need to tone it down. If you bombard people with doom stories they'll think you're paranoid." And then he'd go on about how thousands of people were already using implants to their advantage, voluntarily for medical reasons or for security reasons. He'd get Gavin to give his mangled opinion. Then Brinley, Jamal, Zoe and the rest would prick up their ears. Everyone would suddenly be jabbering and arguing. Almost always this would happen at the point Suzanne was about to release OMNI's publicity pieces. She lost count of the number of deadlines she missed after Lukas had come out of his usual silence to contradict whatever line she'd taken and generally, she thought, to patronize her. At least that's how she'd felt. And that's how it felt right now.

"Change of lifestyle for you, then?" she said. "Smart suit and everything. How come?"

"Well, we all had to change. Move on. Things were messy at the end."

You didn't help, she thought, but didn't say. The protest had been another thing he'd started questioning at the last minute, leading to a general confusion about the route, speakers and collaboration with other organizations. It had been some splinter groups he'd got involved with that had started all the trouble.

"What did you move on to?" Suzanne asked, looking at the pristine attaché case in his hand.

"Vector, you know, the software house."

"Big company." Suzanne said

"What about you? What are you up to?"

Looking after Adam, she thought. Getting my head around the idea of another baby. "I've got an application in with the School of Journalism."

"Oh good," he said, smiling. "You're very good at writing."

"Lukas... I want to ask about Gavin..."

"Gavin? Have you heard from him?"

"That's the thing – we haven't. What about you?"

"Me? No. The last time I saw him was just before he went to Prague."

"He talked to you about going to Prague?"

"Yeah…Why do you sound so surprised? We talked about Prague a lot, especially with that big math conference being there."

"Yes, but I didn't think he'd actually go. I mean, what would he get out of it? He's just not up to higher mathematics any more. And how would he even have the nerve to go?"

"Why not? He had to do something. He was rotting where he was. Oh," he said suddenly, apparently remembering something, "You mean his phobia. His thing about trains? Well, I helped him out…"

"How?"

"Tranx tabs. Otherwise, of course, as you say, he wouldn't have gone anywhere. Of course, I told Gavin," Lukas continued, "that he'd have to go easy on the beer the night before. He wouldn't be able to walk in a straight line if he took tranx and drank the way he normally did. They were strong pills around at the time." Suzanne recalled the footage Ezra Hurst had shown her, of Gavin meandering about St. Pancras concourse haphazardly. Maybe the drugs could account for that. They could also explain how he might have finally got the nerve to go.

"But why hasn't he been in touch?" she said.

Lukas shrugged.

"As I said before, I haven't heard from Gavin either. I wouldn't really expect him to be a conscientious caller…"

"I haven't heard from him at all," Suzanne said quietly.

"I'm sure you will soon enough."

"He's been gone five weeks already."

"Well, look, when I first came to London, I didn't contact my sisters for a long time. That's just the way some people are. I'm sure he's OK, Suzanne. Have you been really worrying?"

"A bit." She didn't want to let on how much. She felt stupid now thinking that somewhere along the line, something underhand was going on. Why hadn't she explained Gavin's disappearance in the most plausible way? He'd talked about going to Prague. She knew Gavin could score tranx and calm himself down for the train ride. Why had she gone to Sense and bothered Ezra Hurst with the half-baked idea that the evidence of Gavin's departure had been doctored? There was the hole in the jacket, but maybe Ezra was right; maybe she'd got confused about the dates of the images.

Suzanne looked at Lukas and saw her own reflection in his sunglasses. Her hair looked untidy and wispy, especially in comparison to Lukas with his perfectly even crop.

"No beard now," she said. "Short hair. You look all different."

"Corporate world – that's what it does to you."

She glanced at his clothes. Tailored suit. Shiny shoes. Pristine attaché. She was surprised by the change. But why should she be? She knew from what had happened to Gavin – serious student to no-hoper – how flimsy personalities were. "Look, don't worry about Gavin too much. I'm sure he's all right."

She checked her watch. 19.20. Adam's bedtime routine would be in full swing. She should get back to help Brin.

"Going?" Lukas asked.

"I'd better."

Lukas flashed her a small smile in response.

She turned quickly and began walking into the diffuse orange light of a very low sun. She was feeling a little calmer now. It was just the hole on the sleeve of Gavin's jacket that troubled her. If she could just get an explanation for that, she'd chill.

***

Ezra was still vexed with John. A lightning drive back to London hadn't changed that. A bleep in his car messaging system sounded; a text-to-voice message was coming through.

"Relay," Ezra barked at the messaging system in his dashboard.

Suzanne Dixon says: Still curious about the jacket problem. Any explanations yet?

Even the machine voice had managed a cynical intonation. Ezra turned it off.

What exactly was he going to tell this girl? He could give brief details of the Feist corruption, about how it had thrown some glitches into a number of recordings, including the one of her brother. That should at least give her the satisfaction of knowing she was right that something was up with the data. He'd tell her that he was currently investigating some of these corruptions. But he'd still insist (and John was probably right about this) that the most likely reason Gavin was appearing in footage boarding a train for the Czech Republic was because that was exactly what had happened. What else did she think might have happened anyway? She said herself that he'd been wanting to go to the conference on – what was it? – mathematical modeling, topology. She'd talked about how he'd considered taking the train to Prague despite his hang-ups. Well, maybe that's exactly what he'd done. Dwelling on the possibility that something else might have happened when there was no supporting evidence would be a total waste of time.

Ezra pulled out into the fast lane, floored the accelerator and hurtled back to London.

12

Saturday 16th August 2059

EZRA AWOKE TO his phone ringing. The night had been warm and the top sheet and light duvet had slid half off the bed. He reached to the floor for his trousers and fumbled for the remote in his pocket. The time glowed on the screen. 6:45.

"You'd better get over here, Ez," Sayle said, immediately.

"Where are you? HQ?" Christ! What was Sayle doing there so early on Saturday? Had he been there all night working out what was going on with the data on Lena?

"You need to get here."

"Why? What have you found?"

"Aberrations."

Too cryptic an answer to know what to do with, but Ezra registered the seriousness and within an hour he was back at Sense HQ.

Marching across a deserted lobby, Ezra heard heels clicking on the marble floor.

Monica. Travel bag in hand.

She stopped her march to the revolving door when she saw him. The last thing Ezra wanted to do was to have to explain a security situation to her before he'd even got to Sayle for the briefing.

She came to a halt in front of him at the side of the ornamental pool. The sound of water zigzagging down the quartz south wall was meant to instill a feeling of calmness. But there was a fault in one of the jets. One spray was overreaching, making the tiles to the side of the pool slippery. A janitor ambled along to place a Hazard sign on the wet floor.

"Working on Saturday?" Monica said to Ezra. "I hope there's not a crisis."

"Busy," said Ezra. He checked the giant clock above the reception desk. It *was* early. It was curious that Monica was here at this time too, but desperate to get some facts on Lena, he wanted to cut the chitchat short. He also wanted to avoid any discussion of the Dixon case.

"And how are our anomalies?" Monica was staring at him all the while.

"Things are in hand." Non-committal answer. Didn't give away the fact that a woman he'd actually drank with four nights ago was an *aberration* (whatever that meant) on the system. Monica was still peering at him, clearly waiting for him to expand. He cast through his mind for something positive to say. He'd already updated her that week on the human trafficking cases and the Passport Office fraud. Distracted by the desire to get to Sayle as soon as possible, he was struggling to find other good news.

"And how are we doing with Suzanne Dixon's complaint?"

Ezra hesitated before saying, "We've had several communications. I've explained to her why there seem to be some glitches in our records."

"Glitches?"

"Minor," Ezra added quickly.

"Really? And is she satisfied?"

"Seems so."

At least as satisfied as she'll ever be, Ezra thought but didn't add. Monica seemed to be waiting for more, but he wasn't prepared to reveal the piece about John's splicing of the data at this stage, so he decided to stay tight-lipped. There was a moment of awkwardness while each waited for the other to speak. She wasn't satisfied. That much was plain. She must have noticed him looking at her travel bag. She said, "I'm just picking up a few papers to take away with me for a weekend trip. Yorkshire Moors," she added. "Have you ever hiked there?" Ezra shook his head. "No? Well, you really should. It's quite rejuvenating. Can be a risk sometimes going alone, though. The weather can change just like that," she said, snapping her fingers. "Mist everywhere. Even if others are on the moor, they might not know you're there. Still, it's a thrill, though."

"Do you ever walk with other people?" Ezra asked.

"Why? Do you like the idea?"

Where had that question come from? He was being general. He hadn't meant to suggest himself as a companion. Was that really how she'd construed things? All right, that would be interesting. Weird though, given that a) she was frighteningly attractive and b) his boss. In any case he was in the middle of a security crisis right now. And maybe he was reading her all wrong. That was probably the safest assumption.

"I like a bit of speed," he found himself saying. "Bike racing, rafting, that kind of thing."

"Not swirling mists, then. And using your instincts. Otherwise," she added, "You can just disappear." She gave Ezra a small smile and a long look with her piercing blue eyes. "I hope you're on top of everything, Ezra," she said, which made him think he was maybe not looking as cool as he'd wanted.

He said, "Things are fine." Then watched her slip out of the revolving door to hail a taxi on the Strand.

He continued marching across the black and white floor. There was a display in the lobby with posters proclaiming the benefits of Resolve, "...a supreme psycho-surveillance system ensuring security." He could do with Resolve in place right now. Tapping into Monica's thought processes was something he'd definitely like to do.

The Anomalies Unit was eerily quiet. The Friday night curtain twitchers would all be in bed now, having finished logging in to

Sense's "Anonymous Crime Report" site to describe suspicious shenanigans on their streets. Ezra clocked one bunch of tracers standing by the far window. One was stretching. Most looked tired. They would have sifted through the gossip, categorized and analyzed the data, ditched the dross, forwarded the facts to the relevant police units. Night shift at an end, some were putting on jackets, getting ready to go. Sayle, though, was separate from them, seated at his workstation, peering at a screen, fingers tapping a control pad.

"So, what's the news?" Ezra asked, pushing aside an empty crisps packet and two Sunburst Soda cans from the space in front of Sayle's computer.

"I haven't traced Lena yet, but ..." Ezra could tell he had some spin – Sayle had been on a continual high ever since Ezra had asked him to see what he could dig up on Lena. "...I've been trying to make sense of the malfunction notices that have been coming up on her records..."

"And?"

"It looks like she has shadow status."

"Are you serious?"

"I said it *looks* that way. See, there's no trace of her at all unless she crosses another person's path, and when that happens she's only a shadow. We have no information. We just know that there was someone there. There's no data on her when she leaves the Tavern because she's not crossing anyone's path, but look here..." Sayle pointed to a clip showing a shadow of a person appear to the side of a young couple on Victoria Street. Ezra gazed at the screen a long while.

"How do you know it's Lena?"

"If you look at the rate she's walking, her direction and the position she's in here, it would make sense that she would have left the Tavern at the time you said she did."

"That's not proof."

"No, it's a hypothesis."

"So... that would mean...that would mean she's covert, working for some intelligence agency."

"Looks a bit like that. Not sure though."

"Why not sure? Who else requests shadow statuses?"

"Well, there's something I don't get," Sayle said. "This shadow doesn't have any information attached it to it."

"That's the whole point of a shadow. The intelligence agencies are the only ones who can pad out the profile."

"Yes, except we should still see a shadow status number and an issue date, since those two pieces of data have to come from us. And with this shadow," Sayle said, pointing to the black profile on the screen, "that information is missing too. There's nothing."

"Are you sure you've looked in the right directories?"

"Of course," Sayle said, glancing around his desk, seemingly looking for something. Finally, he saw his Sunburst Soda cans on a table to the side, reached across Ezra to grab one back.

"How can that information go missing? Jesus Christ! This isn't part of the same Feist corruption, is it? That would be catastrophic if the corruption's expanding to data on protected identities, intelligence workers, people in witness protection programs."

"And there's more…"

"Oh Jesus! What else?"

"Something I noticed early this morning –" Ezra glanced to the clock on the screen. It was still only 7:48; by "early" Sayle must have meant small hours "– when I tried to construct the path of the shadow, by joining up all the points where the shadow appears, there's a certain time on the same night you were at Temple Tavern with her around 11:23 where there's a vague image of a person that appears."

"An image of Lena?"

"Don't know. Look." Sayle found the blurred image in question. "It's not well-formed; there's too little information there for the image to correspond to anyone we have in our database."

"That looks like a regular anomaly, maybe the recording stream is just bad quality." Ezra leaned in towards the screen, tried to adjust the resolution, then the angle of the monitor. The outline of the person could be Lena; the shape of the figure was roughly the same, but the details were too sketchy to draw any firm conclusion. He found himself mentally referring to standard Anomaly Department protocols: "With this footage, we should just do what we normally do to resolve mismatches between the records we have and the actual person it refers to."

"No," Sayle said, "You don't understand what I'm saying. I'm saying this is the same person as the shadow."

"Well, either they're a shadow in the system for security reasons or, like most of us, they have a visible representation of some kind, even if it's bad quality…"

"Not in this case. In this case this person is wavering between the two statuses. And this switching, where they are sometimes in view and sometimes not has been becoming more frequent. This is the last image I looked at – you can see it's clearly a woman here – and the thing about this image, assuming she keeps popping up with some of the visuals filled in, is that there are some oddities that theoretically would make her much easier to trace. Here, for example, see her iris pattern becomes more easily discernible…"

"Enlarge that," Ezra demanded. There were portions of the iris that had the same vivid greenness he'd noticed in Lena's eyes, but the lower sections had taken on a murkier dull tan hue. Sayle enlarged the image, then reclined heavily in his chair, making the back pad strain and creak on its metal stem. He seemed hesitant.

"I don't think there's a problem with our data, Ezra. I think the problem is with her. She's changing. She's…I don't know…somehow corrupt. That's why it's difficult to get a complete trajectory of her movements."

Still gazing at the image of the enlarged eye, Ezra silently considered what Sayle had just said. *She* was corrupt. What did that mean? That she was fake? Flawed? He felt a sudden need to establish facts.

"The upper part of the iris is still the same," Ezra said, placing grid lines over the image to create a triangular section. "This fits with what I remember about her eye color." He had no idea what could account for the dull tan murkiness of the lower iris.

"OK," Sayle said, "but if we try to find a match in the database for a person who has that patterning of the section you're sure about…" he quickly wrote code to set up a search "…this is what we get." He pointed to the words *no results* that had popped up on the screen. "So, what I've been trying to do is home in on some of the features that appear now and again to try and work out the movements, so even if we can't say anything certain about who this person is, whether it's Lena or not, we can have a stab at saying where they are."

"So where are they now?" Ezra said, thinking that the strangeness of the iris patterning was probably a near unique identifier. He nodded towards the screen "What do we get if we put in a real-time search for that pattern?"

Sayle looked at the clock.

"Probably nothing right now. It's early. They're not likely to be out and about." But Sayle began writing a query for a real-time location anyway. "Well, I wasn't expecting that," he said, with sudden alertness. Ezra also moved nearer to the screen when Sayle's script generated a live image of a shadowy figure walking along a narrow street. "Looks like they're out and about after all."

"Wait a minute," Ezra said, alarm in his tone. He checked the coordinate information in the corner of the screen. "That's Victoria Lane. She's just a couple of minutes from here. What's wrong with the gait tracker? Why are her movements irregular?"

"Like I said, I don't think it's our systems. In any case, it looks like she's heading towards this building." Sayle said. "There's nothing else at the end of the lane."

"She's going to the back entrance." Ezra said, standing up suddenly. "But security will stop her."

"Where are you going?" Sayle said.

"I want to be there when they stop her. Find out what's going on."

He couldn't imagine what legitimate business would bring Lena here at this time on a Saturday morning when none of the public-facing staff were around. She had a shadow status. Why? And why had she singled Ezra out in the bar the other night?

Ezra raced out of the Anomalies Unit to the main landing where the night shift tracers from his own department were shuffling into an elevator. He sped over trying to get there in time, but the doors had swished shut by the time he arrived. He jabbed at the elevator button, glancing down to the rear entrance as he waited for another lift to arrive. From where he stood, Ezra had a sweeping view across the atrium to the rear side of the building. Several floors down, far across the lobby, janitors and security guards exited a lift and made their way to the rear entrance. OK, so if she was trying to get into the building surreptitiously, then maybe this timing had some logic; change over time for shift-workers – security would be distracted. Ezra checked his watch. She'd probably be at the back entrance within a minute. There was a ping as an elevator arrived. It would be cutting it fine, but he should hit ground floor before she appeared.

Once down on ground level, Ezra could see six or seven people far across the lobby by the elevators on the rear side. Lena was one of them. How had she got past security? She'd need some kind of ID and hadn't he and Sayle just established that she didn't have any? Ezra had banked on her being held up at the desk for some time. Instead, she was now stretching a finger towards the metal panel on the wall and selecting a floor. What floor? Ezra couldn't see. He raced towards her. She was getting in a lift with a short woman in a navy blue uniform who was carrying a stack of toilet rolls. Ezra could just make out that the woman had selected a lower floor than Lena. He ran faster, but the doors closed before he got there. The lights indicating the two selected floors flashed off. One had been "2". The other was "4". The lift was at "1" now and seemingly held up. He'd be better off taking the stairs rather than waiting for God knows how long. Running four levels was no sweat. He barged through some side doors and charged up the stairs. Floor 4. What was on that level? Ezra didn't come over to this side of HQ often, but he knew that the Contracts department was located there. He'd had meetings with Cunningham a couple of times.

Used to taking the stairs at a light jog, Ezra was surprised to find himself panting when he sprinted out to the fourth floor. Catching his breath, he saw Lena in the sparse white corridor. She was already far down heading towards the Contracts department. She'd come to a stop now. Whose office was that? Looked like Cunningham's. What could she possibly want there on a Saturday? Cunningham wouldn't be there. His office would be well and truly closed. No one was as guarded as Cunningham about security.

Arguing for the need to protect white papers and proposals, he'd even convinced Monica of the need for the ultra-expensive Impenetra locking system. But what the — Lena didn't look like she was struggling to guess a combination. She seemed to know exactly what to press. How could she know the code? Jesus Christ! She'd opened the door. Ezra sped towards her. She'd already disappeared inside. If he didn't get there before the door swung shut, he'd have no way in. Time slowed down or so it seemed; the heavy door was closing, smoothly, slowly. Ezra was still a distance away. A sudden surge of speed brought Ezra to the door just before it hit the frame. Quickly he stuck his foot out and stopped it clicking shut. He barged into Cunningham's office intent on demanding answers to the multitude of questions noisy in his mind.

She was standing stock still far in the office, facing a wall straight ahead with multiple screens. The screens were all on, showing an array of surveillance data. In Lena's hand was the same black cloth bag she'd had in the bar. Ezra walked up to her immediately. He was shocked to see that her complexion was unexpectedly dull and rough. There was a lesion on her neck, where a patch of ivory dry skin was visible. His bombardment of questions went on hold.

She swung around to face him, taking her gaze off one of the images on the wall ahead, an image of a fair-haired slim woman in jeans, carrying a Lewis Store bag strutting along a busy high street.

"What do you all do here?" Lena hissed at him. "Running all this footage — who gives you permission for this? *Who?*" Her lips were cracked, cracking more as she yelled.

He'd been thinking about calling security, maybe medical help too, but derailed now he was on the defensive. "I'm not the one who needs to explain myself. You're showing up on our system as an anomaly. You've broken into HQ. I need to understand that."

"Aren't you omniscient? With these screens and all your cameras..." Ezra couldn't tell whether the tremor that came with the response arose from anger or illness. "Don't you know everything?"

"No. I don't. I don't know why you met me the other night or why you're in Vincent Cunningham's office now. Security will be here soon and you're going to have to fill in the details, right from the beginning."

"The beginning," she repeated, contempt in her voice. She pointed back to the screen showing the woman in jeans walking along a busy street. "Like that beginning. I didn't know anything about *that* one. That was two years ago. *Two years.*" Ezra read the data in tiny white typeface at the bottom of the screen. There were several dates listed. The only one from about two years back said *Retrieval date: 3/5/2057. Subject Last Name: Heaman. Subject First Name: Cleo. Data Accessed by: Cunningham.* "I'd never even met him then," Lena said. Quickly, Ezra glanced at all the screens. Each one showed the same fair-haired white woman – Cleo Heaman – in different settings: street scenes, underground stations, department stores, show rooms, design studios, various rooms of presumably the same large Victorian house. Why was Cunningham running a dozen or so films on this one specific woman? And what was her relation to Lena? Why had she said *I'd never even met* him? Ezra scanned the rest of the office, generally spacious and spare. What was that small statue on his desk? The reports and the spreadsheets, they were expected, but this ivory figurine – was this a portrait of the same fair-haired woman too?

"So, which beginning do you want?" Lena said. Her lips were so dry, Ezra didn't like to look at them.

"Let's start with your version," he said.

Her line of vision settled on a frozen frame of footage showing an interior scene of a pale-walled study with French windows and a cluttered desk. Cleo Heaman stood before a large mirror that was hung above a fireplace. She had a phone pressed to one ear as she looked at her reflection and tried to tidy a flopping strand of hair with her free hand. She was barefoot and wore loose lounge clothes. Expensive, Ezra could tell.

He faced Lena again and found her wincing. There was another tremor and beads of perspiration broke out on her forehead. She seemed like she was struggling to keep standing. The black bag in her hand fell to the floor.

"OK," Ezra said, reaching into his pocket for his mobile.

"What are you doing?" she replied.

"Calling security. They will get you an ambulance."

"No!" She grabbed his arm. "You can't. I'm in danger. Not just me. There are many of us in danger…"

"What… what danger?"

"No ambulance…no! No! No!" She grabbed at his arm. "I've taken such extreme steps...please…please don't let it be for nothing."

"Look, sit down. Have that chair, there."

"Yes, let me sit a while." She slumped onto an office easy chair. "Just a few minutes," she said.

There was a water dispenser to the side of the office door. Ezra yanked out a paper cup from the plastic tube and poured her a drink. When he returned to her side, her head was resting on the back of the chair and her eyes were shut. Along the crease of one eyelid, her dark brown skin was cracked. He should call security; the thought kept recurring. Or maybe even 999. He'd give her a couple of minutes to rest there. No more.

He turned back to the screens, to the last image she'd fixated on – the reflection of the floppy haired woman making a phone call. It was a frozen frame. The metadata showed the date of the footage as 14th July 2059. There was a link to a separate audio file. From the file extension he knew that it was a telephone recording, presumably a recording of the call this woman was making as she stood before the mirror. Scrolling through the panel of information, Ezra saw the telephone number that the woman had dialed. It was a Central London code. He pulled his mobile from his pocket and ran a search on the number. Vision Advertising. Several departments were listed. Looking up to the screen, Ezra saw the extension she'd rung. There was a match on his mobile. Human Resources Department. What was Vincent's interest in this data? What was Lena's? In what way was this footage from five weeks before a beginning?

Lena's eyes were still shut, her head slumped back.

On the control pad, Ezra hit *play*.

Part Two

(six weeks earlier)

13

Monday 14th July 2059

"WE ARE LOOKING for someone with at least five years' senior experience," said the Vision Advertising HR woman on the other end of the line. Her tone was friendly, but firm. Maybe she was sitting primly, professionally at some minimalist desk. Turning on the video would show if this were true. But then there'd be an obligation to put myself on show, and I'd be doing what? Stopping, as now, in front of the fireplace and mirror where she too would see this old baggy blouse and messy hair, the annoying strand flopping into my eye; my obvious unemployment? "Do you have such senior experience?" she asked.

"I do."

Actually I do would have been a more satisfying response. But my reactions were blunt; no one in the daytime to try them out on and Vincent, in the evenings, insisting my "taking stock" at home, "not rushing back into things" had to be for the best.

"Recognized creative talents are very important," said the woman in HR. My e-portfolio board lay on the table in the corner.

Its power light was blinking red. A hand wave over the sensor could launch any number of 3-D demos. Maybe it was a mistake not to have selected the best as my backdrop and have had the video on after all; there were ads in that portfolio for some big name companies that Miss Human Resources was sure to recognize. But the way this call was turning out – its seriousness, the job's increasing appeal – wasn't something I'd anticipated. Just start putting feelers out, find out a bit about the position, about the job search scene in general: that was how I'd been expecting to play it, especially with Vincent wanting to put the brakes on any move forwards.

"...Project management skills and problem solving ability are, of course, of prime importance."

"Of course."

"We expect stellar references and..."

Ah...references. What to do about those?

The pleasant-voiced woman continued spieling words: "...team leadership...delegation...deadline-driven..."

Deadlines, targets – God, was it really nine months since I'd had all that? Nine months since Max had summoned me to his office, disappointment etched into his face, and said that "despite what had happened he wouldn't bad-mouth me." What exactly had he meant? That he'd only say good things about my work record and leave out the part about my getting fired? Or that he wouldn't say anything at all?

"How many references?"

"Pardon?"

There was indignation in the voice now. There was also a faint click on the line.

"I'm sorry. I didn't mean to interrupt you. I wondered how many..." For a couple of seconds there was a hum, a quiet mechanical background noise coming through the earpiece. On a phone call yesterday, there'd been a similarly strange sound. When the noise died down, I said, "How many references are required?"

"Three. One must be from your last employer – that's essential." Shit – that was bad news. "And, aside from references, an impressive portfolio is very important." I found myself motioning the portfolio-board to turn on and selecting the ad for Proteus Jewelry. A 3-D graphic of a single diamond, magnified ten-fold, rose from the surface of the board and rotated to reveal glints and strobes of brilliant light streaming from each facet, forming ever-shifting arrays. I had a portfolio; that was no problem.

"Just so you know," the HR woman said, "we're looking for people with experience of quickly adapting to new market demands and applying a range of techniques."

"I think I have that experience."

When Max was about to leave me out of the Sphere Gaming project because, as he'd put it, action didn't seem to be one of my strong points, I'd made some enhancements to the Proteus diamond to give him a little surprise. Even now pressing the *backdrop settings* on the remote and selecting *shadow hand* made me smile. Surely Miss HR would like this too – the hand looming over the diamond about to snatch it. And the defense – oh, it made me smile remembering how Max's eyes had widened in surprise as each vertex of the diamond extended outwards and transformed into laser arrows. A self-defending diamond – what fun I'd had with that. Such a mistake not to have dressed up a bit and have put the video on for this call.

"Another thing we're impressed with is initiative. You called us to make enquiries. That's good. Most candidates don't do that. We have a small exhibition space in the lobby area. Some of our latest projects are on display there. We would recommend anyone interested in applying for the position to take a look at the kind of work we do. We have a few extra tables too so prospective applicants can show off their own work."

"I'd be very happy to do this. What are the opening times?"

"Well, today…" Today? I checked the clock. It was one. I'd have time to smarten up and make it into the West End, but this was moving quicker than I'd anticipated. "We're open late because we have some grad students visiting."

Possibly some of these grad students might have novel ideas, new techniques that might get attention, even if they didn't have the desired senior experience. And they would be there on the ground, mixing and schmoozing. Getting there in person, portfolio in hand, was crucial. Possibly references could take a back seat if I could plant designs such as the Proteus diamond (still twirling on the portfolio board and generating its brilliant arrows) right under their nose. It was still good to see how squaring the portfolio base with the corner of the table eliminated all surface reflections. Now the luster was satisfyingly pure. One of the good things about "taking stock" at home was the time it allowed for experimentation. Now was the time for feedback. If this exhibition space was open until late, there'd be plenty of time to prepare.

"What time do you get off work?" the HR woman asked.

Careful now. Don't give away the unemployment part.

"I have time in my schedule to come today, but it couldn't be until later."

What fraudulence was I pulling here? But the woman, seemingly detecting none said, "Or another day, if today is too tight for you."

Expedience, not fraudulence. There were going to be hurdles, maybe more for me than most; giving myself a positive spin would help me take them more cleanly. Hadn't the mentors at the Oasis Centre continually drummed that home? There had to be some kind of culmination to all my work in this room, the programming and designing for three months solid. The only stoppages had been for the odd glance through the French windows during coffee breaks (maybe more than usual recently now that the hydrangeas were splashing the garden with purple). No matter what Vincent might say about taking things one step at a time, this Creative Director job was an opportunity. An exciting one. It would be foolish to delay.

"Today should –" There was a loud click on the line and my voice became distorted.

"Pardon?"

Speaking louder I said, "Today should be fine."

After the HR woman had given directions and finally hung up, the interference died down. I listened intently a few seconds more. Another faint click, then silence on the line. Some technical glitch perhaps; maybe there was no need to feel so on edge about it.

But what to say to Vincent?

Straight facts were probably the best thing to give. I texted "going 2 talk designs. vision advertising. dering st. back 5ish " The message seemed blunt. I put an "x" at the end.

***

Combing my hair at the dressing table, I noticed a movement in the mirror. In the reflection, beyond my image, beyond the silky crimson expanse of bed where my smart work skirt and top were laid out, was Vincent. He stood in the doorway in a dark suit, with a loosened tie. Silently he watched me.

He was early. I checked the watch on the dresser. Very early. Out-of-character for him to take a half-day break from HQ when he was normally working late on the Resolve contract.

"I didn't hear you come in," I said. He gave a half smile. "Did you get my message?"

He nodded, watched me comb my hair for a while. It was still wet from the shower and making the neckline of my dressing gown damp.

"Why the sudden decision?"

"I have to go back to work at some point."

A long moment of silence. Why was it so hard for him to accept this?

"How are you thinking of getting there?"

"Tube." Vincent shook his head. "What's the problem?"

"Underground's down."

I checked my mobile. A code orange security alert, another hoax probably.

"I'll get a cab," I said.

"Will you be out long?"

"Not sure."

While I was putting in a pearl earring, he moved towards me, past the dark red bed. He pulled a chair right up to my dresser and sat down, his thighs either side of my stool.

"You know what I'd like?" he said.

He was peering at my earring and so close to me now – this

large, dark-suited presence – I could feel his breath on my neck. He reached for my earring.

"What would you like?" His hand brushed my neck as he fingered the pearl. My skin began to tingle. "What? Tell me."

"An Ost piece."

"Ost? The bone jewelry?

He nodded. "Whose bone?"

"Yours."

"You want my bone?"

"Yes…look."

"Look at what?" He pulled his scroll screen from his pocket and unrolled it. He tapped on icons and pulled up Ost's site. "Seriously – you've been looking into this?"

"Why not? It's simple. They extract a minute amount of tissue from the jawbone." He held my chin up and ran his finger gently along my jaw line. "Just a little prick, that's all. No more than a second. And from that sample they get the cells to replicate, then they mold the new tissue into whatever jewelry or item you want."

There were several bone items displayed on the scroll screen: earrings, necklaces, an exquisite chain of miniscule cubes.

"And what would you like to turn *my* bone into?"

"A portrait." He switched the image on the scroll screen to Ost's art collection. *Portraits by Federico Hernandez.* Small profiles of men and women – cameos, figurines, some pictures in relief, all made of bone and mounted on whichever backdrop or base the customer cared to specify. Mahogany, ebony, redwood. "You can have the bone stained," he said. "I'd stain yours a warm ivory."

"Why?"

"To match your skin."

"And what would you mount me on?"

"Oh," he replied, giving one of his smiles, "something red."

Why had I even led him down that path? What was wrong with me that I was so susceptible to being waylaid? And Vincent *was* waylaying. He was powerful and knew so and that knowledge made him more so. Self-control – why was it so hard?

"And…where would you keep this figurine?"

"At work. On my desk. Or maybe on the windowsill. I know

how you like a nice breeze." His lips moved nearer mine. "So, what do you think? Can we go to the studio?"

"So you can get some of my bone?"

"It doesn't hurt. You can have some of mine if you like."

"To make a little art piece out of you?"

"If you want," he said.

"You're insane."

"I'm serious about wanting some of you."

He wasn't the kind of person who'd waste time surfing sites about procedures he wasn't minded to start.

"Why do you want it so much?"

"Would keep you near," he said, pulling me against him. "I was hoping we could visit the studio today."

"So, it looks like we're both being impulsive."

"Well, what do you think?" He glanced to his scroll screen. "Can I have your portrait?"

"Not with my hair the way it is."

"I like your hair. It's fine like that. Hernandez is actually in the studio today. We have the chance to specify exactly what we want with the artist himself."

"It's all a bit intense," I said, blocking the side of me that was whispering, *You like all this. Go on – just open up that bathrobe.*

"What's wrong with intense?" he said, moving his hand toward the slit of my robe.

I caught his hand. Held it tight for a while, then nudged it away from my thigh.

"Today…" my voice came out small. I took a breath and spoke louder. "… as you know, I've already made plans."

Now our closeness was awkward. He gave a long sigh and shunted his chair back a fraction.

"Can't you see about this job another day?"

"I just have a feeling that would be a missed opportunity. It's time for me to move on."

His stare was so piercing I had to look away. A damp strand of hair fell in my face. I grabbed a band. Pulled my hair back, twisted and tied it up.

"Well," Vincent said slowly, "what about I drive you to this company of yours, then we go to Ost after? It will probably still be open. We can at least have a look."

"And what will you do while I'm showing off my portfolio?"

He shrugged.

"I suppose I can wait in the car."

"Not sure that this all needs to be packed into one day." Neither would it be helpful to have thoughts of bone jewelry and cell extraction and syringes lurking in my mind while trying to make an impression on a possible employer. But Vincent, staring at me via the mirror, was clearly expecting a compromise. "Oh, OK, if you want it so much – let's go to Ost too."

He nodded and scooped his scroll screen off the dresser. "I'll sort out downstairs." He looked at the clothes laid out on the bed. "How long do you think you'll be? Twenty minutes?"

"Something like that."

Strange that he required such a precise lead time simply for leaving the house. He headed to the stairs, presumably to start his usual check of locks and windows.

By the time I came down, the house was unusually dim. Just gone two, but so dark already. Through the French windows of the spare room, there was a slate grey cloud dominating the sky. Vincent had already checked the room: the burglar alarm beeped quietly, and the power lights on the video, the speaker unit, even my e-portfolio were off.

"I pressed 'save,'" Vincent said, his voice coming suddenly from the doorway.

He held keys and remote lock controllers in his hand. I felt Vincent watching me as I rummaged through drawers looking for the e-portfolio case. He must have seen the Proteus design glinting on the table when he came down. Couldn't he say something encouraging – *They're bound to be impressed with a piece like that* – anything that would show some support? Silently he left the room as I inserted the e-board into its cover.

Out in the hall he was entering the code on the security panel by the front door, making sure the alarms were set, that the real-time video and the remote lock option were on.

"I think we can change that now," I said to Vincent as we

headed to the car.

"Change what?"

"The live security feed to your office and the remote lock."

He continued pressing buttons, then strode through spitting rain towards the car on the drive. He didn't answer even as we settled into our seats and buckled our belts. He turned on the car lights and flicked the wiper control. The blades left a smear as they swept across the screen.

"Did you hear what I said about turning off the live feed?"

"Well," he said slowly, putting the car into gear and onto the road, "you agreed that it was good for me to have a real-time view of people arriving at the door. And we know that some of the types you used to hang around with are very bad news. Why on earth would you want to be less secure?"

It was true that the live feed hadn't seemed like a problem before. So, what was the difference now? That I was thinking more of a life outside the house and worried that Vincent was going to challenge the various new moves I might make? And what about the interference on the phone – was there any possibility (was I really going to consider this?) that Vincent might be listening in to my calls?

"What's the matter?" he said suddenly, peering at me intently. A siren was wailing in the distance. The rain was heavy and the wipers were on full. He waited for a gap in the traffic before edging out onto the main road.

"I don't think we need the remote locking option either."

"What? Oh come on – it would be very foolish to turn that off." He looked incredulous. "How many times do people leave the house unsure that they've locked up properly and then have to go back and check? Well," Vincent said, tapping his pocket where he kept the lock control, "I don't need to worry about that, do I? If the remote says 'no – the locks aren't set' I press a button and voilà – they are. What on earth do you want me to change that for?"

I had no answer lined up. I'd just blurted the concern; I didn't even know where that one had come from. Remote locks, live video feeds, interference on the phone – maybe it was just paranoia casting Vincent as a threat?

"Never mind. I don't even know why I'm thinking about this. I need to focus on the job."

His eyes on the traffic in front, he said, "So what makes you so sure that you're ready to go back to work – that the pressure won't send you back to your old ways?"

"That's a risk…but Vincent, I'm going to meet a possible employer. It's not helpful having you fill me with doubts before I get there. What do you think I've been doing all these experiments indoors for? Just to sit staring at my designs at home?"

"I just worry about who you'll come across. It might be a new job, but it's the same industry. You'll run into people from your past – all the dissolutes you've left in the background."

"*Dissolutes*…is that even a word?"

"Stop avoiding the subject," he said, sourly.

"Well, even if I didn't think you were being dramatic – the crucial point is that they are in the background."

"For now, yes. But will you go looking for them the moment the pressure builds up?"

"Like I said, this isn't a helpful…"

"Take Hurst at work," Vincent cut in with a spine-chilling sneer. It was always startling how the mere thought of Ezra Hurst could demolish his composure. "When Hurst first started at Sense he sniffed out the party-heads: John Durrant, Clint Scarman – two loafers propping up the local bar every night. Gaming, strip clubs, drinking, drugs – that was what they were all about. Temple Tavern must've made a packet out of them."

"What's that got to do with Ezra Hurst? I thought he was gung-ho for promotion. Your main rival – isn't that why he worries you?"

"Yes and that's the thing – he has two sides. He's torn. He's ambitious and when he puts his mind to it he can make smart moves. But he also likes to play, which is why he used to waste his time with Durrant and Scarman."

"*Used to.* So he changed things, then."

"He's been trying – you have to give him that. That episode when he took over the Anomalies Department, he had to grow up then. And when –" a short strangled sound came from Vincent, part sneer, part snort, "when he had to cut staff – well, you can see it made sense to cut Scarman; anyone else would have made the same move. Scarman was shady – his database management was questionable, potentially a security threat. He had to go. But Hurst was supposed to be his friend."

"So, what point are you making?" Obviously, Vincent was drawing a parallel between me and this Ezra Hurst, who seemingly had some vices and was struggling to rein them in. But didn't everyone have flaws? "What's the moral of the story?"

"He's a liability for the company. He ditched his friends and now they have a grudge. Scarman in particular – he's a piece of work. Who knows what he's plotting in his barge…"

"Barge?"

"Yes, barge," said Vincent, nodding mechanically. "He's holed up on some battered boathouse in South Dock. Maybe he'll want to get even with Hurst. Potentially, the whole company could be hurt, just at the time I'm trying to win the Resolve contract. So, I have to keep my eye on Scarman – he could be a killer for me." Momentarily, the only sounds were of window wipers rhythmically sweeping rain off the windscreen. "Meanwhile, Hurst – " again the snort of derision " – Hurst carries on having a couple at the Tavern after work. Presumably, he sits there by himself, since he's knifed his friends. The problem with profligates – " *profligates* – why did Vincent choose such melodramatic descriptors? " – they destroy so much more than their own petty worlds. What's really contemptible is their obliviousness – that's the part I can't stand." A road-hugging Lotus slowed in front of us. Its reverse lights flicked on as the driver parallel-parked into a gap by the pavement. Vincent was shaking his head now, "No doubt Hurst'll head off to the Tavern tonight – park himself on a barstool, not a care in the world…"

"You don't know that, do you? You can't know what he's thinking."

Vincent threw me a little smile, the kind you throw a kid. "So, you want to defend him?"

"I don't want to *defend* him. I don't even know him. Why should I care?"

"Because you have some of the same traits. You're trying to see things from his point of view. It worries me that you get defensive so easily. It makes me think that you're not really ready to take the step you're thinking about."

"I cannot stay cooped up at home. That's no more freeing than addiction, is it?"

"You haven't been *cooped up*."

"Look, if a person feels ready to take on new challenges but all they find is a series of barriers – that is being cooped up. Obviously, I might make mistakes and, yes, maybe I'm more prone than most, but I intend to stay out of trouble and put my career back together. That's where I'm at. And, honestly Vincent, if you can't accept that... Look, if you can't accept that, then I don't know how we'll survive."

"So that's it, is it? I help you get better. You're clean for nine months and you're off?"

"Look, I know how much you care for me. More than anyone else – I know that's a fact. I'm just feeling ..." *strangulated, suffocated* – these words were all too strong to say. "I really hope that's not it, but..."

"And what about my ambitions?" Vincent cut in. "You used to be so supportive and listen to my plans at work. Every executive meeting – with Monica Parks, with the other directors – you used to ask for the details. You used to ask how I was shaping up for promotion against Hurst. What happened to all that? You've become so self-absorbed. Do you know how many messages I had today from Monica about the Resolve contract?"

Vincent was gripping the wheel tightly, his eyes fixed on me instead of the road. I shook my head.

"Twenty-three. Budgeting breakdowns, technical reports, ethical committee amendments, updated risk assessments...twenty-three! She's being unreasonable."

It was true I hadn't sensed this level of pressure. It was also true that we used to talk more about his ambitions. He'd always sounded so powerful plotting his path to promotion, expecting to win the Resolve contract, expecting to take over the Operations Division as a result. That confidence, when we'd first met, had been a real turn on. There'd just been one occasion an alarm bell had rung: we were dining at The Criterion and he'd taken a long sip of wine, then said, "It's a strange thing to contemplate, but you know what the Resolve technology will deliver?" He'd created a dramatic pause, then said, "Everyone's thoughts. And I'll have the keys."

The windscreen wipers swished noisily across the glass. One was now making a hideous screech.

We drove the rest of the way without speaking until Vincent pulled the car up outside the Vision Advertising building. Nodding to a solitary parking spot further along the road he said without looking at me, "I'll wait over there."

14

THE LOBBY AREA was light and airy with a few exhibition stands dotted about. There was a rotating hologram of a self-drive Audi. Further along on a display stand was a 3-D set of Carver knives. One of the walls carried a flat screen ad for Cartwright's Hotel. The receptionist, tall, East Asian, asked if she could help me. She wore flared trousers and a wraparound top. If this was the woman I'd spoken to on the phone, she was radically different from how I imagined her. Disarming how an imagined appearance could be so far off the mark.

"I phoned earlier," I said. "I was invited to have a look at some of the current projects and bring my own portfolio."

"Oh yes, I recognize your voice. Here –" she peeled off a visitor's badge from a sheet and proffered the label to me. I unglued it from the tip of her index finger and stuck it on my lapel. "Feel free to look around. If you have anything to show yourself, there are a couple of small tables at the back there. We're expecting a group of students a little later, so it may get busy."

There was already a handful of people milling around. One man began strolling over to the rotating Audi. Made sense he'd be attracted. The imagery was a draw: blood red, sleek, lights glinting off the highly polished hubs. At the back of the room a couple of people were huddled around some piece on a podium. A woman, her back to me, was heading towards a nearby spare desk. She wore a fitted black jacket with square shoulders, knee-length skirt and heels. Her posture was upright and her walk was brisk and familiar. Swinging her portfolio case onto the surface, she turned into profile. Shit! Sarah Coulson – it had to be; the short angular cut of her jet black hair was instantly recognizable. Now she was looking at me, doing a double-take. It was definitely her. Shit. She pulled her e-board from its case – same model as mine. What was she doing here? Had she had enough of working for Max? Was she after a new job too? From the way she was throwing glances my way, seemed like the sussing was mutual. Better go over and talk to her; it would be less awkward.

"What brings you here?" I asked, trying to look friendly, knowing my smile was false.

"Job search," she said. Deadpan.

"Have you had enough of working for Max?"

She threw me a sharp glance with cold, narrowed eyes.

"I was laid off."

"Laid off? What? Really?"

"Well," she said after a moment's silence, a moment dominated by her look of incredulity, "that's just great that you didn't even know. Oh, but that's right – you've been in rehab for the last few months. It's one of the methods, isn't it – ditch all the people in your old life and start afresh? So, it's true then, that ignorance is bliss."

"I…" But the tirade stunned me into silence.

"Well," she continued, "I just don't think that's fair. So, let me fill you in on some details. The contract that you managed to screw up – that was the most lucrative contract the company would ever have had. That was the contract that would have funded my job. And David's. And Radhia's. So we were all part of your wreckage. Oh, don't look so innocent. You might not have been around long enough to see the collateral damage, but you must have known it was there."

"I...I didn't know.... No, I –" I could feel my cheeks flushing. It was difficult looking Sarah in the eye " – I didn't know anyone else had lost their jobs."

"Well, you do now," she said. "And, Radhia, God bless her, she was even prepared to cut you some slack; said I shouldn't judge you so harshly, that I hadn't bounced around foster homes the way you had. Even as she was losing her job she was excusing your behavior. Well, I'm sorry, I'm not so kind – you're an addict, a junkie, and I'm part of your train wreck. If you want to make amends now, the best thing you can do is leave."

She gave a long hard stare, then turned her back and began squaring the base of her e-board on the table.

Jesus Christ! I'd only just arrived and this was already going so wrong. This was supposed to be about moving forward, not going over my failings. Again. There was nothing to do but edge away from Sarah. She didn't want me near her – that much was clear. But the only spare table was still at her end of the lobby. Keeping our backs to each other was the best we could do.

I knew I'd screwed up that contract. No-one else had got out of control at the pre-presentation party. So what that some prankster had spiked my dust and turned what should have been a confidence booster into a draw I couldn't handle? It wouldn't have mattered that it was mixed with shit if I'd just left it alone and had an early night. Nor would it have mattered that the person offering it (God – he seemed so witty and easy-to-talk to) was a put-up job from our main competitor. Max and Sarah and David and me wouldn't have had to watch our concept being pulled apart piece by piece if I hadn't blabbed about it the night before. That was my fuck-up. I accepted that. When Max had said, "I hate to fire someone as talented as you, but I'm afraid I have no choice," I'd understood. But he'd never suggested that Sarah (she still had her back to me), Radhia and David might end up jobless too. Jesus Christ! Was that really the impact I'd had?

"Are you OK?" the receptionist said. I hadn't realized that she'd sidled up to me, nor that I was standing frozen and stupid-looking. I nodded that I was OK. She looked unsure, but thankfully moved on.

What would my Oasis mentor have said? Acknowledge that guilt had muscled its way in (again), then decide what to do with it. Deal with it constructively, not wheel out once more the idea of my own intrinsic badness – that was all pain and pointlessness, a slippery road back to drugs or drink.

Yes, it was horrible having Sarah (jobless, unforgiving) standing to my side. But now put things in perspective. What were the facts? Was I totally to blame for her misfortune? Sarah, offering nothing but her black-jacketed back, obviously thought so. But was she right? Was it really *all* my fault that she was out of work?

Vincent had only just been talking about people losing their jobs at Sense HQ too. The economy was tough; all the news feeds said so. And that was not my fault. And the fact that Max had laid all his eggs in one basket, that the health of his company was so dependent on one big contract – that was a mistake, but not one of mine. As for the people he then laid off: Sarah Coulson, Radhia Alsawaf, David Shaw – if I had been in Max's position, then I'd have picked these three too; they were the weakest players in the company, brutal though it was to say. Radhia – yes, she was a lovely person (God! Had she really stuck up for me? I'd forgotten how sweet she could be. It seemed like only yesterday she'd been planning a birthday bash for her youngest, wondering whether a dry ski run party at Olympia was too extravagant and dangerous for a bunch of ten-year-olds. Shit! That would be extravagant if she had no job). Design-wise, though, Radhia just wasn't remarkable – there was no escaping that fact. And David – well, he was definitely talented, but all about partying. Cruising around Drugland with him, I'd realized early on, was just too dangerous a game. I actually missed him, but he was no career-head. He only had half a heart for hard work and didn't care if it showed. And Sarah… So, she was setting up that old creation was she? The 3-D mannequin with the Cureaux dress. Well, it wasn't bad. But by now she should be able to show better command of resolution and depiction of texture. Viewers should be able to look at that display and "feel" the cloth with their eyes. Sorry Sarah, but these were factors. Your situation was not *all* down to me.

There was a soft ping on the far side of the lobby, where an elevator was coming down. Sarah jerked her head up to look. The sharp angle of her bob hairstyle pointed to the corner of her downturned mouth. She peered at a man with rolled-up sleeves and hands in his pocket, stepping out of the lift to begin milling around the lobby. Quickly she began pressing controls on her e-board, enlarging her Cureaux dress display.

Assuming this man was talent scouting, he'd see she knew the fundamental principles of design. True, the mannequin gave a little disarming wink from time to time. But it was a pretty static piece, not especially original. If the mannequin had gradually transformed from female to male, that would have been more interesting. She could have shown off the Cureax business suits too. But there always was a limit to Sarah's imagination and technical abilities.

The man with rolled-up sleeves was eyeing people with visitor's badges, leaning over to look at their displays, asking a question, making a comment, moving on to the next person. Definitely talent-scouting.

He was getting nearer.

I placed my own e-board on a little table, uncomfortably aware that Sarah was now peering at me from the corner of her eye. She'd seen early versions of the Proteus diamond, but not the gaming version I was about to beam up now. I could tell she was anxious and I didn't feel good knowing I was about to outshine her, but I had to put my own house in order too.

The scout approached the mannequin. Sarah's downturned mouth transformed into a smile. She became vivacious, demonstrative. She was very good at the social stuff. Much, much better than me. Now was the time to launch the diamond.

I pressed, *Open hologram*, then selected *Proteus*.

The hologram failed to appear. The only thing visible on the e-board was a message saying *awaiting input*. I pressed again. Nothing. Checked the control – the casing wasn't loose, the little red power light was on. Other functions looked like they were working just fine; selecting *create* made a white grid pattern appear with an array of holographic shapes to choose from. The malfunction centered on one thing only: making my saved creations materialize. It wasn't just Proteus; every hologram I selected failed to appear.

A shadow fell over the empty e-board; the scout was standing before me.

"Problem?"

"Please give me a minute," I said, stalling for time, hoping some obvious solution would spring to mind. He stayed put. I fumbled and fidgeted, mumbled and muttered. Eventually he walked off.

"So," Sarah said. The word came out slow, oozing with sarcasm. "You still can't perform on the day."

***

"What's the matter?" Vincent said, looking up from his info-remote with a jolt.

"This," I said shaking the e-board at him before throwing it onto the back seat of the car. Vincent used his sleeve to wipe a fallen raindrop from the gearstick. "I've never had problems with this software before." I plumped into the front seat and slammed the door. "Why today? Why?" Unable to look at Vincent, I focused on the Duke of York pub across the road: the sign swinging in diagonal rain bearing the portrait of the white-wigged noble; the blackboard saying *Cask Ales, Fine Wines*; the geraniums (magenta and lilac) in a box by the door. A man carrying a pint stepped outside. He balanced his glass on the windowsill, pulled an umbrella from under his arm and lit a cigarette. I could have done with a drink. Or better, some dust. It was times like this I could do with a draw.

"Look at the way you're breathing," Vincent said, sounding alarmed. "I'm not sure you're ready for this kind of competition when you get so het-up…"

"What did you do when you turned my portfolio off?"

"What?"

"You turned it off before we left the house."

"I pressed *save* and pressed the power button."

"Nothing else?"

"What do you mean?"

"Oh, forget it. It doesn't matter. It's too late."

We sat in silence. The man outside The Duke stood under his umbrella, smoking his cigarette, not giving a shit about the rain.

"Parking warden," Vincent said, nodding into the distance. A woman, smothered by a yellow anorak, was heading our way. "We have to move on." Vincent hesitated before saying, "Shall we go to the Ost Studio? It will take your mind off things."

The word *whatever* reverberated around my head. At least I'd stopped myself from saying it; curtailed Vincent's stock response that it made me sound like a child. Neither had my mentor at Oasis liked the *whatever* attitude, the carry-on as you please approach no matter how self-destructive. She would have pointed to the man standing outside the pub under his umbrella and said, "It's that important to him, is it? He needs that fag so much he's out there getting sodden in the rain. He's in the world's fastest city and is that all there is to do? What's wrong with trying something else? Choosing something new?"

"Is that a *yes* for the Ost studio?" Vincent said. It had no appeal. But it would be "something else." "Well?"

Well, we had to move somewhere, do something, not sit here festering, much as I wanted to. Reluctantly, I gave a nod. He turned the key in the ignition and pulled the car away.

15

IN THE OST showroom, I was still silently fuming. Vincent was strolling past glass showcases, scrutinizing the cameos and jewelry on display, the e-board debacle at the back of his mind, at least that's how he was acting. I couldn't help but replay the episode and could barely restrain myself from swinging my portfolio up on the nearest glass case to fiddle with the controls to work out what had gone wrong.

"You like this piece?" came a falsetto voice. A short, stocky man was standing beside me. Caramel skin. Beady eyes. *Federico Hernandez, Ost Artist* were the words on a label pinned to his shirt. He was nodding to the case, to an ivory ring studded with emeralds. I might have been looking in the direction of the piece, but it was only now that its details stood out. The stones were tiny, translucent and impossibly round. "I made another one very similar to this for my wife. She likes to have green jewels. If you have green eyes, you should always go for green gems – that's what she tells me anyway. She's an avid jade collector, and green diamonds – very rare, you know – she likes those too, but emeralds…"

Federico looked down at the glinting ring, "…emeralds are her favorite. Now your eyes," he added after a pause, "your eyes are…"

"Hazel."

Probably there wasn't such a thing as a very rare hazel gem to recommend for me.

"Hazel, yes, but if you look closely," and he was looking very closely, "you'll find your eyes have little flecks of yellow. Now, amber…" he said, nodding to an Ost ring with a single honey colored jewel, "…amber might suit you very well." But the piece he was indicating didn't seem so impressive. No doubt skillfully cut, but all angles and razor sharp edges. "What kind of piece are you looking for?"

"None in particular." I gestured to Vincent. He'd been on the far side of the showroom by the window, absorbed by some collection for a good ten minutes or so. "He's the one with the interest."

"Oh, you're with Mr. Cunningham." His line of vision dropped down to the portfolio I was holding. "And I see you are an artist yourself, so I imagine you will have some interesting ideas for the order."

"The order?"

"Yes, he texted the order – a five inch figurine, a portrait of you."

"A figurine – let me get this right…" the discussion at home about bone jewelry seemed a long time ago and now that I was recollecting it I couldn't help a half laugh "… Vincent's already ordered a figurine that you are intending to make from my cells."

"That's right, but…" Federico looked confused "I assumed you had both discussed this."

"Only vaguely."

I headed towards Vincent. He was bent over a display case containing dozens of ivory colored rings, some plain bone, some intricately meshed with jewels, all half-submerged in a thick liquid. There was a notice to the side with the title *We Are One – Wedding rings combining cells from two lovers into one unique band.*

I could feel Vincent's eyes upon me as I read the notice, gauging my reaction.

"I hear you've already made an order."

"For the figurine? Yes – why not?"

"Well, it's all very sudden, isn't it?"

"But why delay?"

"Maybe I need to think about it." I was hit by a memory of Vincent in the bedroom, holding my chin up, showing how the skin was pricked to procure some bone cells. "It's invasive."

"Barely," Vincent said dismissively.

"Actually," again Federico's falsetto loomed unexpectedly, "Mr. Cunningham's right – it is a very minor procedure. His beady eyes flashed between me and Vincent, before focusing on a passageway at the back of the studio. "Shall we begin the consultation?"

"Come on," Vincent said. "What are you so worried about?"

The consultation room had little more than a couple of seats, a sink and a blue table with a tray of mini-syringes. Federico asked whether we were familiar with the bone jewelry craft and the process involved.

"Roughly," I said.

Vincent nodded his yes. Federico passed me leaflets and described further details of the procedure.

"So, tell me, what would you like me to design?" Federico had addressed Vincent, who took my face gently in his hands. He turned my head, so Federico could see my profile.

"A portrait," Vincent said. His hand was smoothing my hair, stroking it downwards, "a little figurine, showing all this nice hair, which she keeps threatening to cut. The whole piece mounted on redwood and..." he indicated a five-inch stretch with his fingers, "...about this high."

Federico pulled a pad from a drawer and began jotting notes and quickly sketching images of my face from various angles. It always surprised me how, sideways on, the angularity of my nose and lips took center-stage. It seemed strange, looking at Federico's soft pencil strokes, that there were aspects of my own appearance that other people had greater familiarity with than me. Weird that Vincent should want them immortalized in such a bizarre way.

"I will be a little while," Federico said to Vincent, "finishing sketches, taking some cells – if you want, you could take a look around the showroom."

"Maybe I will. I saw some interesting items."

Once Vincent had left Federico, he glanced down to the portfolio positioned by my feet and said, "So, what kind of creations do you have on your e-board?"

"None." I could see the sharp retort puzzled him. "It's a long story." One that was still unexplained. Exactly how could all my designs just suddenly have disappeared from the system? How...

"Well, OK, in that case," Federico said, sounding awkward and suddenly busying himself with pulling a steel trolley towards him, "Shall we proceed?"

I caught myself shrugging. The whatever attitude had kicked in. I shouldn't be taking anything out on this Federico Hernandez. He wasn't the reason for the portfolio debacle. An image of Sarah Coulson's triumphant expression in Vision's lobby sprang to mind. "OK, OK..." I needed to do something to dismiss that memory "...I'm ready. Let's proceed."

"You need to jut out your chin a bit, so I can get a good view." He held a small syringe with one hand and positioned Petri dishes, gauze, vials on the desk surface in front of me. He plucked these items from the trolley on wheels. A small handheld device lay on the top shelf. The words *Decay Reading* were visible on its screen.

"What's that?"

"Oh, we don't need that. I used that for my previous customer." Federico's hand and the syringe came towards my chin. "It's just a prick. Try to look away. There's not much to see and you'll go crossed eyed, won't you – trying to look at your own chin?" The prick of the needle tip was only slight. "See, it doesn't really hurt much." He put his free hand on my shoulder. "You're very tense, aren't you? Try to relax a bit. This will only take a minute." With his hand cupping the ball of my shoulder, I became aware of how hunched I was. I straightened up and let my shoulders drop.

"What kind of piece did your last customer want?"

"She wanted a pendant made from her husband's bone, but her situation was different from yours and Vincent's."

"How?"

"Her husband passed away a month ago. So for her, it was a case of finding cells he'd left behind. She bought in some of the items he frequently used: his comb, his phone – we tried to find DNA that way." Federico nodded to the gadget on the trolley. "We had to look for the cells with the least decay. That's what that device is for."

"How does it work?"

"Well, the cells have some static charge left in them when they're left behind on insulating surfaces like plastic. But the charge decays over time. It's knowing that rate of decay that's key. That device can tell me which cells were deposited last, even the time they were left. We can find the cells with the least decay and fashion the pendant from those."

"So…." Maybe it was the fact that I'd said the word so slowly or my uncertainty about continuing the thought, but when Federico removed the needle from my chin, he faced me square on, bright-eyed, motionless, clearly waiting for me to speak. "So…" I picked the e-board off the floor and opened the control pad "…is it possible to find Vincent's cells, the most recently deposited on this keyboard display?"

"Oh," Federico threw a big smile, "You want to fashion something from his cells too."

"No. Not fashion something. Check something. Can you find the keys he touched most recently?"

"Well, yes, I suppose I could. It's just you and him who have access to this machine, is it? Well, that's pretty easy." Federico swiveled around on his stool to scoop up the device from the trolley. He pressed a series of buttons, then ran the device lightly over the keyboard. "The newest cells are on the *enter* key. That's not really surprising though, is it? That's always the last key people hit."

"What key did he touch before that?"

"Oh, what fun! This is like being a detective, isn't it? Let's see: he pressed "w" at 13:55:09 – there are a nice batch of cells there."

13.55. That was about right. It was just gone two when I'd followed Vincent into the spare room; the room that had seemed so surprisingly dark that I'd checked the clock. He'd said all he'd done was press *save*. So where did the "w" come from? Looking through the doorway of the consultation room, I couldn't see Vincent. He must still be absorbed with some artifacts outside, but he could come in at any moment. God! What was I doing encouraging Federico to play at "being a detective" and run his scanner over the keyboard and jot down letters in his sketch pad. A lot of letters! What on earth was he writing? Maybe nothing meaningful. Vincent might have accidentally touched random letters as he'd turned the e-board off. Maybe I was being paranoid. Vincent was outside (looking at wedding bands!) while I sat here all suspicious. What kind of person was I?

Federico had put the scanner down and was turning his sketch book so that I could read the letters he'd scribbled with his 2b pencil.

"Chronologically, these were the last keys, that were touched." *run[space][shift]temp[shift]delete[shift]utility[space]* dir contents *MyCreations* *[space]* duration:2hr *[space]* start: *now*

I read the whole string slowly and out loud. I re-read *run TempDeleteUtility* several times. "A program to delete files?"

"I believe so." Federico's voice was quiet now. He glanced to the doorway and pushed his chair back from the table, as if he were trying to create a distance between himself and the keyboard. "And it looks like the deletion is only temporary – 2 hours in this case."

"Temporary? So, what…?" I checked the clock on the wall behind Federico – I'd been out of the house over two hours now "…so my portfolio will be back there now?"

"Well, I don't know, I …careful! Careful!" Federico said, reaching over to grab one of the syringes that got snagged on my sleeve when I reached out for the e-board.

I turned the keyboard to face me and opened the directory of saved designs, selected *Proteus* and pressed *Open hologram*.

"My God!" Federico said, leaning across the table as the diamond appeared. "You designed this? But it's beautif…."

"I don't believe it. I don't fucking believe it."

But Federico, looking panicked now, had laid out the evidence. Momentarily, I found it hard to breathe, then I found myself saying, "Is this really happening? Federico, is this really true?" Then Federico, all flustered, was fidgeting and saying "Well, I may have…maybe my analysis was wrong…I am not a forensics expert. I may have made a mistake." His gaze switched from the keyboard to the notepad, back and forth, then at last he sat still and said, "But I don't think I did."

I was unable to say sorry to Federico for making him uncomfortable or thank him for doing what I asked; welling rage had made me speechless. Compelled to leave, I jabbed the *close* icon, scooped up the e-board and strode across the main showroom. Vincent was still bending over the *We are one* wedding bands. His head swung around as I headed towards the exit.

"What…you're leaving?" he said, as I shoved open the glass door.

Exactly right. The thought of being near him was repulsive. That taxi swerving around the corner, coming my way – I was getting that taxi right now. Vincent could walk to his fucking car by himself. Thank fuck it was parked a good few minutes away. I could get back to the house. Pack my things and go. What the hell did he think he was doing destroying my portfolio and claiming that he'd just pressed *save*? No one had ever lied to me like that before. He was unhinged.

"Drive fast," I said to the taxi driver once I'd scrambled into the cab and blurted the address. The cab lurched forward and I was thrown against the back of the seat.

16

I RUMMAGED THROUGH drawers looking for my passport, birth certificate, bank cards, account details. Threw them into a case. Snatched up some clothes.

There was a beep on my cell phone. I thought it would be Vincent, but the number was unfamiliar. I pressed *talk*, recognized the slight sing-song behind the "Hello there," but it took me a while to place it. Then I remembered.

"Radhia!"

"Sarah said she'd seen you at Visual Design. Sounds like it was all a bit awkward there, so I wondered how things are."

"Things are…." Suddenly, the front door slammed and Vincent called out my name. "Radhia," I whispered into the phone, while listening for Vincent's approaching footsteps, "things are not good."

"Well, thank God I have a new phone and new number and

this one's not blocked. All the other times I texted or phoned I couldn't get through. But, what is it? What's wrong?"

Quickly I processed what she'd said: she'd contacted me before, couldn't get through, her number was blocked. My eye on the bedroom door I said, "I don't think I can talk now."

"Do you want to meet?"

"Yes…." Vincent threw the door open and stared at me and stared at the phone. "I'll call you back."

"OK, but you're sure you're OK. What…."

Vincent lunged forward and grabbed the phone. His eye twitched as he stared at the screen.

"Who are you speaking to?" he demanded, casting around the room, registering the open drawers, the open case on the bed, sundry clothes and documents strewn around.

"Where do you think you're going?" He switched back to the phone as if glaring at it would provide an answer. He began jabbing icons and keys and before I could ask him what the hell he thought he was doing, he said, "Radhia, you're speaking to Radhia? We have one argument and immediately you're running back to your old crowd. What about David? Are you going to meet him too? How long will it be before you're back to being a junkie?"

"You must be insane if you think I'm the one who needs to explain myself. You destroyed my fucking portfolio."

"It's not *destroyed.*"

"It was destroyed when it mattered!"

"I just want to protect you. Same way I want to protect you from meeting up with these so-called friends of yours." He looked at the screen of the phone. "I mean, Radhia, come on," he said in an incredulous tone. "Don't tell me you're thinking of meeting her?" He shook his head a long time, then the hardness of his expression faded into a sigh and the look of someone hesitating, struggling with a decision. "Look," he said, "you won't like this, but, I don't think it's good for you to stay so naïve."

He pressed more keys on my cell phone, then tossed it near me. It landed with a small thud on the bed.

"Here's some history on your *friends*," he said.

I saw some kind of reference number on the screen.

"What's this?"

"A storage number."

"For what?"

"Publicly accessible footage."

"You mean surveillance footage. Have you got this through work?"

"It was data I came across shortly after we met."

"You mean you've been sifting through Sense intelligence? Checking me out? Checking my friends out? Checking information…" and the thought made me anxious "…information that no one outside of Sense HQ can access or corroborate."

"I wouldn't put it so crudely."

"Then how would you put it?" Was he serious? He'd rooted through my past, rooted through David's past, Radhia's as well. And he'd only just told me. "I don't care what you've found, Vincent. You had no right. You're…" I began tripping over my words I was so indignant.

I yanked up a glass from my dresser and gulped down some water. Drips ran down the edge of the glass. They collected in a pool on the dresser when I thumped the glass back down.

"Why is it so bad?" Vincent was casually mopping up the spill as if that were the most important issue. "I wanted to know more about you when we first met. You excited me. I was curious. Wouldn't you be curious to pull out stuff on me if you could?"

"Not personal security data. There's such a thing as asking. Talking."

"I would have told you, but…."

"But what?"

"Look, I just don't think you should spend time on people who clearly haven't worried about making you look a fool. I could have shown you earlier, but since you'd all drifted apart I didn't see the point in hurting you." He hesitated and I found myself retreating, wondering what data he'd found. "Don't you demand loyalty from your friends? Well, take it from me," Vincent said, staring at the phone on the bed, "I do. And you should too. In fact, I'm disappointed that you don't. Any sane person would want to know who to trust."

He turned the cell phone so that the reference number on the screen was the right way around for me to read, then held it out before me.

"Look at the data before you judge me. You can't seriously want to be friends with these people."

He pressed the phone into my hand and walked out, quickly, frustration clearly propelling him to the door.

Anxiety made me motionless, but my mind was racing, wondering what Vincent had found. Whatever it was, there was a chance Vincent might not even understand what he'd seen. A moment's vacillation, then I clicked on the link. The download was quick.

There were nine icons on the screen, each simply entitled "Datum" and attributed a number. I pressed "Datum 1".

Close-up of David in his armchair, the chair in his studio flat in Kentish Town. Vincent never had been able to handle the idea that I'd been involved with men before him; it shouldn't have surprised me that he'd bring up something about David. But Jesus Christ! – I found myself zooming in on David's face – in this footage he looked so startlingly ill. Clammy skin, deathly pale. Eyes mostly closed. Blonde greasy hair. Head lolling forward. A streak of smeared powder under his nose. Oh my God! This was painful. Why did Vincent have to show me this? I continued scanning the imagery. There was an ashtray full on the side table, Ziploc dust bags crumpled on David's lap. Beer cans, more dust bags, strewn on the floor. What was that bottom right of the screen? Hair. Long hair on the carpet in some kind of spillage. Jesus Christ! It was vomit. Someone passed out on the floor, someone wearing a Celtic-style hair clip. Oh my God! Oh my God! It was me.

I jabbed the "close" icon on the screen, took some deep breaths, tried to calm myself down.

Vincent had forwarded other clips to my phone. I hesitated a long while, feeling sick and nervous, then I found myself pressing "Datum 2."

David's car – scarlet, old. The long thin scratch running diagonally across the driver's door made it clear it was his. I braced myself, before pressing "play." The camera angle shifted around to the windscreen. David. Radhia. Talking. Her head tilting back onto the headrest. She stared out of the windscreen. Neither talking now. Twisting towards each other. He swiveled further towards her, then lightly he turned her face around. Her hands, her rings, her thick gold wedding band, loomed towards the camera, then her arms, bent at the elbows engulfed David, for whom only the creases on the back of his crumpled shirt were in view.

I checked the date of the recording. 7th November 2057. Quick mental calculation –this was about the time David and I had started going downhill, the time he'd begun distancing himself. Had this been the reason? He'd been seeing Radhia on the side and was more interested in her? Radhia! Who was married to Ahmed and had two kids and was always so lovely? Radhia who only ten minutes ago had phoned? There were words with the footage. They were muffled and faint. When I turned up the volume on the cell phone I heard David say, "I can turn things around. Come off the drugs. Leave her and get myself clean."

Leave her and get myself clean. By "her" had he meant me? What – so David was saying that I was the reason he was such a mess? Angrily, I pressed "close" then opened Datum 3.

Bridge. Great criss-cross iron buttresses. Train groaning, creaking over an arthritic track.

David. Radhia. Both swathed in long coats. Hers, leather and expensive. His was a Crombie. Arm in arm they stood backs to the camera facing a murky Thames and a horizon containing St. Paul's, the Shard and Gherkin. How could I have had no inkling about this? David and I were supposed to have been together. Radhia was supposed to be so nice. But here she was nuzzling him while her kids were at home. Had she and David found it amusing that I'd been so ignorant? Got some kind of sick kick out of it? Or was I somehow getting everything wrong?

When the camera focused on their kissing, a string of saliva glistened between their lips. I hit *Close.*

"Datum 4." No. That was enough. I exited the program.

Vincent loomed towards the bed where I sat.

"Your reaction?"

Vincent's bluntness jarred. I already felt sick. Sick and stupid. I was better off not knowing any of this.

Turning on Vincent, I said, "This was none of your business."

"Listen...." His tone was more gentle now and knowing he was about to go into one of his velvety spiels, I snapped.

"What business is it of yours to go skulking off to work and dig out stuff on me and my friends?"

"Your *friends*. You'd still use that term? You treat these people with a lot of respect. I just don't think they deserve it."

Well, maybe they didn't deserve it. But maybe, also, I didn't want to know. Maybe I didn't want someone else muscling into my past and altering my recollection of it. Yes, David and Radhia had betrayed me. But Vincent had too. Justifying what he'd done with the idea that he was protecting me didn't wash.

"Time and time again..." I found myself saying suddenly, "I find I worry that you're interfering, controlling things. What you did with my portfolio – that was the last straw."

"So, what do you want?" he said, lunging towards me. "Please tell me that, because I, for the life of me, just don't understand."

A single fleeting twitch of his eyelid threw me off guard. I suddenly couldn't get a grip on my thoughts. The footage I'd just seen, my new knowledge about Radhia and David, and Vincent's sudden physical strangeness – all too disturbing. Why was he twitching that way? Standing so upright and rigid? I felt an uncomfortable prickling in the pit of my stomach and I had an overwhelming desire to be away from him.

"What I want is some space," I said, heading towards the bedroom door.

He blocked the doorway and wouldn't budge. Head tilted as if he were about to swoop, he towered over me. I tried brushing past. He grabbed my hand.

"Let go of my hand. Let...what...." He clutched my wrist so tightly I felt a searing pain.

"What are you doing?" I yelled, incensed.

His eye was twitching and his teeth were clenched. His clutch stayed painfully tight.

"Vincent –" I said in a voice I forced to be quiet. There was no point both of us losing control. I had to establish some order.

"Just calm down a moment. Calm down."

He peered at me a long while, then exhaling loudly, he released my wrist.

"What was it you wanted?" he said, his frame filling the doorway, his gaze now falling on the suitcase on the bed. "Ah yes, space." He paused. "Well, you can't go elsewhere because I will always find you, won't I? I'll always know where you are." Now he'd played it – the card I'd always known he'd had. "Besides, there's no need. You have space here. Here in this house. There's no need to leave. Plus, we know that you will only destroy yourself."

"You're out of your mind."

"You'll stay," he yelled, then he composed himself and said more quietly, "You'll be safer if you stay."

"Who are you?" Vincent was already turning into the hallway, heading towards the stairs as I said this, more to myself than to him. This Vincent was an imposter, not the man who when we'd first got together I couldn't wait to see. This Vincent was unhinged.

Standing motionless behind the bedroom door, my heart was thumping. It took several minutes for my anger and anxiety to subside.

"I'll always know where you are," he'd said. Did he always know what I did? Did he have cameras on me now? I scanned the room – the windows (newly daubed with the yellow-white smear of bird shit), the wardrobe, the light fixtures and moldings. Were there covert cameras in any of these places? I fixated on the idea that I was being watched. It was possible that I was being paranoid, but there was a limit to the number of times I was going to dismiss my suspicions, and given his destruction of my portfolio I knew that limit had been reached.

I had to leave. But how? Where would I go? My "friends," it seemed, were not to be trusted. Who exactly was I in touch with?

I snatched up my mobile and scanned the contacts list. The room was dark now and the screen glowed in my hand. The list was pathetically small. I'd culled all the contacts connected to drugs. And virtually each foster family set-up I'd known had been fraught.

Even If I had somewhere to go, Vincent would trace me, know all about me and turn this – the only relationship I currently had into a one-sided virtual stalk. My mind was on hyper-alert, listening out for Vincent's movements, mentally running through ways out of this situation. Time seemed to slow right down.

The swelling and throbbing of my wrist spurred my resolve to leave. Not tonight though. Tomorrow would be the best time, while he was out at work.

Picking up my remote again jarred my inflamed wrist. I typed the word *flats* into the search field. Tonight I'd consider options, downstairs in my workroom. No way could I stay up here in this room, nor sleep in this bed. The crimson duvet was now a glaring danger sign. No, tonight I'd move to the sofa in my workroom. Tomorrow I'd leave the house for good.

17

IN THE MORNING, from beneath crumpled covers on the sofa, I heard Vincent striding through the house. My wrist was doubly painful and my head was foggy from a fitful sleep, but from the moment I woke up I listened intently to the noises outside my workroom, trying to gauge Vincent's behavior. He was on a phone call. Talking loudly. Irritably. The name Dixon was mentioned several times. A Suzanne Dixon, and also her brother. There was a problem – I gathered that. "Don't the data streams show where her brother is?" he was saying. "What's she complaining about? Oh, for fuck's sake – the last thing we need is some juvenile OMNI protester raising suspicions just as we're about to get the Resolve contract." There was stomping towards the kitchen and I didn't catch any more. Instead I heard Vincent slamming cabinets now, shunting drawers hard along their runners. A clanging of something – cutlery maybe – hitting the floor.

Glancing across to the side table where I'd quickly scribbled details of apartments to check out, I resolved to call the landlords. If Vincent thought it was all right to march out of the house, as I could hear him doing now, without offering a single apology for his behavior, I'd start on that task straight away. As soon as I heard the closing click of the front door I scooped my mobile from the desk to tap in the number of the first landlord. No ringing. Just silence. The line was dead and yet, when I checked, there was a functioning dial tone. I tried the second landlord on the list. Again silence.

Vincent had done this. I was sure of it. He must have set up some block from my number. Enraged, I raced to the hallway, to the front door, ready to yell after him, but the door wouldn't open, no matter what codes I punched into the Impenetra panel. Same for the back door. All the exit codes, I realized with sudden alarm, had been reset. Or maybe, in my panic, I'd tapped the wrong numbers.

Keep calm, I told myself. Breathe slowly. Re-entering the keys on the Impenetra panel, slowly this time, I tried opening the main door again. It wouldn't budge. I tried with both hands, tried ignoring the pain in my wrist. Impossible – the bruise was purple and big. The windows – I tried the keys in all the locks. Hall, dining room, living room – every window was jammed. Knowing the panes were unbreakable, I wrenched at the handles until my hands were sore.

Exactly how unhinged was Vincent? Was he ill? Should I be calling GPs? Psychiatric departments? The police? But if he'd put a block on my line, how could I call? My only option – and I felt anxious and impotent with the realization – was to wait for him to get back. I'd have to reason with him somehow. But I had no idea what I'd say or how to begin reasoning with someone so deranged.

My stomach prickled and ached through tension and my forehead felt as if it were being constricted by a tight elastic band, but I moved back to my study, determined to get a handle on things.

A message from Vincent popped up on my cell screen: "We need to talk. I've booked a table at Sullivan's. Parkway, Camden. Meet me for lunch at 12.30," it read.

"Have you unlocked the door?" I typed back immediately.

For several moments there was no response. Then finally came the curt response. "Yes."

I went to the front door to check. It opened without a problem. Thank God. But something about the message seemed warped, something about the style of writing. Was he having some kind of breakdown? Is that why his behavior yesterday had been so extreme?

"I'm worried about you," I typed, though I was also still worried about myself. "So, yes, I think we should meet." He needed help, perhaps serious. Professional help. That's what I would tell him. And it was good that he'd suggested a public place to meet; that was safer for me.

It was only after I'd sent the message that I focused on his lack of signature in both the notes he'd sent. He always signed off "Vincent." Was his failure to do so this time another measure of his instability? The uncertainty made me nauseous.

***

It was surprising that Vincent had chosen this restaurant. His preference was for formal venues with heavy glinting cutlery, starched cotton tablecloths and matching napkins molded origami style into miniature spires. Shuffling across a velveteen-cushioned bench into the corner of a booth, I took the choice of this place to be another sign of his confusion.

A teen band song wafted from a speaker too close to my ears. Its percussion was tinny enough to be irritating, yet sufficiently infectious for a thin-hipped waitress to swing by, head nodding to the drums.

There was a woman sitting alone in the booth opposite, tall, blonde, fortyish checking messages on her mobile.

Vincent was now a few minutes late. When I began calling him to check where he was, the blonde woman in the booth opposite shuffled across her velveteen seat and approached my table.

"Forgive me for interrupting," she said, looking at my mobile, "but Vincent's not coming."

I had the phone to my ear. It had not started ringing. In a serious voice, she said, "Turn off the phone." While I sat there indignant and baffled, she took the phone from my hand and pressed the "end call" control. "Forgive me," she repeated, through a see-through attempt at an endearing smile, "Vincent never was coming. He knows nothing about this meeting. I sent you the message to rendezvous here."

"Pardon?"

The woman was still standing in a gangway between the booths. She indicated the bench opposite me.

"Do you mind?" She sat without waiting for my response. "Please give us a moment," she said to the waitress who had appeared between the two tables and whose confused glancing from one table to the other eventually transformed into a shrug. Once the waitress had gone, the woman looked directly into my eyes and said, "I'm Monica Parks."

"You're Monica Parks?"

She was the executive demanding reports from Vincent.

"Now, this is going to seem strange to you, but Vincent doesn't know that I'm here."

"What do you mean?"

"Ordinarily, I wouldn't approach outsiders in – how shall I put it? – matters of internal surveillance, but in your case I feel some, well, let's call it moral obligation."

"You're making no sense," I said, but I suspected this Monica must know something about Vincent. The woman beckoned the slim-hipped waitress, who was still stepping in time to the music, back to the table and asked for two menus.

"Please," Monica said to the waitress, "a bottle of water for the table, some coffee and what?" She looked over to me. "Oh, just coffee," she said impatiently when I failed to respond. "We have to order something. We cannot just sit here without eating." Again, the see-through smile, this time fleeting. "So, let me explain myself." She paused for a moment. "One department I oversee is called Reassignment."

"That doesn't mean anything to me."

"No? Probably not." She paused. "We establish new identities for people."

"Which people?"

"It varies. Informers, usually. We give them new tags, fictitious histories, personal data, employment and educational backgrounds – we rewrite them all. Any traceable data – credit histories, medical histories – we can amend them all. Physical traits, appearance, even DNA, can all be transformed. Rapid phenotypic modifiers – they can change not only a person's genetic makeup but also its expression. This can be temporary or permanent."

I didn't know why this woman was telling me this, but I found myself saying, "This work you do in *Reassignment* – " I labored on the word; I was fascinated by what she'd told me, but at the same time I had my own matters to comprehend " – what does this have to do with *me*?"

"I have many responsibilities at Sense Surveillance, but one job is to monitor all our personnel, not just Vincent, but all employees."

"Monitor for what?"

"To check that personnel sifting through data-streams are concentrating on Sense's work and not their own private business. As you can well imagine, there is enormous scope for, let's say, getting distracted. Unfortunately, what we find is that Vincent spends only fifty percent of his time procuring Sense contracts and tackling adverse publicity from the likes of OMNI. The other fifty percent of his time he spends monitoring you."

"What?"

Somehow I sounded and felt genuinely surprised, even though I'd been hit with a confirmation of something I already knew. "Are there hidden cameras in the house? I…I couldn't see any. Are they invisible?"

"Vincent receives data streams of your movements at home, undoubtedly from miniscule cameras, but other means too…"

"Such as?"

"Perhaps from several sources: signal emitters he's added to your body lotions or hair products, he may have added tracers to your food…"

"So he knows I'm here now."

"No," Monica said, her lips snapping together suddenly. "We've overridden his import and retrieval system, devised content that makes it seem that you are still just as you were…" Monica glanced at her cell and read the time "…some forty-five minutes ago when you were in your study, in your dressing gown, standing by the French windows."

Jesus Christ. She'd been intruding. Invading. She must have seen the horror expressed on my face, yet she was carrying on all matter-of-fact.

"We've reused images of you at home," she said. "That's what Vincent will see if he wants to check on you. And he probably does." I realized I was staring at the woman with my mouth agape. I closed it and reached out for a glass and swigged some water.

"Another thing I've noticed," said Monica, "is the number of texts you should have received that Vincent has blocked. Here, look." From her handbag she pulled out a small scroll screen and showed me a list of messages. The list was enormous, some of the messages dated back to last year. There were several from David and Radhia, one from Aunt Jade, a handful from recruitment agencies. The anger that had welled up yesterday at the Ost Studio after Federico Hernandez had proved that Vincent had destroyed my portfolio reared again now. I'd even come to this restaurant, willing to concede that he might be so pressurized at work that his thinking had become warped, that he might need some help, but instead I was finding that this was his basic character, and only my own stupidity had stopped me from realizing.

Monica switched off her scroll screen, then said, "So, I know Vincent was filtering your contact to the outside world."

"So, what happens now? Has he been reported? Will he lose his job?"

God alone knew how he'd handle that. The prospect of promotion had been an enormous drive.

Monica shifted in her seat and said, "Not so simple, I'm afraid. For all Vincent's stalking, he has still succeeded in getting Sense in prime position to get the new psycho-surveillance contract, which as I'm sure you're aware is a state-of-the-art security tool. The thing is…" she said, with a hint of sheepishness. "he's needed right now."

"What? He won't be fired?"

Was she serious? One of her senior employees had manically

abused his power, had abused *me*, she'd come here to tell me this, and she was going to do nothing.

"Not right now, no. This is the biggest psycho-surveillance contract in the world. You have to understand that."

"So I put up with him. I endure this...." I tripped over my words, and swallowed to clear my throat. "I mean, what is this meeting all about? Why have you given me all this information?"

"No, you don't have to endure any of this." She took a sip of coffee. "I can help you do something you will not be able to do yourself."

"Which is?"

"Leave without a trace."

"And how are you going to do that?" I said.

"I can reassign you. Give you a new ID, new trace information which Vincent won't know about, enter you into the system under a different tag."

"I go underground, you mean." The woman said nothing. "I have done nothing wrong and *I* go underground, while Vincent keeps his job and suffers no consequences at all."

"With Vincent in the position he's in, it is surely understandable that any departure from his house will require a certain level of, let's say, covertness."

"You mean with Sense about to get its contract, it's better that my boat gets rocked than his."

"Look, I know this is hard to take in." She reached inside her bag, picked out a pen and tore some paper from a small notebook. Scribbling numbers, she said, "This is my private line. If you want to get back to me, call." She slid the paper across the table. "It's an untraceable line, straight to me. It gets round all Vincent's blocks."

"This is madness," I said, looking at the neat black numbers on the paper, "I don't even know who you are. I mean, why are *you* so concerned?"

"It's just that I have some connections to organizations that can help. I work for one – New Way – that helps people in your situation."

New Way. The name rang a bell. Where had I heard it before? Through Vincent somehow, I was certain. Yes, it was a charity

Christmas card with the New Way logo – a highly stylized image of a pathway leading to a distant sun – in miniature on the back.

"I know this is hard to take in, but –" she shrugged in a what-more-can-I-add? kind of way, "if you need my help, well, just consider it." Monica was already standing and snapping the clasp of her bag shut when she said, "Don't sit here too long. I've wiped the records of your journey here. I have less than an hour to cover your journey back home."

"Is that how you'll help me if I decide to leave? Wipe off my final departure from the house."

"Probably too simple."

"Why?"

"If he checks up on you this minute, he'll think you're at home. I've spliced in old visual surveillance footage. When you get back I'll smooth the content so he won't know you've been out. But if this had been your final departure, as you put it, he'd get back from work and find you're not there, but there would be no data showing you leaving. In the same way that there's no data showing that you've left the house today."

"Isn't that good? There would be no scent."

"On the contrary – there would be a very strong scent. He would know you had inside help, that someone at Sense was covering your tracks."

"So, how could I leave?"

"Think about whether you want to first, then we'll make plans." Monica gestured towards my untouched cup of coffee. "Will you be wanting anything else, something to eat?"

"I'm not hungry."

"Then I shall pay for this at the front. And remember what I said. Don't stay here too long."

I could hardly get my head around this meeting, let alone the idea of being reassigned. Reassigned into what? Someone completely different from myself, someone with a fictitious history, a different set of personal details. Job, family, friends – would these all have to be changed? Would I have to live a lie? Become an actress? How could I pull this off?

Walking from the restaurant out onto Parkway and back

towards the glass façade of Camden tube, I scanned streetlights, bollards, the doorways of public buildings, anywhere there might be surveillance equipment, hidden or obvious. Exactly how could someone, even someone as confident and apparently expert as Monica, override a security system so complex to completely cover my tracks?

I scrutinized objects on the street minutely. The battered red hydrogen car discarded by the curbside, the vertical crack on the wall of the Bank of India – how many of these were loaded with security equipment?

The white plastic help point at the tube station entrance blinked a yellow light. Had this Monica really rendered me untraceable? I hesitated before testing her claim, before placing my index finger on the identification pad of the help point. I'd used these devices so rarely, I could barely remember their usual response to a finger depression. The last time I'd used a help point was after I got lost in some seedy part of East London. A digitized voice confirming my name, ID number and current location had followed my finger depression.

But that didn't happen this time. Instead there was silence, followed finally by an on-screen message saying "System Malfunction." Did that mean that there was some fault with the device or something peculiar about my finger ID?

A ginger haired man headed towards the station. I stopped him in his tracks.

"Excuse me. I'm not used to these things. How do they work?"

"Just stick your finger on the pad," he said impatiently. "You'll get instructions after that." He was already turning towards the staircase leading into the tube station.

"Just here," I said, pointing in the vague direction of the black fingerplate.

"Yes, yes, just there. Your ID number will come up on the screen. Look, like this." He put his finger on the pad. The digitized voice came on immediately. "Martin Chadwick. How can we help?"

Martin Chadwick hit the "cancel" control.

"OK?" he said. "Got it?"

He scurried away.

So, the help point was working, but something had happened to its recognition of me. Apparently, I had ceased to exist.

I walked slowly into the tube station. My chest felt tight. I felt almost powerless to move. I took deep breaths and tried to take stock of my surroundings. Remembering Monica's instruction not to waste time getting home, I snapped out of my trance and hurried down the station steps.

***

Back in my workroom, my paranoia increased while waiting for Vincent to walk through the front door. Continually clock watching, it was alarming to think he might tear home early to say that he knew I'd met with Monica and inform me that her attempts to cover my tracks and edit fictitious data into the footage he received had been a waste of time. I imagined him warning that any plans to leave "without a trace" (I could just see him sneering as he repeated the phrase) were futile. Paranoia turned to anger – anger at Monica for creating such a potentially explosive situation.

A sudden loud thwacking noise left me standing immobile in the middle of my room. I concentrated on the noise, trying to determine its source. Probably next-door. Next came a screech. A baby's single sharp scream? But there were no children at this end of the street. I moved into the hallway and opened the door to the garden.

The huge sunflowers were bent precariously at the end of Vincent's impeccably kept lawn, but my focus shifted quickly to the continued smacking and shrieking coming from next-door. I heard a hiss, prolonged and intense.

Cats. Two, I imagined, all claws and canines. Most probable explanation, but there were no cats in sight. Frozen in the doorway, straining to identify the noise, I was jolted by the bleep of my mobile. Every noise was making me jump.

"Hello."

"You need to move inside," came an authoritative female voice. "Remember Vincent left you locked in. I have to relock the doors remotely. He must find you as he left you."

I scanned the doorway, the moldings around the ceiling of the hall, the basement door bearing assorted coats on hooks. Where was the equipment that was transmitting data to her? How did she know I was standing in the doorway? I saw no evidence of surveillance gadgetry anywhere.

"How are you seeing me?" I asked.

"There are cameras everywhere in this property. Everywhere except the bathroom. If you want privacy you should go there. But now, just move inside."

Catching the urgency in her voice, I stepped inside the house and pushed the door shut. A split second later there came a click, seemingly of its own accord.

I returned to my study, to the clock, to thoughts of Vincent returning supercilious and thunderous.

Exhausted from tension, the thought of bathing appealed. The bathroom had no cameras and, thanks to that big, black bolt, could be locked.

18

THE BATH WAS uncomfortable no matter how much I shifted and stretched. The water slurped as I fidgeted, then stilled and quieted into a total silence. I stared at the bolt on the bathroom door. It stunned me to think that this was the only space that wasn't invaded by cameras, by Vincent, by Monica. And even then, I wasn't sure.

My muscles were tense and my wrist was still sore. Closing my eyes, an image of Monica formed: in the restaurant, looming up to me, taking control of my phone, sliding across the opposite bench. Exactly who was this woman whose power to monitor me seemed even greater than Vincent's, who (and the memory of this made my breathing quicken), had wiped me off the metropolitan surveillance system? She had rendered me a nobody, an official non-entity. Did I still have that status? How could I check?

Reassignment. What the hell did this department do? Issuance of new IDs, usually for informers – that's what she'd said. There were so many questions to ask this Monica, but the ones that blared most concerned the RPMs she'd mentioned. Rapid phenotypic modifiers – they could transform a person's appearance. How safe would such a treatment be? How effective? And exactly how rapid was rapid?

The bath water rippled and gurgled as I tried to get comfortable. A clump of froth and bubbles slipped slowly around my ankle and dripped noiselessly into the water.

Then Vincent's voice. Urgent. In the hall? No – coming up the stairs. Gripping the rim of the bathtub, I glanced at the bolt on the door. Locked. His voice was nearer now. I heard the words "Resolve report," then a thunderous yell, "What do you mean there are issues?" A moment's silence, then the sound of something hard (Vincent's phone?) hitting a wall or floor maybe. He stormed to the stairs. My heart beat fast as I strained to hear him. Three steps creaked sharply, one after the other. The opening jingle of his computer now played. "Welcome," it said. He was up in his office.

Quickly I got out of the bath, toweled and threw on a robe. From the landing I saw the door of his office was open. He was sitting legs squarely apart, elbows on knees, phone pressed to his ear. Knowing I was in his line of vision, I swished quickly down the stairs. He was too embroiled in his phone conversation to pay me any attention. If Vincent knew of my meeting with Monica, he wouldn't be preoccupied with some work matter concerning reports; he'd be yelling in my face instead.

There was a prickling discomfort in my stomach. I'd had nothing to eat in the restaurant. I'd had nothing all day.

In the kitchen, I pulled the fridge door open, but eating didn't appeal. The pasta with its congealed tomato sauce, the squashed quiche portion, the olive loaf and plastic-wrapped brie – it all seemed repulsive.

"You OK?" Vincent's voice came from the doorway. I closed the fridge and turned to face him. He was still gripping his mobile. His face looked haggard and a light sheen covered his forehead. "I'm not going to insist we talk," he said, his eyes fleetingly glancing over my bathrobe. "I can see that's not going to get me anywhere. I'll just wait, wait till you're ready."

As if expecting someone to ring at any moment, he checked the screen on his mobile.

"Why all the calls?" I asked, feeling fraudulent throwing out such an ordinary line in such an ordinary tone when my mind was still swirling with the memory of meeting Monica. Staying calm was imperative. Vincent was too unstable to make any false moves.

"So, now you're asking me about my work, are you?"

Was he serious? After everything he'd done, he was casting me as the one who needed to make amends?

"The locks," I said, so suddenly I confused myself. Then, trying to regain composure, I said in a deliberately measured voice, "I couldn't open the doors or windows. Do you know why that might have been?"

A small wall light highlighted the sheen on his forehead and when he raised his face upward to meet my gaze, the movement was accompanied by a momentary but distinct tremor.

"It's just that I don't want you to leave," he said, before pausing. "In any case," suddenly he was speaking more brightly, "it's not warm in this house, is it? What does it matter if the windows are closed? It's not like my office. It's so insufferably hot. I have to keep the windows open all day...."

Leave it, I told myself. Don't argue. He's deranged.

"...I can't think without air, especially now." His facial muscles tensed again. "The directors want stats everyday on Resolve. And they always want them instantly. What am I supposed to do? Magic these numbers out of thin air?" Vincent was talking rapidly, gripping his phone tightly, standing bolt upright. His eyes were wide and wild. "Monica keeps demanding information. If you're asking for information about vulnerabilities and health risks on the most complex psycho-surveillance program imaginable, that's going to take more than a day to produce, isn't it?"

Health risks. Vulnerabilities. I'd not heard mention of these issues before. All I knew was that Vincent was apoplectic. The veins in his temple were big and pulsating, and his jaw was all clenched.

I didn't know how my expression was set, but he said very suddenly, "Well, I see you're not going to be sympathetic."

I picked up a glass from the draining board and filled it with tap water. Even with my back to him, I could sense his peering eyes. There'd be an issue about me exiting the kitchen; it was bound to be awkward.

"Where are you going?" Vincent asked when I made my move to the door.

"The bathroom."

"Again?" he said, his gaze sweeping the length of my bathrobe. Top to toe, he was taking me all in. He was doing this here in front of me and, with all his surveillance equipment, he could do it from afar. But what if I modified myself? Turned myself into someone he didn't even recognize? I could pass right by him, unnoticed, unhindered.

I returned to the bathroom with my mobile and the number for Monica's private line.

Sitting on the rim of the bathtub, facing the bolt on the bathroom door, I waited for Monica to answer her phone.

"So, you want my help," she said immediately. "A new ID."

"Tell me more about the modification treatment." While waiting for an answer I listened out for Vincent's footsteps. I heard nothing but the drip of a bath tap.

"It's an option for people in special circumstances."

"I'm in a special circumstance," I whispered, holding the mobile so close to my mouth I nudged it with my bottom lip. "I'm trapped by someone you need to secure your Resolve contract. He obsesses about keeping me here. You want to shoo me out of sight, out of mind, so he can get on with his work. I want to change my appearance, temporarily anyway."

Sitting on the side of a cold bath, continually checking the bolt on the door, whispering to a woman who had as much ability to trace me as Vincent, I felt totally powerless. Monica's long silence only added to that feeling. Exasperated, I said, "You met me in the restaurant, offered ways of helping me. Are you going to do that or not?"

"I will send you the information you require. Read it and I will see what help I can arrange for you."

The slit under the door revealed a band of hall light. Anticipating Vincent's shadow, I continually glanced there.

"Send it covered to this mobile. That's your speciality, isn't it?

Making things happen without anyone knowing."

"I will send you the files. Read them thoroughly. Modifiers are powerful drugs."

Vincent's muffled voice came from the landing. He was heading back to his upstairs office again. While he was engrossed with his phone calls and bellowing about reports, I hung up and swept downstairs with the mobile stuffed in my dressing gown pocket.

In my study, I waited for a transmission from Monica, again unable to stop glancing to the door with the expectation of Vincent's shadow lurking beneath.

His preoccupation with reports would have given me time to absorb information about RPM treatment. That such safe reading time was going to waste was infuriating.

Trying to collect myself, I flicked on the hologrammer and caught smatterings of random programmes. The comedy hour on the Intersex channel transformed into disassociated elements: audience cackles, unintelligible dialogue, actors with grotesquely exaggerated expressions of surprise. Vincent's voice was audible. He was in the hall. Arguing on a call. His voice reached a crescendo then faded as he passed by my work room.

Again, I checked my messages. Nothing.

Restless, I turned the hologrammer on again, flicked from channel to channel, registering nothing except Vincent's occasional pacing.

How different could modification make me look? How different did I want to look? As dark as Radhia? As blonde as Monica? Which person did I want to model myself on? Could I specify particular elements from different sources, then turn myself into their amalgam? If so, how natural would that look? None of this would matter if reassignment were only temporary. I could go for a radically different look and once Vincent was finished at Sense I could revert back to my natural appearance.

Monica said he'd be fired after he'd won the Resolve contract. God! That would kill him. *I* would kill him. Could I really do that?

Maybe that's what was needed. Not just for me, but for a saner, healthier Vincent to emerge. My list of doubts was enormous, but right now Monica's plan was the only one I had.

I checked my mobile. Nothing. Jesus Christ! Where was this transmission? Why was it taking so long to come? My head was throbbing, my restlessness maddening. It wasn't until three that I sat back on the sofa and dozed.

19

Wednesday 16th July 2059

THE TRANSMISSION ARRIVED just as Vincent left for work. Still embroiled in heated phone calls, he again said nothing before the front door slammed shut. I checked the Impenetra control panel. He'd set the locks again. What was he thinking? That he could do this every day? He was insane. Getting more so each day.

I marched back to my study and, following the instructions in Monica's message, downloaded the information on modification. "Don't worry, he won't detect this," the message had said, "I've rendered this transmission untraceable. Make sure you delete all files when you've finished."

She had sent numerous reports on non-surgical modification, but the one I was most interested in was entitled "Somatic Transformations and Permanent Phenotypic Alteration." It outlined ways in which new cells acquiring spliced and customized DNA could determine a specified trait. Bone structures, pigmentation, body mass and dimension – a sophisticated mix of gene therapies could manipulate each of these.

Subject 908, a middle-aged squat male, with creamy freckled

skin and brown eyes, was fascinating; his computer generated target appearance (elongated bones, darker, more even pigmentation, green irises) was, so far as I could see, totally indistinguishable from the photo-image of the man after treatment. In the multitude of cases covered in the evaluation, the target appearance was identical to the result. All day I scrutinized the reports and found no serious side effects listed. In cases of minor side effects, the technology for treatment reversal was so effective the Department of Health had ruled that there was no serious cause for concern.

But was the fact that Vincent had put traces on me, monitored me obsessively enough of a reason to go down this road? Maybe Vincent would come round and unlock the doors. Maybe he already had. I ran a file deletion program to wipe Monica's transmission as I carried the mobile to check the front door. It wouldn't open. I strode through the house testing windows and doors, wrenching and pulling and finally slamming my fists on the panes as one after the other window failed to open.

"You're never going to leave," he'd said. Well, he was wrong about that. Not only could I get away from him, I could devise things so I could approach him, stand right in front of him and he wouldn't even know I was there.

One of the sash windows in the living room seemed to budge a fraction. I placed the mobile on the windowsill in order to pull the lower sash with both hands. But it just wouldn't open further. Outside, there was a blur of something small shifting behind a yellow shrub. Stepping gingerly, next-door's tabby – one of the fighting cats? – came into view. Its tail was shaved and stitched, and presumably unused to negotiating spaces with the plastic Elizabethan collar buckled around its neck, it collided first with a euonymus bush and then a statue of a frog with bulging eyes.

Along the street, came a tall figure, heading towards the house. Vincent. I glanced at the clock on the mantelpiece. Six. Determined to get to the one space in the house he couldn't invade, I slipped upstairs to the bathroom, stood frozen by the bolted door, listening. No noise on the landing outside. No footsteps coming up the stairs. He was probably in the kitchen by now, making himself a drink. Or maybe he'd gone to the living room.

The living room.

Shit.

The mobile.

It was still on the windowsill. Had I wiped the files or not? The deletions were still ongoing when I'd put the phone down, but they'd been taking a long time. Had there been some kind of problem?

I was opening the door when my mobile gave a series of short shrill beeps. My heart lurched, but I willed myself to focus and get the phone. Quickly, I headed for the stairs.

Vincent's voice came from the living room when I was halfway down the stairs. Distinct above a news stream, it passed through the slit of an almost closed door. He didn't call my name or raise his voice at all. He simply said, "Your phone." Seemingly he'd made a calculation that since I'd reached the point on the stairs nearest to the lounge, he'd have no need to shout. To me, my movements were noiseless, but somehow he knew my precise location on those steps.

In the living room, he was slumped in the sofa, still in his suit and his shoes. The phone, thank God, was still on the windowsill. But had he leapt up to read the screen, then scurried back into a surreptitious sofa-slouch before my appearance in the room?

"Ringing's been going on a while," he said, as I headed straight for the mobile.

He spoke matter-of-factly, like there was nothing about the mobile to be bothered about. Possibly he was assuming that it was some kind of sales pitch. But his eyes were fixed on me as I crossed in front of him.

Scooping up the mobile from the windowsill, I kept my back to him while checking the screen. The file deletions had finished, thank God. There was nothing showing evidence of any communication with Monica. The beeps of the incoming call were still sounding.

"Are you just going to stare at that phone?" Vincent asked.

I switched my attention to the incoming message, turned and headed back to the door.

I didn't recognize the flashing number. But the voice that

drawled "Hey" to my guarded "hello" was very familiar.

"David?" I whispered, hoping I was far enough out in the hallway now for Vincent not to hear me.

"Long time, eh? Radhia said she'd called you. I thought I'd see how you were."

"David! God!"

My mind filled with the surveillance images of him and Radhia groping. On a bridge. In a car.

"Wait a minute," I said, entering the kitchen, trying to order my thoughts. I wasn't up to light-hearted banter, but as David was currently my only connection to the outside world, I felt compelled, desperate even, to keep him on the line. I poured tap water into a tall thick glass, wondering where the best place was for me to take this call. Not here, Vincent could easily walk in at any time. Locking myself in the bathroom would make him suspicious. Best place was my study with the door shut.

I wondered how David had managed to get through.

"New number?" I said, after checking the screen. I still knew David's old number and this wasn't it. I headed back to my study.

"Radhia told me to try a different phone. This is a friend's. No one's been able to get through to you."

"There've been some problems." I whispered into the phone, fearful that Vincent was already tapping into this call.

"Look, this isn't a bad time, is it?" David said.

"No," I said instantly, not wanting the call to end. "No, I think we can talk."

"Radhia was concerned about you. What's with the blocks on our numbers? I thought you were doing the rehab thing of avoiding us. But Radhia said that something seemed wrong."

Hearing footsteps outside my door it was difficult to respond.

"Look, do you want to meet?"

"Yes," I said, instantly, though how I'd manage to leave the house was beyond me.

"Well, Radhia has an exhibition. It's in the Loft gallery at Moorhouse. We'll be there tomorrow at noon. Why don't you come?"

"An exhibition at Moorhouse?"

"Yes, she's been doing very well for herself. You know graphic design was just a temporary stop for her. She's really all about fine art. That's where her talents are. Will you come?"

"I…I'm not sure." It was difficult to process this new information, especially with the possibility of Vincent creeping outside the door.

"Well, the offer's there. Think about it."

"Yes. I will…."

There was a metallic creak of a turning door handle. Vincent loomed in the entrance. Quickly, I hung up.

Wanting to deflect any questions about the call and feeling my stomach prickle, I said to Vincent, "I suppose I should eat." I passed him awkwardly, silently, in the doorway and made it to the kitchen. I still wasn't hungry, despite my churning insides. Mindlessly staring at an onion half wrapped in cellophane on a shelf in the fridge, I heard a scraping noise behind me: Vincent was dragging a chair away from the table across the marble floor.

"Sit down," he said.

"Why?"

"I want to talk."

"About what?" I remained standing by the fridge. Had he listened in to my last call? Realized I'd been speaking to David? Is that why he was standing there so hard-faced and rigid?

"I want to talk about your avoidance, all this pointed shutting of doors."

"What? I can't take a call in private?"

"It's not just the phone call."

"So what is it then?"

"Well, this is an example." He was gesturing at the chair he'd pulled out. "I say I want to talk. You act like that's a lot to ask." He looked at me steadily. "Why can't you sit down?"

"Just tell me what you have to say. I can listen standing up." He glared momentarily. "What is it then?" I said impatiently. I felt in my pocket for the paper scrap with Monica's private line. As soon as I was done with Vincent I would call her up.

"Is this your idea of getting space? Not talking to me? I've been out since six, I'm trying to start our first conversation of the day and...."

Clutching the paper scrap in my pocket, I said, "I don't want a conversation. There's no point to it." I started to walk towards the door. There was a horrible scraping sound as he pushed his chair backwards. All my muscles tensed.

"Oh great," he said, "walking off really helps things. At least one of us here is trying to work things out."

"Let's just leave it, Vincent." I skirted around him, watching out for any sudden movements he might make, especially a grab for my still sore hand.

"How does leaving it solve anything?" He peered at me intently. "Jesus Christ," he said, "I can't believe I'm repulsing you." He shook his head and gave a long sigh. "You know that as long as you stay here...."

That made me stop.

"And what if I don't stay here?" The question was provocative, but I had to find some way of gauging my situation.

"Why would you think of leaving?" he said.

"You destroyed my portfolio. You've set up locks so I can't leave the house. And you think all of this is justified when it's not. It's really not. That is why I don't want to stay. Do you understand that?"

Wanting to see how much insight he had into his own behavior, I looked him straight in the eye.

"I won't cope if you leave me." His voice sounded plaintive until he added, matter-of-factly, "I'm just not having that. Oh, well, walk off if you want to," I heard him say as I quickly left the kitchen, "but you're not leaving this house." He was shouting after me now. "You have to get your head around that."

20

BOLTED BACK IN the bathroom, I quickly dialed Monica's private line.

"You have read the literature?" she said immediately.

"I have," I whispered, mindful of Vincent's lurking, "and this is what I've decided. I read that genetic modification is fully reversible and also that it is safe. So, for as long as you need Vincent at Sense to secure your contract, I need complete reassignment. Not just a fictitious history, but an altered appearance, modified DNA. When Sense drops Vincent..."

"What do you mean *when Sense drops Vincent?*"

"This is one of my conditions. He has to go. I cannot re-establish my identity while he still has access to live surveillance data streams."

When Monica answered, she spoke slowly, as if weighing everything up: "So long as you realize that the security of the Reassignment department is paramount and that you are a special case I am sticking my neck out for, I may be able to help you. You ask for a complicated process but...I believe...each element is possible. It ties in, in fact, to the proposal I had for you."

"Which is?"

Mentally, I pictured the blonde woman sitting calm and elegant, listening to me through her earpiece.

"OK, here's the deal: you need a cover, a relative to meet...."

"What?"

"Someone in your family?"

"They're in Australia."

"A friend then?"

When the jolt of her authority faded, I thought of David and his invitation to meet at Loft tomorrow at noon.

"Possibly," I said, wondering where this was leading.

"I need a definite *yes.*"

"OK...yes." Picturing a meeting with Radhia and David, knowing what I did about them, wasn't easy, but I had to say *yes* to Monica. There were no other friends for me to meet.

"You meet your friend. This is traceable in the normal way. Then I send you an untagged car to take you from there to one of our modification specialists, a Doctor Liu, at our clinic. I will wipe all relevant surveillance of this part of your journey. Instead, I'll scramble some data that shows you returning home."

"Why do I need a friend?" I asked. "Why doesn't the untagged car take me straight to Doctor...Doctor? What was his name?"

"Liu."

"Why don't...." I thought there was a footstep outside the bathroom, but, straining to hear more, I detected nothing. I glanced to the big black bolt. It was securely locked.

"Yes?" Monica said.

"Why can't I go straight to this Doctor Liu and have the modification as quickly as possible."

"I understand your impatience, but the more complicated your trajectory, the better."

"Can't you just make up a complex trajectory, create a fictitious one."

"I can and I will, but it is good to have at least some elements of it grounded in reality. Then, when Vincent finally becomes suspicious, he will have difficulty working out the story."

"But won't he have the house under surveillance? Won't he find out my movements?" Even today, the mere suspicion that I was about to leave had turned Vincent aggressive. Psychotic even. What would he do if he caught me mid-escape? "He cannot find out, not at any cost."

"I monitored him yesterday," Monica said. "I thought he might watch you, but he hardly checked the house. He'd locked the doors, remember? There was no need for him to worry about you making any plans for leaving. So far as he was concerned, you couldn't get out. I'm assuming he'll continue to lock the doors…."

"In which case I won't be able to get out."

"But I can override the lock codes, remember? Like before."

"And suppose he does watch me leaving?" He'd be maniacal if he saw me in the middle of some elaborate plan to leave again.

"But what will he see?" Monica said casually, as if the potential problem I had raised could be flicked aside as easily as a piece of fluff.

"I don't know. I suppose that depends on what you give him to see."

"He will see you leave and, if we can arrange it, meet a friend. Of course he will wonder how you got out, but when I've rewritten the log for the lock codes, he will think that he made a mistake and failed to set the lock properly. No doubt he will then monitor you intensely, but I'll make sure he sees data of you returning home."

"But I won't be returning home. Is that the idea?"

"That's right. You will be on your way to the clinic in one of our untraceable cars. I doubt it will be long before he starts trying to work out the Sense connection, but throwing in the extraneous element of a meeting with a friend should keep him off my back, and yours, for a while."

God. I was getting David and Radhia wrapped up in all this. Much as their betrayal fazed me, the last thing I wanted was for Vincent to get weird on anyone else.

"Vincent mustn't follow me. That's the main thing. How can you make it certain he won't leave his office and trace me?"

"I can arrange for him to be in a crisis meeting that will keep him at work and away from his monitors. OK," she added suddenly, "no more questions. You have the plan now."

"You've really thought this through, haven't you?"

"Why the suspicion in your voice?"

I couldn't immediately supply an answer, then, after a few moment's reflection, I said, "You seem to have everything fully worked out."

In the moment before her response, I thought I heard a creak. I listened for noises on the landing outside. There were none.

"It is not all worked out. I need the details about the friend you say you have an arrangement to meet."

Still seated on the edge of the tub, I shifted on the porcelain rim.

"I didn't actually say that I'd made a definite arrangement to meet a friend."

"Then why bring it up, waste my time, play games?"

The sudden snapping silenced me. Finally I said, "I'm not playing games. I'm thinking out loud."

Then as if she had telepathic access to my anxieties, she said, "Look, you have a lot to think through. This is a serious undertaking. But you have to understand that I am sticking my neck out too. So, let us start again. You need to meet with a friend, sooner, presumably, would be better for you. Who could you meet and when?"

"David," I said. "David and Radhia at Loft gallery."

The meeting would be awkward and tense. I'd be using them as a decoy, this pair who'd deceived me. But I needed them right now. I had no other choice.

"What time is the meeting?" Monica asked.

"Tomorrow at noon."

"So soon? It will be difficult to make arrangements so quickly. What other plans do you have?"

"I have no other appointments."

"Then...we'll have to plan things for tomorrow. That's not much time. But it's OK. Pressure's good. It focuses the mind. So, you need to prepare."

"Prepare how? What should I bring with me? How long will I stay at this clinic?"

I knew nothing about the clinic. That fact suddenly hit me and I knew, given its covert nature, there was not much I could do to prepare myself for my stay. It wasn't as if I could run a search and find some slick site showing me images of its facilities and its healthful, smiling staff.

"You will stay there many days, weeks even.

"Weeks?"

"Yes, a couple or so. This is not magic. This is a complex procedure. What do you think happens – that we say *abracadabra* and you become instantly unrecognizable? Be realistic. This is not sci-fi."

"So...what should I bring then?"

"You needn't bring anything with you. You are to receive a new identity, remember? You will get new things, papers, clothes. These arrangements can be made after admission."

"I just bring my self."

"Yes, and we will swap it for a new one. How does that sound?" Put so starkly it sounded surreal. "So, you will meet Doctor Liu tomorrow, OK?" Monica said, cutting into my sudden anxiety.

How much would I be modified? Which of my features would I be sorry to lose? These were issues I hadn't thought through. Probably, Dr. Liu would fill in the specifics. And I could always make clear my concerns and demands. I whispered into the mobile, "OK. Tomorrow I'll be ready."

21

EARLY THE NEXT morning, from my sofa bed, I listened intently to Vincent's padding down the stairs, a cabinet closing in the kitchen, a brief burst of a muffled news bulletin, silence, then finally a click of the front door.

Out in the hallway, I shook the door over and over, just as I'd done yesterday, using both hands until the rising pain in my wrist became too much to bear. How could things have come to this? The signs were all there – clear as day now: the encouragement to move into his house, to make a studio here away from other designers, the criticisms of my friends. What kind of idiot was I? I was incensed. With Vincent. With myself.

Striding back to my study, I mentally ran through the details of human appearance modification and the arrangements I had made with Monica. Down by my side, my mobile rang. It was Monica.

"I've unlocked your doors," she said.

"Good. I will leave for Loft at eleven. When will you send the car to pick me up from there?"

"Twelve fifteen, let's say."

"Fifteen minutes. I just pop in to say hello and that's all."

"Is that a problem?"

Again, imagery of David and Radhia in the car, on the bridge, lying about me, and kissing arose in my mind.

"Maybe not," I said. Then suddenly compelled to finalize arrangements, I added, "Yes, let's stick with twelve fifteen."

**

Once Monica had unlocked the door, I took a taxi to Moor House in the city. We pulled alongside the curved skyscraper with its numerous glass panels that reflected drifting clouds.

"Probably that way," said a security guard when I asked for Radhia Alsawaf. He pointed across a wide foyer with thin humanoid statues to a painting collection at the rear consisting of large panels of oranges, yellows and blues.

I headed towards the paintings, picking up a leaflet that read:

Façade Collection

> *The abstract portraits in Radhia Alsawaf's collection of paintings appear to have multiple surfaces. The artist experiments with layers consisting of contrasting patterns and perforations to build multi-faceted subjects. Influenced by Kandinsky's theory of color, Alsawaf uses color combinations to delineate the various façades or versions pertaining to each subject. The primacy of any single façade depends upon the angle from which the painting is viewed. A major theme in Alsawaf's…*

"Well, well, well, long time, no see," Radhia said, smiling broadly. Her hair was high, like a mini ziggurat, and decorated with a thin and glistening gold and red thread. David stood beside her. He wore jeans and a black t-shirt. I felt disconnected walking towards them, like a character finding herself in the wrong play alongside an unfamiliar cast. Radhia hugged me first. David followed immediately, his hold lasting longer and pulling me close. Probably their greetings were as enthusiastic as they'd been in the past, but now, inexplicably, their behavior struck me as a series of gross motor movements, their smiles a complex set of muscular contractions.

"Didn't think you'd come," David said, "you being so unavailable these days."

"Didn't think I would either." The words tripped out of my mouth – an unemotional response to a stimulus. "I had no idea about any of this," I said, gesturing to the paintings.

"Well, you've been out of touch, haven't you? Is everything OK? You seem distracted."

Probably my detachment wasn't helping. In any case quickly conveying everything that had happened over the last few days, let alone the steps I was about to take, was impossible. It was only a matter of minutes before Monica was to send a car that would take me away from my old world.

"I'm all right," I lied. Then changing the subject, "You've done really well for yourself, Radhia, workwise, I mean."

"Yes, things have picked up. Of course, if you replied to any of my messages, I could have told you that." Presumably the broad smile Radhia was throwing my way was an attempt to soften the criticism. I was aware that I was supposed to be updating her on what was going on with me. But hadn't I just learned from Vincent that these two could not be trusted?

"How's the family?" I said to Radhia.

"We're all fine. Kids both at big school now. Growing up too fast."

"And Ahmed?"

"He's good too."

She was smiling. Which façade was she presenting here? I glanced over to David. He pulled on a quick smile too.

"You look very well, David." Was that Radhia's influence? Had he only let himself go when he'd been with me? That's what he'd implied in the footage that Vincent had shown me. *Leave it,* a voice within commanded. *Keep focused.*

"We weren't sure whether you would want to come for a drink," David said.

The best bet for modification treatment, I felt pretty certain, was to avoid alcohol. I found myself mentally running through each element of my recent diet, querying anything that might affect my treatment. The fact was I'd barely eaten over the last few days.

"I can't," I replied. "Besides, I'm afraid I don't have much time."

"Well, what about this man you're living with?" David asked. "How's that going?"

They were both staring at me.

"It's complicated." Behind the statues, through the glass walls, a black car with dark windows pulled up outside the foyer. "I think that car's for me," I checked my watch. It was twelve-fifteen.

"You're going? Already?"

David sounded disappointed.

"Something to sort out," I replied. "I'll be out of action for a while, but I'll get in touch when I'm back. I'd...well, it would be interesting to find out what we've all been up to, wouldn't it?"

I headed back to the foyer entrance, leaving their bemused expressions behind. A security camera light blinked when I crossed the threshold. Was Vincent onto me yet? Anxiously, I checked my mobile, my hand all clammy gripping the plastic casing. There were no messages from him. There were no messages from anyone. This felt just as fraught as the tube journey back from the restaurant where I'd first met Monica, when she'd wiped me off the metropolitan security system and rendered me a nobody. I'd panicked then about Vincent finding out and had been on edge that whole strange day. And yet, Monica's arrangements had all worked out perfectly; he'd suspected nothing. These arrangements too were, so far, going to plan. To the second, this car had arrived on time.

Approaching the black car that was purring by the curb, I heard the click of the passenger door. I had barely sat down when the taxi started down the road. The glass on the inside of the cab was blackened, as was the panel dividing the passenger seats from the driver's compartment.

I leaned forward and knocked on the dark panel. The cab swerved around a bend. Awkwardly, I grabbed a ceiling handhold above the window. The hatch in front opened.

"Yes?" the voice was female. I made out a headscarf, mainly black but patterned with yellow swirls.

"Is this…" I felt stupid asking, at this point, where the car was going. "Is this going to Liu's clinic?"

"Liu?"

The name clearly meant nothing to the driver.

"It's a big place," she said. "I don't know the names of everyone who works there."

"Reassignment? We're going to Reassignment?"

"Yes. Reassignment. No more questions."

The hatch closed.

In the glass panel now, I saw only my vague reflection. Neither could I see anything through the matte black windows. Two-way blackness. No looking in. No looking out.

"Why are the windows…."

There was no point in continuing. The hatch was shut. In any case, I supposed that Sense Surveillance would need to keep its Reassignment facilities undisclosed, even from those who were to be admitted. With the windows closed and the car's A/C on, it was impossible to hear any outside sounds, no matter how much I strained. Already, there'd been too many swerves and turns for my sense of direction to handle. The car began to slow, stopped, presumably in a sudden traffic jam. Probably we were on the border of zone one, going into two.

It seemed like I'd been in the car ten minutes or so. It would take that long to zip through Central London until hitting traffic at any of the Central London borders. But which border? Old Street? Elephant & Castle? White City? Or any of the umpteen others? I didn't even know which direction I was headed in. When I pulled my mobile from my bag, the driver immediately read my mind.

"No GPS," she commanded.

In the blackened windows I scrutinized my own reflection. God! What had I arranged to do? What was I going to look like? Would I be given a choice? I should insist on one. I was certain of that. If points of the procedure didn't make sense to me, I would ask for explanations. If alarming decisions were made, I would refuse to agree.

Resolved to take at least some control, I felt less anxious sitting in the corner of this car taking me for reassignment.

22

TALL, GANGLY, WITH glossy black hair pulled taut in a pony tail, Dr. Liu did not look as I'd imagined.

"What's the matter?" he asked. "Nervous?"

He was standing behind a huge wooden desk in the corner of his windowless office. Towards the centre of the desk was a whitish circular blemish. Coffee cup stain? Probably too big for that. The smear of some caustic medicine? What medicine could be that damaging?

Dr. Liu loomed from behind the desk and advanced towards my seat.

Had he caused that stain? If so, what did that signify? That he was clumsy? Careless? But he seemed poised as he stood by my side and everything else was pristine – steel sink, glass-doored cabinets, white walls.

He was peering at my face now, his eyes darting about as he scrutinized my hair, my forehead, my eyes. He stared at my lips for several moments, then his gaze swept quickly down my body, to my paisley skirt-shrouded lap, then to my calves. My bare calves. I was conscious of crossing my legs. His gaze hovered around my ankles, then swept upwards, lingered upon my lips again, and settled, finally, upon my eyes.

"So," he said, sitting back on the edge of the table, folding his arms across his abdomen. "You want my help."

"Yes," I replied.

"And what precisely do you need from me?"

Of course, he must have known already; this was a highly specialized unit – people didn't walk in off the street.

"I need a radically different physical profile, different enough to throw the tracers, different enough for me to walk right up to someone, someone I know well, walk right up close…" I stood up and positioned myself a footstep away from the doctor "…as close as this but remain unfamiliar to them. I need altered external characteristics, different histories – employment, finan–"

"Not my department," Dr. Liu said curtly. "The histories. Employment, financial, educational, personal, residential – Monica will help construct those."

"I'm just giving you the whole picture," I said, taking a few steps backward.

"I don't need the whole picture. I effect physical transformations. It is solely with respect to these that I require clarity."

"Then I have told you what I require from you."

"On the contrary, you have told me very little. I asked you to tell me *precisely* what you need from me."

Mentally I began putting together some concise version of all the events that had led to my coming here. Dr. Liu cut in with his own train of thought.

"What definite appearance would you like?"

"It doesn't matter."

He gave a short snort and a nasty smile. "Of course it matters. The specification of your target appearance and my ability to deliver – that is the most interesting thing."

"Not for me." It was irksome that Dr. Liu had reduced me to a fun little experiment. "This is a temporary treatment enabling me to go wherever I want unimpeded. That's why I need a new ID. The only thing that matters is that my appearance should be very different from how it is now." Dr. Liu might not want to go into my personal details, but he should at least be aware of my primary motivation.

But he wasn't listening. Instead, he was waving me over to the opposing corner of his office where a spindly stool was situated in front of a hologram platform. I hated sitting on stools at the best of times, but perched now in the middle of this white walled room I felt vulnerable and precarious.

The doctor focused a camera eye on me and with the jab of a computer icon my double appeared on the hologram platform. Looking her over, I noticed the embroidered strap of her top was slipping down her shoulder. I glanced down at my own shoulder and pushed the fallen strap up. The virtual me made identical movements.

"So, how would you like this?" He flicked a button and my doppelganger now had skin the color of cinnamon. "How would you like this for your target appearance?"

"That would work."

Vincent would *never* trace me if I had such a radically different complexion.

I waited for Dr. Liu to give advice. Advice on the psychological and social consequences of extreme transformations of appearance. The numerous reports I'd read on modification had urged the need to counsel subjects on the implications of selecting a radically different look.

"So, this would work, would it?" he said quietly, seemingly to himself. He manipulated a control until the head of the doppelganger was encased in a grid of white luminous lines. "You're sure you want this skin?" he asked, while showing me other complexions – darker, lighter, redder, creamier.

"The first was fine. Is it possible to have it?"

"Certainly."

Again, I waited for questions about my preparedness for such an extreme change. But the questions he should have thrown at me: Do you expect your prospects to be the same with a different color skin? Are you prepared for the prejudice this change will bring? Liu asked none.

Highlighting one square of the grid, a square that covered a region in the middle of the left cheek, and importing a data-table onto a connected screen, he engrossed himself with analyzing the constituent colors of the hologram's ersatz pigmentation. Several minutes were spent on this.

"You are aware," I said, "that, ultimately, I will want all modifications reversed."

"That is what Monica relayed to me," Liu said.

"And this is possible?"

Dr. Liu nodded. "Yes," he said, casually, as if the possibility I was enquiring after was as unproblematic as organizing a cup of tea.

His analysis of skin color complete, Dr. Liu deleted the white grid around my double's face.

"Of course," he said, "we will have to go further than this. After all, she still looks like you. Just like you, except for having a much darker complexion."

"Yes," I agreed. "All the major identifiers need changing. Not just skin color, but hair as well — texture and color. I suppose I should have dark hair, curly or wavy maybe."

"Like this," Dr. Liu said, pressing buttons to produce in the model shoulder-length ringlets, all glossy and as close to black as brown could be.

"Now that definitely is a disguise."

"But is it what you want?"

"If it renders me untraceable, then...it makes sense, doesn't it?"

Then looking at the large hazel eyes peering back at me from the hollo platform, I said, "Now, we need to change the iris color too."

"And what color eyes would you like to have?"

I looked up at Dr. Liu. His eyes were the color of milk chocolate with a distinct black ring bordering the irises. They were different from mine, but not strikingly so. I thought of eyes I knew well. Radhia's were a darker brown than Dr. Liu's. David's were a pale sky blue. Vincent's...God! Vincent – what would he be thinking right now? What would he be doing?

"Here," said the doctor offering a chart of eye colors, "here...what's the matter?"

"Nothing."

The bright beauty of Vincent's eyes could switch into deadly coldness – I needed to remember that.

"Then look at the swatch and make a choice." I forced myself to focus on the colors before me. There was a continuum to consider but one section of color stood out – a bright, bright green. Similar to the emeralds I'd seen at the Ost Jewelers, emeralds that the gene-jeweler had insisted were especially complementary for green eyes – green eyes, he'd seemed keen to warn me, that I didn't possess. Well, now I could change that.

"I'll have this," I said.

Dr. Liu tapped icons on a computer pad, then looked to the hologram. The model's eyes were transformed to a striking green. "Now what would you like next?"

Peering at Dr. Liu's eyes again, I said, "Your eye shape."

"You want an epicanthic fold?" said Dr. Liu. "Times have changed." He smiled to himself. "You know not so long ago, plastic surgeons were sometimes asked to remove this fold." He was pointing to the corner of his eye. "Some women wanted to make themselves look more...European."

He began a nimble and rapid succession of icon manipulations until an image blazed onto the screen. The image was archival. It showed the doctor's long face, framed by loose black hair, glossy and thick and parted at the middle.

"So you want eyes like mine?" he said.

The face persisted for a second. Then transformed into eyes only. Oval and large, beneath fine, tidy brows. A grid appeared over the top of the image. Arrows. Numbers. Another imported data-table with reference codes. Zap.

The double received new eyes.

"You are not asking whether this look is beautiful." Dr. Liu said. "Most women do ask."

"As I've told you already, beauty is not my aim..."

"You are not concerned with the merits of this appearance because you are not yet thinking that this appearance will be yours."

I stared at the hologram. It was a creation. A virtual sculpture. Dr. Liu was right – she wasn't me.

"What do *you* think about her beauty?" I asked.

"Beautiful, ugly – I'm not interested. I'm only interested in how to change one human appearance into another."

The doctor moved to a metal cupboard on the other side of the room. He retrieved a flexi-screen, powered it, then placed it on my lap. I shifted my position on the spindly stool to hold the computer more comfortably. Pointing to a row of keys, Liu leaned over me.

"You can use these controls to manipulate the appearance. When you have made the refinements you want I will determine the relevant codes."

Liu returned to his desk, picked up a long, folded printout and began to mark it with a pen.

Pressing one control for several seconds, I noticed a slow vertical elongation of my double's face. Pressing the adjacent key narrowed the space between the eyes. Hitting the "all angles" control initiated a slow 360-degree rotation. As the model turned on her spindly stool, I focused on her posture. She was crouched over a scroll screen, her shoulders hunched, her back severely curved. I straightened my own posture. In sync, she straightened hers.

I experimented with the dozens of controls that Dr. Liu had indicated and watched the kaleidoscopic changes to my double until finally I'd had enough. Further changes were pointless. I didn't even know what was motivating the changes I'd made.

"Here," I said, turning to the doctor.

"You have decided."

He approached the dark brown hologram in front of me. His gaze swept over her ringlets, long and black; her green and oval eyes; her pinker, bigger lips, her longer neck, her rounder breasts. The doctor turned and peered at my breasts. His eyes narrowed as he peered. Then continuing his sweep of the hologram, he scrutinized the newly elongated thighs and calves.

"Taller, bustier – you say it doesn't matter, but still some things are predictable." Again a nasty smirk. "So our consultation is finished." He jabbed a control on the hologram platform. "I will authorize the production of a suitable modifier."

"When will it be ready?"

"Tomorrow. Probably the afternoon."

"That soon? It sounds so simple."

"It's not simple. Your specification will require a complex amalgam of vectors which all have to work in concert. But you have nothing to fear – I am good at concocting appearances. So now you need a fictitious history, one you'll have to remember if you want to pull off the identity change."

Solely focused on changing my appearance, I hadn't run through the ins and outs of having a fictitious history. Now that Dr. Liu had mentioned it, the issue overwhelmed me. What would I even be called?

"My name – what will it be?"

Dr. Liu tapped some controls and said, "I'll feed in all the specifications for your target appearance, then we'll see what name our machine throws out, shall we?" Only a second or so passed when he said, "Here you are."

"My name?"

He nodded.

"You are Lena Mae Cho."

"What?"

"Lena. Mae. Cho."

"Lena," I repeated quietly, trying out the sound. "Lena."

Dr. Liu was gesturing to the door, indicating that I should prepare to return to the sparse and private room into which I'd been ushered when I first arrived. And while I stood and walked towards the exit, my mirror image remained frozen, looking faintly uncertain, on her hollo-stool.

23

Friday 18th July 2059

IN A TINY white changing room to the side of Dr. Liu's office, a short, squat nurse gave me a coral gown. I read the badge pinned to the breast pocket of her uniform: *Siobhan Keane, Assistant Nurse.*

"All your old clothes, shoes…" she looked at the gold band on my little finger, "… jewelry, you have to put them in here." She placed a clear plastic bag on a chair before me, which was the only item of furniture in the room. "Dr. Liu and Monica Parks," she continued, in an Irish accent, "they'll be waiting for you outside." Not once did she make eye contact before she left me to undress.

When I finished changing I entered the consulting room and found Monica sitting primly to the side of the large oval desk. Her head was swiveled to the corner of the room to face the hologram of my target appearance. Cocking her head at different angles, she was looking at it as if it were an art piece. She said, without turning to me or Dr. Liu, "You know there is a famous Korean screen painting, eighteenth century, where the central character is a peasant girl whose eyes are just like that."

She turned to watch Dr. Liu, who was fixing a drip to a gurney that had been positioned, presumably while I'd been changing, near to the main door of the consulting room.

"What is in the drip?" I asked.

He completed his check of the drip line, before turning and saying, "Sedatives." Walking towards me, he added, "You'll need them, otherwise, psychologically, you'll feel that you're falling apart." Monica turned to listen to him too. I felt uncomfortable standing there in a flimsy medical gown, holding onto a trash bag containing my clothes. "People are destined to view any sudden and unnatural change to their appearance as the mark of something going wrong. You are psychologically pre-programmed to view the treatment as the onset of some terrible disease and then you'll wish to stop the treatment, and start making demands halfway through the administration of the modifiers. Our experience shows that the treatment is best administered while you are relaxed, not frightened by what is happening to you. And for that reason it is best that we make you calm."

I remembered reading something about this in the literature Monica had sent, but, concentrating on the safety and efficacy of the modifiers, I hadn't paid attention. Now I wished I had. "Will the sedation be very heavy?" I'd spent a long time in the doctor's office only the day before, finely manipulating the dimensions and hues of a multitude of features, having some control.

"Think of it this way — when you look in a mirror after the treatment, you will, so your mind will tell you, not see yourself, you will see somebody else. I got the impression you rather liked creating an appearance for our model. But the fact is that will be *your* appearance. That's what people will be looking at when you walk into a room. That's what you will see when you look in the mirror." He paused. "You will be shocked. That I guarantee. That's what we need to help you with."

"Even if I have the knowledge that I'll be reverting to my old appearance — you think I'll still be unable to cope?"

"Don't some women collapse into floods of tears over a new haircut, though they know that it's all going to grow back.?"

"But for how long will I be sedated?"

"The heavy sedation will be in the region of six, seven days. Then the dose will be reduced, allowing you to get used to your appearance.

"This was all in the literature," Monica said, gently. "But, I suppose, you had a lot to take in. It's a big step, isn't it?" She added, glancing over to the hologram – the virtual Lena Mae Cho with her bright green eyes and deep brown skin.

Finally, she picked the brochures from her lap, pushed them across the desk towards me, and said, "New Way has counselors, properties, financial services – all to help people move on...."

"*Counselors?*"

I looked to Dr. Liu, but he was crossing back to the gurney, checking the tubes.

"It's not going to be easy starting all over. Talking it through might help." She tapped the brochures with the pearly-varnished nail of a slender index finger. "The information here should help."

I hadn't worked anything out. The thought suddenly hit me. In an instant I'd extricated myself from one situation with Vincent without any thought about what the next one would be. How would I, as Lena Mae Cho, spend my time? Where would I live? Who would my friends be? David, Radhia – how could I turn up to wherever they were with a completely different appearance? It was a certainty that Vincent would follow up anyone who contacted them. He would be waiting for me to turn up. At least I thought he would be.

"Was Vincent looking for me last night?"

"He's in your past." Monica said flatly. "You've moved on, haven't you?"

"But has he been looking for me?"

"He's been engrossed with the new contract and dealing with opposition. OMNI look set to start a new campaign," Monica continued. "Obviously that's a threat for the Resolve contract. Vincent's focused on his business. You have to focus on yours. This reassignment you've requested is a highly covert procedure. It is extremely risky for me to arrange this for you. I need to know you are resolved to move on and make a new life for yourself, and not have any second thoughts."

Monica gave a lot away by saying that. Vincent couldn't be *totally* occupied with the contract whatever turn OMNI's campaign had taken. How could he possibly switch from obsessing over my every move to having no concern for me at all? Monica was being disingenuous, fobbing me off with a dismissive account of his behavior.

And the idea that I could just blank my past and step into discontinuous future without batting an eyelid was ridiculous. Opting for modification treatment was an enormous decision.

It had life changing consequences for Vincent too.

God! I'd not really thought about those consequences at all – what impact my leaving him might have, how he'd react, how he'd cope.

"It is imperative that you stay committed to this treatment, Lena."

Lena.

Monica was the first person to use my new name. It jarred and I knew that in using it she'd wanted to make a point. She must have gambled that brusqueness would stop me getting distracted from the agreed procedure.

The trash bag to my side, full of my old clothes, contained remnants of a me I was about to discard. Dr. Liu, fully dressed, efficiently assembling equipment, seemed utterly unmoved by the atrociousness of this. Nothing exceptional. Just a run-of-the-mill identity exchange, not the extreme measure it was for me.

"You need to stick with the plan, Lena. Not waver. Look forward. Not back. Act in your own interests."

Act in my own interests. That was right. That's what I had to do.

"So," Dr. Liu said suddenly, beaming uncharacteristically, "When you wake up, you'll be Lena Mae Cho. I hope that you're ready."

"Yes," I said, looking into his excited eyes and feeling encouraged by his smile. "I think that I am."

***

Friday 25th July 2059

Though the room was spare, I didn't register this as coldness or bleakness. It was pleasing that it seemed so clinically clean. The sheets were bright white. The tiled floors were spotless. All of this was a relief. And this bed was so comfortable, the temperature perfect. This pillow was just right and, feeling content, I closed my eyes.

I awoke again to the sounds of muffled voices. There were two doors to the room – one set in the wall opposite and another to my side, from which the voices came. One small cabinet stood by my bed, with a single drawer at the top and a little door. A clinic-issued toiletry bag lay on the surface. Nothing else, except the bed and monitors and wires and drips around me.

There was a strange sensation in my back where it pressed against the bed. Not a pain, but a distinct, heavy sensitivity. I dwelled on this feeling, from curiosity, not discomfort. It was a sensation I couldn't name.

I scanned the metal railing around the edge of the bed and saw a button that would raise me upright. I pulled my arm from the covers to press the button. Stopped mid-movement. Dark hand. A cinnamon brown. The fingers were slender, long; skin was smooth, pristine, the ridges of bones only faint, veins – invisible. I willed this hand to flex. It flexed. It was…mine, this strange, dark hand. The nails had been clipped short, and their ends consisted of straight little edges. The wrist was slender and the hairs on the forearm were ultra-fine and black.

I scanned the walls of the room for a mirror. There was none.

I pressed my hand on my hair. It wasn't straight. There were the kinks that I'd specified. But remembering my complicity in specifying this hair type didn't make its presence less strange. Craving a mirror to check the transformation, all the transformations – hair, complexion, eye shape, iris color, bone structure, I fixed on a plain wooden door in the wall opposite. A bathroom maybe. But, now having guessed as much, I had an overwhelming apprehension about finding a mirror there. When, sitting more upright, I realized that my arm was hooked to a stationary intravenous drip unit. I was relieved. And yet I still wanted to know more about my looks. I grasped one helical strand of hair and pulled it round before my eyes. The color was almost black.

The swish of a door. Dr. Liu approached my bed, carrying a clipboard with a pen hanging over the edge, dangling from a string.

His hair, slicked back in a ponytail, seemed so straight now. I'd never noticed that before. Holding my hand before me once more, comparing his skin to mine, his complexion seemed much lighter too.

"Taking it all in," he said, "your new appearance."

Something about his looking over me, peering at my face, scrutinizing, judging, when I hadn't yet seen my appearance myself spurred me to say, "Is there a mirror?"

Dr. Liu hesitated, then said, "Remember your target appearance, the one you devised, you said you wanted...."

"Yes, why – has something gone wrong?" The color of my hand, though I could barely believe what I saw, was, from what I could remember, precisely as specified. Worried that the treatment might have failed in some terrible way, I ran my fingertip over my brow, my cheeks, my lips. In each case there was a jarring hypersensitivity. The lightest touch was accompanied with a distinct, distracting tingle. Not painful, not unpleasant. Just strange. But what was this a hypersensitivity to? To this – this dark brown hand. *My* hand. I looked to Dr. Liu. "Has something gone wrong with the transformation?"

"No. I just want you to remember what you asked for, otherwise you'll look in the mirror wondering what happened to your old appearance. You know how it is when you have a new hairstyle – you look in the mirror, with an unconscious expectation of the old style, and, until you get used to the new one, are surprised by your own reflection...."

"We have had this discussion before."

"I know. I just want to make sure you are prepared for…."

"I'd like a mirror," I said.

He walked to the bathroom, then returned with a large hand mirror with a blue plastic frame and handle. When he offered the handle first, it seemed that he'd deliberately kept the angle of the mirror horizontal. I would have to raise it myself.

Slowly, I positioned the mirror before my face.

Lena Mae Cho stared back.

My heart lurched so hard I felt a pain in my chest. There was a sound of smashing glass – the mirror was in bits on the floor.

Dr. Liu carefully picked up the pieces of glass. His movements were robotic. I watched until I was distracted by the peculiar tingling in my skin. I said, "This strange feeling…."

"What feeling?" he asked, as he dropped the mirror pieces into a waste paper basket. He turned to me and watched the movement of my fingertips tracing the contours of my chin. "A pain?"

"It's like a tingling. But not quite. I can't describe it. I've never had this feeling before."

"A paresthesia?"

"I don't know. What is a paresthesia?"

"A change in sensation…."

"Yes, I have that."

"An unusual feeling."

"Yes."

"That might be normal," he said. "It's difficult to say. You have a different type of skin now, a new kind of dermis. This feeling that seems abnormal to you might be the norm for people who naturally have this dermatological make-up." Dr. Liu gestured to the array of contraptions around the bed and the clipboard on the little cabinet.

"We are watching you very closely," he said. "Everything is good."

Dr. Liu checked the monitor, adjusted the drip, and told me I should sleep and that things would become more comprehensible over time.

***

Friday 1st August 2059

Now when I looked in a hand mirror, or the full length mirror in the bathroom, I expected to see epicanthic eyes, dark brown skin and ringlets hanging wildly around my shoulders. But I was also getting critical: "The eyes," I said to Dr. Liu, "they are *so, so* bright." I'd been sitting in front of the telescreen waiting for the doctor to enter my room when, along with Siobhan, he'd appeared in the doorway. I turned the telescreen to mute.

"Your eyes are as specified," Liu said. "They are perfect."

But I knew the two things, for Dr. Liu, were linked: my eyes, to him, were perfect just because they were as specified.

Siobhan was standing by the bathroom door, holding a coral gown.

"You need to put this on," she said. The very color of the gown stopped me in my tracks; with my old ivory skin I'd never have worn a color like that – it was the kind of shade that washed me out. I'd have to rethink what to wear. God! There was so much to think through. One thing at a time though. The weird sensations I was experiencing needed sorting out first.

"The strange feeling…with my skin," I said to Dr. Liu after I'd put on the robe to stand before him, "it still hasn't gone."

Smoothing his hand over my arms, seemingly feeling the skin, then taking my face and holding it up to the light for his inspection, he said, "No? Well, it is my belief that this little tingling…."

"It's not really a tingling."

"Well, whatever it is, it should go before long."

"It concerns me," I insisted.

"Yes? Then shuffle around and sit on the edge of the bed."

Something on my neck seemed to have caught his attention.

"What is it?"

"A very slight discoloration, a pale patch, but probably nothing to worry about. The cell exchange is so rapid at the moment, this kind of patching is probably to be expected."

I noted the "probably," but was more caught up with the

strange sensations I experience as he fingered around my neckline to see how far the discoloration had spread.

"This feeling is so hard to describe."

"But not painful?"

"No."

I concentrated on the feel of his fingers around my collarbone. What *was* this feeling?

"Not uncomfortable. Not aching. Not...." I could only describe it in terms of what it wasn't like. Then, still focusing on his touch, trying to class this strange sensation, I realized that it wasn't a different sensation at all. It was the same *kind* of feeling I would expect from pressure on my skin, it was just far more pronounced. "It's the equivalent of turning up the volume of noise – same sound, just louder. Yes, that's what it is – it's just a lot more intense. Why would that be?"

But Dr. Liu didn't seem to be listening. Instead he was smiling broadly, looking at the skin on my neck, his eyes all bright with excitement.

"The results look excellent to me, at least," he added, while his eyes fixed on the tie of my gown, "they are in the areas I can see." Moving closer to me, eyes still trained on my gown strings, he seemed impatient to see more. But something was holding him back – a conscious effort to draw out the moment maybe. Clearly this was exciting for him. Overly so, it seemed. How long was he going to stand there all wide-eyed? Was he ever going to step out of his hesitation and begin examining me? He'd generally seemed so emotionless and clinically efficient in the past – what would he do now? What was he going to say? What would anyone say to someone they'd just created? He was standing so close I felt his trouser material brush against my leg. The sensation was intense.

Surprisingly, he said nothing as he made for the bow. He pulled the ends of the tie and gently but deftly nudged the gown apart.

He looked down at my body. His eyes were darting about taking everything in, then he took his info-remote from his pocket and uploaded my target appearance, and he said, "Yes! Oh yes! You are as specified. Aren't you very pleased?"

There were faint patches of a slightly lighter brown spread over the left shoulder, running down to the side of the left breast.

"What about these?" I said.

Siobhan was also leaning in, looking at the blemishes.

"As I said before, all this should go." He sounded confident, but it seemed like Siobhan, whose expression was serious, had doubts too.

Dr. Liu cupped his hand over a patch on my shoulder, smoothed over the skin. "It's magnified," I said, "– the pressure on my skin."

"But not intolerable?" he said, after a moment's silence.

He didn't want to hear that anything was wrong – that much was clear.

I pulled the flaps of the gown together. Siobhan, who was preparing a blood pressure gel pad, glanced from me to the doctor. It seemed like she was waiting for more of an explanation too. But other than, "You are doing very, very well," he had nothing more to add. He smiled and made his way to the door.

When he'd gone, Siobhan approached and stood to the side of my armchair.

"I know you're very concerned," she said, constricting my upper arm with a tight band before placing the gel pad on my vein. Her face was round and friendly looking.

"It's just that this tingling isn't going." She nodded slowly. I understood that she was listening carefully. I trusted this Siobhan. "I mean, he may be right, the feeling may go, everything may settle down, but…" I knew this would sound alarmist, "…what if something's gone wrong? I mean, well, they were highly complex transformations applied to my DNA…."

She was nodding. "Yes, they were complex," she said, quietly. "I will definitely be keeping my eye on things."

"What if there's been some kind of mistake? What happens then? Does he have a look at my DNA and check for some error he's made?"

Siobhan bit her lip. The motion was slow but distinct. Her eyes, now focused on the clear gel pad around my arm, were a muted jade color, a naturally gentle shade. Her lips parted as if to speak, then there was a hesitation. What was she holding back?

The gel pad changed color from clear to a creamy white. The constriction around my arm grew painful. Very painful. "Does that hurt? I'm sorry." She released the band, peeled off the gel pad and applied a blood pressure reader to score the color code and translate it into a standard BP measurement. "I'm finished now. Are you all right?"

I was rubbing my arm, wondering why such a simple procedure as taking blood pressure had caused such an abnormal sensation. "This is what I'm concerned about," I pointed to my forearm, "somehow this doesn't feel right."

She took my forearm and peered at it. There was nothing unusual to see.

"I have listened to your concerns," she said, then peered at me as if she wanted me to really understand her. "I've registered them. You can trust me. OK?"

It was only when I said *OK* back that she put the blood pressure equipment away.

24

Monday 4th August 2059

I YANKED THE covers back and began looking frantically for the emergency alarm. The pain in my leg was so severe I was desperate for Dr. Liu to come in and treat it immediately.

"Why has this treatment gone wrong? The blotches and sores?" I demanded as soon as he appeared. He pressed around a sore, near the ankle.

"That is something to determine," he said.

He didn't know what was wrong. That fact caused a spike in heart rate. Why didn't he know? None of the articles I'd read had mentioned side effects like this. "For now," he said, "we need to stop the deterioration. Then we can consider its cause."

The door swung open. A male assistant carrying a tray with gauze, vials, little white packs, a hypodermic in cellophane. There was a bead of sweat on his temple. His eyes were darting about, seemingly looking for space to put the objects. Sweeping a pile of papers at the end of the bed aside, Dr. Liu said, "Put it here." The assistant obeyed, then in response to a sudden shrill ring, he pulled an info-remote from his pocket. "Room 13?" he said, "OK, coming." He left at once, leaving the door ajar. Through the slit of the doorway, a gurney was visible. It was being quickly wheeled away. There was a person on top, draped with a white sheet. Person? Or body? I processed the visual data, tried to make sense of it, while Dr. Liu sorted through the items on the tray. He, she...whatever it was, whatever it had been, was covered. Completely. From head to toe.

"What's happening?" I shouted.

Dr. Liu didn't answer, just continued swiftly preparing something at the end of the bed. There was a small gauze pad to which he applied a brown substance. He was working quickly, too quickly – the gauze wrapper fell from the bed to the floor, as did the plastic container of the brown preparation. The doctor left them there.

Now there was a buzzer blaring faintly outside. A siren?

"What are you giving me? Tell me...tell me!"

"A stabilizer," Dr. Liu said, sticking an adhesive pad to my arm. "This should normalize some of the sensations you're feeling. It might feel very strange...."

"I already feel strange. I hurt."

"This preparation contains powerful catalysts. They repair cells at an incredibly fast rate." He pressed the patch onto the skin and immediately there was an intense tingling, like cold water was spreading under my skin all the way through my arm. The feeling radiated through my body: neck, shoulder , chest, waist, belly, hips. My heart was still pounding.

"The effects of these drugs can be so sudden. You will probably feel alarmed."

"I do. Help me. I *do*."

"This will help then," he said, injecting something into my arm. "You see, it's all very well us developing these drugs with rapidity factors, but we have to consider the psychological impact such intense, fast treatment can have. Fortunately," he said, removing the syringe and holding it up to the light to check that it was empty, "we have powerful tools to keep our minds in sync.

You will feel calm in a little while."

Right now, though, there was a spreading coldness, unbearable in intensity. I was compelled to stand and wrench the gown off my body. Even the touch of my hair dangling around my shoulders became unbearable. I grabbed it and twisted it up, trying to secure it in a bunch on the top of my head. It fell down all at once, causing another excruciating tingling.

Dr. Liu picked something off the top of a little white cabinet and moved towards me. I couldn't help but jerk away from him. His arm was stretched my way. In his fingers he held a turquoise band.

"For your hair," he said.

I snatched it. The pressure of holding the band in my fingers radiated through my skin but I grabbed at my hair and managed to tie it up.

Then, over a few seconds, the tingling subsided. I felt so drained I could barely stand.

"You should be stable now. And the lesions will heal very quickly. By tomorrow they'll be gone."

Dr. Liu picked the coral gown from the floor, threaded my arms into it and fastened the ties. He nudged me back to the bed, propped me against the pillows.

He began stuffing preparations into his pockets, gauzes, packets, capsules – all were squirreled away.

There were two new buzzers blaring now. What *were* these alarms?

Dr. Liu gathered up the papers lying on crumpled covers at the end of the bed then said, "The sedatives should kick in soon."

"No more sedatives. I…."

"She will be all right," Dr. Liu said.

She? Why was he talking about me in third person. Craning round, I saw Siobhan, severe-faced, standing silently by a trolley. I didn't recall her coming into the room. Presumably, she'd done so during the earlier commotion, when I'd found my own skin too unbearable to be inside.

"I will keep watch," Siobhan said.

"Do," Dr. Liu replied, bustling quickly from the room.

"What's going wrong with the treatment, Siobhan?" She was at my bedside now, looking me over, squinting at the diminished lesions. "Why all the alarms?"

Quickly, Siobhan glanced to the door, then back to me.

"You need to leave here as soon as possible." Her tone was shot through with chilling urgency. "The stabilizers you've been given – they'll work well, but only for so long. It might be just a matter of days before you deteriorate again…"

"What?"

"Listen to me. Your treatment here is dangerous.…"

"Dangerous?"

"Yes. Very. The RPMs you were given, they're extremely unstable. They should never have been administered. That's why all old DNA samples have been destroyed. Dr. Liu is so eager for his research to be a success, he's blind to negative effects." Siobhan once again glanced over my body. "Monica's worried, I know. She keeps asking Dr. Liu questions, but he keeps wanting to try new solutions, new combinations of drugs – " Siobhan was speaking so quickly, I had to concentrate hard to catch everything she was saying. "I've been watching him for a while now, checking records and dosages and noting the compounds in the drugs."

Siobhan *had* seemed meticulous in recording patient data and scrutinizing medicine labels. Prior to this instant that had actually been reassuring. But now what was she saying? That she'd suspected the modifiers were dangerous and that she'd felt a need to keep tabs on Dr. Liu's treatment?

"I was beginning to get a picture," Siobhan continued, again glancing back to the door, "beginning to get an angle on the experiments.…"

"Whoa! Wait – you're speaking too fast. Experiments? What are you talking about?"

"They may know I'm onto this, Lena. One of the technicians saw me in the storeroom just now, checking out the modifiers, the compounds in them. I'm trying to tell you as much as possible now, because I don't know how long I can speak to you."

With Siobhan's wide, darting eyes and her hushed and rapid speech, her panic was clear. So clear, I became scared too.

"Why would anyone conduct…*experiments?*"

"Modifiers with rapidity factors are potentially *very* lucrative. That's what Dr. Liu is working on. And of course, the set up here is perfect, perfect for running an underground trial. The problem is getting enough subjects. There's a limit to how many informers come through this place. And if you're limited in experimental data obviously there'll be unforeseen consequences. These RPMs you've been given, they're pretty new treatments anyway, but Dr. Liu, well…."

"Well what?"

I could feel some of my background suspicions making a sudden shift forwards. The way Dr. Liu had looked me over, smoothed my skin with no regard to how I might feel, like I was some artifact he'd created – that *did* fit with what Siobhan was saying.

"Some of the compounds he tried using before contained base agents that are known to have very adverse consequences. I looked up a couple of those agents, and they don't have Department of Health approval. And here's the thing, he's started playing with them again. And once again there are serious problems."

"What about Monica? What does she say?"

"I know she's challenging Dr. Liu; I heard them arguing. But she's not the one with the scientific expertise, so she keeps deferring and assenting to his methods. He's convinced her to remodel part of the clinic to bring in new personnel, new technologies.

They're keeping a lot of these new technologies under wraps. All I know is that there are scanners that we've not had a need for before. They've also built new living quarters, an apartment of sorts. I've heard there are new personnel. This has all been rushed and urgent. It's typical of Dr. Liu to be demanding and impatient. The thing is it's yet another new treatment he wants to try out and Monica's given him the reins."

It sounded, now, as if Siobhan was getting carried away, dishing up an increasingly incredible story. Before deciding on reassignment I'd spent an entire desperate night in Vincent's house reading through the research and hadn't come across anything documenting serious side effects.

None of this was ringing true. Why would Monica take such a risk? Indisputably, she had many flaws – a coldness, an insensitivity – but she was far too careful to risk employing a risk-taking scientist, especially in a department which by its very nature, dealing with informers, needed to operate under the radar.

"Monica sent me all the scientific literature to make sure I knew what I was doing…."

"All the scientific literature except for Epstein's later papers outlining the problems with the rapidity factors."

I hadn't seen any such articles. That was true.

"But still, on the phone…" I was sure my memory was correct, "…Monica warned me of the extremeness of the procedure."

"Yes, I'm sure she went through those motions," Siobhan said. "And then she let you go ahead with the procedure anyway."

"But still…" for reasons I couldn't fathom, I felt an overriding desire to shine an ethical light on Monica's actions "…she wouldn't take this kind of risk, surely. She just wouldn't do that."

"But she has," Siobhan insisted.

"For what reason? Developing a lucrative new drug to make money?"

Vincent had frequently made comments on the time and money she'd put into her various charities. Her *own* money. Someone motivated by greed wouldn't give her wealth away.

"No. I can't be some kind of guinea pig. That's ridiculous. Monica and I discussed the possibility of a reassignment and I agreed to the procedure…."

"She threw you some bait, Lena." Siobhan paused before adding quietly, "And you took it. You were supposed to get a temporary reassignment. But that went wrong. Now they've covered their tracks, destroyed all the old DNA samples and left you with little hope of reversal…."

"What are you saying?"

"Look," Siobhan said, speaking more urgently, "I don't know why Monica's agreed to all this…."

"What do you mean – little hope of reversal?"

Noises in the corridor silenced us both for a moment.

"At least you have the luxury of questioning me," Siobhan snapped in a way that jarred. "Believe me, there was another woman – her name was Deborah – she was here some time ago and she does not have that option anymore. Dr. Liu's given you a similar compound to the one Deborah received that, so far, is keeping you relatively stable, but it will not last. It's a temporary measure, but that still makes you luckier than most – you have time to get help. Understand that."

Coldness radiated through my body.

In the pandemonium of sirens and bustling medics there'd been a person – a body – on a gurney, draped from head to foot with a sheet. Goose bumps, in waves, spread across my skin.

"Listen to me, Lena. You need to go to the basement section on Wing D and take the back exit. Everyone's distracted now. The best thing you can do is leave." She pointed to a black cloth bag on the floor by the bed. "I brought you some clothes, shoes. There's cash and a pre-paid credit card. You need to get treatment in a regular hospital. Somehow you need to get a sample of your old DNA and take it to Dr. Epstein at Central Hospital. He worked with Jason Liu on RPM treatment. But," Siobhan continued, after a lightning glance to the door, "when the modifiers looked like they had unacceptable side effects, Epstein stopped his main line of research. Dr. Liu, though, he continued working at one of the big pharms and then came here."

"Why haven't the police been called? Have you called…?"

"Impossible," Siobhan cut in. "Monica's sitting on all the surveillance data, the police are dependent on her for information. I tried raising alarms with someone I knew at Sense before. He worked in the Training Division. I really thought I could trust him, but he just came back and said there was nothing untoward going on. I didn't believe him. And, now I think I'm under suspicion."

"So what should I do?"

"You should leave this facility at once, while you feel well….you are feeling OK, aren't you?"

"Yes." It was incredible how fast the treatment had suppressed the hypersensitivity of before.

"Security guards on Wing D change over at 1pm. This is your best chance of leaving unnoticed." Siobhan began packaging syringes into a small plastic box. "Here's some more of the medicine Dr. Liu gave you. It will keep you stable for just a limited time. These syringes with the white label contain relaxants. The other ones are so potent, you'll need to dull your awareness of their effects. That's what the relaxants are for." She pressed the plastic box into my hand. "It's only a matter of days before the efficacy starts to wear off. So you need to act fast. Dr. Epstein at Central Hospital…."

"Central – the new one near Liverpool Street?"

Nodding, Siobhan said, "Epstein may be able to help, but he will need a sample of your original DNA. Focus on getting that sample then take it to him as soon as you can."

"But how will I find a sample of…."

There was another noise outside in the corridor and Siobhan interrupted my question in a hushed but urgent voice.

"Go to the basement exit. I paid Nisreen, one of the drivers, to get you away from here." She glanced at her watch. "You've got another twenty minutes to show up, that's all – this is a big risk for her. You must…."

The door burst open. A tall security guard entered the room.

"Get to the corridor," the guard commanded Siobhan.

Turning to me, Siobhan tried whispering, "You need to…."

But the guard snapped, "No talking," and then added, "*You* need to hand over your ID." He pointed to the badge pinned to Siobhan's breast pocket. When she refused to pass it over, he grabbed it. "You shan't be needing that anymore," he said. A pink plastic highlighter that was clipped to Siobhan's breast pocket fell to the linoleum floor.

"Siobhan!"

The plastic of the highlighter cracked under my foot as I ran after her. If Siobhan had uncovered serious malpractices in this Reassignment clinic, was she now in danger? Where was the guard taking her? What was he going to do?

Reaching the door, my heart pounding heavily, I saw Siobhan being frog-marched towards an elevator where two more guards were waiting. There was a ping of an arriving lift. A swish of a door.

Siobhan was out of sight. One guard turned to face me, marched towards me, shunted me back into the room and locked the door.

Shit! Wrenching at the handle was useless; the door wouldn't open. I had just under twenty minutes to find this driver to get me out of the clinic. And I had to do this with no idea where the basement exit was, where wing D was, who the driver was, and on top of that the door was locked!

Even if I got to this waiting car, where was I going to get a sample of my old DNA to take to this Dr. Epstein? All samples here in the clinic had been destroyed. Inevitably, there would be hair strands back at the house where Vincent was, but that was out of the question. After all these lengths to get away from him, the idea of walking straight back to his house was unthinkable. There was the Ost Studio, where Federico Hernandez had extracted my cells. But there were no further samples of DNA there. "Once we've made the piece you require we have no further need for the cells, besides, we don't want unwanted cross-contamination." Federico had been very clear about that.

There was the Ost piece itself, the figurine that Vincent had ordered and wanted to put in his office. Even if he'd gone ahead with the order and taken the piece to work with him, getting hold of it would be impossible. That would mean breaking into Sense HQ, the country's leading surveillance company, with all their sensors and covert cameras. The idea was preposterous.

But devoid of other plans, the image of the statuette kept stirring in my mind. Was there any way to get it? Any way at all?

Vincent had said that with the Ost piece in his office, he'd have me near. There'd been such calmness in his voice as he'd said these words, as there'd been when he'd admitted destroying my portfolio. Why couldn't he have been less dangerous and insecure? For God's sake – why was all this happening to me?

There were voices in the background. When I swung around I caught my reflection in a mirror on the wall. Lena Mae Cho, downturned mouth, hard eyes, was staring back. I found myself kicking the door, over and over, unable to stop, until a stinging sensation spread from my toes, to my sole, ankle and calf. The pain focused my mind on Siobhan's warning about the urgency of finding Dr. Epstein and taking him a sample of my unmodified cells.

The figurine in Vincent's office….

Break into Sense HQ….

Think. Think. Make it possible.

Vincent wasn't always in his office. Squash games at lunch time, the Monday executive meeting, the Thursday webinar – he wouldn't be in his office at any of these times. Ordinarily, anyway. There were also weekends. Even so, how was it possible to even get into HQ? Let alone Vincent's office. Walking in as a visiting Lena Mae Cho was out of the question because Vincent wasn't the only one with a radar to avoid. There'd be Monica's radar too.

The only way to get through security was as a Sense worker and for that I'd need someone else's Sense ID, some kind of forgery. Jesus Christ! How was it possible to wangle something like that? I didn't know anyone who did things like forgeries. Didn't even know *of* anyone, let alone know them personally. But…hold on…maybe there was someone. What about the person Vincent had mentioned? What was his name? The one Ezra Hurst had fired. He knew about Sense security, had worked on their databases. That's right – he'd caused some kind of vulnerability. What was his name? Kurt… no.

Klein…?

Clint.

That was it. Clint Scarman. He was supposed to be holed up on some battered barge somewhere, a battered barge in South Dock. Maybe the driver waiting at the basement exit could take me to this Scarman, who I would then persuade to find a way of getting me through Sense security, through the main entrance, and into Vincent's office.

This was insane. Impossible.

Leaning back against the door, I shut my eyes. But the memory of Siobhan being shunted into the elevator smothered my negativity. I had to try something; I owed it to her.

The electronic clock by the bed blinked red. Only fifteen minutes to get to the waiting car. I pulled jeans, trainers and a top out of the cloth bag Siobhan had brought in and quickly got dressed. There was a cheap wallet with a bundle of cash and a pre-paid credit card in the bag. I grabbed the medicines and shoved them in too.

Casting around the room, I fixed on the alarm on the opposite wall. If I rang it, someone would come and open the door, and so far as I could see, there was no other way of making that happen. I rang the bell, having no clear plan what to do when anyone arrived. Seconds passed. No response. Then minutes – it seemed like several. What were the medics doing that they couldn't come immediately? Were there too many emergencies elsewhere, in other wings, with other *guinea pigs*? It wouldn't matter who came to my room in answer to the emergency bell – they couldn't be trusted, that seemed certain. They would only serve as a means to get the door opened and for me to make an exit as quickly as possible, but, if everything Siobhan had said was correct, they'd try to prevent this. Try hard probably. Thinking I might need to fight my way out of the clinic, I scanned objects in the room, quickly assessing their usefulness. There was a drinking glass on a cabinet by the bed and coat hangers in the empty wardrobe. There was also a metal stand supporting an IV fluid bag. I wrenched the bag away, letting it splat on the floor, then went to pull the metal pole from its support.

A movement at the door made me jump.

It was the same guard who'd taken Siobhan. He was peering through the window. Now coming in. He was a tall, angular figure, treading on the pink pen that had fallen from Siobhan's pocket earlier, crunching its plastic casing with his heavy black boot. His expression was quizzical as he stared at the fluid bag in the middle of the floor. He raised his head slowly redirecting his gaze towards me. I lunged towards the IV unit and pulled the pole from its stand. He came towards me, fast now, his eyes wide and focused on the pole. Gripping one of the ends, I summoned all my energy and swung it hard across his face.

A crack of bone. A violent roar. He was clasping his face, teetering towards the bed.

I snatched up the cloth bag containing the medicines and raced to the open door, then out into an empty white corridor. Wing D – where the hell was that? Running rightwards I saw a staircase. Knowing I needed eventually to get to basement level, I ran down, past a "Level 4" sign, then "Level 3."

Voices. Urgent. Male and female.

A man and a woman, both in white medical uniforms were coming up the stairs. I pushed through the swing doors to enter the level 2 corridor and hurried past several more doors. All locked. An entrance further along looked open. I sped towards it. The swing doors from the stairway opened and the voices I'd heard earlier were now just outside in the corridor. I ran to the entrance, into a huge space – a ward with a dozen people, most lying close-eyed and dull-skinned. There was a faintly putrid smell in the air. Behind were the voices again, echoing in the corridor. The male one saying, "Monosetum 8 is too unstable. Let's try another base," each word growing louder as he approached the ward. There were curtains around some of the beds. Darting to the nearest bed, I slipped behind the drapes, hoping while my heart was thudding, that the medics would pass by, go deeper into the ward, to some other patient. Not stop at this one, this – I froze at the sight of her – this grey-skinned one. Vacant-looking. Small. *Very* thin. Jesus Christ! A youth. Maybe fifteen or so. A child so disconnected she seemed utterly unmoved by my sudden appearance at her bedside. There were flashes of light as a malfunctioning fluorescent fixture sputtered above her bed. Each flash spotlighted the deterioration of her skin.

A see-through plastic bag hung at the end of her bed. A comic was packaged inside, a fold-screen game too. I edged towards the foot of the bed, listening out for the medics. They seemed to be further into the body of the ward, still discussing monosetum doses.

I drew close to the girl and gently took her hand. She jolted at my touch. Immediately, I put my finger to her lips, wordlessly pleading for quiet.

"Don't be scared," I mouthed. Worried that she'd make a noise, say something too loudly or cry out, I implored, "Please don't be scared." She squinted as she gazed at first my face and then my arm where there were dry patches on my wrist. Calculating that she'd guessed I was a patient myself, I whispered, "How did you get here?"

The girl parted dry lips and coughed loudly.

I listened for footsteps, for one of the medics to rush over and yank open the curtain. There was no sound. "How did you get here?" I tried again.

From her look of puzzlement and the shaking of her head, it was clear that she didn't know.

"Where were you before?" I tried instead, torn between wanting to comprehend things and the drive to get clear of the clinic as fast as possible.

"New place," she said.

"New place?"

"Safe house."

"You mean New Way?" The girl nodded. "You were in a New Way safe house?" Slowly, she nodded again.

"Did Monica Parks set this up?"

She winced, and in a strangled voice that was too loud, she blurted, "She said this would help me."

I put my finger to my lips again to get the girl to quieten down.

Hadn't Monica said that she was making an exception for me, offering a procedure ordinarily reserved for police informers, not the kind of people she was running into through working in her New Way charities?

Heavy footsteps. I froze, expecting the curtains to be pulled apart. But the footsteps continued past the girl's screened space towards the voices further in the ward. I crept softly to the edge of the curtain and pulled it aside a fraction to see who'd come in. A man, forties, broad face, short black spiky hair. He wore a dark suit and his expression was grave. Who he was just wasn't clear.

What *was* clear was the need to find outside help, get to the Dr. Epstein Siobhan had mentioned. He'd stopped working on phenotypic modifiers once their adverse reactions had become evident. He'd documented the problems and was now working in a regular hospital. He'd worked with Dr. Liu in the past and might, more than anyone else, have an insight into Liu's methodologies and be able to help normalize the treatment and help this ashen-faced girl by my side.

"I'm going to get help, OK."

With the medics distracted and huddled around another patient on the far side of the room, this was a good time to slip through the parting in the curtain and back into the corridor.

Immediately, I saw a security guard standing a little further along the hallway. He was too thickset to be the guard I'd lashed earlier, but from the way he was pushing open doors along the corridor and cocking his head to see inside, it was obvious he was looking for something. For someone? Me? The security officer was entering one of the far rooms now. Once he'd crossed the threshold, I bolted the opposite way, back to the stairway, and raced down the steps to the lower level where, despite a frantic scan for exits, I saw nothing but rows of tall black cabinets lined against the wall. Finally, I reached a corner with another stairwell around the bend.

Thank God – a sign on the wall saying *Wing D* with an arrow underneath.

I ran quickly past several closed doors, looking for the way to the basement exit. One set of swing doors led to a smaller corridor that turned to the right. But instead of a parking area, there seemed to be labs on this level. There was one large room with what looked like a compact MRI scanner. There was also a desk covered in reports, several computers and wall screens. Squinting at the reports I could make out part of a title. The first words were obscured, but the last said *...and Priming in Neural Technology.* In the corridor outside were discarded cardboard packages, the wrappings of new equipment. Siobhan had said that Dr. Liu's latest demand had been that a new research unit be built. It looked like this was it. On the far side of this room with the scanner was another room. The door between the two was slightly ajar. There was the sound of a faint radio that seemed to come from that room and what looked like the back of an armchair. Just as I strained to see more I heard a cough. I pulled sharply back into the hallway, then veered away and back into the main corridor again.

A loud grating sound made my heart lurch. Quickly, I slid into a space between two tall cabinets and tuned into the noise. It sounded like metal moving mechanically. Peeking out from behind the cabinet, I saw a shutter rising in a wall further along the corridor. Had to be an exit, but whether it was the exit that Siobhan had meant, there was no way to tell. A tall security guard began striding along the corridor. Then a faint ringing started, a distant alarm. Frozen, I listened for approaching footsteps. Adrenalin made my stomach prickle as the alarm grew louder and drowned out other sounds. Unable to hear footsteps, voices or anything, I tried to estimate the time it would take the medic to stride the thirty-foot distance between us. But time had become warped. I seemed to have been standing an eternity with my mind racing. Maybe, by now, the man had taken some turning. Peeking around the cabinet again would be a gamble, but the drive to know what was happening was overpowering. Thank God; the guard was turning into a smaller passageway. With the entrance clear, I forced myself to run to the shutter. My heart was lurching uncontrollably. There might be no other opportunity to get out. That thought propelled me towards the exit. Eyes fixed only on the shutter, I dashed as fast as I could along the corridor, hoping that there'd be a car outside waiting for me.

I was almost retching from pushing myself so hard, but continued to race along an alley leading to deserted grounds, eerily quiet, with newly clipped grass. Checking to see whether I'd been followed, I found no one behind. Trying to slow down my breathing, I was hit with the smell of grass cuttings.

A black car with darkened windows pulled up on a lane beside me. The lock of the passenger door clicked. A woman's voice said, "Get in."

The headscarf of the driver was instantly recognizable.

"It's you!" The glass partition between the front and back of the car was open. She was peering at me in her rear-view mirror, looking puzzled. "What? You don't recognize me? Don't you..."

Of course, she wouldn't recognize me. Why should she? I was utterly transformed.

"Just tell me where you're going," she said.

Where *was* I going? I scrabbled for ideas. The words "South Dock" spilled out, then, "I want to go to the marina there." I stared at the back of the woman's head, waiting for a response. She said nothing.

"Are you...."

"No more questions, OK. This is dangerous for me. I will take you to the marina. There's nothing else to say."

She closed the panel between us and put the car into gear. That was it? She wasn't going to talk to me? I banged on the partition.

"What do you mean there's nothing else to say?" She'd heard; her eyes had flashed up to the mirror to cut a hard stare, but within a few seconds she regained composure and reset her focus to the road ahead. Thumping the partition again made my fist throb with pain. "How much do you know about what they're doing in there? You take people in...." The image of an abattoir formed in my mind; of groaning cows stumbling towards a black box building, being shunted into a single file at a doorway; of enormous brown eyes wide with fear, of a gun pressed directly to the middle of each forehead.

One by one.

Bang. Bang. Bang.

"Do you turn a blind eye to these experiments?" I should have kept my mouth shut, put a lid on this tirade. Siobhan had taken enormous risks to set up this escape. It was stupid and dangerous to jeopardize everything by blowing up like this. But the calmness of this driver, cocooned in her headscarf, was infuriating. And she'd been the one who had driven me to the clinic. She must have had suspicions, but she'd chosen to keep tight-lipped. "Why do you do this? It's good money, is it? Do you...."

The plastic panel between the driver and passenger side slid open.

"Don't judge me," she snapped. "You went there," she said, jerking her head back in the direction of the clinic, "with ideas about changing your appearance; wanting a new eye color, a change of complexion. It's all trivial."

"It wasn't a trivial decision to...."

"It's trivial," Nisreen cut in, sourly. "The trials they're doing in there – they hold out hope of a proper life for some people. A *life*. Not just a change of look."

A screen on the back of the driver's seat flickered on. The word *loading* appeared, then an image of a young boy, maybe ten or eleven years old, sitting awkwardly in a wheelchair, his neck contorted to one side, his face pressed against a head support.

"Do you know what I want for my son? I want him to be able to hold his head up and feed himself. To pick out his own clothes and to be able to put them on. That's the kind of change this technology could bring. I'm sorry if your focus on looks gets in the way of seeing that."

"But don't you have any questions about what's going on in there?"

"Look, I'm not going to throw myself out of work without solid facts." There was a short silence, before she added, "Oh, I'm glad you're having a good look at that picture. You see that wheelchair..." I could see that it was made of modular components that had been arranged to suit the boy's scoliosis. "...that cost three-and-a-half thousand, three-and-a-half thousand that I've had to find all by myself. So, yes I do need a job that pays well." Looking up to her rear-view mirror, I saw her hostile, piercing eyes. "I don't know what you're thinking of doing at this marina, but you're the liability here, not me."

The image of the boy disappeared and the screen on the back of the driver's seat went blank. Nisreen closed the partition with a slam and drove on.

25

THE SKY WAS going a dark blue by the time the car pulled up at South Dock. Across the water, orange wall lights glowed in a row on apartments lining the north bank of the Thames. Their reflections shimmered uniformly on small rippling waves and the towers of Canary Wharf, with a multitude of office lights, loomed over the scene.

At the entrance of the dock, the driver of a white delivery truck, scrunched-up paperwork in hand, strolled over to the security guard. The gate opened slowly and automatically. Nisreen reversed and drove out of sight as soon as I got out of the car. While the guard was distracted with the truck driver, I picked up pace and headed towards the water's edge.

Hundreds of cruisers, speedboats and yachts were moored. Most seemed empty, tethered with chunky ropes. A few faint voices were carried by the breeze. Sounds of laughter came from the upper deck of a spectacular white cruiser some eighty feet long, shiny and sleek. Its occupants were sitting up high, wine glasses in hand, too engrossed in their jokes and opulence to care about the bobbing boats below.

Busy glancing back and forth trying to find Clint Scarman, I caught my leg on a thick wet rope restraining a speedboat. I braced myself for a hideous pain in my shin, a nauseating tingling sensation. Surprisingly there was only the simple kind of grazing that would normally be expected. Except for this graze, the skin on my legs, my hands, my arms seemed unusually smooth. The lesions from before were healing fast. Thank God! – the stabilizers were working; in the pandemonium of escaping the clinic I hadn't even registered that fact. But Siobhan had warned that the stability would be temporary, that another deterioration was inevitable. Remembering the ashen woman lying lifelessly in the clinic spurred me to focus on finding Scarman.

Where was he? Where was his battered barge? It was difficult scanning the marina in the dark, especially with all the wires and mastheads and sails obscuring my line of vision. Finally, eastwards, a group of narrowboats came into view. One was dilapidated with black and red paintwork. Quickly, I headed towards it.

"Can I help you?" On the deck of a nearby yacht a light brown skinned man, sixty-something, looked at me with suspicion. "You seem to be lost."

"I'm looking for Clint Scarman." The words came out before I'd thought through how much I should be telling anyone what I was doing.

"Scarman with a visitor!" The man stared hard. "I've never heard of that before, except for the harbor officials wondering when he's going to move off. Let's hope he's in a fit state for you."

"Is that his?" I said, pointing to the rusty red and black barge.

The man nodded before adding sourly, "It's easy to tell, isn't it?"

His whining and nosiness irritated me. I carried on towards the barge.

There were raggedy curtains covering each window of the boat. They were precariously hung and all mismatched, little more than filthy rags. One was made of a lighter cotton and the flickering lights of a TV or hologram platform shone through. On the boat's small stern deck there were several empty beer cans, each one bent in the middle. A tattered hoodie hung on the tiller. There was a smear of bird shit dried on one sleeve. Some tangled rope, a wooden pole, a lifebuoy covered with a gelatinous weed. A face was now pressed up against the nearest window. A torch was blinding my eyes. Heavy, even footsteps. A bang of something wooden. The boat began rocking back and forth and a large man in shabby clothes clambered from the cabin, up slippery steps and staggered onto the deck.

"What do you want?" He was loud and slurring. "Are you from the authority? I'm not moving anywhere. I'll tell you now. You want me to move, you're going to have to fucking tow me. You – "

"I'm not interested in moving you anywhere."

"So, what do you want then?"

His torch was blinding.

"I want to talk to you."

"Why?"

"I thought we could work together...."

He snorted. "*Work together.* Well, there's a fucking eumeph ... fucking euphemism. Oh, I get it – this is some kind of softly-softly approach. Is that your game? Butter me up, get me to agree to sign some eviction paper." He was swaggering dangerously on the tiny deck of the stern. An empty beer can crunched under his boot and when the boat rocked he fell against the metal tiller. "Think I was born yesterday...." His voice was now carrying across the marina. The man on the yacht was standing severe-faced, hands on hips, staring our way. Scarman needed to quieten down, get back inside his boat, anything to deflect attention.

"Can we go inside?" I said.

"Like fuck!"

"Look – " there was no alternative but to get him to focus his rage on the thing that would help me, "I want to talk about Ezra Hurst."

"Hurst?" His eyes had narrowed. Once again his torch was directed straight at my face. "What do you know about Hurst?"

I moved closer to him, nearer to the point of the splintered stern. One long jump down and I was on the deck, standing just two feet before him.

"What the...."

My movement was so sudden, he nearly toppled backwards.

"We both have grievances with Sense Surveillance."

"Sense... Too right I have a grievance. Oh yes, I have a grievance all right...." He staggered and threw me a cold stare. "What the hell's it got to do with you? What's your grievance? How do you know about Hurst?"

At the bottom of the steps that led from the deck were open cabin doors. Inside was nothing but disarray. Papers, clothes, gadgets strewn all over the floor. Going inside the cabin had no appeal, but the old man was still watching us and Scarman was too loud.

"I will tell you what I want, but not out here. Inside."

Scarman looked at me suspiciously then shuffled through the doorway. The cabin smelt of mold and rancid food. It was impossible to go in without treading on unwashed clothes, papers, rope, tools, congealed tissues, computer parts, discarded beer cans. There were plates with dried food on every side table and stool. There was no need to venture further than just inside the door.

"So, what's this about?" Scarman said.

His breath was beery and his eyes were red.

"I need to get access to Sense HQ without being detected."

"What? What did you say? Why?" he added, his eyes narrowed in suspicion.

"I need something."

"What?"

"It doesn't matter what." The conversation needed to be twisted back to something that would appeal to Scarman, something that would get his buy in. "I need to get into HQ without being traced by Hurst's department."

Scarman was a long time processing the words, then finally he snorted and said, "And how are you planning on that?"

"With your help." With Scarman brewing up a sneer, I cut in quickly, "He stitched you up, didn't he?"

"Stitched me up...."

He was swaying a little and taking too long to process this suggestion.

"Isn't that what he did?" I said putting an end to the silence.

"Too fucking right." The sudden vehemence in Scarman's voice was intense. "Do you know what he is?" He stared at me with his reddened eyes. "He's a traitor! A traitor! We'd known each other for years. But as soon as he wants promotion he throws me out. Years of friendship snuffed out – just like that! Suddenly, I'm not good enough for him. He doesn't want me around. Just like that fucker outside wants me out." Scarman lunged over to the window and yanked the curtain aside. "Look at him standing there on his yacht. Captain Interference. And the oligarchs over there on their personal Titanic, look at them quaffing their wine, looking down their noses...."

"Wouldn't it embarrass Hurst if I managed to break through Sense's security and show a vulnerability in his systems?"

"What? Break through...fuck Hurst over...."

"You have knowledge, you know the databases there – if you can make this happen, we'll both get something we want."

"Listen, lady," he said quickly. The suspicion was back. "How come you know so much?"

"I *need* to know. You have to believe me – this is a really serious situation for me." Whether it was psychosomatic I didn't know, but I felt a sudden strange twinge in my shin. "This is urgent. I don't have much time. I have to break into HQ. It has to be possible. I mean no system can be one hundred percent secure, can it? It's possible, isn't it? Can't you help?"

"You want to break into HQ undetected." Scarman said the words slowly, robotically – finally, he seemed to be thinking this through. "You think it's easy, that I can just magic a way in out of nothing. I'd need something to go on."

"Like what?"

"Like a password, especially of a senior manager...."

"Like Ezra Hurst?" I said. Scarman broke into a small smile that I couldn't read. Either he liked the idea or even in his drunkenness he thought that I was stupid. "So, you get a password of a senior manager...." I prompted, desperate for him to keep thinking things through.

"...then it might be possible to find out all the User IDs and attach one to a false access card."

"Can't you hack into the system and get this information?"

"You've been reading too many fucking novels. It doesn't work like that. You have to engineer things so that people give you the password without realizing they're being set up. And here's the thing that you haven't factored in, lady – Ezra Hurst is very smart. The chances of him falling for some internet scam, if that's what you're imagining, are zero."

"So, what would catch him off his guard?"

Scarman seemed to drift off thinking of an answer.

"Games used to," he said finally.

"Games?"

"Computer games. Used to be obsessed, know every game, every level." Scarman looked over to a broken game controller on the surface of a cluttered stool. "Any new device – he'd be the first to get it. But since he's got all gung ho for promotion, he's been giving that a miss. Been forgetting all about his mates too…fucking traitor…."

"What else might distract him?"

Scarman jerked his head back towards me.

"Birds, of course." He looked me up and down. "A bird could get him distracted, get a hold of his remote."

"Steal it?"

Scarman was shaking his head. "No, not steal it. Too obvious. He'd know who'd taken it."

"What then?"

He gazed upwards, seemingly thinking the scenario through. "Spray it," he said finally.

"What?"

"Spray it."

He staggered further into the boat, pulled up clothes on benches, rummaged behind heaps of papers, yanked drawers open, scoured through the contents. The boat rocked as he swaggered around the cabin. Cupboard doors were wrenched open. More papers, gadgets, empty packages, spilled onto the floor. He rummaged through a box by the side of the bench and retrieved a small canister. Lumbering back towards me, he knocked over a mug. Brown liquid spilled and stained the corner of a threadbare rug.

"Get hold of Hurst's remote," Scarman said with beery breath. "Spray it with this. Short blast leaves liquid on the surface. Dries into a film, not even visible. Won't even feel the difference if he's distracted."

"How will that help find his password?"

"If he gets an urgent message, something that will lead him to check a record, he'll start tapping in various codes and leave his skin cells on the film. You peel the film off and bring it back to me."

"And you'll read the static charge that's left, compare the rates of deterioration and be able to work out which letters he's pressed and in what order."

Scarman's eyes widened.

"Clever girl." He pushed the canister into my hand, then turned to retrieve an almost empty bottle of rum from the top of a bundle of blankets on the nearest bench. He took a swig and said, "Maybe we'll make a good team, after all."

"You have the device that reads the deterioration rate?"

Glancing over the clutter, he said, "Somewhere in here. Don't know where right now."

"So I should try and get the spray on his mobile? How would I do that?"

"What? I have to work the whole plot out? Nah. That's your part."

He guzzled more rum, then turned his back and shuffled over debris to a room further along the narrowboat. Lights flickered on and there was the sound of a TV.

Part Three

26

IN CUNNINGHAM'S OFFICE, Ezra rewound the footage, stopped the video mid-stream, played one section after another. Where was it? Where was that frame? She'd said something that had jolted his memory.

While Lena was still slumped on the office sofa, her eyes shut, Ezra cut back to an earlier section of footage. The fair-haired woman shown on the screen was standing in front of the mirror listening intently as the Human Resources employee gave information about a vacancy. It was somewhere around here that this Cleo Heaman had said it. He didn't really need the video, just the audio file; it was the words she'd used, or the way she'd said them. Feeling perturbed, he hesitated to press *play*. He was trespassing in Cunningham's office, interfering with Cunningham's things, intruding on his fixation with this woman. Eventually, Ezra reached out for the control and listened again.

'We would recommend anyone interested in applying for the position to

take a look at the kind of work we do. We have a few extra tables too so prospective applicants can show off their own work."

"I'd be very happy to do that. What are the opening times?"

Ezra rewound two seconds and pressed *play* again.

"I'd be very happy to do that...."

It was the same. Not just the words, but all the intonations, the strikingly heavy stress she placed on the first syllable of "very." He'd noticed that in Temple Tavern when Mo had egged Lena on to prove that Ezra might not be the best gamer in the world. "I'd be *very* happy to do that," she'd said, in the same theatrical drawl.

OK. OK. Ezra willed himself to slow down, put a brake on his thoughts. It was the same manner of speaking. But the same person? That would be insane. He edged up to the sofa, where Lena was resting. Standing over her, he scrutinized the dry patch on her closed eyelid and the peculiar ivory lines that had formed along the creases of her otherwise brown skin. OK, that was alarming and strange. It was some kind of weird change that had come on in the few days since he saw her last, but no software would ever get a visual match between Lena and the woman on the screen. So, why was his mind insisting they were the same person? That the one had somehow transformed into the other.

In the bar, she'd mentioned having a medical procedure, though she'd kept quiet on the details. And right from the get-go he'd been baffled by her appearance. But it was still the voice he kept coming back to, that phrase about how *"very* happy" she would be.

The same enthusiasm was in both utterances. Over-enthusiasm. Made sense in this clip about the job; sounding keen with a prospective employer was a smart way to act. But what about in the bar, though? There'd been something too familiar about her response. And, there'd been an outright audacity to the way she'd helped herself to the fries on his plate, same with the way she'd given his mobile a good swish with a tissue before pressing the controls. The screen hadn't even been grubby. What was that all about? Was she up to something with his mobile? He'd been thick not to have queried that before. He'd even received a message from Systems that night warning that there'd been some kind of breach. It was supposed to have been minor, but he'd still tapped in an ID and a password to find that out. Was that something that Lena had engineered starting right from the moment that she'd arrived at the pub? She could have sat anywhere that night. Instead, she'd made a beeline straight for the stool next to him, messed around with his remote. It was clear as day now; she'd strung him along. The question was *why?*

She had a massive grievance with Sense – that was obvious from the way she'd demanded to know, vitriol in her voice, what they all did here in HQ with their screens and their scanners. Stalking on a massive scale – that must have been her assumption. It was a shock for Ezra to find that Cunningham, running a multitude of recordings of the same woman, was guilty of that. Lena's shock (and this assumed that Lena was the same person as the woman on the screen – an assumption he was still having problems with) was discovering that the stalking was more pervasive than she'd expected and had started earlier than she'd imagined. She'd said she needed to take extreme measures. Extreme measures to avoid him. Like changing her appearance? Cosmetic surgery? But if she'd gone to such extreme lengths to slip off Cunningham's radar, wasn't it counterintuitive for her to walk right into his office? What could she want in here?

True there were classified documents: white papers and contracts. That was how Cunningham had persuaded Monica of the need for an Impenetra locking system and insisted on there being no internal surveillance of his office, though it now seemed probable Cunningham had other things he wanted to hide. "Possible Adverse Effects of Resolve Technology," a report with a "sensitive" label glued on its cover, was lying on Cunningham's desk. Monica had exploded over being kept in the dark about the details of that report, so the contents had to be controversial. If Lena had been interested in lifting that particular document, she could easily have slipped it into her bag before Ezra had followed her through the door. But the report was still on the desk and her black cloth bag was scrunched on the floor, looking pretty much empty as far as Ezra could tell.

He knew he should be bringing in security, but what would he end up admitting? That his sense of vigilance in the Tavern had been sidelined by his hots for some skirt? That despite hours drinking with Lena he had no idea who she was or what she was doing in Cunningham's office, looking so sick and distressed by what she'd seen on the screens? Well, that was the state of play – there was no getting around it. He'd just have to say how it was. Ezra pulled his mobile from his pocket ready to call security. He'd deal with each question one at a time and answer what he could.

"Ezra, wait." He swung around and found Lena, eyes open, looking dull-skinned and panic-stricken and pointing at the black cloth bag. "There's medicine in there. Please...please bring it here."

A moment's hesitation, then he cut the call to security, scooped up the bag, wrenched it open to look inside. There was a small oblong box, plastic and white. He flicked the catch open, saw two small syringes. One of the syringes was tagged with a thin sticky white label and the single word *relaxant*.

"Quick," Lena said. Beads of sweat had formed on her upper lip. "Bring them here." She was rolling up her sleeve, then reaching out to take the box. Immediately, she grabbed a syringe, pulled off the plastic cap and stabbed the needle into her arm. Her face became red and contorted and every muscle and sinew grew rigid and big. Repulsed, Ezra stepped back. He snatched only the briefest of glances and willed the hideous contortions to pass. In one convulsion the plastic box fell from her lap and the remaining syringe fell to the floor.

"Do you need this one too?" Ezra demanded. Certain she must, he was already taking the cap off.

"Yes..." another convulsion and a grimace of agony, "... yes. Give it to me."

She snatched the syringe, then stretched out her arm again ready for the prick. Ezra saw a tiny globule of blood that had formed at the point of the last puncture. She was taking aim again, more hesitantly than before. She drew a deep breath, then the needle changed direction. The action was smooth, but fast.

"What the...." Ezra saw the point of the syringe coming towards his bicep. He was too late to catch it. The needle punctured his shirt, sank deep in his arm.

He lunged towards Lena to grab her wrist, but his strength rapidly dissipated.

He heard, "I'm sorry. I'm sorry."

Nothing more.

***

Through waves of pain, Lena willed herself out of Vincent's office to a deserted Saturday morning Strand. She clutched her bag tightly, afraid of losing the figurine it contained. Desperately, she waved at the sole taxi coming along. The driver slowed. She saw the narrowing of his eyes, his look of suspicion. What? He wasn't going to stop? She yelled at the driver who'd chosen to ignore her, then swiveled this way and that looking for other cabs. There were none that she could see. She took deep breaths and forced herself to think.

Embankment – that was the nearest tube. Which lines? District or Circle. Either would do. Change at Monument. Then what line? Northern? No. Central. Central to Liverpool Street. Then walk a couple of minutes to Central Hospital, to Doctor Epstein. God, she hoped that Siobhan was right that he could help. Not just her, but the others back at the clinic like the young kid she'd seen earlier, too weak to even move. Quickly, she turned into Villiers Street, and fumbled through her bag for cash as soon as she saw the station at the bottom of the sloping street. All the cafes and bars were shut. She hurried past empty beer bottles strewn in the gutter, a couple of cigarette butts, a broken food carton.

In the station, she inserted cash into the machine and pushed her way through the barrier, then hurried down to the platform.

A train was already hurtling in, pushing a strong blast of air into the station.

When the doors swished open, she walked into an almost empty carriage and slumped into a seat. The train set off, left the lights of the station, and made a high speed entrance into the blackness of the tunnel. She caught her own reflection in the window opposite. It was patchy, blurred, hazy. Was that a warp in the glass? Or were those creases and dark sections part of her skin.

She felt her face. There was a hideous dryness on her cheeks and cracks on her lips. The injection may finally have helped with the pain, but her appearance was still deteriorating. She needed treatment fast.

The train hurtled into Temple station where two young women stepped on and settled in seats on the opposite side.

She was hit with a wave of memories: Temple, the Tavern, Ezra.

Oh God! She hated what she'd just done to him, but what alternative did she have? He'd been about to call security, would have stopped her getting to Epstein. She couldn't tell him about the clinic, the experiments and Dr. Liu. No one at Sense could be trusted – Siobhan had driven that point home. Lena had to stop Ezra raising alarms. She didn't like what she'd done, but she'd really had no choice.

The train had been stationary for a few minutes now and Lena couldn't help giving a long, loud sigh. Both women opposite were staring. Hard.

There was a crackle over the PA system. Please no, she thought, not a delay, not now.

We apologize for the delay….

One of the women opposite tutted. Lena, jerked her head back against the window in frustration, wanting to yell and scream.

***

Suzanne awoke to the sounds of quiet clicks, though she was too sleepy to immediately place the noise. The electronic clock showed 8:05 in glowing red. A gentle breeze blew through the slit of the open sash window and made the curtain give a little flap. In the corner of the room, Adam was curled in his crib, still fast asleep. She heard more faint clicking. Turning over, she found Brinley lying on his back, tapping into his mobile and reading some text on the screen.

"What's so fascinating?" she said, nuzzling up to him.

"Interesting rumors."

"About what?"

"Resolve Technologies – one of their scientists has blown a whistle. And get this – OMNI's got hold of the report. There's a meeting this afternoon. You could get a really good piece of writing out of this. You have to come."

"What's in the report?"

"Well, all along, Resolve have been insisting that because their implants are as fine as dust they make for a really subtle brain-machine interface. Turns out that having thousands of microscopic chips acting in concert can be overwhelming and lead to unpredictable psychotic changes. Uncontrolled aggression being the main one. That's what Sense has been keeping quiet."

Brinley angled the screen towards Suzanne.

"Ew," Suzanne said, grimacing, "What's that?" She squinted as she tried to make out the image of a wild-eyed ape, bearing its teeth. Part of its head was shaved and there were wires poking out from its temple.

"This is the research that Resolve never talked about. These chimps were all wired up with thousands of dust-like implants…."

"Jesus! What's that?" Suzanne asked, pointing to a plastic penny-sized object attached to a sore on the chimp's shaven head. This was not what she wanted to see first thing on a Saturday morning.

"It's a transceiver. It carries signals between the implants in the chimp's head to an external computer. The Resolve scientists found that increasing the strength of electricity to the implants made the chimps really focus on working out how to get rewards. But their focus was so intense, they became utterly determined and aggressive. Sense wants us to believe the implants are innocuous and passive…" Brinley had now changed the image on the screen to one of a wired-up chimp manically wrenching a metal grille. "… but can you imagine what power they'll have, once they've wormed their way right into our heads."

"Turn it off. It's horrible," Suzanne said, turning her back to Brinley. "It's too early for this."

Would seeing repulsive images trigger some stress hormones in her that would pass onto her unborn baby? It couldn't be good, she was certain about that. She pulled the sheets tightly around her and focused on Adam across the room curled calmly in his crib.

For a minute or so she heard nothing but the faint clicking of Brinley's mobile. Then she felt him press against her body and smooth his palm over her belly. "We publish this stuff," he said, "we could kill off Sense's whole psycho-surveillance shebang. Don't you want to come to the meeting and hear about it?"

"I'll come to the meeting. Just don't show me pictures of vivisected chimps right now."

27

EZRA WAS COLD and uncomfortable on the floor by the sofa in Cunningham's office. A paper cup was crumpled on the carpet. A small plastic box was open and empty. Something was glinting: the needle of a syringe. Now he remembered the needle coming towards him. What the fuck had she stuck into him? How could she poison him like that? He felt heavy trying to pull himself up and twist around to see where she was.

She'd gone. The figurine on Cunningham's desk had gone.

He picked both syringes up from the floor, found their caps, covered the tips. There were still globules of liquid inside their plastic containers. He pocketed both, resolving to get them checked out. Apart from a little sluggishness, he basically felt all right.

A small sharp bleeping caught his attention. Ezra found his mobile under the sofa.

A call from Sayle.

"What the hell happened?"

"She's gone."

"Gone where?"

But Ezra was too distracted by another beep on the line to

answer the question. A new message was coming through. The words *Car Break In* flashed in red across his screen.

"Gone where?" Sayle asked again.

"Don't know," Ezra said. "Just trace her. I'll get back to you."

Quickly, he cut the call to Sayle to focus on the break in notice. Someone was breaking into his car? Right here in the Sense HQ car park? He dug into his pockets, expecting his keys to be missing, that Lena must have taken them. When his finger ran against the jagged edge of the car key he was surprised.

Quickly Ezra accessed the local security network for camera recordings. Bay Q125. He could see the image of his car in the space where he'd left it. But then he noticed the car roll backwards at a snail's pace, then forwards again.

"What the...?"

He peered at the windows, but since they were tinted he couldn't see through.   Ezra sped out of Cunningham's office and took the lift to the basement level where he shoved the heavy car park door open so hard it swung back violently into its frame. He could hear the purr of an engine, *his* engine in the distance. He was close now, watching the Viper slide slowly in and out of its parking space. Ezra strode over, grabbed the handle on the driver's side, wrenched the door open.

"Ez," said John.

"Jesus! What are you doing?"

"Thought I'd check things over while I was here. Seems OK. You must be driving calmer at last...."

"What are you doing here?"

"Get in," said John. Ezra stared back at him. "Get in. Can't talk to you with the door open. Shut the door. You keep it open, then any parabolic microphone will pick up what I say." Ezra slammed the driver's door shut, strode round to the passenger side. How the hell had John got through security? Why hadn't he been stopped? Ezra threw quick glances around the car park. There was no one about. Nobody walking around. No security staff or police. Ezra quickly opened the passenger door and slid into the seat.

"How did you get in?"

"Don't worry about it," John said, while Ezra was twisting

around, checking for guards that might be coming. "We should be OK in here. I've had a mini-bot go over the car," John gestured to the back seat where a small cuboid device lay, "check for bugs, put blocks on if it finds any. Should be safe to talk."

"Talk about what?" Ezra said.

"About this." John pulled out the rolled up picture of Gavin Dixon from his jacket pocket. "After you left, I had a look at it." John smoothed the picture on his lap with the palm of his hand.

"What about it?"

"OK," John said, slowly, "This is a still from the St. Pancras footage…" Ezra glanced at the picture. "…well, here's the thing," John said. "I *did* use con software to insert plausible stories when the real recordings got scrambled, but I didn't do this." John was pointing at the image of Gavin Dixon.

"What do you mean you didn't do it? Your name's on the footage. You admitted you did it before."

"Not this," John insisted, nodding towards the picture in front of him.

Reaching into his trouser pocket, Ezra shuffled in the passenger seat and pulled out his mobile. He tapped in a series of passwords until he was finally able to access the stored footage of Gavin meandering about St. Pancras station. He retrieved the file's metadata. *Data reconciliation – John Durrant.* "So, whose name is that?" Ezra asked, not bothering to disguise the sarcasm as he pointed at the white text on the screen.

"It's mine. And it's true that most of this footage is my responsibility, but not this rendition of Gavin Dixon. I don't know who did this." John paused, before adding, "I'm surprised, Ez, surprised you even thought I'd do something as shambolic as this."

"Why?"

"Well, I hadn't looked at this picture of the boy properly. And neither, it seems, had you."

"Listen John, just make your point. What is it I'm supposed to have seen that shows you didn't fix the data on Dixon?"

"This," John said, "pointing towards Gavin Dixon's belt. "Look at the glare on the buckle, and here on his watch…" Ezra looked, but saw nothing remarkable. "…now compare these sections to other sections with metallic surfaces – the gold chain on this Chinese woman, the barriers here at the gates. No glare there." Ezra studied the image. John was right. It was only with Gavin, his buckle, his watch, that there was any kind of glare. "When I used the con software to reconstruct the station footage I used a low-glare medium. Same medium I use at home for the nudes. Gets you a nice luminescence. Nice and gentle. You pretty much need to be an art specialist to know about this kind of stuff, how to get the best renditions of metallic surfaces. I understand this very well. The person who spliced in this stuff on Gavin, however, does not."

"But your name's on it. And you've admitted some fabrication…."

"…which," John interrupted, "must be a handy cover for whoever is responsible for this."

Ezra stared and squinted at the picture, held it at different angles and compared it to the image on his mobile. Finally he nodded. The difference John had pointed out was definitely there.

Ezra remembered nights they'd go back to John's after a heavy session at the Tavern, to sit about playing music, John with a beer, Ezra on scotch. John at some point would start editing his nudes, altering their metallic skin tones. To him, Ezra conceded, the difference was probably glaring.

"So, let me get this straight," he said. "The station surveillance footage gets scrambled by Feist. Then you, instead of unscrambling it, use continuity software to fill in for the corrupt data…."

"…which in all probability," John interrupted, "told Dixon's story like it actually was."

"But…" Ezra closed his eyes trying to get his head around the twist.

"But," John cut in, "someone didn't like the sequence of events I put in, the true sequence."

"The *probably* true sequence."

"Ok, the *probably* true sequence. In any case, the point is, someone didn't like it. So they edited it. Except their editing skills," John said, angling the paper to catch the light from the car park wall-lamp, pointing to the image of Dixon's belt buckle, "are very poor."

"So what *was* there? What *did* the con software put in?"

"Of course, that information has been erased from Sense's database, presumably by someone who wanted a smooth, coherent trajectory for this boy. Not a sequence that would raise questions. What do you know about this boy? Why would anyone worry that questions about him might get raised?"

"What *do* I know about him?" Ezra said, quietly, slumping back onto the car's headrest. Maybe he was still in a daze from whatever shit Lena had jabbed into him, but it seemed like eons ago that Suzanne had first come into his office to talk about Gavin. In the dimness of the car park, Ezra didn't have a clue why anyone would be interested in altering the St. Pancras footage. In addition to John's tweaking and Feist's corruption he was now supposed to be contemplating some different version of events. His head felt too fuzzy for this kind of mental gymnastics, but somehow he felt compelled to pull whatever pieces he could into place.

The Dixon boy's tendency to wear the same jacket and jeans all the time had made it easy to fix in spliced footage into a reconstructed data stream. Only someone who knew the minute details of his physical appearance, someone very close to him, could spot the differences. Suzanne Dixon had said it was her son who'd spotted the hole. Ezra could see that. Little kids always picked up on those kinds of things. They were always fascinated by irregularities. Why? Why? Why? That's all Ezra had got from his own little niece, at least until the encephalitis. If Suzanne's kid, Adam, was anything like as inquisitive he could see how the hole would be jarring to him. Jarring until it had been explained. The problem was that the original footage had come from six months previously, when Gavin had lived in some dive with the OMNI hippies before the protest at Hyde Park, before they'd all found themselves proper places to live.

Ezra stayed slumped in his seat, eyes shut.

"You look like shit," John said. "What's the matter with you?"

An image of the syringe coming towards him formed in Ezra's mind.

"Don't ask," he said, forcing his eyes open again. He tried refocusing on Gavin, but saw nothing there but a dead end. "If everything's been corrupted and erased, we'll never know what was there, will we?"

"Now that's where you're wrong," John said, shifting in his seat to reach inside the pocket of his jeans. He pulled out a disk. "When I was trying to work out how to smooth things out, I made my own copies of Con's reconstruction." Theatrically, he held the disk between index finger and thumb. "We can see what story the software put in on here."

"Jesus Christ! Why didn't you say so earlier?" It was so fucking irritating the way John dragged everything out. "Put the disk in," Ezra said, with an aggressive nod towards the laptop.

Career-wise, Ezra thought, watching John help himself to Sense's files, this could be catastrophic. He was supposed to have smartened his act up since John had left, made himself look a serious candidate for promotion to directors' level. How was John sifting through files in the car park going to look if it got out?

A sound, half snort, half laugh came from his side. John was smirking and looking across the mostly empty car park in the direction of Sayle's grey car.

"What's so funny?"

"Dexter Sayle – I suppose he's in there, isn't he? At his desk, working all hours, supposedly maintaining security. Nine o'clock on a Saturday morning. Can't keep away, can he? But what good does it do?" John snorted. "I mean, here I am, walked straight in, all cloaked."

"Yeah, I have questions about that myself."

"Don't worry about it. I'm not going to blow your move up to exec level."

From the passenger seat he looked at John who was quickly manipulating keys and scrolling through reams of code. How *had* John even got on the premises? Somehow he must have got past Internal Security, Personnel, even his own Anomalies section and its security wall headed by Sayle. He'd have to have used a whole series of security markers belonging to a known employee. There was no other way. Same explanation for breaking into the anomalies database. If this got out…. Ezra shut his eyes.

"I've got it," John said. He shifted his info-remote towards

Ezra, held it over the gear stick.

But Ezra was tired of seeing images of Gavin Dixon veering haphazardly around St. Pancras.

"I've seen this," he said, impatiently.

"This bit, yes. But not from here. Look. This is what *I* came up with using Con to reconstruct the data after the Feist corruption. See, it differs radically from this footage of Dixon getting on the train that was spliced in." Ezra watched the sequence on the screen. It showed a disheveled-looking Dixon in his torn green jacket meandering around the station. He was checking the indicators, pacing about the concourse, fidgeting with his ticket, glancing to the gates, then back to the indicators. He headed towards a barrier at one of the gates, then suddenly faltered. Seemed like something at the information desk had caught his eye. He was frozen now. Staring. But not at the assistant behind the desk. Ezra couldn't tell what had made him so wide-eyed and panic-stricken.

"Is there another camera angle?" he said.

"Nah. This is the best there is."

Ezra scrutinized the images on the screen, trying to find the cause of Gavin's panic, the reason why he was veering backwards from the information desk. Gavin was shaking his head manically as if he were trying to shake something disgusting away from his face. He collided with an elderly woman who frantically clutched onto her walker to stop herself toppling.

"What's his problem? What did he see?"

"Dunno," John said. There was nothing at the information desk other than folded timetables and glossy brochures. "He looks wrecked. Is he off his head or something?"

"Possibly." Suzanne had described in vivid detail how out of hand he'd got in her flat. She'd said he did drugs. Ezra leaned over his gear stick, to adjust the angle of the screen for a better view. John put the machine up on the dashboard. "Wait! What about this woman? Replay the video. Look, this one. Short. Asian. See how she looked like she was approaching him? Then here – she backs off when he starts getting weird. She's pulled out a phone and she's still following him. Who is she? Get the metadata on her."

John placed gridlines around the image of the woman's face and tapped database commands trying to get a biometric match across a range of her features. The message *Shadow Status* flashed across the screen.

"What?" said Ezra. "She's with one of the intelligence agencies?"

"Well, her data's protected – that's as much as we know."

"Fast forward," said Ezra. "Does she meet up with Gavin or not?"

John pressed controls on the keypad. Gavin, in the later footage, appeared to have calmed down. He'd stopped shaking his head and was walking more smoothly, but still away from the platforms.

He was heading towards the Betjeman Arms, picking his way past outdoor seating, pushing his way through the door of the bar. The short woman followed and disappeared inside too.

"What next?" said Ezra.

"Well, obviously we don't have data from inside the bar."

"What about when he comes out? Where does he go? What happens to her?"

John fast forwarded through the footage, searching for the points that either left the pub.

"Nothing," he said, after several moments of manipulating controls and scrutinizing the images.

"What – they don't leave?" said Ezra.

"There's no data on them leaving. Maybe that's not such a surprise. She's got a shadow status and he's acting irrationally half the time. We already know the Con reconstructions are having a hard time putting coherent trajectories for him together. Looks like Con just couldn't cope at this point."

John had pulled the laptop towards him and was engrossed with tapping in a new series of commands.

"What are you doing now?

"Just wondering something."

"Wondering what?" Ezra snapped, irritated once more by John's habit of continually keeping him in suspense.

"I'm…won…der…ing, wait, don't interrupt me. I need to

think about how to set up this query." John sat frozen for a few seconds with an expression of intense concentration etched on his face. Then his fingers flicked across the keyboard until finally he said, "There – " he angled the screen towards Ezra, where in small yellow typeface ten or so names were listed on the screen. "I just did a search on whether there were any more cases of this glitch that shows up with metallic graphics, where someone's spliced in footage with a high glare medium…"

"And there are all these?" Ezra said, his eyes running down the list. *Dixon, Gavin* was the first person named. Then Eady, Farmer, Harrington. Getting on for halfway down was a name that captured all his attention: *Heaman, Cleo.* "What's the location for the footage on this woman."

John uploaded the clip of Cleo Heaman exiting a solid detached house and walking towards a taxi. "Hampstead," he said. "Hang on – this house…this is Vincent Cunningham's house. Hey, this is interesting…" John was accessing current Sense data "…Cunningham's running a massive search for this person. Has been for several days now, weeks even…."

Temporarily John's screen went blank.

"What happened?" Ezra asked.

A new message appeared on the screen. *Network access denied. Code Ano1.*

"Well, well, well," John said, relaxing back in the car seat. "It's Sayle. He's onto me. He's realized someone's hacked into the anomalies system. He'll probably block me…yes…shit – he's blocked me." John relaxed his head against the headrest. "Took his time about that, eh?"

Thinking Sayle might already be registering an emergency security breach, Ezra quickly got out of the car saying, "I'll speak to him. You wait there. What are you doing?" Ezra added, seeing John suddenly pick up his info-remote.

"I think I know a way to unblock myself."

"Leave it," Ezra hissed. He looked around the gloom of the car park to make sure he hadn't been heard speaking to John. Nobody was there.

***

Ezra strode across the concrete floor, took the stairs to the Anomalies Floor and burst into Sayle's workspace. Sayle was already on his mobile making a call.

"Security breach. Someone's hacking in," Sayle said to Ezra.

Ezra took the mobile from him, saying "It's John Durrant."

"Durrant? Are you serious? What's he doing here? Does he think I'm not going to pick up on this? This is actually a serious criminal offense."

"Listen," Ezra said, suddenly thinking of a way to calm him down, "remember Lena, I need your help finding her." Sayle brightened. Ezra reckoned he could make him brighten some more. "John's been helping out on this, but hasn't got anywhere. Take over, will you? I'll handle John's breach, OK."

"And what exactly is the latest on Lena?" Sayle said, immediately taking the bait. "How come she got away? What happened earlier?"

Strangely, Ezra was reluctant to go over the incident with the syringe. He was still incensed that Lena had spiked him, but he found himself wanting to get to her motives. Given Cunningham's stalking, Ezra could see that she'd consider Sense employees a threat. But there seemed to be more to it than that. She'd said "others were in danger" and had been convinced that Ezra's calling security was going to make the situation more dire.

Ezra limited the information he gave to Sayle to Cunningham's massive data trawl for details about a woman called Cleo Heaman, which was, so he conjectured, a previous ID for Lena.

"You're sure about that, are you?"

"That's what I think."

"And," Sayle said after a long moment of silence, "you want me to check on Cunningham's personal relationship with this woman?"

"Lena is an anomaly in our system. Your job is to smooth anomalies out." Though Sayle nodded to this, he looked far from convinced. Ezra continued, "It looks like there's a connection with Cunningham. Maybe I'm wrong. For Sense's sake, I hope I am. But that's what I need you to determine."

Sayle continued nodding slowly, taking it all in. Eventually, he asked for more details about the supposed Lena-Cleo identity, then swiveled in his chair to face his keyboard.

With Sayle occupied, Ezra headed across the Anomalies Floor to the quiet of his own office. Slowly, he paced back and forth across the carpet, thinking things through. His orderly Anomalies Unit was in disarray: John had trespassed into HQ, hacked into various systems and even picked his way into Ezra's car, where he was probably still sitting in the dark of the basement car park trying to save his pride by attempting to dismantle the block Sayle had put on him. Ezra could handle these two. Give them something to get engrossed in and they'd forget their squabbles. That was easy.

But what was the story with Gavin and Lena and the other eight or so people who'd shown up on John's list of individuals with reconstructed histories? One version of events had shown Gavin getting onto a train bound for Prague and another had shown him just disappearing into a pub, never to come out. And both those versions were contrived: one reconstructed by John who'd try to put things together after the Feist corruption and the other all spliced by some unknown person. And then there was Cunningham? What was his game? He'd spent hours stalking Cleo Heaman and now he was obsessively trying to find her. Jesus Christ! Ezra hardly knew where to start.

"Ez," Sayle shouted, from across the Anomalies floor. Ezra strode over to the doorway of his entrance, saw Sayle, looking excited, beckoning him over. "This Lena," he said, as Ezra approached. A couple of tracers looked up from their workstations.

"Keep it down, Sayle." Ezra shunted Sayle over to the desk where a wall panel screened them from the teams of tracers outside.

"OK, OK," Sayle said, reducing his voice to a whisper. "But this Lena or whoever she is…."

"What about her?" Ezra headed, with Sayle, towards the desk terminal.

"One of the search engines Cunningham's running – it's come up with a hit. He knows where she is."

"He can't do. She's physically different."

"What?"

"Take it from me: he's looking for her under her old ID. I've seen the searches he's running in his office."

"It's the gesture monitor," Sayle said, after a long silence. "It's registering a hit."

"The gesture monitor?" Ezra thought it through. Even with new a new appearance, Lena was sure to retain some of the gestures of her old self. Earlier Ezra himself had picked up on a particular way of speaking that had led him to posit the identity. So why wouldn't Cunningham make the same kind of inference? What gesture had he picked up on? Did Lena have any identifying mannerisms? Hair flicking, nail biting – he couldn't remember her performing any of these.

"This is what Cunningham's looking at," Sayle said, cutting into Ezra's memories. He enlarged a picture of the ivory-skinned woman onto the screen. Ezra still found it hard to accept that this Cleo was Lena. Absolutely nothing was similar about their facial features. He'd never come across cosmetic surgery as radical as this before. "It's this movement," Sayle said, pointing to the woman's hand and how it was smoothing down the fabric of a black dress, which lay upon her thighs.

Instantly, Ezra remembered Lena in the bar. There'd been the smoothing of skirt, those slow strokes along the length of her thigh, just like this ivory-skinned woman's gesture.

"And this," Sayle said, "is the woman he's comparing her to." He clicked a button on his workstation and the screen was filled with a live image of Lena Mae Cho.

"Shit!" Ezra said, shocked that Cunningham had traced her. There was a dullness to her skin, and, squinting for a better view, he detected dry patches. But the hideous rawness he'd seen in Cunningham's office had pretty much cleared away.

"Is that Lena?"

Ezra nodded, despite being dumbfounded.

"Where is she?" Ezra asked, looking at the backdrop shown on the screen. "On a tube? A tube to where?"

"Looks like a Circle Line carriage," Sayle said. "Yes," he said, tapping the metadata table showing the location as Temple Station.

"Train's not moving though."

Ezra remained silent as Sayle split the screen to show Lena Mae Cho as she was now next to footage of how she looked before. Both depicted women were making the same gesture: slow strokes along the thigh. The movements were identical, even when Sayle hit the slow motion control.

"And this is what Cunningham's discovered?" Ezra asked. "So, he's been accessing real-time surveillance footage and knows what train she's on."

"Yep," Sayle said. "He keeps flicking from one image to the other, enlarging the images, trying different angles. See how many times he's accessed this data. Looks like he's having a hard time believing that it's really the same person, even though that's what his search results are telling him."

Ezra could understand that; he was having a hard time accepting this himself.

"Seems like Cunningham's been following this up for the last half hour or so," Sayle said. "Look at this video: he's just arrived at Bank Station. He's put in an apprehension request with Transport Police."

"What?"

"He'd already alerted the police before he got to the station. See the transit reports," Sayle said, pointing to a separate window in the corner of the screen. "These delays on the Circle Line – that was Cunningham registering a security threat from an imposter."

"That's a total abuse of his power. Transit Control should have questioned that. How's he getting away with this?"

"Doesn't he have connections to Transit Security?" Sayle said.

That was right. That's where Cunningham had worked before he joined Sense. He'd run the whole surveillance operation when he was there.

"So, what's he doing?" Ezra said, "Using his old connections to intercept her at Bank?"

Sayle nodded slowly.

"Looks like it, doesn't it?"

Ezra silently conceded it did.

28

AT LEAST THE train was moving now. The delay at Temple Station had seemed interminable with the two women opposite filling the carriage with a series of increasingly loud tuts and sighs. They would be late for a choral concert, Lena had heard, as well as *London Transport was such a shambles. Our underground used to be the envy of the world. Everything's gone to pot. The country's gone to rack and ruin.* The tension of the train delay, the monotonic whinging, the fear that time was running out to help the lifeless fifteen-year-old back at the clinic – all of this clogged Lena's mind, forming an intense pressure at the front of her head. The women fell silent, thank God, when the train began to move, so slowly at first that Lena could feel the thud of the wheels over every join in the track. She willed the train to build up speed and at last it clattered through the tunnel. Just six more stops to Liverpool Street station, to Central Hospital. Lena squeezed the bag on her lap and felt the outline of the figurine through the cotton cloth. What if Dr. Epstein wasn't there? It was Saturday and early. He might not be on duty. She'd have to insist that he be immediately called, somehow convey the importance of this to whatever staff were there.

There was a sound of a violently rushing wind; a Transport Police Officer came lurching through the door that connected Lena's carriage to the next. The door slammed shut and the windblast was muted.

Average height, young, neat black beard, the officer grasped at a handhold as the train hurtled noisily along the track. He scanned the carriage, looking this way and that. Routine check? It was possible, Lena thought – he scanned the two women opposite. One was now dozing with her head lolling forward with every judder of the train. But when his eyes fell on Lena, he stared so hard she was instantly panicked. Had she set off some alarm at the Reassignment clinic? Was she now being traced? If so, by whom? Monica? That wouldn't make sense. Monica, seeing the experimentation at the clinic collapse, wouldn't be calling in regular Transport Police Officers to find her. No, that didn't square, not given the covert way she'd been transported about before. Unmarked cars, undercover taxis. Monica did things on the sly, not out in the open like this.

The young policeman, still staring Lena's way, seemed unsure about approaching her. He began speaking into a mouthpiece, then listened carefully, it seemed, to a long reply. Desperate to know what was being said, Lena strained to hear. But the juddering of the train and screeching of the wheels obscured all words. He began walking towards her. His eyes were focused on something on her lap. There was the bag, but that's not what he seemed to be looking at. He seemed more interested in her hands. She kept them still now – it was only his staring that made her aware she'd been rubbing her thigh.

"I need to ask you some questions," he said, now towering above her.

Momentarily, she froze. Finally, she managed to say, "Why? Questions about what?"

"Some questions on behalf of Sense Surveillance."

Sense? Lena was convinced it wasn't Monica's style to have her pulled up in such a public way. It was possible that Ezra might have put a trace on her, especially since she'd jabbed the syringe into his arm. She was sure she could explain things to Ezra. Maybe she should have done so already. He seemed sympathetic, but it was so difficult to know who to trust. If Ezra was the one who was after her now, that would be the best possible scenario because the only other Sense person who'd be interested in finding her was Vincent. And she could barely countenance that.

But what if it were true? Her heart began racing. Had Vincent somehow seen through her identity change and somehow traced her? Oh God, no! She wasn't going to let herself be taken to him, not after everything she'd been through. She felt a sudden surge in her stomach and a quickening of her heartbeat. She willed herself to stay cool and focused and consider the facts.

She'd changed her identity. Vincent couldn't have found her. There must have been some confusion.

"I think you've got the wrong person," she said, struggling to sound calm.

The policeman spoke into his mouthpiece again, then fell silent presumably to listen to the response. When he turned to her again, he said, "Lena Mae Cho?"

Lena couldn't speak.

"You have to come with me. I have a warrant."

"Why? What is this warrant for?"

"Anomaly investigation. Your ID is unstable and needs to be verified."

"My ID will become stable," Lena said, trying to quickly think of a way to get out of this situation, "when I receive medical treatment." She could see from the way the officer was scrutinizing her face that it was clear she needed some kind of treatment.

"Medical assistance can be arranged, I'm sure." He turned away to talk into his mobile. "I have Ms. Cho. I am bringing her in now."

"Please," she said. "It's essential that I have treatment, you can see that can't you?"

The guard spoke into his mouthpiece again. He was repeating everything she'd told him. Who was he talking to? Straight to Vincent?

"If you tell us what we need, I'm sure we can arrange for

medical services to treat you."

No. She wasn't telling them anything more. She'd already said too much. Why had she mentioned getting treatment? Her plan to get help, so surreal and complex that she hardly dared reflect on it, was the only plan she had.

"Well, you can stay tight-lipped if you want. But now you must come with me."

"To where?"

"To Bank station," he said. Lena tried craning around the official to see the tube map opposite, but a jolt of the train threw him even closer to completely block her view. "A Sense official would like to speak to you."

"Who?"

"A Vincent Cunningham."

Coldness swept over her body.

"You don't understand," Lena said. She was imploring with her eyes. "I can't come with you. I have to...."

"Like I said before, I'm sure that all the medical help you need can very quickly be arranged...."

Suddenly Lena stood and yelled right into the policeman's face, "I *cannot* come with you." The man clasped her shoulder. She tried wrenching herself out of his grip, but couldn't break free. "It's impossible. Can't you understand?" The hold on her shoulder tightened, a sharp searing pain gripped her. She jerked her foot straight into the policeman's crotch. He yelped, then angrily shoved her down into a free seat by the central doors.

Incensed now, the policeman was calling for assistance on his mobile. Lena looked to the women opposite. They stared back at her as the policeman pulled her up again and dragged her towards the door, drawing their legs in to make room. Another noisy blast of wind as a second man in uniform lunged from the next carriage and through the connecting door. Sandwiched between these two, it was pointless to struggle. Best bet was to wait until they got to the next station when the doors would open up. Glancing at the tube map, making quick mental calculations, Lena reasoned that there were three stops prior to the Bank-Monument interchange, where Vincent was waiting. Three stops where the doors before her would swish open, and through which she could conceivably run. She'd made this kind of escape at the clinic, against all the odds. She just needed to think it through. As if he'd read her mind, the new policeman pulled a remote control from his pocket and pressed a button. A red light flashed above the nearest door of the carriage. The word *Doors Locked* appeared. Standing squarely on either side of her, both policeman gripped her biceps so hard, she winced. Blackfriars, Mansion House, Cannon Street – the train slowed and drew to a stop at each station. Each time the door nearest Lena stayed shut and the men's hold on her remained so vice-like that she was incapable of any movement at all.

When the train hurtled into Monument station, Lena saw more security guards among crowds on the platform. She found herself being forced off the train and shunted along the Circle line platform towards an exit that one of the guards was indicating. The platform was crowded, but seeing her flanked by security staff, most people stepped aside to make room. She felt like flotsam being sucked by a strong current with people steering themselves away from her. The policeman and guards were speaking in jargon either to each other or into their mobiles. Their talk was of containment, coordinates and codes. There was a constant bleeping of calls against a backdrop of speaker announcements about train delays, line closures, and information about alternative routes. Posters along the tunnel announced the *Temporary Northern Line Closure*. She tried pulling away from the men holding her arms when she heard all the carriage doors close automatically in sync. "I needed to be on that train," she yelled, hearing the hum and swish of the train as it built up speed. She needed to get on another, get to Liverpool Street. She tried wrenching herself free, but the guards' grip tightened and she was shoved towards a passageway that was deserted and decked with *no entry* signs.

"*Where* are you taking me?" she yelled again, utterly bewildered that she was being pulled into a construction area in a deserted passage that led to the closed Northern Line.

"Sense are here."

"Here?" Lena said, glancing at the huge rolls of cable and sheets of steel strewn along the passageway. At the end of the passage way she saw the light blue and white tiles with crown motifs lining a tunnel wall. *Northbound Northern Line* – she was forced onto the platform. Giant reels of cable and the train tunnel entrance were to her left. Dozens of huge metal brackets were piled against the tunnel wall on her right side.

The guard clasped her arm. "We understand you need urgent medical treatment. I'm sure Mr. Cunningham will understand too."

"He mustn't know about that," Lena hissed. The guard seemed confused.

"What's happening?" came a deep male voice.

It was Vincent's.

Shit – he was coming towards her.

"You have her?" he said. "You're sure it's her?"

She pressed herself against the wall, behind the reel of lining material, hiding from his view.

There was no way she could explain the urgent need for treatment to him. He'd delay and twist things so that her needs would become something he could barter with. She hadn't been through everything at Reassignment – the treatment, the escape from the clinic – to land right back at square one. Heart pounding, she pulled away from the one guard left holding her when his grip momentarily loosened. He grabbed at her bicep. The action incensed her. She clenched her fist and put all the force she could muster into a punch aimed straight for his eye.

"Bitch!"

The word reverberated through the tunnel.

Holding his face with one hand, the guard lunged towards her. Knuckles throbbing in pain, she dodged him and ran back the way she came to the main passageway.

More yells followed her through the tunnel and then footsteps, pelting over the concrete floor. She took several turnings, then stood panting in one archway, looking at a moving escalator. Construction workers at the bottom were huddled around a suited man holding several papers.

Lena glanced around, desperate to get her bearings. She saw a passageway leading back to the Northbound Northern Line. Gambling that Vincent wouldn't think she'd go back to the line she'd just left, she turned to head there. But immediately she saw him ahead. He was holding a mobile in one hand, barking instructions into the mouthpiece.

"Get personnel down to the construction area," he said. "I need people on the ground keeping an eye on things; the cameras aren't working down there on the platform."

He retrieved a slim remote device from his pocket. Lena recognized it as a trajector, a tool for tagging people's movements. Her mind was racing, thinking through what to do. If she threw an object far from her person, into the view of a camera, then it might get picked up by the scanners, serve as a distraction and give her a chance to run to the platform. The cameras weren't working back there. She'd just heard Vincent say that. But what could she throw? Out here there was nothing on the ground and she had nothing on her person except the bag containing her wallet and the figurine. Quickly, she yanked out the wallet, pulled out cash and stuffed some notes in her pocket. Would the wallet, if she threw it, get picked up by the scanners? She had no idea. But there was no other choice. Heart still thudding, she willed herself to step out of the shadows of the passageway and toss the wallet onto the moving escalator. The risks were enormous: Vincent might see her, so might the construction workers. But when she peeked around the passageway entrance again, she saw that Vincent was engrossed with his trajector and tapping its controls. She had time to act. That thought was enough to propel her forwards. Within a split second she focused on the escalator, leaned back for maximum thrust and threw the wallet across the station hallway. She heard the tinny clatter of the attached key ring hitting a metal surface as she pelted back to the Northbound line. Somewhere behind her there was a crescendo of shouts. Back on the platform now, she saw the tunnel entrance to her left, giant reels of cable to her right. Frozen, she listened for sounds, heard voices far back in the main crossway. There was a movement on the track. Mouse. Running over the concrete sleeper. Then another scurrying first over one rail, then along the electric line. Vincent's voice, bellowing, "Check back on the Northern Line."

Footsteps.

Someone was approaching. Lena looked into the black chasm of the tunnel face. The footsteps drew nearer. The mouse on the track was still sitting on the electric line. The power had to be off. She stared down at the track, at the scuttling mice. Hearing voices now she raced forward, jumped down onto the line and merged with the shadows of the tunnel.

29

SAYLE, STARING AT a screen in his workstation, looking first puzzled, then intrigued, said, "Sudden projectile."

"What?" Ezra asked.

"One of the station security alarms has picked up an unidentified projectile." Sayle wheeled his chair over to make way for Ezra. "There's supposed to be something here." He pointed to the image of the top of the escalator, to the metal teeth under which each upcoming step disappeared, "but there's nothing there."

Ezra studied the screen, nudged Sayle's hands off the keyboard and hit the control for enlarging the image. Pieces of litter were caught at the top of the escalator; paper shreds and dust clumps, too big to pass between the metal teeth of the escalator's landing plate. Ezra enlarged some more, fixing on a small square object. It was a heavily pixilated image now, but unmistakably the image of a red wallet.

"That's the cause of our hit," Ezra said. "Question is how did it get there?"

"Dropped it, you think?"

"She can't have dropped it at the *top* of the escalators. It's a construction site there, out of bounds." Lena was somewhere down on the lower level, as was Cunningham, who was busy looking for her. "What about the sequence showing us how the wallet gets there? Do we have that footage?"

Sayle ran a search, retrieved a data stream with a time five minutes earlier. No wallet on the escalator's landing plate. They stared at the footage and the timer counting seconds at the bottom of the screen. At 12.10.04 a small red object sailed through the air on an arcing trajectory, landing halfway up the escalator. The parabolic microphones had picked up the muffled voices of construction workers. The words *OK, let's test it* were followed by the conveyer starting suddenly with a clank and a judder. Ezra peered at the image of the wallet being transported upwards on a metal step until it reached the top where it became trapped.

"Somehow it was thrown," Sayle said.

"*She* threw it," Ezra guessed, "to send Cunningham on a wild goose chase, buy herself some time. She must want him to think she's at the top of the escalator." Ezra fell silent. "I just can't work it out," he said. "She's going to all these lengths to avoid him. So, what was she doing in his office?"

Sayle leaned back in his seat. His belly was straining against the buttons of his shirt.

"Problem is," he said, "that decoy with the wallet has made it more difficult for us to find her too."

"Why can't we use Con?"

"Con software?"

"Yeah. John put things together after the Feist corruption. Why can't we fill in the details for Lena? The system might have problems matching Lena to any records in the database, but we can still tag her as a new entity to trace."

"Yes," Sayle agreed, "it's theoretically possible."

"And we can factor in certain details that will help predict her future trajectories."

"What details?"

"That Cunningham is in the station, somewhere down on the platforms where the cameras are out of action. And she will do anything to avoid running into him."

"Is that a certainty?"

Ezra thought about it.

"She's not going to move towards Cunningham," Ezra said to Sayle. "That's the last thing she's going to do. You can feed that into the calculations as a certainty."

"OK, then," Sayle positioned himself more squarely over his keyboard, "so let's see what possibilities that gives us." He sat there, hands poised, remaining motionless for several minutes.

"Come on, Sayle. I need this information fast."

"I'm thinking."

Sayle started slowly writing various tags and symbols across the screen, faltered, erased, began again. Slowly.

Disguising his impatience, Ezra concentrated on the other screens around Sayle. They showed the uniformed men, who'd been called to the escalator, beginning to disperse. Cunningham was consulting with security guards, then dispatching them to more passageways. His forehead looked clammy. He was barking orders. Ezra tuned into the parabolic microphone to hear. Cunningham was yelling about locations he wanted covered and giving station grid references.

"OK," Sayle said, suddenly. "This might work." He began typing furiously, then waited for a results table to appear.

"What have we got?"

"With the meager input we started with – a whole host of scenarios."

Ezra scanned the data table. The list of possible trajectories that Lena might have taken filled the entire screen. There were percentage scores by each possibility on the list.

"Yes," Sayle said, when Ezra pointed at the 67% figure at the top of the list. "That's the most likely story."

"Which is what?"

"Let's see," Sayle said, while pressing the *run* icon.

Ezra saw an image of Lena standing on a station platform, then jumping down to the track. Leaning over Sayle, he pressed the coordinates and location details. Bank Station. Northern Line. Northbound tunnel.

"That's the most likely scenario?" Ezra said, disbelievingly.

"That she's gone *into* the tunnel?"

"Like I said, if you start with unstable input, you shouldn't be surprised if the output is weird."

"But is it true?"

"Well, as you know, Con is the best reconstruction software we have, and that's Con's story."

"And what about Cunningham? Where does Con put him?"

Sayle fed in prior footage showing him in a section of the Bank-Monument interchange with functioning surveillance equipment.

"Now feed in all his recent trajectories at the station and an overriding determination to find Lena," Ezra said.

Sayle hesitated for a long while, scribbling notes, then writing and rewriting several lines of code on the screen.

"Here," he said finally.

The computer image showed Cunningham standing on the platform of the Northbound Northern Line, staring into a pitch-black tunnel, then moving back along the platform looking into the exit passageways, then, again, returning to the tunnel mouth.

OK, Ezra told himself, she's in the tunnel and moving away from Cunningham who's standing just outside wondering whether she's in there. But if she'd do anything to avoid him, she wouldn't come out. Somehow Ezra knew that; he'd seen how adamant she'd been.

Ezra stared at the screen. Con software showed her still moving. The same software showed Cunningham heading to the main exit tunnel, then directing police to look for her. Now Ezra could check the verisimilitude of Con; since the real-time surveillance cameras were working in that part of the station, they should show exactly the same scene.

He switched a control to relay live data from the working cameras. Cunningham was, as Con predicted, in the main exit passageway, directing transport police to look for Lena. And if Con was right about Cunningham, it might be right about Lena – she might *really* be in the tunnel. He sat motionless thinking about the danger involved, about the high voltage in the underground's power line. She wouldn't be able to see where she was going, for

Christ's sake. Several screens showed an array of officers scouring the station, all presumably looking for her. Cunningham was shown as a grave-faced solitary figure pacing through the station. When he paced out of range of the working cameras, Con filled in a story of where he was: platform three. His backdrop was the arch of the Northern Line tunnel and the blackness inside. On the screen, Cunningham was turning towards the tunnel, looking into it now.

"He's considering it," Ezra said quietly, "considering the possibility that she's in there."

"Well, that will be easy for him if she is in there," Sayle said.

"Why?"

"She won't be able to get anywhere. Look," Sayle pulled up transport security data. "Here's the schedule of station closures. The environmental health people are working on the tunnel section by section. They're testing how pathogens get carried in the ventilation systems. And, for each section that's tested, the ends are carefully sealed. Moorgate is the next station along the line, but it's closed."

"What? So Lena's going to find she has nowhere to go?"

"That's right. So the only way out is here," said Sayle, pointing to the screen showing the tunnel face that Cunningham was staring into.

"So how far along the tunnel could she get?"

"All the way to Moorgate. She could get right into the station. Onto the concourse even, but there's nowhere for her to go once she gets there. The whole station is sealed. Every exit out onto the street, every passageway leading to connecting lines." Sayle tapped into transport security records and pulled up a calendar outlining the Northern Line construction schedule. "You see," he said, pointing at the calendar, "the construction people have made some preliminary investigations about new materials, new linings for the tunnels, new concrete compounds – they've been trying those out. But what they've been doing for the last few weeks is carefully sealing sections bit by bit. So Moorgate's all sealed up now." Sayle switched the screen back to the original image. "And the only way out," he said, tapping his finger on the glass monitor, "is back here at Bank, where Cunningham's waiting."

***

Gripping an arched iron girder in the tunnel, Lena watched Vincent pacing on the platform. She was too afraid to move. Too risky to have her feet scuffing over the dust of the track; any movement might attract his attention. So, she stood still in the tunnel, beads of sweat forming on her forehead, mind swirling with action plans: advance further into the tunnel, away from Vincent, who, if he saw her there, was bound to start the sweet-talking; or continue standing there just as she was, petrified against the tunnel wall until he left the platform. She could then find station security staff, police…. But the guards were already taking orders from Vincent, as was the policeman who'd marched her off the Circle Line train and delivered her to the platform where Vincent was waiting. No, somehow he'd got security to take instructions from him. Her heart thudded harder with the realization that she was completely on her own.

Footsteps scuffed over the platform. A security guard, female, young with blonde cropped hair.

"Central, Northern and Circle Lines – no trace," she said.

"Shit." Vincent replied.

Panicked by the prominent vein she could make out on his temple and the single twitch in one of his eyes, Lena pressed herself even harder against the tunnel wall.

"We have guards covering every exit," the woman said, "and we're combing the main forecourt…."

"This whole construction area," Vincent said, pacing away from the tunnel entrance, past deserted passageways that led away from the platform, "you've checked everywhere?"

"Nearly."

"Nearly's not good enough," he said harshly.

There was desperation in his voice. And another noticeable eye twitch.

His gaze was sweeping along the platform again, towards the entrance where Lena stood. She was pressing so hard against the concentric wall, she felt thick cables against her neck and an iron bolt pressing into her shoulder.

"Are there lights for the tunnel?" Vincent asked, from out on the platform.

She felt a sudden lurch of her insides. Oh God, it's over, she thought.

"Must be," the female guard said, "probably the builders outside will know where the control is."

"Get the builders," Vincent commanded.

"All right, but I'm not sure how much use the lights will be. There's only a few feet before the tunnel curves...."

"Just get the builders," Vincent shouted. "Where's the foreman?"

"I'm here," came the response. His eyes were narrowed with suspicion. "What do you want from me?" he said, coldly. "This is a construction site. There are dangerous materials here."

"I need the tunnel checked."

The man was hesitant, seemingly wanting to object, but eventually he said, "Well, everyone has to be kitted up." He pointed at a warning sign saying *hard hat area* and another saying *Protective clothing required – it's the law!*

"Then get the protective clothing," Vincent snapped. "Get it now!"

His shout was so loud it propelled Lena to move. With the guard's feet scuffing over the concrete floor and Vincent back on his mobile again, Lena moved further into the tunnel, feeling the arch of an iron girder and a series of thick, rubber-coated cables pinned to the tunnel wall. In the dark, her hearing and touch were on hyper alert. The further she went in, the more horribly black it became. She ran her finger over the cables, moved gingerly, trying not to make any noise as she moved. Edging forward slowly, using her toes in her trainers as sensors, she felt for obstacles that might block her way or trip her. The more steps she took, the more she got a sense of the ground: staying close to the tunnel wall, she could avoid stumbling on the rail or the sleepers or any of the bolts or brackets holding the track in position. Edging along at an excruciating rate, she felt as if she were going nowhere, groping along slowly, breathing rapidly, too rapidly to feel like she was in any kind of control.

Hearing murmurs behind her coming from the platform, she was surprised to find, when she turned to look back, that she'd moved so far from Vincent that discerning his words was difficult. The sounds of her own panic, her thudding heart, her frantic breathing, were the main things she could hear.

Still pacing the platform, Vincent was talking into his mobile, seemingly unaware, so far, of her whereabouts. But if she could still see Vincent in the station lights, then she wasn't yet in the curve of the tunnel that would wipe her completely from his view. If he were to switch on the tunnel lights, she'd definitely be seen. Panicked, she scrambled along the track even faster. Pressing her palm against the tunnel's side, she used the thickest cable running the length of the tunnel wall, as her guide, and forced herself to walk faster. Almost immediately she stumbled on something hard, a metal bracket, a dislodged bolt, she didn't know what. She yelped as she fell, then glanced back to check whether Vincent had heard. He still had his back to her. Lena picked herself up, moved forwards fast. There was nothing but pitch black ahead, and now behind her, several voices. The construction workers. Soon they'd put the lights on. But when she turned to check next time, the curve of the tunnel had taken the platform side of the station from view. When she scrambled a few more steps along the tunnel, she found, once she'd looked back to check, that the entire station was out of sight.

Lights flashed on. Dimly glowing bulbs in rectangular plastic casing.

Dusty grey arching walls, thick cables pinned to the tunnel lining, a series of arched iron girders, stretching forwards infinitely, shining steel rails, concrete sleepers on thickly greased brackets.

Still audible, just, were voices behind her. Frozen, she listened, trying to discern whether they were getting nearer. They weren't. Instead they faded into silence. If Vincent was combing the Bank-Monument station complex to find her, she'd be unable to go back. Her mind was on overdrive, working out a plan of action. She couldn't stay here. Casting around the tunnel, she was disgusted by the filth. The cables pinned to the side of the tunnel wall held inch-high layers of dust. Looking at her arms, Lena saw that a large sore by her wrist was choked with dirt. She winced, strangely feeling pain only now that she'd looked at the wound, now that she'd stopped picking her way along the tunnel. But she couldn't flag now. Had to go on. To where, though? What was the next station on from here? Moorgate? Yes, she was sure it was Moorgate. Probably not too far; most of the city stations were packed close together. But maybe the station was closed? Was the whole line down? When she'd been frog marched off the Circle Line towards Vincent, there'd been a boom of a PA system, giving details of station closures and alternative means of transport, but she'd been so panicked she hadn't taken any of that in. Focusing on the thick silver rails now, she tried to calculate how long it would take to get to Moorgate. Her eyes followed the line of one of the rails. What was that object?

Jesus!

A rat. Dead, flattened, blackened – it was lying next to a metal bracket. The sight spurred her on. She moved forwards quickly, scanning the tunnel frantically, for any other rodents. A small black shape, in the distance scurried silently away. Had there been mice running past her before? Rats? The thought horrified her – so much that she scoured the ground, the walls, every nook until she became paralyzed just thinking through what might have run around her. Just move fast, she told herself. Don't think about what's here. Concentrate on what you need to do. Just keep going away from Vincent, get to the end of this tunnel and get to Central Hospital. Any moment someone back on the platform at Bank could flick a switch and make that light disappear. The thought propelled her forwards.

Feet either side of the left rail, she paced her steps to avoid tripping on the concrete sleepers, their bolts or brackets. Adrenalin drove her on, that and the fear of being stuck in darkness.

A rumbling sound. Getting louder.

Lena froze.

A train coming towards her? How could that be? The line was closed. And there'd been a mouse running along the central electric rail. She'd seen it in the station. The power was off before. Why was it back on now? If the line had closed down for engineering works, why would there be a train? Was it an engine necessary for construction work? To shunt the equipment and materials?

Her temples throbbing, she imagined an engine laden with heavy machinery, great rolls of cables like the ones she'd seen on the platform. Jesus Christ! The construction crew would *have* to use an engine to transport those. Was that what was happening now?

The rumbling was more distinct now, close enough to make the tunnel's wall reverberate. Lena swiveled her head, looking all around the track for somewhere to escape. Pressing herself against the side, onto the cables – would that leave enough space for a train to pass without hitting her? She didn't know, couldn't think; desperate for air; it took all her powers of concentration to bring her breathing under control.

Trembling now, she focused on each facet of the rumble, the speed it denoted, its distance from her, until finally it dawned that though the reverberation could be felt, the noise seemed muffled. She felt no dust being blown towards her. And now, yes she was sure she was right, the sound was passing somewhere overhead – another tunnel crossing over the one she was in. She remained frozen. Listening until finally the noise faded.

Desperate to get out, she scrambled onwards, through a section of tunnel with a pristine white lining. She fixed her eyes to the track, on a seemingly infinite number of concrete sleepers. She'd fallen into a rhythm, was advancing at a decent pace when she caught site of a brown, irregular object in the distance. A large paintbrush, bristles congealed with some thick compound from which came a faintly nauseating stench of ammonia. One tunnel sidelight flickered, immediately setting her on a check of other lights. Were they all about to go? She checked the lights ahead, swiveled and glanced at the ones behind. Each continued, thank God, with their steady yellow glow.

Further along, Lena could see large tubs by the tunnel wall. *High performance coating*, read one of the labels. Presumably the tubs contained the compound she'd smelled and seen congealed on the paintbrush earlier. Brush marks were visible on the tunnel wall – vertical strokes along the joint between each sheet of lining. And the nauseating smell was stronger here, unbearable, as if the compound had only just been laid. She covered her nose with her palm to cut out the stench. A large iron plate lay on the track. It was slightly curved as if it were a grate or cover to fit an opening, a vent perhaps, in the tunnel wall.

On the track – a filthy mask. The acrid smell was overwhelming now, she immediately stooped to pick it up. The smell was so horrid, she didn't think twice about wearing it.

She lurched forwards, desperate to get out of the tunnel. Desperate to reach ground level. Desperate to see the sky, feel a wind, to breathe in cool, fresh air.

***

Con software represented Lena as a red dot moving through the underground tunnel towards Moorgate. Sayle had repeated the query several times now. Each time a trajectory showing her avoiding Cunningham by entering the northbound tunnel came out as the scenario with the highest probability.

"So what do you want to do now?" Sayle asked.

"We have to block Cunningham's access to all surveillance data."

Sayle pulled a soda can from his bottom drawer, ripped off the ring. His face was clammy. His hair was greasy. He'd been here all night and it showed. He was leaning back in his swivel chair taking a long sugary swig.

"Why are you siding with Lena?" he said, before giving his mouth a big wipe with the back of his hand. "I mean, who the hell is she?"

"Good questions."

Ezra could see where Sayle was coming from.

"I mean, she broke in here," Sayle said. "Came waltzing in to Sense HQ with some kind of shadow status. But you're more worried about Cunningham."

"He's abusing his power. She thinks that's what we all do. She doesn't trust any of us."

"If you ask me, she's a risk," Sayle insisted. "I think we should call security right now. But you're concocting excuses for her. Why? Rivalry? You against Cunningham?"

"No." But the question had thrown Ezra and the answer had come out in a small voice.

"What then?"

Ezra pointed at the screen showing guards all suited up in protective gear, plotting to follow Lena into the tunnel.

"Cunningham's getting guards on her for personal reasons."

"She's a liability."

"You might be right. And if that were the reason Cunningham's tracing her, and he'd gone through appropriate channels, convened a meeting about the situation, collaborated on a plan, then fine. In that case I'd have no qualms. But this is personal. He's fixated on her, has been for well over a year. He's accessing our department's records to set up a trap. I say we should take away his access rights now."

"And what about her? What are we doing with the fact that she was an intruder here?"

"One thing at a time. Let's deal with Cunningham first."

"Why?"

"Just do it," Ezra snapped.

He couldn't exactly explain his thinking. It was just gut instinct.

Tentatively, Sayle twiddled with controls, before saying, "He's senior staff. We should get Monica's buy-in on this."

Monica would be incisive and thirsty for facts, whereas gut feelings and suppositions were the only things Ezra had. He could hardly interrupt her jaunt to the Yorkshire Moors to dish up that kind of vagueness. Instinct had got him interested in Lena right from the off and instinct was operating now. His rational side was screaming the same questions that Sayle raised. More questions, given that only a couple of hours before she'd assaulted him with some kind of sedative. Yes, she was dangerous, but something in him was rooting for her. It was inexplicable. Persuading Sayle was going to be difficult; this needed insistence. He was just going to have to pull rank. When Sayle brought up a telephone keypad on his screen and started dialing Monica's number, Ezra jabbed the

End Call icon and said, "No. Forget Monica. Cut Cunningham's access to our databases. Do it. Now."

30

LENA WAS BREATHING heavily, and felt sweaty and hot as she stumbled forwards along the track.

Get out of the tunnel – the amalgam of perverse images of rats and mice and grease and dust crystallized into that single thought, a thought that propelled her past newly installed concrete lining and tubs of *High Performance Concrete Coating*, then finally out of the tunnel face into a deserted Moorgate station.

The lights were dim and the only motion Lena detected was that of a swiveling security camera. Its lens aimed straight towards her and its little red power light was blinking. What if Vincent was able to see her and trace her, give the order that she be brought to him again? She scrambled up from the track onto the platform, determined to leave the Northern Line, and merge with the crowds of the station.

She scrambled past a neatly stacked pile of concrete sleepers, through an exit leading into the main body of the station. Silence all around. Just her own hurried footsteps and panting.

No crowds.

No one.

The passageways leading to the southbound Northern line were all sealed with wooden panels. Both the escalators were frozen.

Builders – they must be somewhere around. Glancing to the motionless escalators, she headed to the ticketing area up on street level. She gripped the rubber belt to help pull herself up. Her legs felt heavy now, and she was hot and exhausted. She stopped. Gulped in deep breaths of air. Felt aches in her legs and her feet. Keep going, she told herself. Get out. Looking at the next metal step, she forced herself to move up.

Siobhan had warned her that the stabilizers would only last so long. She had to keep going before all her paresthesia returned to paralyze her.

"Come on!" she yelled.

Angry with herself for flagging, she took the rest of the escalator determinedly and made it, sweating, to the top.

Heavy tools, cables, a ladder – all positioned by the escalator's landing plate as if they were waiting for someone to switch the escalator on and transport them down. Why wasn't anyone here? Why were there lights on an underground line that wasn't in use? Were the builders out on a break, due to come back sometime soon?

Natural light streamed through high windows flanking either side of a heavy, closed, station doorway.

The inspector's hut, the main concourse, the ticketing office – all deserted. The entrance, she confirmed, shaking it, was definitely sealed. In the empty ticketing office she saw an analog clock on the wall. Five past nine.

A bank of phones to the side. Who could she talk to if she made a call? Emergency services to come and get her out? No. The police had escorted her off the Circle Line straight to Vincent. They'd help him, not her.

Head throbbing, she stared at the heavy steel barriers sealing the entrance. Her entire body ached and her eyes were watery from pain and the sheer effort of climbing the escalator. Despite the perspiration on her forehead, the drip of sweat forming on her temple, she began shivering, had to force her teeth to stop chattering. She needed to keep moving, keep doing things. What though? *Come on! Think!* But her thinking was distracted by a coldness on her forehead, a coldness that seemed to have an external source. She tuned into the feeling – the feeling of air mingling with perspiration.

Air? From where? It must have been coming from a decent opening for her to sense it so strongly. It felt fresh too, unlike the stuffiness of the tunnels. Turning her head slowly, focusing on the angle at which the breeze hit her damp brow, she determined its direction. It was coming from the far right of the concourse. There were men's voices; builders coming through a side entrance. One was hanging back, calling out to someone outside. Lena edged closer, pressing herself against the glass casing of a ticket inspection booth. The pressure of the hard glass against her arm felt intense and was tinged with a nauseating heat. She willed herself to concentrate on the open entrance, to focus on getting out of the station. The builders, with their backs towards her, were strolling casually over to a motionless escalator ahead. Lena scurried to the entrance, quickly peered outside. There were two large white vans parked right up on the pavement, one with its side door open where a grey haired construction worker was leaning in, cigarette hanging from his lip. He was pulling on thick plastic cables. They fell in coils around his feet. No one else was around. She slipped out of the entrance, ducked under hazard tape and hurried along the street.

***

Hunched over his keyboard, Sayle quickly typed code. Ezra was standing behind him, looking over his shoulder, checking the array of dialog boxes and windows open on the screen.

"Cunningham's still accessing data, Sayle. Why's it taking you so long to block him?"

The growing list of queries with the user ID *Cunningham* was making Ezra nervous. It was there in writing that Cunningham was still trying to find a real-time match for anyone with the same appearance as Lena just as she'd looked on the Circle Line just an hour or so earlier.

"Shit! Look – there's an anomaly registering at the entrance of Moorgate. Someone with shadow status. It's got to be her. She must have made it all the way through the tunnel." Ezra accessed footage of the station, saw images of a blocked off pavement, of construction workers, a couple of white vans, cables. There was a glitch in the footage, then the word *Anomaly*. "If Cunningham picks up on this…."

"He won't," Sayle said, flamboyantly hitting the return button on his keyboard. "I've blocked him."

Under the list of queries showing on the screen were now the words *UserId Cunningham – Access Denied.*

"He's going to go apeshit," Sayle said.

Ezra shrugged. It was Lena that concerned him. Flummoxed him. She'd come out at Moorgate Station. Where would she go next? And how would it connect to her being in HQ earlier and taking that small statue, the one thing that had gone from Cunningham's office? That was a mystery. At least it seemed like progress to Ezra to simply acknowledge as much. *Mysteries are interesting, but distracting.* When Ezra was at university specializing in biometric detection his tutor frequently dealt that line, before following up with: *Always start with what you know.*

What Ezra knew was that Lena was sick. Sick people seek treatment and probably won't travel too far to get it. What were the nearest hospitals to her current location? National Neurology, London Bridge. She'd had that strange discoloration in her eyes, so maybe Moorfields was a possibility too. He could ring around, see if she'd been admitted in any of these. There was also Central and Royal London and the Hospital for Infectious Diseases….

There was a beeping from Ezra's pocket.

"Here we go," Sayle said with a knowing grin. Ezra pulled out his mobile and read the name of the caller. "Don't tell me – Cunningham?"

Nodding, Ezra turned the mobile off and stuffed it back in his pocket. Cunningham was out of the picture. Ezra would keep him that way.

***

Moorgate was quiet. Bleak rectangular buildings were empty of office workers. There were no buses and only a few cars. Only one person: a newspaper seller in a kiosk along the street who was gawping at her dirty clothes. The magazines hanging on the roof and sides of his stall made a multicolored frame for his face. He looked her up and down and eventually called over, "You OK?" He was inspecting her face, scrutinizing her skin. "You want me to ring 999?"

"No!" Lena responded so loudly it stopped the man from pulling his mobile from his pocket. "No 999." She didn't want anything official being recorded anywhere. She glanced up at the streetlights. Shit. Cameras. Maybe she'd been picked up already.

"Central Hospital – do you know which way it is?"

The man came out of his stall, grabbing a water bottle, twisting off his cap and passing it to Lena. Gratefully, she glugged the water. Some spilled down the sides of her chin and dripped onto her chest. When she finished gulping, she found the man pointing into the distance and saying, "You could cut through Finsbury Circus over there." She saw the trees of the park space, reasoned they'd provide good cover. "Central's just a couple of minutes on the other side. Near Liverpool Street."

Lena gulped some more water, said thanks to the man and clutching her cloth bag tightly hurried off as fast as she could. She was praying that Vincent would still be looking for her at Bank Station, that she'd have time to get the DNA sample to Dr. Epstein. For five minutes or so she kept a good pace, keeping close to trees as much as she could. But as she exited Finsbury Circus and dodged traffic to cross the street she felt horribly hot and began straining to breathe.

She came to a standstill near an approaching young couple, who silenced their chatter to look her over, who slowed but didn't stop. There wasn't any oxygen – it made no difference how fast and hard she snatched at the air. She grew hotter still and her forehead became sweaty. She felt terribly tired and sore.

The hospital was visible now in the distance. It was just a couple of hundred yards away — a huge tower made of turquoise glass panes, big rectangles set in steel. She forced herself to breathe as slowly as possible and focused on reaching that tower. It was a legitimate medical facility. Not like the secretive reassignment clinic to which she had been delivered in a soundproofed car with windows that displayed nothing but her own reflection. This tower was a beacon for everyone to see — the passengers who were crammed into double deckers, the motorcyclists, taxi drivers, all hurtling along the street. This hospital was out in the open and signposted with a big letter H and an arrow showing the way to a car park.

She forced herself towards the entrance where the words "Accident & Emergency" were displayed in bold, bright red. She wanted Dr. Epstein in the Gene Therapy Institute, but if she could just make it to A&E that would be something. At least it was the right hospital and he could probably be found. That thought spurred her towards the entrance.

Once inside, she fixated on the reception desk and willed her way towards it until she felt a sudden pressure around her bicep and found a nurse holding her arm. She heard, "Let's do paperwork later. Come with me. Let's sit you down."

She was asked what her name was and what had been going on and how long she'd been feeling sick and whether she had any pain. But she found she couldn't breathe and talk at the same time. A curtain was swished around her. A flurry of medics appeared and disappeared. A thermometer was inserted into her mouth. A blood pressure cuff constricted her arm. She heard "tachycardia," "systemic inflammatory response," "anti-virals," "skin lesions." Too weak to listen, she turned her back to the people, the equipment and commotion. She couldn't help but shut her eyes.

***

She was in a bed with a polka dot curtain around her. She'd never seen this curtain before.

Or slept in this bed. Where was this bed?

What was this tube sticking into her arm? Strange how it didn't feel uncomfortable.

Polka dot curtain – *had* she seen this before?

***

She awoke again and her skin felt sore, but the lesions were less ragged than before. Light footsteps and a child's high voice coming from the other side of a polka dot curtain. Now an adult voice: "Stop running. This is a hospital. People are sick in here."

That's right – this was a hospital. A proper hospital.

A thickset doctor with dark brown skin and tight curls that were grey poked his head through the slit in the curtains.

"Ah, good. You're awake again. I'm Doctor Epstein. I introduced myself before. I'm not sure you remember."

"Again? I woke up before?"

"A couple of times, in fact, which we were all very relieved about because you were a very sick lady when you turned up in A&E." The doctor pulled up a stool and sat by her side. "The first time you woke up you were quite insistent that you needed to speak to me, which is very interesting because I am probably the only person in London, and certainly the only person in this hospital who could have any insight into your condition. We still need to find out what has happened to you...."

"It's not just me," Lena blurted, "There are others too, all the others who've been experimented on...."

"OK, now wait a minute."

"They're in danger. They need help."

"Where are these others?"

"I don't know. I can't answer that."

"Who can answer?" said Dr. Epstein.

Lena exhaled loudly. How was she supposed to explain this? She was devoid of salient facts.

"Well, why don't we just take one thing at a time. Before we talk about these others you mention, let's see if we can clarify some things about you. First off, we have no record of who you are. There was no ID on you and when we scanned your fingerprint and iris, we found no match. So my first question to you is: what is your name?"

"That's not so easy," Lena said slowly. "I was given the name Lena Mae Cho."

Dr. Epstein turned to his computer and tapped "Lena May Cho."

"M.A.E," Lena said.

The doctor corrected the spelling and submitted the name. The message "No medical records" appeared. Pressing more keys, Dr. Epstein ran another search, this time for birth records. Another message appeared: "No data." The doctor turned to Lena and said, "You were given this name by whom?"

She suddenly felt panicked and remained tightlipped. How was she going to explain things about the reassignment clinic and the covert practice of creating new identities? And exactly how much should she reveal anyway? If she blew the whistle and revealed what she knew about the illegal experimentation there, would Dr. Epstein be duty bound to report it? Would the details she gave be made available to the surveillance people? The very people she believed were involved?

"What about relatives?" the doctor asked. "You came in by yourself. Is there anyone we should call, anyone…."

"No! No one. And if anyone comes looking for me, you must stop them coming in. No visitors. No one at all."

Dr. Epstein looked at her uncertainly, but didn't question her.

She began scanning the furniture around her bed, searching for her clothes, "If you were looking through my things looking for my ID, you must have found the Ost piece."

"The Ost piece?"

"The little figurine made of bone – it was in my bag. I had it with me. It is the only sample of my original DNA. Where…?"

"You mean this," said Dr. Epstein, pulling open a drawer by Lena's bed and taking out the ivory statuette.

"Yes," said Lena, reaching out to take the piece. She stared at her old profile, trying to work out the best way of asking for what she wanted. "No matter what your records say or don't say about my name and my birth – the way I am now is not the way that I was. You must know that I have been genetically modified and the treatment is unstable." When the doctor nodded, Lena tapped the figurine. "Well, this is how I used to be and this piece is made of bone cells that were extracted from me before I had any treatment. I need to know that reversal is possible – that eventually I can get back to my old self."

After a long silence, Dr. Epstein said, "My first concern for you is that your current condition is stabilized. Now I don't know why this has been done, but you've been injected with several viral vectors containing different gene modifiers and your body has launched a massive immune response to that. You're still very sick and I have to tell you that you are not fighting this viral infection by yourself." He pointed to the IV stand and the clear fluid by her side. "This is what is keeping you stable. We need to work out how you can stay well by yourself. That comes before any…" Dr. Epstein hesitated, "…reversal."

"But it is possible, isn't it?"

"Like I said, let's take one thing at a time."

"Isn't a sample of old DNA all that's needed?"

"Look…."

"No!" Lena said, her voice rising. "Don't shut me down. " She held the figurine before him. "Reversal is possible from the DNA in this piece. Tell me – yes or no."

Dr. Epstein gently bit his lip, then said, "It is not sufficient just to know what your previous genome sequence was. We'd also need a roadmap of how to get there."

"But this is your area of expertise. I thought you had promising results."

"We've made some inroads, but…look, let's concentrate on making you stable first, OK? Before we discuss anything else, can we agree that that's the priority?"

He'd used the word *but*. He'd changed the subject. Feeling all hope dissipating, she turned away from him. She was tired, so, so tired of treatments and procedures and doctors and hospitals. There was a pulling of bedclothes and she felt a wire being placed across her.

"Here's an alarm," Dr. Epstein said, putting a small plastic unit by her hand. "If you feel suddenly feverish, which you might, ring this buzzer and someone will come."

Lena stared at the button on the buzzer, but didn't respond. She didn't want to talk any more.

She wanted to be alone.

There was the sound of a chair shunting backwards, a ruffle of papers being gathered.

"You should rest," said Dr. Epstein. "We can talk again later."

A quiet woman's voice came from far across the room, probably from the entrance.

"Someone's called and asked about a Lena Mae Cho." Lena's eyes shot open. Her heartbeat quickened. "Is that the patient in here?"

Lena grabbed the doctor's hand. "Is it Vincent? He can't come here. No one can see me. No one at all."

"It's OK. Calm down. Our security is strong. This Vincent – we can make sure he doesn't cross the main entrance. What's his surname?"

"Cunningham." She was shocked by how immediately she'd divulged his whole name, cut through all their history to cast him so decisively as an enemy. By now he must know what drastic changes she'd made to her appearance. He must have worked that out to track her down in the tube station. And with his access to surveillance imagery, he'd probably seen how she was deteriorating. Yet, he'd still wanted to find her. What was she to make of that?

"What's the matter, Lena?"

Treachery – it was a choice. "If not to him, then to me."

"What did you say?" Getting no response, Dr. Epstein turned to the woman at the door and said. "You can get the name and number of the person who's calling, but you must tell them *no visitors*. Give no information. Confidentiality is key."

Footsteps shuffled away. There was a closing door, then silence.

31

STALLED ON THE Dixon case, barred from visiting Lena at Central Hospital, Ezra paced his office. Politely but firmly, the information assistant had told him Lena wanted no visitors – *none whatsoever*. Even personally helping out with the hospital's formal request to set up a CCTV intercept order on Vincent Cunningham hadn't changed things; he still found he was banned from seeing Lena himself.

He sat heavily in his chair, uncertain what steps to take next. All these screens surrounding him, the scanners, the surveillance systems – all useless to him right now. A smudge on one of his monitors annoyed him. He grabbed a screen cleaner from his drawer, sprayed the acrid fluid and wiped the smear away. The smell was noxious and powerful enough to stir memories; memories of the training room where he'd taken the biometric tests.

Harrington.

The name came to him suddenly. When John had compiled the list of spliced footage instances, that name was associated with one of them. Preoccupied with Gavin and Lena, he hadn't registered that fact before. The initial was "D," he was sure. Deborah

Harrington? In the tests he'd taken when he first started working at Sense, Alex Fenton had pulled up footage of a woman with the same name and had asked him a series of questions. Was it just a coincidence that the name had popped up for John this morning? Quickly, Ezra tapped into his computer to run a search. The episode with the examiner all that time ago had been so bizarre that Ezra found many of Deborah Harrington's details were easy to pull from his memory: she was thirty-four, lived somewhere in Walthamstow. She had one kid, wasn't married, as far as he could recall. The footage he'd been tested on had had a Camden location. Ezra had no difficulty retrieving the relevant clip. Quickly, he scanned the footage, fast-forwarding, rewinding, not exactly sure what he was looking for. It was all coming back: her brunette hair, the Hynek travel bag. Wait, what was that? Now, that was something he hadn't noticed in the test: the big brass buckle in the middle of the bag, how it caught the sun and gave off an unnatural glare. Was that what John had seen earlier?

It was possible that John might still be sitting in his car, engrossed with dismantling the block that Sayle had put on him. He might even be looking for more cases of splicing. Ezra hurried towards the Anomalies Department exit, calling out to Sayle as he went, "Take the block off John."

"What?" Sayle said, his mouth full of hamburger.

"Just do it."

Ezra hurried down to basement level and across the concrete floor of the car park towards his Viper. He was unable see through the car's darkened windows whether anyone was inside. Wrenching the door open, he found that John had gone. He checked his watch: just after noon. He pulled out his mobile and dialed John.

"Where are you?"

"Tavern. Fancy a pint?" Predictable that John would be there. And no, the last thing he wanted was a beer. The drugs Lena had injected into him had largely worn off, but he didn't want to risk triggering another mental slump. "So," John said, before a sequence of glugging and swallowing noises, "I see you're not number-one gamester any more. I see your score...."

"Never mind my score. Just wait outside."

Ezra thrust the car into reverse, screeched out of Sense car park and sped around the corner to Temple Tavern.

Pint glass in hand, cigarette on lip, John was waiting by the curb. Ezra rolled down the window.

"Drink up. Get in."

"What's so urgent?" John said, leaving his pint glass balanced on the narrow ledge of the pub's windowsill. He slid into the passenger seat, hoisting his shoulder bag full of disks and gadgets onto his lap.

"Remember that whole business with Alex Fenton, from a couple of years back?"

John sat expressionless for a moment, then a light bulb flashed on: "Oh, the test where he got weird?"

"Yeah. The woman he was making me trace in the test was called Deborah Harrington."

"Harrington? Wait a minute – wasn't that name...?" John was already unzipping his shoulder bag to pull out his computer.

"Yeah, it was on the list you came up with, people with new histories spliced into their records."

"Hah! Looks like I'm not blocked anymore. I can get into the data now. Let's see...." John shuffled in the passenger seat to set the angle of the screen for optimal viewing, then began typing in commands. "Harrington. Yes. She's on the list."

"10th October, 2057. Bus stop on Camden High Street. Get the data of her in that location. It looked to me like the footage had the same kind of problem with rendering metallic surfaces."

John found the video file and fast-forwarded through sections.

"Yes, it does." John confirmed, scrutinizing the imagery on the screen. "This is definitely spliced. Fenton made you look at this?" Ezra nodded. "Why? Did he know it was spliced?"

"That's what I'm wondering." Ezra pulled out his remote, looked for public contact details for Fenton. Wasn't surprised to find there were none. "Be good to ask him directly, but looks like he's been keeping under the radar."

John glanced to the clock in the car. Ezra copied the action, saw the glowing red numerals: 12:25.

"Saturday lunchtime," John said. "Race time. Pretty safe bet he'll be at the bookies. Think a lot of Sense people were surprised to find stalking was his thing, but one thing I knew about was his gambling. Talked about races with him a couple of times. Phew," John said, shaking his head, "he was hardcore."

"So?"

"I'll put money on him being in one of the bookmakers. He lives somewhere in Kennington. Should be easy enough to find if you drive over there."

For John this was clearly all high adventure, a riddle that needed delving into immediately, full speed, no reflection. Ezra felt more circumspect, unsure of what he was getting into.

"Let me see the list again," Ezra said. Having been slow to contextualize Harrington, he now considered each name carefully. Dixon, Eady, Farmer, Harrington, Heaman, Patel, Patterson, Stevens, Tusker, Volks. Most still had no resonance, and the three he could say something about – Dixon, Harrington, Heaman – were all known to Ezra via unrelated contexts. There was no connection between Gavin Dixon and the two women that Ezra could see.

The one commonality was that Deborah Harrington and Cleo Heaman seemed both to be victims of stalking.

"So, why did Fenton make me watch this footage of Deborah Harrington?" Ezra had asked the question quietly, posing it to himself.

"Well, you can ask him, can't you? Just hit the road, Westminster Bridge…" he pointed westwards to the pale green bridge with Big Ben and parliament in the background "…just ten minutes or so to Kennington. What is it? What are you waiting for? Come on. Let's go!"

***

There were signs in large blue typeface on each wall of Rackers Bookmakers. *Greyhounds, Horses, Lottery, Pools.* Underneath each sign were large sheets of paper outlining runners, riders, courses, odds, breeding information, handicap ratings, draw times, race times.

This was the third betting shop Ezra had called in; they all looked much the same. His car was outside with John still sitting in the passenger seat. Just before they'd stopped at Rackers, John had been typing some commands into his machine and had pulled his usual trick of discovering something interesting in the data without letting on exactly what. Irritated, Ezra had left him running his queries and typing feverishly in the car.

Inside Rackers he stood amid betting slips that had been scrunched and tossed to the floor. An elderly woman with a hunched back sat in front of a betting machine, her eyes fixated on the screen. One man, twenty-something, sat at a circular table in the middle of the room. A newspaper was spread out on the surface with the man leaning over it to read fixture details in fine print. A chunky, bored looking woman in a striped uniform sat behind a plastic screen at the cash register. Four men, different complexions, all thickset and middle-aged stood with their backs to the main entrance. Their eyes were all fixed to one television screen that showed jockeys in bright yellows and turquoise and checkers, crouching over their runners' necks and brandishing whips. Mud flew up as the horses stampeded around the course. Ezra edged towards the TV. Heard an increasingly animated and loud narration: ...*and coming from the outside is Cougar. Pistachio in hot pursuit. Madagascar, unbelievable, all the way back in seventh now. Fahrenheit's going to take the lead. Half a furlong to go....* The crowds on the television were cheering more loudly. One of the thickset men turned and tossed his betting slip on the floor. His face was ruddy. He wore big black glasses, which Ezra immediately remembered. Fenton had already ambled over to the fixture listings to read the stats for his next bet.

"Remember me?" Ezra said, sidling over.

The widening eyes and raised brows said *yes*. Fenton was silent a long while, then finally said, "What's brought you here?" His words were tinged with suspicion.

"Wanted to ask you about the test on biometrics you gave me...." Fenton's eyes flashed up to the surveillance cameras in the corner of the shop.

"That's all behind me now." He was already turning his back to Ezra to read the listings.

"No, wait...."

"Look," Fenton said, moving close to Ezra, speaking in a harsh but deliberately quiet voice. His expression was menacing. "I have nothing to say. I thought I just made that clear."

Thinking Fenton might say more without the security cameras and microphones around, Ezra strode out of the entrance, banged on the side of his car, got John to scroll down the window. But, engrossed with his own investigations, John pointed to some new footage he'd pulled up on his computer and said, "You need to look at this." The angle of the screen was awkward; it was impossible to see any images in the sunlight.

"Never mind that," Ezra said. "Fenton won't talk. I need to deal with that first."

"Why won't he talk?"

"There are cameras in there. He's nervous about them. Run a check, find out whether Rackers is relying on a Sense network." John opened another window on his machine and ran a new query. A few moments later, he said, "Yes."

"OK," Ezra said, "Then let's have Sense declaring a need for urgent maintenance, and giving some reason to take the local Rackers' surveillance down for a little while." Seriously below board, but Ezra felt compelled to get more information; he leaned in through the car window and started tapping his way into various servers. "Do the rest," he said to John, before striding back to the shop.

"Are you deaf?" Fenton said, after Ezra pushed his way through the entrance and approached him again.

Ezra nodded to the camera positioned in the far corner of the ceiling. The "recording" light was green. "It's going down. Watch."

"What – "

"The surveillance cameras – they're being turned off." John was taking his time disabling the unit, but at last the green light disappeared, then changed to red.

"No monitors. No mikes. OK?" Fenton still looked suspicious, was trying to see through the windows, presumably to find out who Ezra had spoken to outside. "In the test you gave me, there was something strange about the footage of Deborah Harrington. I want to ask you about it."

The stare that Fenton gave Ezra through his thick-rimmed glasses was hostile and hard. He began shaking his head.

"You've only just realized, have you? After all this time! What is it that you've *just* noticed?"

Ezra felt exactly the same kind of discomfiture he'd felt in the exam room all that time ago.

"Seems like the footage of Deborah at the bus stop is fictitious...."

"Clever boy, you got there in the end then. Well, you're too fucking late." The words were so cutting and accusatory, Ezra hesitated to ask Fenton to explain "What? You still don't know the whole story? Are you still buying the idea that I was stalking her?" Ezra was annoyed with himself for not checking more of the footage and establishing more facts before he'd come racing to Fenton. "Deborah Harrington's whole journey from the New Way shelter to the bus stop at Camden...."

"New Way," Ezra repeated the words quietly and slowly. "One of Monica's charities?"

Fenton sneered, before saying, "Monica gave people the promise of a new life away from abusive situations. She covered their paths as they went to Sense's reassignment clinic with fictitious footage that showed them going elsewhere. They thought they were getting help to a new life, but they all became guinea pigs in genetic experiments." Fenton paused. "I can see this is all news to you."

Covert genetic experiments.

On vulnerable subjects.

Organized by staff at Sense Surveillance.

This was preposterous, except Ezra could almost feel certain facts clunking into place: the spliced data John had uncovered, Lena's deteriorating physical appearance, and her strange insistence that "others were in danger."

"I knew a nurse who worked at the clinic," Fenton continued. "Siobhan. She was very cagey about saying too much, mainly because a lot of the people who go to Reassignment are involved in one covert operation or another and the data they deal with are classified, but she was getting worried about what was going on, about the way some of the treatments were being run. She asked me to look into it." Fenton gave Ezra a withering look. "That's what I was trying to do in those biometric tests. I thought the tests would make a good cover while I investigated. No one was going to look into what trainees were doing in exams. How could they be doing anything questionable? They wouldn't know enough about the data. It was the best way for me to see whether there was any truth to back up Siobhan's suspicions. But you," Fenton said, through a caustic sneer, "you ruined things. You were such a stickler for the rules, wouldn't look into the things I wanted to check out. You brought all my investigations crashing down by going directly to Monica to complain, just as I was getting somewhere, just…."

"OK, stop there!" Ezra snapped. The man sitting at the circular table looked up from his newspaper. Ezra reined in his voice. "You're saying…." He floundered; it was virtually impossible to conceive that Monica (Monica! – with all her charitable work and art foundations and impeccable manners and elegance) was herding people from refuges into illegal genetic experiments.

"You're fooled by her politeness, are you?" Fenton cut in.

"If what you say is true, then yes I am," Ezra said. He looked through the smudge on Fenton's thick glasses, tying to find the truth in his eyes. "Here's the difficulty I'm having: if everything's as you describe, why didn't you take this higher up?"

"You mean blow the whistle?"

Ezra held a steady stare.

Fenton gave a quiet snort, before shuffling slightly. He trod on a crumpled betting slip that had been tossed to the floor.

"Don't you have any vices?" Ezra chose to say nothing, waited for Fenton to continue. "Well, as you can see I do. Compulsion," he said strangely, gesturing to the space around him. "I don't like it. I can't seem to help it, but that's what this is all about. I have a compulsion to come here. Then there's a compulsion to celebrate a win by having another flutter, and there's a compulsion to counter a loss by placing another bet. D'you see the problem? No? Maybe you don't then. But let me tell you – this takes a lot of money and I've done a lot of bad things to get it. I thought I'd been clever about it. But Monica dug up some footage on me I didn't want to come out." Fenton's voice was quieter now. "You take advantage of people when you're this out of control, even people really close to you. It would be horrible for all the people I know to find out exactly how I've screwed them. Most already think I'm shitty enough. So," Fenton said, after giving a long sigh, "I agreed to go quietly and keep my mouth shut."

From across the other side of the room came another crescendo of cheers and racing narration from the television.

Fenton was beginning to turn once again to the fixture sheets pinned to the wall, but Ezra still had questions. He blurted, "What about the nurse…" temporarily, he struggled to remember her name, then it came "…Siobhan – did you get any more information from her?"

"I reported back to her that there was nothing untoward going on. That she was worrying needlessly. Then I severed all contact with her. For Siobhan's sake I thought that was for the best."

"Is there anyone else who suspects anything?"

"Possibly a driver. Female. She's pretty tight-lipped, though. Siobhan sensed that she had some suspicions, but seemed like she was too afraid to rock any boats."

"And what about Lena Mae Cho, Gavin Dixon, Eady, Patel…"

"Who are they?"

"They're other people with fictitious histories."

"Lena Cho, Gavin…." Fenton was repeating the names without any flicker of recognition.

"Lena's like Deborah; she was in an abusive situation…" with Cunningham, of all people! "… but Gavin Dixon," Ezra continued, "he doesn't fit this picture. He lived with his sister who was very supportive. Do you have any information on him?" Fenton's expression remained blank. "OMNI activists," Ezra added, "at least his sister was." He began sifting through his memory, trying to pull together all the information Suzanne had given him when she'd arrived at Sense HQ in her baggy clothes to spew a torrent of accusations. Then there was Monica – what precisely had she said about the Dixon case? She was the one who'd raised the whole matter with him in the first place. She'd stood by that antique Chinese bottle in her office and insisted on Ezra's prioritizing the Gavin case. "No," Ezra said suddenly, fixing on Fenton. "Your story doesn't mesh. Monica insisted that I help Suzanne with her concerns about her brother. Why would she do that if she'd had something to do with his disappearance?"

Voice tired, matter-of-fact, Fenton said, "To get a heads-up when things are getting sticky – you proved yourself good at that in the tests. You're a siren, I suppose, though you don't seem to know it." Shaking his head slowly, he continued, "So many more people involved in these experiments now... I tried... I did try to raise the alarm. You didn't hear it though, did you?"

Ezra's grip on everything that Fenton had told him was too feeble for guilt. Each piece of information he assembled, rather than clarifying things, only made the mystery of the anomalies even more pronounced.

Quietly, Fenton said, "I'm afraid for some of these people, people like Deborah. I really worry about her. The experiments they're performing in this clinic are very dangerous. Siobhan described some of the terrible side effects. This realization you've finally arrived at, that there's something up with Deborah's records – it's probably too late."

Looking despondent, Fenton glanced up to the surveillance camera. The light was still red. He said, "There's nothing more I can tell you."

The memory of Lena's cracked skin as he'd seen it in Cunningham's office had taken center stage in Ezra's mind. When he left Rackers and returned to his car he felt nauseatingly on edge.

John, once Ezra had slumped back into the driver's seat and given him the low down, stopped tapping the keys on his laptop and said, "If what Fenton says is true...."

"Do you believe it really is true? I mean, Monica!"

John shrugged. "She was always a cool one. A hard nut to crack."

"Playing Frankenstein? Why would she do that?"

It was clear from his blank expression that John had no idea.

"Well, someone's playing games," John said, nodding towards the computer on his lap. Ezra saw the list of anomalies was back on the screen. Gavin, Lena, Deborah, then the seven or so others he knew nothing about. "And whoever it is knows how to access Sense data and work their way around it."

"So has to be an insider."

"Looks that way."

"Wait – how did that happen?" Ezra said, leaning across to scrutinize the list on John's screen. "Eleven entries. There were ten earlier. Where did this entry eleven come from? And why does it say 'name to be confirmed'"?

"That's what I wanted to show you earlier. A new case just appeared within the last twenty minutes. There's a false trajectory, another anomaly, being created just as we speak. Starting point is Euston. But that's pretty much all I've got a hold of right now."

"Is that male or female?" Ezra said, squinting at the shadowy figure shown walking along a station platform.

"Dunno," John said. "It's so blurred you can't really make out the person at all. Not yet anyway. Presumably, the details will get filled in. That's what I'm waiting for. I'm keeping my eye on this."

Fixated with the latest anomaly, so absorbed with scrutinizing the imagery, Ezra took several moments to acknowledge the series of sharp beeps coming from his pocket. Eventually, he pulled out his mobile and checked the screen. The number was unfamiliar and he felt trepidation when he answered the call.

"Dr. Epstein from Central Hospital," came a clipped authoritative voice. "It's about Lena."

"How is she?" said Ezra immediately, straightening up in his seat.

"Serious…you know I'm not permitted to say too much. The thing is, I need information from you. Someone has given her treatments that we don't fully understand. It's crucial that we analyze the drugs she's been given. A little while ago she mentioned you knew where some of these drugs were. Is that true?"

"The syringes? Yes…" Ezra knew all too well about the syringes: the white plastic box they'd been contained in laying open on Cunningham's office floor, the repulsive contortions of Lena's face after she'd injected herself with one of the fluids, the minute bead of blood that had formed on her arm, then the syringe coming towards him with the label *relaxant.* "…yes, I know about the drugs. Wait…."

Hadn't he picked the syringes up? His thinking had been cloudy when he'd come round, but he was sure he'd put the caps over the needles and taken them from Cunningham's room. Ezra shifted in his seat and gently felt inside his pockets. Eventually, he felt the long plastic stems. He pulled them out. Both syringes were near enough empty, but there were still minute droplets of fluid in each. Probably enough to do an analysis.

"I can bring them to you." Ezra said quickly.

"Thank God!" Dr. Epstein said, before cutting the line.

"What the hell are those?" John was eyeing the syringes Ezra had placed in the cup-holder between the two front seats. "And where are we going?" he added, as Ezra's sudden swerve into the flow of traffic thrust him against the window.

"Central Hospital. This drive'll be fast."

32

SUZANNE AND BRINLEY walked among the shadows under the Westway. They passed concrete pillars daubed with angry red graffiti, and the whoosh of cars speeding on the flyover above echoed all around.

"I'm glad you're coming today," Brinley said. "You should try and meet up with the OMNI crowd more often. Just because you're pregnant doesn't mean that you can't be active."

"I know, but in case you hadn't realized, I had been feeling pretty rough…."

"But…" Brinley looked uncertain whether he should continue, "it's just the first couple of months, isn't it?"

"Probably." Actually, she was feeling better today. No nausea. Her mum was looking after Adam and she and Brin had relaxed over a rare brunch on Ladbroke Grove. She nuzzled against Brinley's side. He slowed to put an arm round her.

"You're in a good mood," she said.

"Well, it's a nice warm day, you seem perky and we might have a lead that means we can nail Sense…."

"And you're going to enjoy that, are you?"

"Every last minute," Brinley said. "If they want to use their technology – untested technology! – to alert us every time we have a devious thought...."

"What they *deem* to be a devious thought."

"... then they're gonna have a fight on their hands. They think they know enough about neurology to tell when it's a thought I'm likely to act on rather than one I keep in my head for my personal titillation, which quite frankly is no one else's business."

"Not even mine?"

"I might share some deviousness with you...."

"Ooh, go on, then."

"Well, I might just do that. But that's up to me, isn't it? I don't imagine you tell me everything that's on your mind. I mean you can if you want. I don't expect it, though. But Sense – a massive corporation that I have no say in – wants to make access to my thoughts compulsory. What shit is that? *But the devices are just as small as dust*, they argue...."

"Ooh, don't do that spooky voice, Brin."

"But that's what they argue, like the fact that the chips are microscopic makes it OK."

"Well," Suzanne said, "we know the bit that they're going to concentrate on when they try and sell this technology is the fact that can transmit a warning signal to someone who's having an errant thought and is about to actually do something wrong. They'll say they're there to help us stop breaking laws."

"But who are these people who have this control? What business...?"

"I'm just stating their argument."

Suzanne could feel Brin's body getting tense. He stayed silent for a while.

"You're right," he said, finally. "That's why it's good you're coming to this meeting. You keep a level head.... You've gone quiet," he said. "What's the matter?"

Suzanne's line of vision was directed at a large man on a bike coming their way, but her thoughts were on Jamal and Bohdana and all the old OMNI crew.

"They're not all going to start teasing me about being too idealistic, are they?"

"Oh, just ignore them. We need idealism anyway. We need strong arguments. There's a lot of momentum building again now. This leak about the dangers of Resolve – this could be a real success story for us. We could completely overturn Sense's whole microchip program. It's still incredible to me that they're even *thinking* of going down that road."

An image of monkeys with wires poking into their shaved heads flashed into Suzanne's mind. It was those sorts of images that got the public riled. She imagined placing them in adverts. Posting on a big billboard would get the message across.

Strangely, the cyclist up ahead was scrutinizing the concrete pillars of the flyover and checking lampposts along the street. He slowed down some twenty yards ahead, close to a battered white van. His bike was a London hire cycle, blue with a sturdy frame. The rider looked out-of-place and fidgety. Through thick-rimmed black glasses, he was staring Suzanne's way.

"Suzanne Dixon?" he asked.

Suzanne and Brinley stopped before him.

"Yes?" Suzanne said, after a moment's silence. "How do you know my name?"

The man gestured further along the street.

"I just called in at the OMNI office, they told me you were about to arrive and which way you'd come." Pointing to a broken surveillance camera fixed to the nearest pillar, he said, "Look, I don't want to move from here. This is the safest place for us to talk."

"About what?" Brinley said, his voice shot with suspicion.

Looking at Suzanne, the man said, "It's about your brother, Gavin...."

"Gavin?" She pulled away from Brinley, though she could feel he was tense. "Where did you hear about Gavin?"

"Ezra Hurst mentioned him."

Suzanne felt inclined to keep away from this strange, thickset man who'd cycled across shadows to meet her. But the mention of Ezra Hurst had sidelined that concern. What connection did this man have to Ezra? And what exactly had they said about Gavin? "Do you know what happened to Gavin?" she said finally.

"Whether he went to Prague?"

"Prague?" Suzanne registered the confusion in the man's expression and felt her fleeting moment of optimism slithering away. "No, nothing to do with Prague," he said.

"So what do you know about Gavin?"

"I heard you are looking for him. His name has come up in connection with Sense's reassignment program."

"What program? Reassignment – what's that?"

Distracted by something high up on the underside of the flyover, the man was now keeping silent. When Suzanne looked to where he was focusing, she saw a camera swiveling on a metal arm, its lens pointing their way.

"Look, I don't have a lot of information," the man said, while quickly reaching into his pocket. He pulled out a folded piece of paper and pressed it into Suzanne's hand. "This woman may be able to help," he said, nodding to the piece of paper. "She picks her son up from day care at four, usually parks at FreshFoods next door, often gets some shopping before she collects him."

"Who is this woman? Hang on…." Suzanne said, seeing the man position himself back on his saddle.

"Wait. Who are you?" Brinley demanded, gripping hold of the handlebar, stopping the man from pedaling off.

"Don't make a scene," the man hissed. "This is dangerous. For me. For you." Suzanne saw how he'd glanced to the camera again. Instinctively, she tried to pull Brinley away from him. But he stood his ground, clasping the handlebar even more tightly. Suzanne gave him another tug, more urgent this time. At last he let go. "I suggest you go there now," the man said, putting his foot back on the pedals. "FreshFoods. Notting Hill. If you're lucky, you'll catch her. She might not want to talk. But she knows more than me."

"What is this about?" Brinley said, aggressively.

But Suzanne was still holding onto Brinley, willing him to give the man some space, keep him at ease so that they'd get more information. Instead, the man quickly put his whole weight on the pedals. He was unsteady at first tightly turning the bike around to go back the way he'd came, but then he built up speed, weaved around a dumpster and cycled out of sight.

Quickly, Suzanne unfolded the piece of paper. Though it only had one fold now, it looked like at some point it had been completely crumpled. Faint grids, numbers and times covered one side. She saw the word Rackers, realized the numbers were betting odds, that the word *Madagascar* must be the name of a horse or a grey hound, she wasn't sure which. When she turned the slip over she found the handwritten word "Nisreen, Grey BD 53 SRL."

"Car registration," she said, peering at the slip. "So…this woman, Nisreen…" Suzanne checked her watch, "…she'll be arriving at Notting Hill FreshFoods any second. He's telling me that I should go and look out for her car. She might know where Gavin is or what happened to him…."

"What? You're thinking of doing this, no questions asked?" said Brinley, staring at her in disbelief. "I mean, who is this Nisreen? And who the hell was *he*? He didn't give us his name. He didn't tell us what his connection to Hurst is." Brinley was staring in the direction that the cyclist had gone. "You don't know what you're getting into here. You can't just go shooting off on some escapade on some stranger's say-so."

"You think we should just ignore him, then?"

"I didn't say that."

"So, what do you suggest?"

"That we think this through, think about what just happened. Maybe go to the meeting at OMNI see what the others think…"

"He said this Nisreen was going to be at FreshFoods at four. We haven't got time to go to OMNI and have a discussion."

"Look, I'm not just going to follow some stranger's orders…."

"Well, I don't know who that man was either or why he was acting so shady. But maybe I'll go to FreshFoods…." Brinley let out a long sigh of exasperation. "Look," Suzanne persisted, "Maybe I'll get nothing out of it. No Nisreen. No nothing. But I'm not going to throw away the one tip-off about where my brother might be after all these weeks of looking for him. You know I can't do that. You don't have to come if you don't like the idea. I'll meet up with you later…."

"Don't be daft. We don't know who this man is. He himself said this was dangerous…."

"Well, I just explained why I have to follow up on this...."

"I understand that," Brinley said, "But I can't just go off to the meeting and let you go by yourself." Silently, he turned towards Ladbroke Grove. He was thinking things through. Suzanne didn't interrupt him, just waited for him to speak. She waited a long time, heard him give a long sigh. "I'll come with you," he said at last. "We could cut through Portobello Road."

"You don't mind missing the meeting?"

"I can see this is important."

"Thank you, Brin."

Quickly, they stepped out of the shadows under the Westway, took a side street that led to the fruit stalls on Portobello Road. A couple holding plastic coffee cups sauntered in front of them. One elderly woman bobbed around a stall to bag up some onions. Another weighed potatoes on silver scales. A man with stubble and a cigarette stuck to his lip fixed an awning that had started to droop. Farther along were the racks of vintage clothes. A woman with a beehive held up a tiger print dress, pressed it against herself, checked her reflection in a mirror that was precariously rigged to a spindly clothes rack. Cars were double-parked and the back doors of one van that had climbed the curb for space were splayed open to reveal countless boxes of trinkets and toys.

Outside the Salvation Army building a group of three women were peering at a notice board. Pointing at a flyer, they babbled and laughed. Suzanne and Brinley veered off the pavement to pass them. An oncoming car blared its horn at their sudden appearance in the road.

Away from the market now, the street was much calmer and they heard their own footsteps. They passed the outdoor seating in front of the Portobello Gold. One woman, light brown with an afro, sat there alone, a large glass of red in her hand. Up ahead were the terraced houses that Suzanne usually liked to see. Quaint and pretty at the quiet end of the street; one pink, one yellow, one sky blue, one orange.... Today they were all vague blurs of color as she strode quickly by, Brin in step and silent by her side. The betting paper was still scrunched in her hand. Her mind was racing. There were so many questions. Who was this Nisreen? Would she even be at FreshFoods car park like the weird man had said? And supposing she could be found, what on earth would she say about Gavin if anything at all?

"He said she might not want to talk," Suzanne said to Brinley, who just shook his head in response. "What does that mean?" She didn't expect a reply from Brinley. Neither did she get one.

Striding out to the junction of Notting Hill, they could see the glowing FreshFoods sign on the other side of the road.

"What color's the car?" said Brinley, as they dodged traffic to get to the shop.

"Grey." Suzanne said. She glanced at the cars speeding around her. "God! Half the cars on the road are grey."

"That's fashion for you." Brinley replied. "What is it? 53 reg?" When they reached the other side of the road Suzanne unfolded the piece of paper and nodded. "That was the in color when those cars came out."

They hurried to the upper level car park of FreshFoods. There were no free spaces left and several cars were circling like vultures waiting for a spot. Every other car seemed to be one or another close shade of grey. There was the noise of trolleys clanking and rolling across the concrete floor. Doors slamming. Engines revving. Suzanne saw one grey car's reverse lights flash on. The registration ended in L. She peered through the window. Saw the driver was male. Disappointed, she looked away. She was aware of more than one of the circling drivers throwing her suspicious looks, clearly wondering what her game was, scrutinizing every car.

"You check this side," Brinley said. "I'll go over there. We can both do a sweep, then meet at the far end."

But Suzanne was already fixated on the far end, on a woman in a headscarf wheeling a noisy trolley towards a shiny grey car.

"What about her?"

"Is that an L?"

They both edged nearer, squinting at the registration plate.

"Yes," Suzanne said. She unfolded the crumpled betting paper again. Checked the registration number, squinted once more at the car in the distance. "That's it. That's the car."

Immediately, they strode forwards, making a driver pulling his car out suddenly slam on his brakes. He blared his horn. The woman with the headscarf turned around from her now open boot and looked their way. Suzanne marched towards her even faster.

"Nisreen?" she called. She was at a light jog now. The woman stared back. She held a bursting shopping bag in her hand. "Nisreen?"

"Yes?" the woman replied, a look of puzzlement on her face. Suzanne saw the woman's gaze switch quickly back and forth from her to Brinley. "Have I left something?" She began checking the bag she was carrying. Its plastic was so stretched it looked about to tear. Then she glanced to the bags in the boot of the car, then at the already emptied trolley.

"No," Suzanne said, "You haven't forgotten anything. I'm...I'm Suzanne... I wanted to ask you whether you knew anything about my brother."

"Your brother?"

"Gavin. Gavin Dixon."

Her eyes widened. Brinley, obviously noticing the glimmer of recognition too, stepped forwards, and said, "Can you tell us where he is?"

"No," she said curtly, turning her back to them. Brusquely, she pushed the groceries in the boot further inside to make room for the last overstuffed bag. The plastic ripped as she swung the bag upwards and a large pack of Comfort Stay-Dry Pads fell to the ground. She snatched it up and threw it inside.

"I heard he's in a reassignment program," Suzanne said quickly. "Is that true?"

The woman slammed the boot shut and pushed the metal trolley away from the car. It clanked into Brinley's side.

"She's been looking for her brother for several weeks," he said. "If you know anything, *please* let her know."

"Anything," Suzanne pleaded. "Can you tell us what this reassignment is?" The woman was opening her car door now. "Please. We've had no information at all."

"Look, there's been a security breach. One of the clients disappeared and everyone is under suspicion. I'm not getting involved."

"Just tell me whether you've seen Gavin and if you know how he is?" Suzanne said. But the woman was already inside the car. Her door slammed shut. There was the noise of the engine sparking on. The car lunged back so suddenly, both Brinley and Suzanne had to jump out of its way. Swerving out into the exit route, the car caught the empty trolley sending it spinning into a concrete post.

Speechless and still, Suzanne watched the grey car speed towards the down ramp and disappear out of sight.

33

DR. EPSTEIN'S SMALL, cramped office was up on the fifth floor, away from all the wards. His old wooden desk, abutting the far wall, was cluttered and untidy. There was a light knocking at the door and a forty-something woman with gaudy make-up and a beehive hairstyle poked her head around the frame to tell Ezra that Dr. Epstein would be back again presently. Checking his watch, he realized he'd been in the hospital over an hour now. The woman glanced to the desk where the caps of the syringes he'd brought in still lay, disconnected from the needles that Dr. Epstein had placed on a tray and whisked off to a lab for analysis. "He's been running test after test with those drugs you brought here, but he shouldn't be too much longer. If you'd like a drink while you wait," she said, "there's a machine just down the corridor. Coffee, tea…."

"No thanks," Ezra said. The assistant stepped back out to the corridor, leaving Ezra alone with his impatience. So far, everything here had been one-sided; he'd raced over to Central Hospital with the syringes, relayed the little he knew about Lena and answered mostly "I don't know" to the barrage of Epstein's questions. But when he'd asked after Lena he'd heard "she's still critical" and nothing else. Seemed like the doctor couldn't get to the lab quick enough to run his tests on the few droplets of fluid in the syringes, leaving Ezra in the dark.

He stood and moved over to the window. Looking down to the car park, he could see his Viper, parked slightly askew, because he'd been hurrying, no doubt. John, his backpack of disks and gadgets hitched over one shoulder, had got out of the car at the same time as Ezra. He'd said he was going to grab something to eat, find somewhere quiet to investigate the new anomaly appearing nameless on his screen. "Text you when I've cracked it," he'd said. Ezra made another check for updates, but there were no texts on his mobile yet.

He jerked his head up when he heard a creak at the door. Dr. Epstein swept in, his long white coat brushing against the door frame.

"I'm sorry I kept you," he said, waving Ezra back to the chair, "Let's sit." Epstein's dark brown face had a sheen to it and his tie was skew-whiff. Clearly, he'd been rushing around. He dug into his pocket and Ezra was surprised to see him pull out the ivory figurine that only that morning had been an ornament on Cunningham's desk. He set it down next to the plastic syringe caps in front of Ezra.

"She gave you that?" Ezra said. Then seeing the doctor nod, he said, "Why?"

"It's made out of her own bone cells, specially cultivated at the Ost jewelry studio. Have you heard of it?" Ezra shook his head. "This is what her features were like just a few weeks ago and the blueprint for that old appearance of hers still exists in these cells." Dr. Epstein picked up the piece and turned it carefully in his hand. "Someone has transformed her using rapid phenotypic modifiers and the cells in here…" he said, holding up the Ost piece, "… are what she wants to use to get back to her old self." Now Ezra understood – her breaking into Sense HQ, into Vincent's office, the desperation that led to her lunging at him with a syringe – now her purpose was clear. Ezra watched the doctor scrutinize the statuette. "What troubles me is that the configuration of vectors involved in the treatment she's had resembles work that is still only happening at an experimental level."

"How troubling?" Ezra asked, noting the doctor's deflated posture.

Slowly, Epstein sucked in breath through gritted teeth.

"So far all relevant research shows that kind of treatment she's had is flawed. Unacceptable side effects – that's the bottom line. That's why she's been deteriorating. I would really like to help Lena…but I just don't think I can."

The room was noiseless for several moments before Ezra asked, "Who has been conducting these experiments?"

"A few people," Epstein said. "The vectors she's been given…" he turned his attention to the syringe caps, "and these supplemental compounds are very similar to a regimen that one of the big pharms was researching very heavily. Gen-exica…" The doctor looked up to see if Ezra had heard of the firm. Ezra gave a nod back and Epstein continued "…of course pharms like Gen-exica are massively interested in this kind of bio-technology: working out optimal mutation rates in multiple concurrent transformations to bring about changes at the phenotypic level. I'm talking about changes to appearance that are specified and controlled – we've all been struggling to get this for years. Throw in the ability to get reversals and snap back to your original appearance whenever you want…." Epstein exhaled, leaning back in his chair. "Do you have any idea how lucrative this kind of cosmetic genetics would be?" When Ezra didn't immediately answer, the doctor expanded, "Just think about what people already do to change their appearance…." Ezra recalled the assistant who'd popped in earlier with her bright red lipstick, her blusher and beehive. "Make-up sales every year making trillions. And think about the drastic measures some people take to change themselves. Plastic surgery – deciding to break your bones, cut out parts of your flesh, staple parts back together again, all for a different look. The thing about genetic cosmetics is that it has the potential for a far more sophisticated way of altering appearance. At the technological level, highly complex. But to the consumer, potentially it can come in the form of a custom potion."

"Like Alice in Wonderland," Ezra found himself saying. "Drink me for a couple more inches of height."

Dr. Epstein was nodding.

"The computational power we have now is phenomenal. The most complex alterations, all physically possible. And targeted. That's the key. Targeted to work in tandem with a particular person's genome. You have to understand there's enormous commercial interest in this. And, when you get head-hunted by a big pharm or Fortune 500 cosmetic company waving vast amounts of money at you, of course, it's very tempting." He gave a long sigh. "I've been tempted. I confess it. It's hard not to give into the pressure. Organizations like Gen-exica were throwing hundreds of thousands at promising scientists to deliver results. Of course that's when corners get cut. That's what Jason Liu did...." Ezra must have looked quizzical because Dr. Epstein took a detour from his stream of speech to give a description of Dr. Liu. "He worked in the field, but was struck off the medical register for not following ethical protocols. Of course, Gen-exica are his sponsors – they just paid a fine and came bouncing back. They always do, don't they? Whereas I have to beg for government grants...." Epstein pulled a file of papers towards him and flicked its numerous pages. "That's what this is – a long beg for money, for sponsorship."

"What about Gen-exica now?" Ezra said.

"They've been quiet. They have no formal research projects that I've heard of, but here's what's interesting: the treatment Lena's been given, the configuration of compounds that I saw just now, this is just the kind of approach Jason Liu would have taken when he was working for them. Unfortunately," Epstein said, shifting in his seat, looking slightly awkward, "there are still the same problems of stabilization. These are the problems Liu had before. You can't get reversal without stabilization of the initial procedure. And I don't have a solution to that."

Epstein had picked up the statuette again. He was smoothing his fingers over the profile: the brow, the nose, the lips.

"So, she's had procedures that have been banned," Ezra said quietly, thinking aloud. "And there may be others." He visualized John's screen with the ten anomalies, eleven counting the new one that had emerged just a couple of hours ago.

"Yes, she mentioned there were others to me."

"Did she say where they were?" Ezra said quickly. But Epstein was shaking his head. "Anything about them at all?"

"Nope," Epstein said. He stopped running his fingers over the statuette. He pulled open his desk drawer and carefully placed the Ost piece inside. When he gave the drawer a light push, it slid smoothly on its runners back into the desk and closed with a firm, decisive thud.

Back in his car, Ezra sat motionless, hesitating a long while, then he rummaged through his glove compartment to find an old pre-paid remote. When he used to be out till three in the morning boozing and gaming with John and Clint it had occurred to him that Sense might monitor its own staff, especially staff with ideas of promotion. So he used to buy cheap pre-paid remotes which John would then fix to give them "hidden owner" status. That way he'd keep his habits hard to track. Denise used to cut him hard looks when she saw him testing John's modifications. "If you're reduced to hiding your lifestyle, then something's got to be off." By the time he'd come around to her point of view, she'd already left. It was annoying that this tacky plastic remote could remind him of Denise, especially right now when he had so much to get his head around. The last thing he needed was that kind of flashback. Ezra felt drained, which he supposed, could still be a side effect of being spiked earlier. Christ Almighty! What kind of day was this?

Maybe he was being paranoid, maybe he shouldn't be giving any credence to Alex Fenton, but all his suspicions were directed at Sense right now. He pressed the power button on the remote, was relieved to see it still had some juice. He dialed John, put the remote on speaker and reversed the car out of the hospital's grounds.

"Any leads?" Ezra said, as soon as John appeared on the line.

"Yes," John replied, before adding, "I see you're using your play phone. Smart move."

"Why?"

"Fenton might be right. Could be that Monica's involved. Might be a good thing to keep things off Sense's radar."

Ezra hesitated before saying, "Why? What have you found out?"

"That there are only a few places that specialize in the kinds of digital manipulation we've seen with these anomalies. Moore Institute is one of the few. Turns out Monica took some classes a few years back. There's an advert you should look at. I'll send you the link…." John's voice faded a little and the "incoming message" light flashed on the screen of the remote. Ezra braked and pulled over to the side of the road, too quickly for the driver behind who honked aggressively and mouthed obscenities at Ezra as he drove past. Ezra opened the link and saw an online flyer for Moore Institute Digital Show 2057. There were links to contributors. Ezra pressed the one that said *Monica Parks*. "Got it?" John said.

"Yeah. What am I supposed to be looking at?"

"See the portrait of the woman on the bench she's created? Press play."

When Ezra pressed play he saw that though the woman remained stationary with the same fixed and emotionless expression, her clothes, accessories and jewelry transformed every 10 seconds or so, from business attire to jogging clothes, from hair pulled back to spilling over her shoulders.

"You see the bit where the subject's wearing the work clothes?" John said. Ezra rewound. "What do you notice?" It took him a while to see it, but then he noticed the ring on her hand, and the odd way it suddenly began glaring 32.07 seconds in.

"The ring," Ezra said.

"Right. You can see where her splicing techniques are not so hot."

Ezra stared at the image for a while. "But that doesn't prove that all the splicing we've seen is down to her. Maybe that's a common problem."

"But it does show that Monica has exactly the same level of skill as the person who *did* do the splicing?"

"Not sure," Ezra said. "Need more to go on. What about Case 11? What have you found out about the last instance of splicing. It's being created right under our noses for God's sake!"

"Haven't worked that out yet."

"Well, that's a priority," Ezra said, putting the car into gear. "This person could be in danger. If all the other cases have ended up damaged at this Reassignment place, this person could end up that way too. I'm going back to HQ. If you find anything, contact me there."

34

EZRA DROVE BACK to Sense with his car windows wide open. He made a violent U-turn to avoid a traffic jam at Moorgate and took a series of side streets, leaning back against his headrest, breathing in the gusting cool air.

As soon as he strode into the Anomalies Unit, Dexter Sayle jumped out of his seat and lurched towards him.

"My account's frozen," he said immediately. "Systems have shut me down."

Ezra looked over to Sayle's workstation where most of his screens were blank and some were frozen with error messages appearing on top of bright blue backgrounds.

"Why have they shut you down?"

"They're accusing me of having a compromised account. *Me!*" He was almost shaking with rage. "You watched that woman break into HQ. You let John hack into our databases. But *my* account has been frozen? I've done jack shit, but I'm the one with the frozen account!"

Ezra moved to Sayle's desk, where the crumpled soda cans

had multiplied. Sayle followed, short of breath and red in the face. He looked unkempt, but more than that, lost. He had no idea what to do with himself now that his access to computers had been taken away. Repeatedly, he jabbed at his keyboard trying to input his user ID and password, clearly hoping that this time around his machine might just work. But on each smudged screen the same message appeared "Security Alert. Your account has been frozen."

"Did you report that woman?" Sayle said in an accusatory tone.

"You mean Lena?"

"Of course I mean Lena."

."You're jumping to conclusions thinking this has something to do with her…."

"Oh come on! She broke in! Who the hell is she? She needs investigating."

"It's true that there needs to be some investigations, but we might…." Ezra wasn't sure how much he should say, who he should even talk to, but he found himself mumbling, "We might need to look internally first."

"What?" Sayle said, glancing across the department to the handful of tracers who were wearing big headphones and staring at screens across the other side of the room. "Who needs investigating?"

"Probably no one in this section."

"You mean Cunningham?"

"Well, yes at some point I'll look into him. But he's pretty much toast now that we all know what he's been up to. No, I…." Ezra stopped himself. He just didn't think he could let Sayle in on his suspicions about Monica; Sayle simply wouldn't believe him, especially without hard facts. He had to get those first. Ezra glanced at his watch and wondered whether John had had enough time to dig up more information. Ezra backed away from Sayle's workstation to head to his own office. "I'll see what I can find out," Ezra said, then seeing Sayle start following, added, "I'll make some enquiries and as soon as I get some updates I'll let you know."

Sayle headed sulkily back to his work station.

Ezra was glad for the privacy of his office and his almost clear desk. Expecting to have problems logging on, he was surprised to find he had no trouble getting network access. He'd have to be careful how he went about things, but at least he could delve into records unimpeded. What about John? It would make perfect sense if Systems had somehow got wind of the known maverick John marauding through their databases. Ezra felt a small spike of anxiety with the realization that he was incriminating himself by not reporting that kind of breach. Problem was he could barely tell who was trustworthy any more. Plus, he needed John's skills. He pulled out his pre-paid remote and called him.

"Have you had any problems getting into the network?"

"What sort of problems?"

"Sayle's been blocked. His account has been compromised."

"Oh, that was me."

"What?"

"Well, his account is never very secure. He never changes his password. Uses the same one for multiple things. He even has 'remember me' checked 'yes' for some of his passwords."

"Why did you do that?"

"I needed to get access to real-time data somehow. And I know you're not going to give away your account details. I mean look at you right now, using a cover-your-arse device." Through the glass door of his office Ezra could see Sayle still jabbing at keys, desperately trying to log on. It was a sorry sight, one that compelled Ezra to turn away. "I'm trying to look into how footage has been reconstructed. 'Course on my hard drive I've only got old data...." That was another thing Ezra might have difficulty explaining – how an ex-member of staff had managed to leave the company with a disk carrying surveillance records on millions of people. Jesus Christ, this was messy! "So, I needed to get access to live data to help you out with case eleven, find out who is having their history altered by Monica."

"Well, wait a minute, that bit's still conjecture."

"You're still having a hard time believing that, are you? Despite what Fenton's told you...."

"But how reliable is he?"

"And despite what I showed you about her background in

digital splicing? At what point are you going to stop doubting? If you understood as much as I do about manipulating that kind of video media, you'd just accept that she's the one doing it. For me, the main question right now is whose history is she busy reconstructing? Who is Case 11?"

"I think that's an important question too. As is *what is reassignment?* And *who are these others that Lena talked about?* These are all important questions. But the reason I'm having a problem accepting that Monica's responsible is that I can't see a motive. Fenton said money. But she's not motivated by money. I just can't see why she'd do this."

"Or is it more that you're reluctant to denounce a company you work for?

"If I'm going to do any denouncing I need hard facts."

"All right. Well, I'll try and find you some more, while you scratch about trying to find motives. But at some point you're going to have to start whistle-blowing, Ez. You do know, the onus is on you."

Irritated, Ezra hung up. Somehow John had managed to cast himself as the righteous one in all this. Leaning back in his chair, Ezra exhaled slowly. He felt tired and stumped. When his stomach rumbled, he checked his watch, found it was getting on for early evening. He realized he'd barely eaten all day.

"You should go home, Sayle," he said, coming out of his office to set off to the Strand for a coffee and something to eat. "I appreciate all your help earlier with tracking Vincent and Lena…." That seemed like eons ago now, that episode that was so intrinsically surreal. Ezra shook Sayle's shoulder. "I'm gonna try and get things back to normal round here." He was about to say *There's not a lot you can do right now. Why don't you go home?* But he thought better of it. "I might need your help later. Keep your mobile on just in case I need to call you?"

"Yeah," Sayle said, squidging himself out of his chair. "I'd like to get to the bottom of this."

"Me too," said Ezra.

They took the elevator down to the ground floor together. The conversation was short.

"What are you going to do?" Sayle asked.

"I have some ideas," Ezra said.

It was a lie; he had none. He felt a duty to stay positive, especially since Sayle was still looking upset. They crossed the lobby area and went in opposite directions out on the Strand.

Ezra weaved through a throng of pedestrians and dodged taxis and buses to cross the street. He passed by the church, finding it impossible to imagine that the woman who'd once found him quietly sitting there after the bio attack tragedy was involved in illegal genetic experiments and supplying unwitting subjects for the trials. She'd been so charming that day, conveying her sympathies, introducing him to her (somewhat smug) organist friend who'd played Bach's fugue in some key or other a little too fast for Monica's liking. There was no organ playing now, just the sounds of traffic roaring past on either side of the church. Strange to have this solitary building in the middle of the Strand, this oasis in the midst of commotion. Ezra stood by the curb waiting for an old Moto Guzzi, a filthy truck and two buses to pass. He crossed to Antonio's, ordered a large coffee ("just ordinary"), a fat ham and cheddar sandwich and a couple of shortbread biscuits.

Back in his office he avoided all screens, cell phones, and remotes until he'd finished his food and had had a good swig of his coffee. It was only once he'd tossed the empty wrapping and swished the crumbs off his desk that he picked up his prepaid remote.

He found a minor search engine to log into and ran a general search. "Monica Parks," "Jason Liu," and "Gen-exica" – he typed in the terms quickly and hit enter. The first few results consisted of official pages from Gen-exica's main website: its home page, Research Programs, New Technologies and Investor Information pages. A senior staff page listed a Gregory Liu, but not the Jason Liu who, according to Dr. Epstein, had been struck off the medical register for breaching research protocols. Ezra scrolled through more search results until one listed way down caught his eye: *Insider Trading Stats and Facts*. He pulled up a table entitled *Top 10 Insider Buys of the Last Month* and felt a spark of excitement when halfway down he found Gen-exica listed twice. Quickly, he scanned across to the column entitled *Insider Name*, then scrutinized the rows of information, absorbing the details. Monica's name wasn't there, but Jason Liu was on the list. He'd bought a huge shareholding on August 1st. Ezra checked the date on his remote. Just two weeks ago. Another Gen-exica insider, A. L. Grant, had made a much bigger purchase on the same date, but no bells were ringing from reading that name.

Ezra scrolled back to the links on Gen-exica's net site and ran a search on the "People" page. There were a dozen or so directors, each one with a thumbnail image. Bingo! Anthony L. Grant was listed and there was a photo alongside his details. It startled Ezra to think that he recognized the face; he brought the remote closer to his eyes to make sure he was remembering correctly. Black hair (a little spiky), thick jaw, brown eyes, complexion probably in the FDF range. It was definitely him – Monica's friend who'd played the organ too slowly in the church down on the Strand. Had she said his name was Anthony? Ezra couldn't remember. Faces were his strong point, not names. And he remembered this face very clearly, especially the way it had formed a small but supercilious smile.

So, what was Monica's connection to him? Was she his bird? Ezra hadn't picked up on that so much that day in the church. In fact, he'd go so far as to say there'd been something business-like about their interaction. Quickly, Ezra typed in more search terms: both their names again, "Gen-exica," "classical music," "arts." Most of the results were irrelevant, but a couple of dozen or so entries down was a link to the "British Museum – Gallery 95 Appeal."

Clicking on the link Ezra found that there'd been a fundraising dinner on 16th September 2058, that all monies raised would go towards the extension of the Chinese Ceramics section (Gallery 95) and that Monica Parks and Anthony Grant had both been guests. So, they had South East Asian pottery in common. Ezra was aware of Monica's interest; he'd witnessed her enthusing about the restoration of the Korean wine bottle in her office.

But what about Grant? It was a long time ago that Ezra had met him and he vaguely recollected him being interested in ceramics. He typed "antique eastern pottery," and "Anthony Grant." One result leapt out: a link to Sotheby's Sold Lot Archive, where Lot 3243 that had sold in Hong Kong for 4.2 million and was described as "The Celebratory Vase – A magnificent celadon glazed vessel, a sister to the Goryeo Wellness bottle…." Ezra switched to the photo and immediately saw the resemblance between the piece pictured here and the one in Monica's office with its faint depiction of ginseng leaves. Running a couple more searches, Ezra determined that Grant was the buyer.

"Even more precious." Ezra remembered Monica's words about the Celebratory Vase. Still staring at the image – the slenderness of the vase, the depiction of clusters of plump little berries – he leaned back in his chair and slowly exhaled. Was this piece so precious she'd provide guinea pigs to Grant in order to get hold of it? He cast his mind back to that time in her office when the lesser sister bottle was being installed. Ezra couldn't think of a single time he'd seen her more enthused. He shuffled in his chair and clicked the *call* icon on his remote. He hesitated a long while, then finally dialed John.

"I can think of a motive for her," Ezra said.

"Well, that's very good." Ezra heard sarcasm in John's tone, then a deep sigh coming down the line. It was surprising that John hadn't immediately asked what the motive might be. "Thing is – you're too late. Case eleven – "

"What about it? Have you done a reconstruction?"

"Yes."

"Well, who is it? Where are they?"

"It's her, Ez. It's Monica. She left Heathrow this morning and gave that trajectory a shadow status."

"Heathrow? She was going to the Yorkshire Moors for the weekend." To her swirling mists where she'd said it was so easy to just disappear.

"That's what she wanted people to believe and that's the fiction that she spliced into the records. The going to Euston, the getting on the train; she spliced in old footage of herself, just like she did with Gavin Dixon."

"So where's she gone?"

"I'd guess one of the countries Sense pissed off with its cross-border eavesdropping, and there are quite a few of those right now. They're not going to readily cooperate with sharing their intelligence and handing people over." There were sounds of shuffling and John putting the phone down and a muffled popping noise before he came back on the line. "So, I suppose..." there was a cough and the sounds of glugging – Ezra guessed he must have just pulled a ring off a drinks can, "...the best thing to focus on now is this Gavin Dixon lad because, of the ten remaining anomaly cases, he's the one that doesn't seem to fit." There was a long silence where John was clearly waiting for Ezra's response. But Ezra couldn't be that clinical; some of his major beliefs were being shattered and he couldn't just think *Monica mystery solved. What's next?* If the whole Monica thing were true, or even just plausible, he'd have to start thinking carefully about which people to tell, which authorities to bring in, what exactly he was going to say. This could bring Sense down. Ezra's heart started racing as soon as he'd formulated that thought. Fifteen thousand people worked for Sense. Was he really going to start making claims that could put them all out of work?

"I still need to get my facts straight."

"Jesus Ez! You're in denial. How long are you going to stay this way? Well...it's up to you, but like I say, you should look up Gavin Dixon. Because from the little bit of digging I've done, it looks like he might not be such a victim."

That caught Ezra's interest. Immediately he said, "What have you found out?"

"I think he's on the research side of things."

"How can he be?" Ezra had a flashback to the time Suzanne had come into his office and had described how he'd been fascinated with math from a very young age. "He's not a geneticist like Liu was. He's not an anything anymore since he can barely think straight these days. Didn't I tell you already that he'd been in that Maglev train crash?"

"But before then," John said, "when he was in academia he seemed to be devising some theories that had relevance to the kind of genetics that the likes of Liu were working in."

"What sort of relevance?"

"I don't know exactly. I haven't had time to delve into it too much. I was concentrating on finding out what the deal was with Monica. But you were at Central Hospital this morning talking with Epstein. I think this Epstein will be able to tell you something. Contact him. Get him to explain where this Gavin Dixon fits in. Look, I know you want to take your time with things, but this is an important piece, I'm convinced."

When John hung up, Ezra stood up and stretched. He felt heavy. Oppressed. He scooped up the disposable cup he'd got from Antonio's Café, but the coffee was cold. Probably not a good idea anyway; his heart was already beating abnormally fast. He went out to the hallway to the water fountain and had a long drink. He straightened up, wiped the drips away from his mouth and looked down to the floor of the atrium. A couple of security guards were talking and laughing. Was Ezra going to break a scandal that would see them hanging up their uniforms? What about all these offices opposite right up to the 18th floor? Was Ezra going to make an accusation that would culminate in every desk being cleared? His heartbeat quickened again. He took another long drink.

Back in his office he took his pre-paid remote and called Dr. Epstein.

"Is this a good time to talk?" Ezra asked.

"As good as any. What can I do for you?"

"Um...how's Lena?" Ezra found himself asking.

"Well...a fraction more stable than before." That didn't sound great, but a small improvement was something. Ezra waited to hear more, but Dr. Epstein didn't expand.

"So, something else I want to ask – can you tell me anything about Gavin Dixon?"

"Gavin Dixon? Interesting that you should mention him. I've just been reading through some of his old work. Why do you ask?"

"I'm not familiar with his studies, but I gather...and I don't know too much about this...but I gather he used to have some connection to genetics."

"Yes, yes he did."

"Can you explain it to me? In layman's language."

"Absolutely. There are aspects of Lena's treatment that point to his theories." The doctor paused. "Essentially what we're doing in trying to modify physical traits genetically is alter the way that proteins get folded."

"OK," Ezra said.

"Well, folding and unfolding 3-D molecular structures – that's topology…" Ezra immediately remembered Suzanne's description of how her brother had done an entire school project on shoe lace patterns at primary school. "…and that," Epstein continued, "is why Gavin Dixon caused a stir with some of his mathematical models. He'd written a brief paper in the Bulletin of the British Mathematical Society that found some new ways of predicting complex mathematical knots and folds. He was a quiet and unassuming worker – he just published his theory. No fuss. It's possible that he didn't even realize the implications it could have in GM treatments. Obviously big pharms are very interested in this kind of manipulation. In terms of bringing about controlled and complex changes at the phenotypic level – we'd all been struggling for years with this. Gavin gave us something that might not only allow for greater prediction and stability in programming physical changes but also something that allowed for reversal. But then," Epstein hesitated, "he was in that terrible accident and there were no more theories from him. Do you remember the Maglev train crash?"

"Yes, I do."

It was vivid in Ezra's memory since Suzanne had forced him to watch the news footage just a few days earlier.

"For me," Epstein continued, "it was like someone putting a key in your hand that you're sure is going to unlock something special, then just as you're about to try the key out, it melts and slips through your fingers." Epstein cleared his throat. "I know it sounds selfish. I mean, he was just a young man, his career was ruined. I think he found it difficult to accept his limitations, though. He still tried to attend conferences. But…well, it was embarrassing, really, he just wasn't up to it anymore."

"And you say you were just looking at some his old research?"

"Yes, yes. Because some of the analysis I did today showed

that Dixon's model was being applied in ways very similar to the way that Jason Liu used to work, except there have been some interesting extensions to the model, extensions I'm not familiar with. You remember I told you about Jason Liu earlier?"

"Yes," Ezra said. "How he wasn't above board."

"Exactly. And that's what I am seeing in my analysis."

"You mean your analysis of how Lena's been treated."

"Well, er...." Ezra wondered whether the doctor would hesitate to give details. Patient confidentiality was always going to be a top concern, even if Ezra had earlier helped out by bringing the syringes to him. "The thing is though this new application is interesting, I can see that the parameters are still faulty. And it's imperative that this treatment be stopped. I already know that it just can't work. There can only be serious side effects...."

"Like the ones we see with Lena?" Ezra said, recalling her cracked and sore skin.

"Exactly. The research that we're about to launch here also makes some use of Gavin's old model, as far as it goes anyway. If we had the rest of his model we'd have the possibility of far safer treatments than the kind of procedures Liu was devising. And, significantly, reversal should be possible too."

"Are you going to try your own procedure with Lena?" It was a direct question, which Dr. Epstein deflected with a general statement: "We're not able to try it on anyone as yet. First off, we'd need to get approval. Second, we need the missing pieces from Gavin Dixon's model." Dr. Epstein hesitated. "Do you know where Lena was treated?"

Now it was Ezra's turn to be cagey. Gen-exica would destroy all evidence and deploy an army of lawyers in an instant if Ezra started making blatant accusations. And the fact that Anthony Grant and Jason Liu had two weeks previously become controlling shareholders of Gen-exica was not itself evidence of any wrongdoing. "I don't have any definite information," Ezra said.

"It's just that Lena has mentioned others being in danger."

"I'm acutely aware of that," Ezra said. "If I'm able to find out anything helpful, for Lena or anyone else, of course, I'll let you know."

"Please, please do. This is really very serious."

Ezra found himself annoyed by the gravity of Epstein's plea. He switched the remote off feeling sick and tired of voices coming through his earpiece to tell him how important it was for him to act, that the onus was on him to make everything OK. Jason Liu and Anthony Grant were characters he hardly knew about. They were links in a set of search results, names on a list. Who were they in reality? How could Ezra run to the authorities to talk about an illegal experiment when he couldn't even say where this reassignment facility was?

Deep down he knew he needed to start summarizing what he'd discovered. Sense's departmental heads, the Board of Directors – they'd all need information and Ezra was the main holder of that. Damage limitation – ultimately that's what they'd focus on. The only survivors at Sense, if there turned out to be any, would be the ones that could get on board with that. He wished his heart would settle, that he could think more clearly to start the summary. Hands in his pockets, his shoulders aching, Ezra walked to his office window and gazed across the rooftops of Covent Garden to an ominous grey sky.

35

ADAM HAD BEEN whining from the moment Suzanne had plucked him from her parents' vegetable patch where he'd been happily scratching through earth, clogging his fingernails, tugging out the occasional new potato. He hadn't wanted to leave, nor had he wanted to be inserted into his stroller and pushed along the street back to Ladbroke Grove by two irritable, thwarted parents. He continued his whining as their flat came in view.

"Ugh," Brinley said, in a rare growl of impatience. "When is he going to stop?"

"Don't know," Suzanne said, shortly.

It wasn't possible for this day to get worse. Brinley was silently sore about missing the OMNI meeting, and Suzanne was feeling guilty, though she wasn't sure why she should – it wasn't as if she had much choice but to follow the tip from the strange cyclist who'd stopped them. But the Asian woman they'd tracked down had kept her lips sealed, driven off at top speed and left them precisely nowhere. Adam, red in the face from trying to break free of his stroller safety belt, only underlined the day's descent with his grating, continuous whine.

"Maybe he's tired." She looked down the street to their flat. "He might nod off if we put him in his cot as soon as we get in. He might...."

"What?" Brinley said. He followed her line of vision. "What is it?"

"That grey car. Just ahead of our flat. Is it hers? Nisreen's?" Brinley squinted to read the registration plate.

"That's it!" he said. "Why's she come here?"

"Maybe she's got something to tell us." They hurried towards the car. Adam cut the whining and was now craning his neck up at them as if to say, "What's the sudden change of tempo for? What's going on?"

"Come on, quick!" Brinley said. "Looks like she's been at our door and now she's about to get in her car."

They ran, whizzing the stroller along at full pelt, making Adam giggle.

"Nisreen!" Suzanne called out, but the sound of an old fume-spewing bus drowned out the word. "Nisreen!"

Nisreen turned, threw Suzanne a quick glance and seemed to recoil in alarm.

"She doesn't look too pleased to see us," Suzanne said. Then seeing Nisreen turn back to her car, she quickly added, "What? Is she leaving?"

"Maybe she's locking it." There was uncertainty in Brinley's tone. "OK, look – she's coming towards us."

Nisreen was marching towards them now with such sudden urgency Suzanne felt wary and slowed her own pace down. They all converged outside an estate agent with copious 3-D images of Victorian terraced properties in its window. Ordinarily, Suzanne would stop to look at the picture of the one with the glass extension emerging out of its attic. Today she paid it no attention.

"Do you have something to tell us about Gavin?" she said at once. Nisreen fidgeted a little and glanced towards her car. "Well, do you?"

"Is there somewhere we can talk?" Nisreen said, craning to see between Suzanne and Brinley for a view of the street beyond.

"Of course, we can go back to our flat...."

"No...no. I don't have time to come in. What about there?"
she said, pointing to a small garden square with a bench inside.
"Your boy can play in there."

Panicked by Nisreen's gravity and nervousness, Suzanne said,
"Has something bad happened to Gavin?" Nisreen was still trying
to shunt them towards the little park. Suzanne found her physical
closeness uncomfortable, her urging desperate. "Just tell me what
you know."

Slowly, as if carefully picking words, Nisreen said, "I
mentioned your name. I said that you were looking for him.
But...well, he became agitated." Nisreen was avoiding all eye
contact. "The thing is – he needs to be left alone."

"Is it because I lost my temper with him just before he left?"
Suzanne said. "I told him that he should get out of my sight. Is that
why he wants to be left alone?"

"Left alone where?" Brinley demanded with such force that
both Suzanne and Nisreen sharply turned to face him. "You told
Gavin that we were looking for him, but where were you when you
told him this?" Nisreen looked down to the ground in the direction
of a large crack filled with moss. "*Where?*" Brinley's voice was
aggressive now.

"Look, he's been in...it's a clinic. I don't know much more."

"What is this clinic? Is it like a psychiatric institution?" Brinley
demanded, voicing a question that was on the tip of Suzanne's
tongue too.

Given all Gavin's behavioral problems since the train accident,
it wouldn't be implausible that he'd got into some terrible scrape
and been held somewhere. But there was something off about that
idea – surely someone would have contacted her to say where he
was. She was impatient for an answer, but Nisreen still seemed too
nervous to speak.

"What is this clinic?" Brinley demanded. "What do you know
about 'reassignment'?"

Reassignment, yes – the man with the big glasses who'd
approached them earlier on the bike had mentioned reassignment.

Nisreen threw a furtive glance back along Ladbroke Grove
towards her car. Suzanne looked the same way. The car was parked

on newly painted yellow lines on Ladbroke Grove. What – was she worried about getting a ticket? If Nisreen was really that worried about getting a fine, they'd all be better off moving back towards the flat where they could watch out for traffic wardens, then she'd be able to speak more calmly, without any distractions.

Then Suzanne noticed the main doorway of her building, just opposite the car. Usually, the door of the flat, an ugly brash orange, was visible even from this distance down the street. Instead she saw blackness; their door was ajar.

"Is someone in there?" she said, looking to Nisreen and seeing sudden alarm in her eyes. "Is someone in our flat?"

Brinley had barged past for a better view.

"Look..." Nisreen sounded panicked, "you want to talk...let's sit down over there...."

"No. Let's find out what's going on," Suzanne snapped. Nisreen knew something about the door being open. It was clear now that she'd been preventing her and Brinley from getting to their own home. Well, if she wasn't going to talk, Suzanne would march right on over there and find out what was going on for herself.

"Suzanne! Wait!" Brinley said when she set off down the street.

But she wasn't waiting any more. Closer to the door now, she could see that it was wide open. Brinley was close behind her, pushing Adam in the stroller until they reached the main entrance.

From the dark dingy staircase, they could hear heavy footsteps and thuds.

"Close the door," Brinley said. "We'll leave Adam here on the ground floor."

"We'll come and get you shortly," Suzanne said to Adam. She pulled Magnifico Mouse from the basket of the stroller. Adam quietly took the toy.

The thuds grew louder as Suzanne and Brinley climbed the stairs and approached the landing. The inner door of their flat was ajar. A laundry basket that she'd placed in the kitchen earlier was upturned and clothes were strewn across the hallway floor. The sound of footsteps was coming from the lounge. Moving towards the noises in the living room, Suzanne trod on an old long-sleeve top with muted reds and beads on the front. Just a few days before, she'd packed that top up in a bin liner ready to take to the charity shop. Same for those old jeans by the living room door.

"What's going on?" Brinley said in a whisper, while scrutinizing the shredded bin liner.

Suzanne pushed the door open and was startled to find Gavin squatting by another bin liner full of old clothes. He was wearing a denim flat cap that covered all his hair, and holding up one of her old crocheted tops, inspecting the sleeve. Brinley's boot crunched on an old plastic handbag lying on the carpet. Gavin jerked his head up.

"Suzanne!"

Standing up, he was still clutching the top in his hand. His posture was tense and his face was contorted into a look of extreme confusion. He began wincing as if he were experiencing unbearable pain.

"What on earth happened?" Suzanne asked, walking up to him immediately, wanting to reach out to him. Gavin's wincing dissipated as Suzanne approached; his line of vision had dropped to some point on her arm. His eyes narrowed into an expression of intense focus. It was a lightning transformation, so instantaneous and unnatural it stopped Suzanne in her tracks. Gavin took a long stride towards her and grabbed hold of her elbow. His grip was forceful.

"What – what are you doing?" she said.

Brinley rushed over and pulled Gavin's hands away.

"Get off her," he said. "Leave her alone."

Despite his skinniness Gavin had surprising strength and clasped her tightly. She toppled backwards trying to move away, bringing Gavin with her. Quickly, she regained her balance and jerked upright to free herself.

"Everyone just calm down," she said, pushing her hair out of her face. "Everyone…" she felt breathless and tense, "…just calm down."

"Mummy," came a faint cry from the ground floor.

"Did you hear that, Gavin? Do you see why we all need to calm down here? Didn't you just hear Adam?"

Mentioning Adam didn't make Gavin less tense as she'd hoped. Still he peered in the direction of her arm, at the creases in the sleeve, she realized. It was the kind of creasing he'd focused on a few years back when he'd been in the math department, a series of folds that had had a kaleidoscopic effect on the underlying patterning. He'd tried to explain it to her, even showed her computer simulations, but he'd lost her within a matter of seconds.

"I remembered it right," Gavin said, his eyes all wide. "You see," he snatched up a piece of paper on the carpet and pointed to sketch after sketch of complex shapes, some stretched, some deformed, a myriad of folds and angles all marked, annotations by the side. Quickly, he sketched another variation – an array of lines and overlays. Suzanne was stunned by his concentration; he hadn't been that focused in years. But after all these weeks away, of no contact, of worrying about where he was, he was just going to throw himself back into some mathematical problem? Not even say hello. She sensed Brinley, severe-faced and agitated, to her side. She snatched up a cardigan strewn on the floor to cover the creases he seemed so fixated on, to force him to acknowledge her, but that only made him groan. When he stepped forwards again, Suzanne cut in before Brinley could react, "You need to tell us where you've been, Gavin. We're not doing mathematical patterns now."

It was like talking to a child. Still he was fixated on her sleeve, as if he were trying to see through the cardigan to the patterns and creases of the shirt underneath.

"That *is* the formation. I'm sure I have it right."

Momentarily, she was thrown by the sheer intensity of his words. He had spoken as if he were making a crucial confirmation for someone else. Why was he speaking and behaving so obsessively and why did he look so pained? She felt a need to get answers methodically, in a logical order that could help build up a picture she could understand.

"You went to St. Pancras," she prompted, "To go to a conference in…."

"Try more," Gavin said suddenly. "More."

"What do you mean?"

His neck was cocked downwards as if he were talking into a

microphone somewhere on his chest.

"Who's he speaking to?" Brinley said quietly to Suzanne.

She was shaking her head, wanting desperately to do something to calm Gavin down.

"I must be missing something. It is the right formation as far as it goes." Gavin swung around and peered at Suzanne's arm again. "Something's not squaring. I just can't see what it is."

His face was red and beads of sweat had formed on his upper lip.

For a few moments more his body remained rigid, then unexpectedly he crumpled forwards, hanging his head low and panting heavily.

Suzanne reached out to hold him. His shirt was damp with sweat and he was squinting as if he couldn't properly focus, staggering as if he were about to fall. Guiding him to the yellow sofa, she said, "Get him some water, Brin." She was worried that he was about to pass out, but at least felt relief that his hideous contortions had gone.

The sound of running water came from the kitchen, then Brinley quickly reappeared holding a full glass, its water slopping onto the carpet as he moved. Slumped on the sofa, Gavin breathed heavily at first but gradually he grew calm. His redness subsided and he was struggling to keep his eyes open.

"Rest there," Suzanne said. "Have something to drink."

Closing in and towering over him, Brinley said, "You have to tell us what's going on, Gavin."

Eyes opening a little, Gavin looked first at Brinley, then Suzanne. He seemed disoriented and his breathing was labored.

"I think we should let him rest for now." She watched his eyes start to close again. "We're not going to get anything out of him for a while."

She crossed the living room quickly to run downstairs and check on Adam. She scooped up some toys for him on her way out.

***

Still the right words wouldn't come. Ezra paced from desk to window, gazed down to the Strand below where the night lights one by one were flickering on. He barely knew which Sense people to trust, let alone what any memo he designated *urgent* should say. Some departmental heads would just get defensive, dismiss all his claims about corruption and illegal experimentation as paranoia. Going round in circles – that was all he was doing right now. When he felt his info-remote vibrate he was glad of the distraction.

"Sending you an audio file," came John's voice down the line. Ezra immediately caught the urgency and excitement in his tone. He also noticed that the download had already started and that the double encryption indicator was flashing. Clearly, John was going to some lengths to shroud the contents. The question was, why?

"An audio file of what exactly?" Ezra asked.

"Anthony Grant, Jason Liu. They've been having an interesting conversation."

"Where?"

"Over the internet. Just now."

What the hell was John doing now? Hacking into their calls? He didn't doubt that John might have the technology – only a few days before Ezra had seen the intelligence gear he'd filched and stashed in his garage. Jesus Christ – here was Ezra struggling with getting his words just right, while John without any kind of intercept order or warrant went blazing into situations without thinking through the consequences.

"Doesn't matter what you suspect," said Ezra. "You cannot set up a tap."

"No phone tap," John said. Thank God for that, thought Ezra, but the moment of relief was instantly crushed when John quickly added, "This baby's even better."

"What baby?"

"The laser Listener."

"You'd better be joking." John's silence told Ezra otherwise. "What? You're listening to them with that laser microphone you were hiding in your garage?" This was serious: the only entities authorized to use this kind of equipment were intelligence departments with cleared personnel. "Where are you?" Ezra demanded, while making a check of his remote's security app to make sure everything in his own conversation was being encrypted. Thankfully, the double encryption indicator was still flashing.

"Primrose Hill," John said. "From where I'm parked I've got a good view of Grant's house down in Stanford Street. Must earn a packet to have a Porsche like that outside. Spyder by the look of it. Can't see the reg from here; it's parked at the wrong angle. Looks like a 918 model. I'd say about 20 years old." He gave a short derisory laugh. "That Doberman he's got out by his gate – waste of space. It can snarl all it likes; I'm 400 meters away." Ezra imagined John sitting in his white van looking through a zoom lens attached to the laser listening device. "Took me so long to work out what window to target to pick up his speech and to get the angle of the beam just right I nearly missed the conversation. But I picked up every vibration – everything they said – bouncing back off the window back to the recorder in a beam. Dunno what room Grant's in. Study maybe. The only furniture I've managed to zoom onto is a bookcase against a wall. Room's small though, I can tell by the vibrations. Easy to pick up Grant's voice. Can tell he's moving about as he's talking...."

"And Jason Liu's there too?" Ezra cut in with the question, despite wanting to distance himself from John's illicit surveillance.

"He's not there in person. They've been on a call, shielded, of course...."

"How do you know it's shielded?"

"Well, I couldn't tap in."

"So, you did try doing a normal tap, then." It infuriated Ezra that John was always so sly. "It's just that you were blocked. Is that it?"

"So, good thing I've got the long-distance laser, isn't it?" John said, trampling straight over Ezra's question. "In the transmission I'm picking up, I'd say Liu's voice is coming via a speaker phone. His voice is nowhere near as clear as Grant's. Signal's fainter. Seems like Liu called Grant up to discuss the Dixon boy. They're arguing about him. Like I said before, Dixon seems somehow to be involved with their research, but looks like he's left the research site and Grant's not happy about that. You should listen in. Has the download finished?"

Ezra checked the progress bar and read *Download complete.*

"It's finished."

"Then check it out," John said. "See what you make of it."

John hung up and Ezra found himself tempted by the green triangular *play* icon that would start the audio file. He wasn't sure whether the pixels were really pulsating or whether this nerve-wracking day that had started with Lena breaking into HQ some twelve hours before had made his mind play tricks. He hesitated a long while, then opened up his desk drawer and pulled out his big headphones. If he was going to listen in, he wanted to get as much detail as possible, especially if one of the voices John had recorded was coming into Anthony Grant's house via a speaker phone. John had said he'd recorded the conversation from 400 meters away. Exactly how clear was this conversation going to be? Ezra adjusted the headphones so that his ears were completely covered. He attached the lead to the remote, made himself comfortable in his swivel chair and pressed *play.*

At the beginning of the audio a phone was ringing. Each tone was remarkably clear. Then the words: *What the hell are you doing?* London accent: educated and clipped. Aggression, anger – both emotions were in there. Anthony Grant, Ezra presumed.

"I don't understand what happened." The second voice was faint in comparison, younger and desperate. Ezra surmised it must be Jason Liu. "I lost all the EEG readings I was getting from Dixon. He was getting so close to rebuilding a viable mathematical model. He was…."

"It's over," Grant said bluntly. "I turned the transmitter off."

Ezra then heard desperation in Jason Liu's voice: "No. No. It's not over. We have a breakthrough. The models Dixon has been constructing in the last couple of hours…."

"It's over. He's supposed to be remembering his theories in a secure facility. Instead, you've let him out."

"There's a critical piece of information missing, a particular configuration. He insisted it's at his sister's flat where he used to live. He had notes there, drawings, a specific pattern he wanted to see again. He became quite aggressive about it…."

"He's aggressive because of the intensity of the treatment you're giving him. You know full well that there's a limit to how much charge you can use. Thank Christ! I have the ability to pull the plug."

"Look, Anthony, I don't think you realize just how close we are to having a stable, reversible modifier."

"And what if his sister asks questions? You do realize that since Monica has received her compensation, she has little interest in manipulating Sense data to cover any of our tracks anymore."

"I'm sure she would understand that...."

"She's unreachable," Grant cut in.

Though he didn't get everything, Ezra took comfort in the knowledge that he was not the only person Monica had conned. Clearly, Liu was having some difficulty processing the news that Monica had whisked herself away; the silence on the audio file seemed interminable. Ezra heard a muffled cough, presumably from Liu. It was amazing that the laser microphone that John had operated from a hilltop nearly half a kilometer away could work so well, that it could home in on just the subjects of interest and filter out most background sound. Morals aside, John had certainly done his research in setting up the parameters for using the Listener.

"What about Monica's clients from New Way?" Liu's question was underlined with uncertainty. "Wouldn't she want to see that the treatment they got actually helped her clients?"

The laugh that came in stereo into Ezra's headphones was condescending, loud and clear. It was followed by the words, "You're a fool, Jason. She didn't care about any of the people in her New Way shelters. Oh, I suppose she used to, a long time ago. But they always turned out to be disappointments. Her words, not mine."

"What do you mean?" came the younger voice. Again, Ezra was relieved to find that someone else had the same questions he had and felt the same trepidation.

"They always went back — these victims of abuse she stuck her neck out to help. It used to infuriate her that she'd offer a safe place for them to stay, a chance to start over, then before she knew it, they'd shuffle back to their partners, mumbling excuses. She came to the conclusion that they were people who wanted to be controlled. *I've come to despise them.* She actually said that to me."

Coldness spread through Ezra's body.

"So," Anthony Grant cut into the silence on the line, his voice suddenly playing louder on the recording, "We needn't worry about Monica's interest in her clients. What we need to do is fold everything up quietly and lay low for a while."

"No," Liu replied, "We can't stop now, just as we're getting results."

"For the time being that's exactly what we're going to do. Tidy things up...."

"That's a mistake. Dixon's on the point of a breakthrough...."

"Look," Grant snapped, his voice loud in Ezra's earpiece. "Dixon's like you, an over-enthusiastic researcher, so eager to get results he's not thinking about any consequences. It's enough that we have one subject missing without Dixon behaving erratically too, leaving the clinic without authorization. You should never have let that happen. That was utterly stupid. It's thrown everything we've worked on into jeopardy. His sister has been looking for him...."

"The sister won't ask questions," Liu said. "I had Nisreen Ahmed drive Gavin to the flat with specific instructions to make sure there was no one at home, to delay them if they looked to be on their way, so Gavin would have a chance to find what he was looking for."

"Well, you shouldn't have involved the driver. That was another stupid thing to do."

Ezra found himself wanting to visualize this Anthony Grant who sounded so cutting and incensed. He pulled his keyboard towards him, ran a search for the Gen-exica Board of Directors and pulled up the image next to Grant's bio. He enlarged the formal portrait so it filled the monitor. There was no emotion in Grant's expression. His brown eyes looked straight to the camera. His black hair was well-groomed and a little spiky. His thick jaw and neck showed that he was powerfully built. On the recording he continued snapping, saying, "We don't know how much this driver knows. We've already had enough people thinking of talking, forming ideas of going public. Anybody who wants to do that we just stick to the plan: deploy whatever dirt we've got on them to keep them quiet. That worked for Fenton and the nurse...."

"Siobhan?" Jason asked.

Ezra could hear curiosity in Jason Liu's voice. Ezra was curious too. In the betting shop earlier, Fenton had mentioned how a nurse had wanted him to blow the whistle on the illegal experimentation at the reassignment clinic.

"Siobhan – " Liu said slowly as if he were trying to piece things together, "she's stopped questioning what we're doing. In fact, she has been very cooperative for the last few days."

"Of course she's been cooperative. We have her dirt: she's been playing around with a man in her gym and she doesn't want her partner – her lesbian partner – to know."

"I see." Jason said, after a few seconds.

"So, now we exercise some patience. We have what we need from Monica – the subjects, Dixon, the technology to get to his theories. That Korean piece I gave Monica is incredibly valuable and I don't want to find that I've given it away for nothing. There is no need to rush into anything."

"On the contrary," Jason Liu said. The pitch of his voice was lower, the volume louder and his tone now bore unexpected authority. "There is every reason for you to turn the transmitter back on and help Dixon focus his mind." Now it was Grant's turn to stay silent. "You don't see the rush because you haven't been following Epstein's work. Epstein's close to a viable treatment himself. Didn't you read his *Nature* paper?"

"Well, every researcher insists that they're close...."

"He's not just insisting. Look, Anthony, you can gamble if you want. Exercise some patience, as you say. Then you will find that you're too late to the finishing line and yes, you will have given your antique away for nothing." Ezra imagined Grant standing in an expensively furnished study, listening to the younger scientist's voice coming through the speakers, nonplussed by how sharply control of the conversation had changed. "Just as Dixon was settling on a viable configuration you took away the means for him to think it through. You have all the electroencephalogram readings and should be able to clearly see the sudden acceleration in the number of connections he's making. Keep the plug pulled if you want. It's up to you, Anthony. But when you see Epstein develop a modifier before us, that mistake will be all yours."

There were a few moments of silence, then finally a click where presumably Grant cut the call to Liu.

Ezra continued playing the audio file, wondering what move Grant would make next. But the recording was devoid of any noise at all. Nothing detectable in the background, no traffic, no voices; a very quiet house in a sleepy part of Primrose Hill. Presumably, Grant was standing utterly motionless. Ezra checked the time of the audio recording. 20:10 – this entire conversation had been recorded just ten minutes before. What was Grant doing now? Still standing silently in the same spot? The only noise to come through Ezra's earpiece before he hit *stop* was a low background sound of a barking dog.

Ezra wrenched off his headphones. Elbows on desk, he clasped his head tightly in his hands, tried forcing his thoughts into order.

Was Monica the only Sense superior involved in this reassignment scheme? If yes, he needed to alert the Board of Directors to have the police brought in as soon as possible. But exactly how far did the corporate poison extend? It was surreally unsettling that he couldn't tell which employees at Sense were trustworthy. Monica. Cunningham. Even John who was helping him was using filched parabolic equipment to do so.

Though Dixon's involvement made a fraction more sense now, Ezra barely knew how to handle the idea that the boy was subject to a mind control mechanism. If that were true, he should contact Suzanne immediately to warn her of the dangers. All it would take would be Anthony Grant switching on the mechanism again and Gavin (so Grant himself had only just said) could suffer serious damage. To what end anyway? Hadn't Dr. Epstein just a short while ago said that Liu's approach was flawed? Liu might keep on intensifying the treatments, expecting a solution that just wasn't possible.

Immediately, Ezra reached for his remote to dial Suzanne.

Several rings passed before the phone went to voicemail.

"Suzanne," he said, "Ezra Hurst here. Need to talk to you urgently. Contact me as soon as possible."

36

THERE WERE SEVERAL people in the ward: a short rotund orderly sweeping the corridor, two women in the reception area (one young, one old) huddled together over a computer screen, a man wearing shorts and flip flops and carrying flowers asking a male nurse for directions – Lena had felt so numb pacing along the corridor, she'd not noticed any hubbub before. Dr. Epstein had sprayed a compound all over her to soothe the lesions on her skin. She felt rigid somehow, as though she'd been plasticized. She could barely even sense the long hospital gown swishing around her feet as she edged along the corridor. The large mirror hanging on the wall further ahead unnerved her. She didn't want to know what she looked like – she'd felt numerous raw patches on her face before. Deliberately, she looked the other way.

There was an ugly metallic screech as a uniformed worker rounded a corner and dragged a ladder into place under a flickering fluorescent fixture. The light was small and circular. Four small screws held it fixed to the ceiling. Lena stopped in her tracks; there had been the same type of light in the reassignment clinic, in the room she'd run into and discovered the ashen fifteen-year-old lying lifelessly on her bed. She'd promised the girl she'd get help. Had she even told Dr. Epstein that there were others in danger? She couldn't remember exactly what she'd said to anyone when she'd staggered into the hospital earlier that day. God! Was she so wrapped up with her own problems to remember others needed help? She should do something now though, let those women up ahead on reception know there were critically ill people hidden out of sight whose situations were dire. The image of that young fifteen-year-old was vivid in her mind now. The girl barely had strength to speak. And as for the comic on her bed, she'd been too ill to even lift the thing, let alone read it.

The two receptionists were still looking at the computer as Lena approached. The younger one was chewing gum.

"That's right," said the older woman who was short and plump, "touch that icon and you get up a patient's admission records, touch this one and you can create a new record." Looking up to Lena, she said of her assistant, "She's new," before giving a knowing wink.

"And what does *intercept order* mean?" said the young woman who was pointing to some other section of the screen.

"That's a notice for the security staff. It means that they've been given an instruction to prevent someone from entering the hospital. We should all be on alert if we notice this person. Since the cameras capture everything right from the perimeter of the car park, I doubt he'll get near the wards. But just to be on the safe side we should all be aware."

"But who needs to be intercepted?"

"Well, go on, give it a click and it will give the name."

The younger woman extended a finger to the screen.

"Cunningham," the younger woman read, making Lena's heart lurch.

Lena found herself staring at the younger woman, at the contortions of her face as she chewed on her gum before blowing a big bubble.

"Do you have to do that?" said the senior receptionist. "It's really quite grotesque and not at all the kind of thing you should do in a hospital."

The younger woman popped the bubble and sucked the ragged gum back into her mouth. She leaned in to read more details on the monitor. "Vincent Cunningham. Male, thirty-six. Good-looking bloke, isn't he? Why does he need intercepting?" Why…." There was a sudden shrill bleeping noise.

"Is that the intercept alarm?" the young assistant asked, her eyes darting over the screen trying to match sounds to visuals. Lena switched her focus to the older woman, desperate for her response.

"No," she said finally. Lena breathed a long sigh of relief. "There's a patient calling for help," the senior assistant said. "Room 25. Where's Nurse Katharine?" The thickset woman had squeezed past her assistant and emerged from behind the reception desk to look up and down the corridor. The younger woman followed looking vaguely uncertain. Inadvertently, she'd started blowing another bubble, but quickly sucked it in when her superior turned around to say, "Go to Room 25 and tell him we're sending someone as soon as possible. I don't know where Katharine is. I'll go and look for her."

The two women set off in opposite directions along the corridor.

"I'll be with you shortly, lovie," the older woman said to Lena as she bustled past.

Lena's heart was still jumpy from hearing Vincent's name and the news that the hospital had been granted an intercept order to stop him entering the grounds. She must have been stupid to think that he would give up trying to track her down. In the underground she'd seen just how obsessive he was. He'd make excuses if he found her. She knew exactly how he'd justify all his locks and his cameras — *I'm keeping you clean, stopping you hurting yourself, let me show you some video, can't you see how messy you were without me?*

The reception unit was still empty and the two assistants were still out of sight. She reached over the counter to swivel the monitor towards her and was taken aback to find a large picture of Vincent occupying half the screen. The picture was his official driving license image. His eyes were grey and clear, staring straight to camera, staring straight at her. Feeling suddenly cold, she drew her gown around her, then leaned in closer to read the small words at the bottom of the screen. *Intercept order issued 16/8/2059 by E. Hurst.* Ezra – oh God! Here he was helping after all her deception. But the memory that was forming of the Tavern bar with the djembe drum music suddenly shattered when a series of raucous beeps sounded from the computer speakers. The word "alarm" was flashing in red across the still image of Vincent. Immediately, another mini window opened on the screen. Lena's heart started racing when she saw it was live footage of Vincent walking through the car park towards the main entrance. She staggered over to a large window that spanned from floor to ceiling and looked down to the hospital grounds several levels below. There were hundreds of cars crammed into the car park, but clearly she could see him on the far side near the main street. Severe-faced, single-minded, he was taking long strides towards the entrance. Where were the security guards? Why weren't they rushing over to stop him? Lena glanced around the ward looking for the assistants. Where were they? Just like the reception staff who had not reappeared, the security guards might also be busy elsewhere. All these monitors and cameras were useless if there was no one actually manning them. Lena ran back to the reception area and craned over the counter to see the computer. She saw an "emergency call" icon and raised her finger to press it. But she was stopped by the image of Vincent's cool grey eyes. She remained immobile. Torn. How could she do this to him? He had helped her, even if his ways were twisted. Hadn't she been better off with him than before? Stayed clean? Been creative and productive? How did her current situation compare to that? These sores all over her, the pain and physical disintegration – it was not as if she was in a better place now.

Then, from somewhere within, she was silently saying: I'm sorry. I'm sorry. I think you're worse for me than I am for myself.

She jabbed the "emergency" icon and a loud siren sounded. Quickly, she crossed to the window, expecting to see a phalanx of security personnel charging across the car park. "For God's sake, get down there," she hissed to guards she knew must be somewhere but just couldn't see. Then a movement directly below, close to the hospital entrance. Thank God! There they were, crossing the forecourt: three black-suited guards, yellow badges on their shoulders, walkie-talkies hitched to their waists. Still Vincent strode onwards as if the guards who were conferring and cautiously heading his way had nothing to do with him. Lena's hands were pressed against the cold pane of glass so large and clean she had a perfect panoramic view. So, this was what it meant to watch, to monitor, to have the controls. She'd pulled the trigger. Now the chain reaction: the guards fanning out to form a blockade. Even from this vantage she could sense Vincent's fury, could imagine him thinking that these people were idiots getting in his way like this. He tried shouldering past, but then it seemed to click. He was glancing from one guard to another. What was he shouting? *What the fuck are you doing? Who the hell do you think you are?* Some relentless torrent was inevitable, spewing through a scowl. Though none of the guards were as tall as him, it was clear that he wasn't getting past. When was he going to accept that, stop getting into the big guard's face to grimace and bawl? *Who authorized this? Bring me your supervisor?* Lena knew him well enough to predict that he would be demanding to know the power here. That had to be why he was pulling his remote from his trouser pocket. To demand answers from someone. Who though? Had the guards told him that he was under surveillance? Had he somehow tapped into the same information that Lena had seen on the reception monitor: "Intercept order issued 16/8/2059 by E. Hurst." Something had twigged; Vincent had turned on his heels and was marching, fists clenched, back towards his car. Lena's heart was strangely calm as she watched him wrench open the car door, reverse maniacally from his parking spot and speed towards the street where two police cars swerved in front of him and stopped to block his way. A policewoman, all nonchalance, sidled alongside Vincent's car. She gestured for him to slide down his window while unhitching handcuffs from her belt. When he resisted two more officers approached. Finally, he opened the door.

"Phew!" came a female voice from behind Lena. "They took their time, didn't they? How are you feeling?"

The older assistant's face was full of concern.

"There are others in danger," Lena said finally, not wanting to discuss herself.

This stalker, this traitor, this thing she'd become – the idea of examining how it was feeling was totally abhorrent. There was the girl she'd promised to help, the others hidden behind curtains and closed doors. She must focus on them.

"And where are these others?"

Lena swiveled around to face the electrician on the ladder and gestured to the light fixture he was prying away from the ceiling.

"A place with lights like that." Driven to and from the clinic in a car with dark opaque windows, it was impossible to give a location. "It's pathetic I can't say more."

"Well, those lights are faulty. Probably not too many medical facilities installed them before they were withdrawn. Maybe the lights are one small detail, but could be crucial, couldn't it?" She gestured to the sofa. "Let me get you some tea. Or would you prefer coffee? If you sit and relax a while, you never know, you may remember more."

"Yes, you're right. I should put my mind to it." There were coral gowns, pink plastic highlighters, marble-effect linoleum floors. Reassignment didn't exist in a vacuum. It had contractors, decorators, suppliers and vendors. "Do you have paper?" She'd list every detail and help ensure the clinic was found.

***

Gavin was stirring on the sofa. His face was clammy and Suzanne could see that the hair on his nape, visible beneath the cap, had been cropped short. He seemed paler than she remembered as if he hadn't seen the sun for a long time and there were darkish circles under his eyes.

"We were worried about you. Where have you been?"

The question seemed to confuse him. He cast about the living room, trying to get his bearings. Then his eyes fell on his notebook and scroll screen which he scooped from the floor.

While offering him a glass of water she said, "Are you ready to talk now?"

"I'm ready to try again," he said without meeting her eyes. He began leafing through his notebook, finally settling on a sketch with annotations written in a pencil scrawl. "I'd forgotten about this." His voice was quiet and serious. "This configuration – it might work with Liu's parameters. Where is he? I can't hear him." Gavin fiddled with his collar, where Suzanne could see a thin white wire. "Let's try this again." He took a long look at Suzanne's sleeve, then walked over crumpled clothes on the carpet to the table in the corner of the room. Brusquely, he spread out his scroll screen and sketch book, knocking over a tall empty glass. Suzanne saw it was cracked; Gavin didn't notice. Instead, he glanced around until he found the crocheted top, then laid that on the table too. "Stronger this time. I think I can take...."

"Now wait a minute," Brinley interrupted, going straight over to the table, "you're not just carrying on as you did before. You owe us an explanation and that's what you're going to give...."

"Just give me a moment to let me *think*," Gavin said. The sentence started calmly enough but had become menacing by the end. His face was turning red again. The muscles around his jaw were becoming rigid.

"God, this is starting again. Leave him, Brinley." Suzanne hurried to the bay window and looked down to street level. It was dark outside. Vehicles had their headlights on and were swerving around Nisreen's grey car. "She's still waiting down there. I'm going to speak to her."

Out on the street Suzanne hurried over to Nisreen's car and hammered on the driver's door. The darkened window slid down.

"What's happened to him?" Suzanne demanded. "And don't lie to me now. You knew he was in our flat. You were trying to keep us from finding him. He's talking to people with a microphone. Are these people in the clinic? Tell me!"

Nisreen shut her eyes and sighed heavily before saying, "Listen, after you came to find me I looked for him. He was in a different section of the clinic. It was on a separate floor from the other rooms, more like a suite. I was just told to bring him to your flat and when he's found what he's looking for to bring him back. I don't know why he's behaving like he is." She looked up from the driver's seat to make eye contact with Suzanne for the first time. "It was the same when I first had to pick him up several weeks ago.

They told me he was important, he had crucial mathematical theories, that I should pick him up from the station. But when I got there..." Nisreen exhaled and shook her head "... he was so unstable. I thought he was on drugs or something. He was mumbling about logos and blood when I saw him."

"What blood? What do you mean?"

"He said he saw a rail line sign that triggered a memory of a small kid sitting on a train, that the kid's face was slashed right through by a sharp piece of metal which had some of that logo on the side. You know the logo, I mean, the one with the red stripes?" Suzanne nodded. "He kept saying the stripes were the exact same color as the boy's blood. He couldn't tell where the one thing started and the other stopped. He kept repeating himself. Over and over...I didn't know what was up with him."

"He was in the Maglev train crash," Suzanne cut in.

"Oh."

Suzanne could tell Nisreen didn't know.

"Why didn't you ask him?"

"He sounded like he was on drugs."

Suzanne had to concede there was a good chance he might have been. He might have taken some tranx tabs to help calm him down for the ride. Hadn't Lukas told her so much the other day? Even so, what business did this Nisreen have with Gavin? She eyed her suspiciously. "Who told you he was so important that you needed to intercept him at the station?"

Nisreen looked away, remained tight-lipped.

"Tell me!" Suzanne said.

"Look, I was told he had some mathematical ideas that were of interest. They wanted to get to him before he shared his ideas at the conference in Prague."

"Who's *they*?"

Silence again.

"Who's *they*?" Suzanne insisted, anger rising.

"Gen-exica. Someone from Sense."

"Gen-exica? Why were they interested in his theories?"

"They wanted to stabilize some of the treatments at the clinic. Look, I've told you enough," Nisreen said, reaching for the window control. "I've told you everything I know. What's he doing in there? He's been in there way too long."

"Wait!"

The window slid shut. Its glass was so dark Suzanne couldn't make out any of Nisreen's profile. The engine revved up and the car swerved into traffic.

"Shit!" Suzanne said, loudly enough to make a passing cyclist swing around and wobble on his bike. Remembering Brinley's impatience with Gavin, she collected herself quickly and went back to the building. Adam was looking sleepy in the stroller parked in the downstairs hallway. Magnifico Mouse had fallen to the floor. She stroked Adam's hair, told him she'd bring him up soon, then climbed the stairs, hoping she wouldn't find the two men arguing.

Entering the living room, she saw Gavin intensely scribbling notes, gripping the pen so tightly his knuckles looked white. Sweat shone on his forehead and his face was worryingly red. Brinley was standing near the table staring at him, severe-faced. At least he was controlling himself, holding back, giving Gavin space.

There was a faint buzz. Suzanne's mobile. She scanned the room and saw it positioned on the arm of the sofa. A voicemail notification was blinking. The caller was E. Hurst.

"Why didn't you answer?" she said to Brinley. "It's Sense. They're involved in this somehow."

"Never mind the message. Come here," he said quietly, beckoning her over. He was staring at Gavin's denim cap. "Look at that," he said. Underneath the band at the back of Gavin's head was a thin white wire. Brinley yanked Gavin's cap off. There was a massive sore on his scalp and a plastic device at its center. "Jesus!" Brinley was so repulsed he stepped back. Suzanne looked too and winced.

"Who did this to you?" she said to Gavin, who fleetingly felt for his head while looking at his diagrams and notes. "It looks so raw. How can you ignore it like this?"

"What are you doing?" Gavin said angrily, aware now of Brinley looming over him and holding his cap. "Move back, both of you." His voice was getting louder, his face even redder. Turning away from them and pulling his diagram nearer, he said, "This has

to be the configuration. I just can't extend its application. Ugh...."
He was groaning in frustration, screwing his eyes. "Don't know
why...try again. I think I can take more."

Suzanne glanced at Brinley who with narrowed eyes was
scrutinizing the device.

"It's a Resolve transmitter," Brinley said quietly to Suzanne.
"It's the same as the ones I showed you this morning."

"What? In the pictures with the monkeys?"

"Dust implants. Someone must have inserted them." Brinley
was staring at Gavin who was pressing his palms tightly onto the
side of his head, beginning to writhe in pain. "It's like someone's
trying to make him remember things. I'm sure it's Resolve. That's
exactly how it's used: have people receive electrical impulses to
strengthen weak connections. He's going along with it – asking
them to increase the intensity. That's why he's feeling pain. Who
the hell's doing it though?"

"Gen-exica. And Sense is somehow involved. Nisreen just said
so," Suzanne added, seeing Brinley's questioning look.

"Gen-exica? The biopharm company? Why?"

"They wanted to know about some of his mathematical ideas.
She picked him up from the station all those days ago."

"What?"

"She drove off before I could get any more out of her. What
are you doing?" Suzanne said, alarmed at the way Brinley had
closed in on Gavin and was reaching for the device. "You might
cause more damage pulling that plastic thing off."

"We have to take it out, switch it off, something. These things
are dangerous. Aggression. Contortions. Look – he's got all the
side effects the report talked about."

Gavin swung around as soon as he felt Brinley's palms clasping
his head.

"What did you just do?" he yelled. "Have you clicked
something? It's not working now." Gavin shot upwards, knocking
his chair over and shoving Brinley backwards. "I haven't finished
thinking this through. What exactly is your problem that you can't
let me sit here and think?"

"This is dangerous technology, Gavin."

"You don't know what you're talking about. It's the exact opposite of dangerous. For years, I haven't been able to focus on any of my previous research and these dust chips have reversed all that."

"And the people who gave you these chips," Brinley said, "Did they tell you about the mood changes, the aggression, the fact that you've just come bursting into our flat without even properly acknowledging your sister? Just thrown all our belongings around. Did they tell you about the side effects?"

"Why should I worry about side effects? What did I have to lose?" Pointing to the scroll screen and a series of diagrams and formulae, he said, "Do you know what it means for me to be able to put something like this together again? Look at it." He held the screen right up to Brinley's face. "You see how topologically fascinating these chains are...." Roughly, Brinley shoved the screen away. "Can't you see it? No?" Gavin turned the screen towards himself and peered at the diagrams. "My models should account for the kind of polypeptide chains Gen-exica's uncovered. They involve the same kind of structures." Then more quietly, he added, "They really should work with these. I don't understand why they don't." Desperately, he fiddled with the device on the side of his head, jiggling it so frantically a large globule of blood appeared and transformed into a crimson line running down his neck. Turning his back on Brinley and Suzanne, he took a deep breath and said, "Again. Let's try again."

"No!" Brinley said, clasping Gavin's shoulder to turn him back round.

Gavin grabbed the tall empty glass, smashed it hard on the table and swiped a jagged shard full-force across Brinley's cheek.

"Oh my God!" Suzanne said, rushing over to Brinley.

"Now will you let me think?" Gavin said to both of them.

While the pair stumbled towards the door, Gavin put the broken glass down, pulled the wooden chair upright and sat down heavily. Squarely, he set his notebook in front of him.

Suzanne's hands were shaking as she grabbed a T-shirt from the floor, pressed it gently on Brinley's face.

"Are you all right, Brin?" She peeled it away after a few

moments, saw three long gashes, all still seeping. "Oh my God."

"I can't see," Brinley said.

Panic was in his voice.

"I think it's the blood getting in your eyes." She pressed the material against his cheek again. "Yes, that's what it is. He missed your eye, thank God! The cut's right by the side." Brinley was frantically blinking and feeling his face. Gently, he felt the gash by his eye. "That's where the blood's coming from," Suzanne said. "Oh my God! What's wrong with him?" She felt hatred for brother, was furious at him sitting at the table in oblivion, manically scribbling notes.

The mobile on the arm of the sofa began ringing again and Suzanne lurched towards it, expecting it to be Hurst trying her again. It was. She jabbed the icon to speak.

"What the hell have you done to my brother?"

"Suzanne," Ezra said immediately, "Listen, you had every right to be suspicious. We have a lot of explaining to do and you *will* get those explanations. Right now, though I want to try and help with your immediate situation. Is Gavin with you?

"Yes, he's here. He's out of control. He's just slashed Brinley with a broken glass. I have a toddler downstairs…."

"OK…."

"It's not OK. Don't you think of telling me to calm down. You haven't seen what he's doing here."

"Tell me what he's doing now."

Suzanne stared at her brother again.

"He's writing notes, drawing diagrams of distorted shapes and folds." She realized her brother was staring at her again, at her elbow. "What?" she yelled over to him, "What is it about the sleeve?" She threw the mobile on the floor. Angrily, she ripped the cardigan off to reveal the patterns of her blouse and the way they were creased in her elbow. "What? What is it? Is there something mathematically interesting you're seeing here? Is that it?"

His face was screwed up in pain. "It's a simple version of one part of my model. It's not squaring properly. I just cannot see what's wrong."

"Move back from him, Suzanne," Brinley said, struggling to his feet, holding the blood-drenched T-shirt to his face. He pulled her further across the room with his free hand.

Suzanne! She heard her name coming faintly from the mobile. She snatched it up from the floor.

"That's all his been saying since he came here," she said angrily to Ezra. "*I can't see what's wrong. I have the right formation.* What the hell is his problem?"

"It's possible he might be right," Ezra said. "There might not be anything wrong with his mathematical models. It might be the parameters he's trying to apply to them. I want to send you some links to relevant papers, particularly one from a Dr. Epstein…."

"Why should I trust you? Nisreen said Sense is involved in all of this."

"She's right and we've already called in the police to give them as many details as we can. I think it will only be minutes before you'll hear from them too. They'll want to know what's happened to Gavin."

"*I* want to know what's happened to Gavin."

"Gen-exica were interested in tapping into some of his insights, ideas he had before his accident that he never got round to publishing. They've been using neural chips to strengthen the connections he can make to Jason Liu's genetic research. Your brother isn't thinking of making his models work on any other theories because Liu is primarily focused on his own. Gavin's probably forgotten the details of other researchers' work, people like Dr. Epstein. And Liu hasn't done anything to help him remember them. This is not my field, but I've heard that Liu's theories are flawed. Here, I've sent you the links to different approaches that might gel with his models better. At least they might calm him down until the police arrive."

Suzanne saw a number of files downloading on her mobile. She clicked open one by Dr. Epstein. Looking across to Gavin, she saw he was holding his head in pain, he was mumbling into his microphone. She strode to the table, still livid with him.

"Who are you talking to? Suzanne demanded. "Is it these scientists? This Dr. Liu?"

Gavin nodded. His eyes were watery with pain, "I just don't

know what to change for him. Making the charge stronger – it's not helping."

"So take the transmitter off."

"After I've come so far in remembering things? I can't just give up and go back to how I was before."

"You've gone far enough with Gen-exica."

Suzanne placed the mobile showing the Epstein file on the table in front of him. Momentarily, Gavin remained blank-faced. Then he leaned further in and began to read.

"Degrees of occlusion," he said, quietly after a while. "Epstein talked about this some time ago, didn't he?" Gavin pulled the crocheted top towards him. "One entity intertwining with another…" He glanced over to Suzanne's sleeve "…how sections of patterning become occluded or opaque, to greater or lesser degrees."

He began scrolling through the file, uncertainly at first, returning to the abstract, then deeper into the article, back to the abstract again. Suzanne turned to Brinley, who'd picked a different T-shirt from the floor to hold against his face. The first was dark red, soaked right through. She walked over to him and rubbing his back, said, "I'll get some water. Clean you up. Hurst says the police are coming. This should be over soon." When she came back from the kitchen with a bowl and sponge she saw that Gavin was immersed in the article, that he seemed calmer and had sat back in his seat.

"He's taken the transmitter off," Brinley said.

Suzanne nodded. Held Brinley's head gently while sponging his face.

"Mummy," came a quiet voice from down the stairs.

Taking the sponge from Suzanne, Brinley said, "I'm OK. You should go to Adam."

Heading downstairs, Suzanne heard a faint siren in the distance, its shrill pitch rising and falling, growing louder and louder until it reached their door.

EPILOGUE

March 2060

THE WORDS "Lena calling" flashed on the base of the hologram unit that Ezra had installed in his new office up on Director's Level. When he pressed "admit" a 3-D woman materialized, sitting relaxed in a high-backed armchair. The green epicanthic eyes were instantly recognizable, but not the dark beige skin, nor the cropped red hair. The eyebrows – were they more arched than before? Thinner? More defined? The lips were plumper, a darker red than he remembered. He noticed the corners of her mouth slowly turn upwards, then open and move as she spoke.

"Staring again?"

Smiling to himself, he shook his head.

"At least your personality is a constant. But I'm surprised that your name is," he said, looking at the words "Lena Calling" at the bottom of the hologram unit.

"Lena is what you know me as."

"But I have the back-story now, don't I? I can call you whatever you want to be called."

"Haven't settled on my new self yet," she said, raising a china cup to her lips. The skin on her hands was young and smooth, the fingers more slender than before. Steam swirled upwards in front of her face as she sipped her drink. "Name. Appearance. It's all up for grabs, you know. Apart from the eyes – Epstein's treatments are not at all stable on eyes. But other than that – he's near enough cracked it." Ezra nodded. He was aware that Epstein had published accounts of his breakthrough treatments in *Nature*. "Rapid phenotypic modification. It's a reality now. Exciting, isn't it?"

"As long as you're in control," Ezra said. It came out more flatly, more cynically than he'd intended. It was true that Epstein followed protocols, had all his trials go through recognized review boards. But exactly how different was he from Liu with all his excitement about human modification? Why hadn't Lena settled on an appearance yet? Was Epstein the one suggesting changes?

"You think I'm a vulnerable subject," Lena said.

That's exactly what he was thinking but he had to concede and he decided to say because it was diplomatic, maybe even flattering. "You don't sound so."

"And what about you? Don't you fancy a change of look?"

"I'm all right as I am."

"Yes, you are. But here's the thing," she said, "I gather you've been working hard steering Sense clear of all its scandals, even changing the logo...."

Logo, brand colors, the Chinese artifacts that Monica had favored for interior decor, yes, he'd got rid of all those. Even the wellness bottle housed in its own special display case in front of his desk was about to be removed. Any minute Professor Ma would be arriving to discuss moving it permanently to the British Museum. Removing all associations with Monica was a necessary step to get Sense back on track.

"...but ," Lena continued, "the thing is, how are all your fancy surveillance systems going to cope with this new ability we have to change ourselves?"

Mental monitoring, he thought. Neural implants. Microchipped intentions.

"So if you've been following things," he said, "you'll know that Resolve technology is now much safer than before. Has definite advantages, in fact."

"Oh yes, that's right." Ezra read sarcasm in Lena's tone. "I have to say getting Gavin Dixon to testify to the benefits of neural implants, well, that was a complete coup, wasn't it? So, we're all going to be intellectually enhanced while you're busy monitoring our movements? What a marketing masterstroke!"

"I can think of less cynical ways of putting things." But essentially she was right. The whole "Resolve – good for the community, good for you" campaign had been a great success. After the documentary about Gavin's latest theories and his use of the new implants had aired, the 98% of people who were against the idea of surveillance implants was down to 84%. Obviously, there was still a lot of convincing to do, but Sense was heading in the right direction and Ezra was the leader of that. Shame the Dixon siblings had fallen out over the issue. Ezra liked Suzanne. He hoped she'd come round.

The intercom buzzed and a voice came through the speaker. "Professor Ma is here to see you."

Turning back to Lena, Ezra said, "I have a visitor and I'll have to go, but what made you call on me?"

"Monica. You haven't found her yet."

"You have to know that finding Monica is my top priority."

"For both of us then. If there is any way I can help, you'll contact me, won't you?"

Ezra was uncertain about how she could help, but he nodded and said, "I will."

There was a movement in the doorway and Ezra looked up to see a tall skinny man whose gaze immediately fell on the hologram unit and the disintegrating woman.

"Professor Ma?" Ezra said, once the hologram had vanished. "Come on in."

"I won't take up too much of your time, Mr. Hurst."

Ezra waved the professor towards the Korean wine bottle.

"Ah," the professor's face lit up. "I've been looking forward to seeing this."

"You've never seen it before?"

"Of course not. It's been very privately held. It is a travesty, really, when such things end up in private collections."

A premises security person appeared in Ezra's doorway. Impatiently, Ezra waved him in too.

"My predecessor had it brought here," Ezra said.

The one time it had left the premises, for cleaning and restoration, had been the only occasion that Ezra had seen a glimmer of anxiety on Monica's face.

He could take or leave the wine bottle, though he'd wondered whether it would grow on him if he left it there in its glass case, to quietly infuse his consciousness, as the ginseng leaves on the bottle were supposed to have infused the wine. Maybe he'd get it, this obsession Monica had had for the bottle. But it hadn't grown on him.

"I'm sorry," he said. "I don't have much interest."

Neither did he have time for archaeologists requesting viewing time to make notes. Tightening surveillance after November's bio attack, an attack for which no one, as with the 2055 attack, had claimed responsibility – that was one task Ezra should be devoting his time to. Then there was re-establishing international surveillance agreements, overseeing damage limitation after the reassignment scandal, even sorting out this new office.

He'd made a point of changing it, not just to put his personal stamp on it. He'd liked Monica's style, the clean, sparse space. But changing it was part of the rebranding Sense needed to do.

Monica was still an enigma to Ezra, though less so now that Anthony Grant had stated that he hadn't given her the celebratory vase just because she'd provided human subjects ("They were all willing participants," he'd protested in court), but instead because she'd engineered access to Dixon's forgotten theories.

Recently, when Ezra had revisited the church across the street, the old rector had been sitting quietly on the organ stool. "Of course, I quickly took all the New Way publicity down," he'd said. "You know, it never occurred that I should have checked the organization out." It had made no difference what Ezra had said to him – he couldn't help the old man out of his guilt. "But I didn't just let them put leaflets up," he'd said. "It was worse than that: I directed a teenager there, thinking that Monica might help her out of a horrible domestic situation. But she used her for experimentation. Can you believe it? Of course, I'm relieved that she was found, along with the others, but they should never have suffered that way."

Ezra glanced over to the wine bottle, to Professor Ma, in front of it, now taking photographs and making notes – it was objects like this that moved Monica. And the celebratory vase she'd acquired from Grant was even more precious yet.

The professor and the premises security man had begun speaking urgently, carefully turning the bottle. What were they checking for? Hallmarks? Glaze imperfections? Ezra didn't know. He registered the seriousness in their expressions though.

"What's the problem?"

"Professor Ma insists this is a fake," the security man said, "but I have records," he waved some documents in Ezra's direction, "proving Sense's purchase of the genuine piece."

"Whether or not Sense purchased the bottle," the professor said matter-of-factly, "I can tell you quite categorically that this is not it."

Walking around his desk now to join the two men by the display case, Ezra said, "Monica told me she'd had the ginseng bottle repaired and taken off the premises by security. I was here when the security guards were putting it back in the case. It was August." She'd called him up for an update on the Dixon case – Ezra remembered it very clearly.

"Well, this is not the original." Professor Ma was emphatic.

Frantically leafing through papers, the Premises officer said, "There is no record of anyone from my department granting permission to take the piece off site." He looked to Ezra, panic in his eyes. "Who were these people you say you saw?"

Mind rapidly processing everything he'd just heard, Ezra said, "Perhaps Monica is the only person who knows that."

She switched them, he thought. Jesus Christ! There was no piece of work bigger than her.

"So," Professor Ma drawled the word as if saying it slowly would buy him time to comprehend the truth, "the ginseng bottle and the celebratory vase…" Ezra nodded, knowing that Professor Ma had reached the same conclusion he had "…now she has both."

An hour or so later he was alone at his desk, awaiting a detective. Ezra pulled the latest Neural Implant Risk Assessment Report towards him. He'd read it thoroughly, was convinced that the previously reported problems of uncontrolled aggression had all been eradicated, convinced that, as a matter of public security, it was the right way to go. He clicked to his calendar. His implant appointment was May 28th, only two months away.

About the Author

Stella Whiteman was born in London. She studied philosophy at King's College, University of London, then worked as a literacy teacher for several years. She now lives in America with her husband and two children. *Control Alter Delete* is her first published novel.

CPSIA information can be obtained at www.ICGtesting.com
Printed in the USA
LVOW06s2329141215

466604LV00007B/1139/P